In Any Ordinary Life
Clare Stanley
Midgley

I0638950

Dedicated to Colin, Emillie & Mia
To my life line and my angels thank you for
your support
Love you.

To Rosie – thank you so much for your
patience I don't think
I would have ever got through the book
without you.
I can't thank you enough

Contents

Chapter 1   Chapter: 37
Chapter 2
Chapter 3
Chapter 4
Chapter 5
Chapter 6
Chapter 7
Chapter 8
Chapter 9
Chapter 10
Chapter 11
Chapter 12
Chapter 13
Chapter 14
Chapter 15
Chapter 16
Chapter 17
Chapter 18
Chapter 19
Chapter 20
Chapter 21
Chapter 22
Chapter 23
Chapter 24
Chapter 25
Chapter 26
Chapter 27
Chapter 28
Chapter 29
Chapter 30
Chapter 31
Chapter 32
Chapter 33
Chapter 34
Chapter 35
Chapter 36

Authors Introduction

Jeanie sat in her office dreaming of changes to her life. The mundane existence had dragged her down to the point that nothing except routine existed. Her father's death had provided the perfect excuse for her to hide away and nothing she tried seem to change the eventualities of what was to come.

Her seven sisters drain on every resource, and as she Jeanie now pulled between family, business and money realising there is nothing left for her. As her business grows, Jeanie feels the constant pressure and knowing that every decision is under scrutiny from her mother makes her feel trapped, lost and alone.

With her life so fragilely held in an uncompromising state, an old friend suddenly appears questioning the walls that she has built up around her. His kind nature and gentle hand lull her into a security she has never felt before, and before stepping into his world, he provides her with hope giving her a pedestal she feels she deserves.

She had never been in love; men had always been a difficult species that she never quite understood, and as an old flame walks back into town she is thrust back into turmoil. James's promises turn to dust she finds that her only real strength is back amongst the oil of her father's workshop

As Jeanie tries to pick up the pieces, she realises her life is slowly spiralling out of control, and a darkness which had always been hidden takes control almost killing her as a result. Knowing the pressure will eventually consume them all she waits in the background for the day when the truth about her father and the lies that surround her family come pouring out and at last her soul can be free.

IN LIFE, IN LOVE, AND IN OUR QUEST FOR
FREEDOM SOMETIMES WE FORGET WHAT
TRULY MATTERS.

Chapter 1

Dreaming one day her life would change and questioning her existence was nothing new to Jeanie. With one ear reaching out to the alarm and her thoughts deep in sleep she knew her sudden awakening would finally put everything into perspective and knowing she was waiting for her life to start made the mundane routine of her existence even harder to bear. As the clock shrieked, she began the day exactly how she always did. Tired.

Life and existence for the past ten years had revolved around work and waking up at four o'clock in the morning was nothing more than a hard slog. Daring to peep out of the window she noticed the frost gathered around the windows and the intricate patterns which crossed over the fragile pain. As she looked out into the white sky it provided her brain to start it's secondary quest of searching for a reason to get out of bed.

As the alarm began to prattle again, she threw it onto the bed fighting with the noise that had now started to ring in her ears. Dragging on her clothes and tiptoeing down the large panelled staircase she stood at the picture window looking into the gloomy sky. Feeling uninspired she continued to put the kettle on, and as she stepped into her usual habitual practices, the thought of any adventures died in the stirrings of her morning coffee. After taking minimal sips, she braced herself for the brisk November air, and as the door creaked open, the cold wind made her shudder as if it had crept into her veins. As she tiptoed down the garden path, she placed her hands in her pockets, gazing at the sparkle studded road ahead and with all of her thoughts lost in the frost she looked deep into the sky seeing if the answers she needed had been written in the stars.

As they twinkled brightly inviting her into her fantasy, the moon's silver light lit the path ahead, and as she followed, it seemed to light the way ahead.

As much as the moment seemed magical the reality of the harsh cold air bit hard at her cheeks and nose and as the numbness started to flood over her face, it soon broke the spell.

The rows of cottages lay asleep, and as she passed, she longed for the close comfort of her bed. Hiding in the blackness and eradicating her wishes of a desired lay in Jeanie's tiredness soon disappeared in the efforts for keeping warm and feeling her breath plus the wet condensation on her scarf made her quicken her pace.

Rolling up to the gates she sighed exhaling her thoughts into the frosty air and as the foggy mist appeared Jeanie followed in quiet contemplation. It was indeed the start of a beautiful morning.

The factory roof looked like a Christmas card, and the Nordic dangles of the icicles followed a perfect line, and as everything matched the scene, it honestly seemed a magical morning. As her eyes wandered across the sky found herself being brought back down to earth with a solid jolt. Catching a glimpse of her reflection in the main reception window made any moment of enchantment disappear replacing it with the feeling of contempt. As she threw her head back in disgust she traced the grease and oil splattered marks from her antics with pieces of machinery and wondered when the quiet little girl would ever be seen again, and as she turned sideward, her reflection didn't fare any better, and her feelings regurgitated her sensation of utter repulsion

"Look at the state of you. If you walked down the street like this anywhere else in the world, they would think you were homeless."

Jeanie often talked to herself starting as a habit created by an incredibly large family. With a large number of people vying for attention, it made difficult to get a respected answer never mind common sense and having to rely on oneself for advice and talking to her reflection had become a routine morning occurrence.

Now completely demoralised Jeanie knew she always had a way of making herself feel unremarkable even treating herself as if she was nothing more spectacular than a drawing pin, but what she didn't realise or appreciated was the glow she had inside. She captivated even the impatient listener and her ability to pull everyone into a conversation and entice their imagination was the main reason why so many staff had stayed true.

Her father's sudden death had impacted her life more than she cared to admit and in more ways, she couldn't get away from the fact that she was her father's daughter. The mirror had never reflected it, however; inside both were joined at the core. She missed him more these days especially now the dark nights had started to draw in.

Jeanie had always been close to him even starting the business with him, but his contradictory standards always confused her especially when one minute he would say run for freedom and the next saying that he couldn't manage the company without her. Jeanie was in the middle, she was always caught in the middle and after his death, her fate had been sealed and looking through the glass wasn't going to change that.

Gathering herself together she opened the door to the downstairs reception; she could already hear Eric bellowing his orders. Jeanie cringed at these mornings and had regularly scorned him for his nonchalant attitude towards her staff. Climbing to the platform she mischievously put her head around the door waiting for her next scolding for being late for the fourth time that week.

"Good morning to you. You grumpy old bastard!" As he threw his head around he quickly, he slammed the window shut apparently angered by Jeanie's lateness.

"And what time do you call this? This fucking place doesn't run itself you know!" Jeanie knew his bark was worse than his bite and she also knew he was digging for a reaction. Slowly taking off her coat she walked to her desk purposely avoiding looking directly at him. Looking at the papers Jeanie never rose to his commands knowing it would frustrate him more and as Eric hit boiling point she smiled under her scarf, and with that, her muffled reply gave chase to his temper.

"Around 4:30 am why?" Ignoring her comment he walked towards the door with his mumblings getting louder as he made his way around the gantry.

"Number seven has thrown a piston you cocky little shit and don't give me any grief today as I'm ready for you!" Mornings wouldn't be the same without him, and he had made her feel like a daughter even providing her with that security after her father's death. Eric supported her through her dark days and missing her dad felt natural especially when his name was in huge letters down the side of the building. Thriving on the sarcasm and non-specific morning's banter with him was no different to any other day.

Sitting down in her dad's chair the feelings of emptiness began to rise again, and as she stared out of the office window, she sighed heavily wanting at least some direction instead of the catalyst of routine which set out in front of her. Instead, the wind howled around the building as it started to snow and she wished for more. Gazing out over the frost covered hills made it seem as if time had stood still and feeling like an onlooker in her life the world appeared to spin without anyone knowing her existence. She had almost become a passer-by in her life, and as the darkness engulfed the morning, the emptiness seemed to echo with responsibility. However, on hearing a loud bang and Eric's voice jolted her straight back to reality

"Shit number seven!" Jumping out of her seat she made her way down the steps to the shop floor and as she walked past the rows of lockers the roar of a fully fledged working plant was at her feet and in her control.

She didn't feel in control.

The petrol heater in the back luckily masked the noise of Eric still shouting behind her, and with the warmth hitting her face she tried to forget about the emptiness that rested inside.

"Just another day!"

Pacifying her feelings of escape, she disappeared under the press but all she could think about was her nice warm bed and the sound of her seven sisters snoring and chattering in the background.

Jeanie thought about them a lot and regularly worried mainly about how she was going to feed them. The cold floor and the smell of oil filled her senses and as she climbed underneath the resentment at the situation flooded back into mind. "Yep it's ok for me to get covered in shit, but no Jeanie comes to work and looks like a tramp and smells like one too. " As she twisted the bolts she bit down hard grinding her teeth forcing the metal to turn and as the bolts dropped out one by one she couldn't help but think of her family. Jeanie loved them unconditionally, and the only reason she had kept going for this long was that she cared about them so much. Having two older and five younger sisters often made Jeanie feel out of place especially when none of the others had even had a remote interest in the business. The difference was they were all incredibly beautiful, and she knew she stuck out like a sore thumb.

Jeanie's thoughts wavered to her main concern Ivy. Her older sister had become her confident but being heavily pregnant and ill made Jeanie's life even more complicated. A baby in the house was good news, but all she could concentrate on was that it was another mouth to feed. Ivy had rejoined the family over a month ago and had moved in temporarily while George her husband was away. Jeanie ultimately understood that coming from such a large family and living nearly a hundred miles away must have made Ivy feel isolated. Having her home felt like more pressure, and she knew she had to make the plant work. Ivy had become the defining muse she needed to focus her efforts on, and the business had to make money or else all of them would be destitute.

As the oil dripped down her face and along her brow, it acted like a sponge soaking up the small puddle which was now beginning to take shape. While Ivy played on her mind, she continued to feel uneasy knowing something would happen soon if not tonight. Ivy had become more than a big sister, and she was afraid of losing the only confidant she'd had. Ivy knew she would do anything for them and in her efforts to make her sister feel welcome Jeanie had given up her room and bed awaiting the imminent arrival.

Trying to forget and trying hard to concentrate Jeanie ploughed ahead as there was nothing else she could do after all she couldn't have the baby for her.

The only thing she knew was routine and today couldn't be any different.

Chapter 2

At home, Ivy lay in bed unable to sleep, and as waves tightened in her stomach, she could feel the storm brewing inside. As she made a move towards the door, she stopped suddenly almost paralysed in fear feeling unable to shout for help as the pains came and went. The doctor had visited regularly putting Ivy on bed rest, but she knew tonight was different.

Outside the wind howled stronger and the panic washed over her along with the pain, and as she fell to the floor, she screamed out into the still of the night.

"MUM!" The house erupted in a sound of stomping footsteps, and the transition from asleep to awake had been made in seconds as her family gathered. They knew the baby was coming and forcing her to stand her waters broke and before she knew it, she was on the way to the hospital with eight people in tow.

Ivy was given a side room with windows onto the corridor. The room was cold and dark and as the doctor appeared masked and gowned Ivy froze and panicked more. As she looked over to her mum with a sense of helplessness, Irene drew close to hold her daughter's hand.

"Mum I need Jeanie I can't do this without Jeanie. Mum get her now. I can't." As Ivy screamed again, Irene had no choice.

"Get Jeanie now!"

Jeanie by this time was covered from head to foot with oil, and her arms and back ached as the piston was heavy and cumbersome. Eric's bellowings had started to draw on her patience and on hearing his cackles increase she finally poked her head out to see what his problem was now.

"What the Fuck is wrong with you today?" Pissed off, tired and covered in shit Jeanie shouted back not able to understand what his problem was.

"You never listen! I said get to the hospital now Ivy's in labour, and there's something wrong." Eric more flustered than usual threw his clipboard at her as he ran down the gantry. Jeanie didn't need a second chance, and as she ran out of the side door, she didn't stop to catch her breath.

"I knew it I told her last night she looked like shit!" Knowing she had to get there and fast she started to flag down anything which could get her there quicker than her own feet. Waving her hands rapidly a van slowed down and stopped just in front of her.

"What's up Jea?" pausing and panting rapidly Jeanie tried to catch her breath.

"I need to get to the Hospital..."

"Hop in I'm on my way over to that side anyway." Jeanie looked like a cat on hot bricks, and as they reached the hospital, she didn't have time to say Thank you! Stepping out before the van had stopped she waved in gratitude and barged her way through the double doors. As she ran down the grey-walled corridor, her sisters sat in anticipation of her arrival. Jeanie still trying to gather breath rested her hands on her knee's hoping her words would poke out.

"Where is she?"

"Second one down." Not one for waiting she barged her way through and went straight to Ivy's side.

"What's all this about?" The panic was evident in both Ivy and Irene's face.

"I can't do this Jeanie she's stuck, for fuck sake she's stuck!" Tears rolled down Ivy's cheek as the chaos began to unfold in the delivery room. Seeing Irene in the same state Jeanie spoke firmly trying to keep a lid on the emotional ramblings which set around her.

"Calm down you're not helping. Either stay and be calm or get the fuck out and I will deal with this. Doctor tell me what we have to do!" Ivy grabbed desperately to hold onto Jeanie's arm hoping for any sign of comfort. Irene, now fervently unimpressed by her daughter's forcefulness poised before her response.

"Just help." Hesitantly moving to one side and speaking through gritted teeth the small amount of venom rolled off her tongue as she silently saw her daughter take control. Still gripped in panic Ivy looked for reassurance and as Jeanie's presence brought her a small sense of relief she listened intently to the Doctor.

"This baby is just as tired as you mum, but you need to hear to my instructions and push as hard as you can. Do you understand?" As Jeanie looked back at Ivy, she nodded knowing the next few minutes would mean life or death.

"Listen this baby has had enough, and she needs to come out! Now grab hold of me sit up and push with everything you have and don't stop until I say so got it."

The screams of labour could be heard down the ward, and as Jeanie held onto Ivy, she kept eye contact always encouraging her sister. Ivy trusted her so implicitly that the pair worked in conjunction Jeanie to calm and Ivy to push. Ivy didn't want to think anymore, squeezing her sister's hand she continued to coax her lovingly.

"Come on I know you can do it. " As the baby appeared Ivy fell back into the bed.

"Jea is she ok, please?"

"They've had to break her arm to get her out but she's ok she must be tough like you." As the nurse turned around Jeanie jumped in fright.

"Are you holding?" Jeanie stepped back shaking her head, and as she looked back at herself in the glass, she smiled uneasily as the nurse handed the beautiful baby girl over to Ivy.

" I'll leave you to it I stink, and I think I've done my bit." As she tried to exit the room, Ivy extended her arm.

"Thank you!"

"Your turn now." The footsteps of the remaining six sisters could be heard piling into the delivery room, and the screams surrounded the corridor. Jeanie sat on the bench opposite the poster board closing her eyes taking a moment to reflect.

"Can't say it's been boring today what a day."

"You can say that again!" ." Not expecting a voice to appear Jeanie sat up embarrassed of the fact she had just been caught. Recognising that it was the doctor from the delivery room Jeanie's cheeks flushed crimson.

"Sorry Doctor force of habit you know," Blushing more she continued. "Anyway thank you."

"Don't thank me. I don't think your sister could have done that without you." The doctor smiled thoughtfully, however, still embarrassed and still trying to shrug off the compliment she blushed again.

"Smoke?" Extending a packet of cigarettes towards Jeanie's direction she smiled unable to bring a sentence to her lips.

"I know it's a bad habit, and I'm not supposed to offer, but in these circumstances, I think I can bend the rule?"

"I don't, but a little air may be nice." As she strolled back down the grey dimly lit corridor, she looked at the doctor's face with seeming familiarity. Jeanie couldn't quite place where she had seen him before but was confident she knew him. As they reached the doorway, a small congregation had gathered all trying to light cigarettes from frigid frost bitten hands.

"Do you remember me?" Jeanie looked puzzled, and as she shuddered in the cold, she shook her head. Pausing to light his cigarette the doctor seemed upset by her answer.

"Maybe it's this light." As he led Jeanie to an empty doorway at the side of the main entrance, he bent closer making sure she could see his face.

"What about now?" As Jeanie was about to speak the doctor kissed her softly. Stepping back in shock and unable to comprehend what had just happened she came to her senses rapidly.

"James, your James Watson… Why did you? What? I mean why?" unable to string the sentence together James followed with his.

"I've wanted to do that for years and tonight gave me the greatest opportunity. " Pausing to take a drag of his cigarette he looked deeply into her eyes hoping for any response.

"I'm sorry I couldn't help it and after the last time, I just couldn't. I couldn't get you out of my thoughts and with everything that's going on. I'm sorry this is happening a bit fast. "As the doctor paused Jeanie smiled anxiously.

"I remember, how I can't forget, the last time we spoke was at my father's funeral."

"We didn't just talk Jeanie I've been thinking about that kiss for the last eighteen months. I'm sorry it's so sudden, but I asked for a transfer up here so I could find you, now that I have I'm not willing to let you go." As James bent in closer, Jeanie was still unsure of his actions. Trying to pull everything together in her mind she started to unravel where James fitted into the equation.

"I don't understand why? Why would you do that? I mean nothing happened!" As he threw the cigarette into the newly laid snow, he grabbed her hand resting it on his chest softly.

"I'm staying at the Old Cock in town. I finish my shift at midnight tonight, and I'm not going to take no for an answer!" Jeanie watched cautiously as his fingers warmed against her skin.

"You're very sure of yourself aren't you?" Placing his other hand over the top of hers, he pulled her close hoping his sincerity would be more apparent. "I hoped you remember me a little better or maybe it meant more. I just want you to hear me out. Please come to the pub tonight even if it's just to finish off what I need to say. Listen I have to get back. Promise me" Jeanie still dumbstruck at his self-assured assault remembered the kiss and remembered how passionate it had been including the gentleness of his touch. The problem was why now and why had he come to find her.

"I love you, Jeanie, I always have done, and I'm here to make you mine, and I intend to." As he brushed the strands of hair away from her forehead, she felt the small pulses of electric under her skin. As he kissed Jeanie softly on the cheek, he disappeared in the snow and through the main entrance.

"Ok what the fuck just happened. What was that about?"

Jeanie bit her lip not able to understand how she had been caught up in his sincerity and as her head swam with a thousand thoughts she tried to piece some of his puzzle together.

Her sister had just nearly lost her baby, and in the same day, the doctor who had delivered the baby had just confessed he loved her. Sitting on the bench at the front of the hospital she watched the snow, and as the soft, crisp white flakes settled on the ground, she followed the crystal coloured carpet around her feet.

"Dad if you're watching this you taught me well!
You always hear how men don't get women. Well,
guess what I don't get men."
As she walked along the snow-covered lanes, she
transferred her thoughts back to the afternoon in
question. James had been very supportive when her
father had died, and on the plus side, he was a
handsome man. Jeanie toyed with whether she
should or shouldn't go. This kiss seemed different
to the last. Jeanie touched her lips trying to
remember the last time she felt desired or desirable.
" Pull yourself together girl. It's a kiss nothing more
and what's the worse that could happen." Jeanie
struggled with the memories of the day that he left
and no matter how much she tried to justify his
appearance her thoughts always came back to the
same conclusion. What did a doctor want with a
grease monkey like her? He was beautiful, and she
was not the prettiest pebble on the beach. Why?

As she kicked at the snow, she tried to provide an
order to her thoughts which weren't forthcoming.
All of her previous relationships had been disaster's
why should this be any different. She was twenty-
nine years old single and looking after now a family
of nine why did she need to complicate things more.
In the back of her mind, she was looking for
romance a lover or now maybe a husband. She
wanted children or just a life outside of her family
and not being able to comprehend the obscurity of
the situation had sparked her curiosity.

The clock seemed to roll around very slowly after
the morning's events and as the shift began to
change at eighteen hundred Jeanie put on her coat
and headed out of the building. Eric had
disappeared already after being confused by
Jeanie's sudden incomprehensible mood. The
debrief sessions for the evening had started to take
place and leaving them in control Jeanie slipped out

of the back door leaving the instructions with the floor manager. Finding her walk leading back towards the hospital she stood at reception contemplating her next move. She had no flowers or gifts to bring, and she was covered in oil and other than thinking she was the maintenance man she looked like and smelt like a tramp mixed with a traction engine.

As she sneaked past the nursing station, she rolled around the corner where she saw Ivy's beaming face cradling her new child.

"I didn't think you would be back tonight?"

"I know I have had a rather an unusual day so far and this morning was the start." Jeanie looked at the floor trying to hide the confusion inside.

"Come on chick you know you can tell me anything after this morning I owe you a lot more than I already did." Jeanie hated compliments and felt embarrassed and awkward if anyone mentioned good points about her character.

"He kissed me. He barely knows me we worked together for nine months before dad died and he was very charming and quite lovely to look at but Ivy this is me. Give me an engine or a piece of machinery I know what to do but give me a man who is interested and I fall to pieces; I'm just not cut out for this!"

"Slow this down who kissed you when? Start from the beginning because you have lost me already." Ivy placed the baby in the crib at the side of the bed and seeing Jeanie so confused she stroked her cheek coaxing whatever story she had to tell out of her.

"Ok, I see you're talking about the doctor."

"That obvious."

"I saw how he looked at you. You've always been a funny little thing. Jeanie, he obviously has a thing for you. Listen to me remember what you said to me when I met George. This time I'm going to say it to

you. No regrets. Go and see him what's the worse
that could happen. You could even enjoy yourself."
Jeanie started to bite her nails causing Ivy to dig in a
little deeper.

"Jea you've worked with him you should know him
a little for goodness sake. You spent ten hours a day
with him he's not that much of a stranger. He's seen
me a couple of times today, and yes we all
remember him how can you not! Rosie nearly
passed out cause she had no makeup on. He is a
very handsome man, and he speaks highly of you
and mum can't be pissed off about a doctor."

"But it's not normal!"

"Jeanie May Rutherford you're a beautiful and
talented woman any man should be grateful to have
you in their life I am. I don't know what I would do
without you some days so stop being a damp squid
and go and enjoy the doctor, and that's an order."
Ivy pointed to the door, and as she giggled, Jeanie
knew her sister was right, and there was no reason
to hold back she had always been a good girl why
not. As she reached the door of the ward, Jeanie
smirked always having to have the last say.

"He was arrogant you know." Ivy pulled her face
and pointed directly back to the corridor.

"Go away and don't forget to tell tomorrow."
As Jeanie disappeared through the back of the
hospital, she hesitated still confused at the unknown
prospects he offered. Jeanie had settled into a life of
work and responsibility, and this was just going to
complicate matters further. Placing her hands back
in her pockets she hid back in her scarf and taking
two steps forward and three steps back Jeanie
couldn't make up her mind what to do.

Sitting in the bus shelter, she started to reminisce
about her previous relationship; she had been hurt
so badly by one man who had promised to love and
respect her instead all he did was abuse any trust

she had. Trying not to generalise Jeanie waited for a sign and as the hour rolled past the only thing that greeted her was dirty washed up slush from the side of the road. By this time she knew fate wasn't going to make this decision and as she jumped from her seat, she continued to walk to town.

"What am I waiting for a sermon? A burning bush? Not every man is the same, but you never know. Ivy's great words of wisdom! What's the worst that could happen? I can tell you now I could be found dead at the bottom of a field with my knickers round my ankles and strangled by my boot laces!" Jeanie laughed under her breath knowing her self-reasoning wasn't going to help.

As Jeanie walked past the old church, the snow had started to gather around the graves, and a calmness had fallen over the village. The steps of The Old Cock pub beckoned and as she looked at the clock tower across from the grocery store the town seemed to be at peace, unlike Jeanie. Everything had a calm serenity being spotlighted by a silvery moon but inside Jeanie's stomach somersaulted and churned.

The door to the pub was closed, and a dim light from the corner room could be seen through the mock Tudor glass, and as her mind flipped from yes to no, she started to feel butterflies in her stomach. Jeanie felt she needed more time the events of the day had overwhelmed her and even though everything shouted Yes Jeanie still felt the huge pull to NO. As she ran out of time, the squeak of hinge sounded out, and she turned she was forced to jump back onto the road.

"Fucking hell Jeanie, you frightened me to death!"

"I'm sorry Jim I was asked to meet someone here, and I'm a little late."

"I know who you're meeting, and he's been like a hen on hot bricks all night! Get in here, or you will have the whole town talking." Jim closed the door quickly, and as he shivered at the doorstep, Jeanie knew he hadn't finished his rhetoric.

"Right you I'm only going to say this once, and it's about time. James is a nice bloke you're a lovely girl. No funny business in my pub and I'm going to bed. Night Doc!" As he disappeared up the staircase behind the bar, he pulled the door shut behind him. Jeanie now frozen stiff not knowing what to expect, saw James sat at the side of the fire, and as she studied every expression she could see the well-assured demeanour of before now completely out of sight. With a bottle of beer in his hand and an overturned book on the table, Jeanie started to see his inability to concentrate. Feeling intrigued she peered around the corner wanting to see more. He looked like an expectant father, and as he ran his hands through the thick dark hair, his dark eyes seem to pierce the night as if his answer lay in the cold outside. As he looked at his watched his anxiety seemed to increase with each passing second.

Jeanie still hiding behind the main bar and still not knowing what to do she moved closer and as the floor creaked she knew it had marked her position. Knowing she had been heard she saw his head rise from his hands.

"I thought I'd frightened you away. I didn't believe you were going to come I didn't know what to think. Can I get you anything?" Jeanie shook her head half anxious that she had been found.

"I'm sorry about before. I was.....please forgive me? Come and sit down." He seemed agitated and uncomfortable, and as Jeanie shook his hand, he found himself confused by her reaction. Finding a spot, she sat in the corner next to the fire. James still unsure sat beside her trying to gauge her thoughts. Looking at her in the glow of the fire Jeanie's auburn hair seem to shimmer in the dying embers, and as the flames danced around her shoulders, he couldn't help but want her.

She looked at him in silence wanting to look at the floor and feeling more out of place than usual. "Maybe I should go."

"Please don't I've been rehearsing this for months, and now that you're here I've forgotten what to say." He paused nervously grabbing her hand. "I'm sorry. I meant what I said outside of the hospital, and I've not been able to get you out of my head. I wanted to say something before your father died, but it didn't seem appropriate. I mean after everything that that happened." Jeanie breathed deeply letting go of his hand.

"It was just a shock, and I didn't, I didn't know what to do, and after dad had died, things were such a mess. I thought you were just being kind, supportive. Listen I'm not good with this…..I don't know what to say."

"Jeanie Rutherford, I spent nine months with you, and I haven't been able to think or breathe without you. I've missed you, and I know you like talk to be straight, so I'm going to tell you. I fell in love with you, and if I'm truthful I have pictured myself making love to you a thousand times?" Not wanting to hear any further Jeanie grabbed her things spinning on the spot.

"Okay, too much too soon, too quick! This is a lot for me to take in and I'd love to be swept off my feet but back off one minute!" Jeanie looked intently at James unable to comprehend how deep the conversation had become.

" I'm sorry you usually. I'm sorry I wanted to tell you eighteen months ago, I thought you felt the same,"

" I don't know what you expect me to say, James, you have waltzed in after all this time and just expected me to jump into bed with you. How do you think I feel?" James sat at the table taking another cigarette he rubbed his face with his hands. "I understand how this looks, but it isn't the same. I want to love you, take care of you, I want to make you happy Jeanie. In the time that I have known you-you changed me you changed me for the better and for what it's worth I have this," Bending down on one knee he produced a ring. Jeanie now taken aback for the second time watched as the blue sapphire danced in the darkness of the room.

"I love you marry me, Jeanie." Excusing herself, she moved towards the bar, and as she put on her jacket she spun again trying to make a decision "You're asking me to marry you," James nodded not wanting to say anything else just in case she left. "Please don't go I beg you just give me a chance." She was the girl who never took risks and always calculated caution; she was always the good one the loyal one, the one that was always devoted her time to her family. Jeanie was either going to take a chance experiencing life or walk away.

"You love me" James held out his hand trying to reassure her.

"Please come back inside let us talk work things out, please Jeanie" Standing in the cold she tried, to sum up, her next move. Her deliberation and insecurity seemed to pain him deeply. Taking his hand, Jeanie knew she was taking a chance, and as she took off her jacket, Jeanie felt the little electric tingles again in her spine. As he wrapped himself around her, he ran his hand down her face and neck. This time Jeanie leaned into him and placed one hand on his chest she kissed him, and as he pulled her close, she felt his fingers run down her back. "James I know what I did, and I did remember you…" James kissed her neck, and as she closed her eyes, he ran his thumb over her lips.

24

"I want you to be my wife Jeanie I want you. I always have. All I want you to do now is say yes,"
"I'm scared James. I'm scared because I've been here before and I remember what happened that day. I remember how you held me."
"Whatever you want I will give it to you. I left everything just to be with you, and all I could think about during my residency was getting back to you. I've never been in love like this before, and just the fact that you're here now makes me happy.
I don't want a night Jea I want you forever, and I will do whatever you want me to do just to make that happen." As he played with the top button of her cardigan, he felt it slip through his fingers without an interruption, and as each one fell, he brought her hands to his face.
"Tell me what you're thinking."
"Why me? Why now?" Feeling his hands smooth down the inside of her shirt Jeanie couldn't help but catch her breath. He had enticed her into a moment, and at that moment she didn't want him to stop.
"Please don't be scared of me. But the answer to your question is simple. I love you, and I don't want to live without you near me any longer. The thought of coming back to you has kept me going for months, and now I can feel you I never want to let you go." His eyes sparkled wildly, and as they flickered in the dark burning embers of the fire, she felt lost and confused.
"I've never taken a chance before James. I've always calculated my decisions and weighed up every option. With you, I feel it's not possible. I've seen the sunrise with you more than once but always as friends not like this." As he kissed the palm of her hand, he saw the confusion cross her brow, and even though she lay in his arms, he knew he had to convince her.

"I remember the first day I met you. You were this scruffy fowl mouthed little destroyer which made me feel like the biggest prick on the planet. I didn't like you at all." Seeing Jeanie laugh he smoothed the strands of hair once more from her face.

"In fact, you made my life a nightmare, and I hated my father and my peers for putting me with obviously the basest of working class. I was an asshole, and with each new day I spent with you I knew it. Then we had a full machine breakdown, and you only had me to help, and I remember it now. Now it wasn't because you laid between my thighs although I must admit a certain amount of enjoyment that situation gave me. It was the pride and determination you had to see everything through and make sure everyone was alright. From that day I saw you. I felt every mean word and forgot my selfish pride. I fell in love with the woman you are and for the man you want me to be." As she bit her lip, he knew he had captured her thoughts, and as James kissed her softly, he felt her body give in to him.

"Be my wife, Jeanie." As her breathing slowed and her eye glassed over Jeanie could feel her body betraying her and her mind falling for him.

"I have one condition. If this is going to happen, you have to give me six month's before any wedding plans." She couldn't believe what had just come out of her mouth and as he dragged his fingers over her lips, he couldn't understand what had been said.

"I won't let you down, Jeanie." The fire had begun to burn itself out, and as the darkness crept in, neither noticed the impending gloom. Drunk on confusion Jeanie stared directly at James,

"I said yes didn't I?" Questioning herself, James kissed her on her cheek and held holding her tight.

"I'm glad you did." Worrying whether this was a reaction to how lonely she had felt she took James by the hand.

"In that case, I think you better show me your room." As he grabbed his belongings from the fireside, he led Jeanie up the narrow staircase, and as they reached the roof of the pub, he opened the door to a huge room.

An arched window looked out into the snow covered street, and the big double bed filled the middle of the chamber. James kissed her again, and as his lips left hers, she had never felt as alive in a long time. It also beats going home feeling helpless and lonely.

It was evident that he wanted her, and he'd been dreaming about this day for months, however, feeling her tremble again he stepped back not wanting to frighten her away again.

"James I'm dirty, full of oil. I need a bath, and also I need to tell you something."

"You can tell me anything?" he walked back over to the fireplace and took her hand softly.

"You don't have to do anything tonight if you're uncomfortable; I just want you with me that's all I've ever wanted. Listen let me run you a bath."

Jeanie sat in the tub with her head on her knee's she wasn't nervous anymore, in fact, she felt the opposite she was quite content for the first time in a while and taking a chance, and the doctor was surpassing expectations. As the water began to cold, she stepped out noticing that he had left his shirt on the rail and having nothing else available she put it on.

Beautiful butterflies started to emerge in her stomach and thoughts of him holding her and touching her sent sparks around Jeanie's body. Checking the corridor, she crept back towards the doctor's bedroom, and as she slipped through the door, she turned to close it quietly. As she stood with her back to the room, she felt James's hands on her. They were warm and smooth as he kissed her softly the electric shocks seemed to emanate around every part of her body. Moving away Jeanie stood in front of the fireplace, her hair still dripped with water, and as James brought a blanket, he wrapped it around her shoulders.

"I like your shirt." As she sat down in front of the fire, she waited for his next move but unable to wait Jeanie kissed him feeling she was living in a fantasy. As the water dripped from her hair, the white shirt became translucent and the shadow of her body silhouetted through the cloth.

"I'm sorry. It just felt, and I don't. I'm sorry this is a first for me, and I'm just a little nervous."

"You mean the first time with me."

"No, I mean the first ever time." As he lay his hand against her cheek, he knelt in front of her and pulled her close. As they kissed, she felt his hands on her breasts and his breath on her neck. Her body gave way to his touch far too easily, and every stroke made her react more. Wrapped in his embrace, she began to undo his buttons on his shirt, and as it slipped off his body, she could feel his heart beat. As her fingers rolled over his smooth chest, she couldn't help but admire how beautiful he was. Jeanie started to unbutton her shirt, but before she reached the bottom, James caught hold of her hand. "Is this what you want?" Jeanie felt his hands running over her stomach, the warmth of his touch and understanding in his voice made Jeanie want him without reason. As his fingers reached the opened gap near her breast, Jeanie closed her eyes. "Please don't stop," Her words echoed inside distantly remembering the girl she was. Her fear had disappeared and nothing else but feeling him connect with her mattered. Keeping her eyes closed he ran his hands over her shoulders, and as the shirt fell exposing her body to the night.

Jeanie's insecurities fell with it.

No longer self-conscious she opened her eyes as James watched the flames dance along her pale silk-like skin. For him the intensity and desire he felt overpowered how he had imagined her. The thought of making love to her beleaguered with the power of her presence and with Jeanie's still hand rested on his chest she seemed fixated by his heart beat rising and falling with every touch. As he picked her up in his arms, he carried her to the bed, her body now everything he ever wanted or desired he couldn't wait to feel her finally. Sliding her hands down she began to take off the rest of his clothes, and as they wrapped themselves in each other's embrace all the fear, she felt before turned to excitement.

Jeanie arched her body in pleasure and as he kissed her from head to toe feeling his anticipation. His soft kisses connecting with every part of her body made her body flood with the expectation of their union. As she ran her leg down his back, he slowly descended creating the connection she had been craving, and as the pain engulfed her body, with each slow rise and fall, every muscle yearned for more.

As he gently moved his body with hers, she was unable to distinguish where he ended, and she began. Quivering he picked her up from beneath him and as he pressed his hands over the curve of her hip he kissed her ardently. As She slowly lowered herself onto him, he placed his hands on her back feeling the small beads of sweat expire from her skin. Moving the strands of hair from her face he cupped his hand around her cheek pulling her gently towards him. James felt Jeanie arch in pleasure, and as he began to climax, she held him tight as the movements intensified. Looking into her eye's he felt the passion between them heighten and as she rested her head on his chest, she felt secure in his embrace. Her heartbeat raced in time with his, and whether it was right or wrong didn't matter anymore.

AS she touched his brow, she followed the curve of the perfect line above his eye. His gaze hadn't faltered, and as he caught her hand, he kissed it softly.

"What happens now?" holding her hand he placed her fingers back on his chest.

"You stay forever..." Curling up Jeanie felt her eye's start to close, and the security of his arms took away some of the emptiness. Today certainly wasn't another day.

Chapter 3

Jeanie opened her eyes and blinked several times to see what the time was. As she lay slowly down on her pillow, Jeanie knew she was late for work again, but as she stared blankly at James's watch, she could help but gaze at her new fiancé who was still fast asleep. His clothes still lay on the floor at the side of the bed, and it was far too tempting to forget work. As she pulled back the covers, she couldn't help but take a sneak peek at James, his smooth, toned skin welcomed her back to bed, and she giggled at the thought of him still undressed.

As Jeanie moved slowly into the cold, she glanced towards the fire which had burnt to nothing and as Frost gathered on the inside of the window it made any movement out of the warmth painful. Jeanie shuddered as the snow had fallen rapidly overnight and the street outside was crisp clean and white. As Jeanie gathered her things quietly, she started to dress. Her clothes felt wet with cold, and the smell and grime made Jeanie instantly feel unclean. As she moved around the bedroom, the floorboards creaked under her weight, and as she looked back, she made sure she hadn't disturbed him.
"Sneaking out."
"I didn't want to wake you. I'm late for work again, and Eric will think I've gone AWOL." Jeanie blushed as he got out of bed and as he put on his trousers he walked to the door he covering himself around her
"Let me walk you to work at least," Jeanie smiled as he kissed her still caught up in the fantasy of last night's events.
"You don't have to its cold, and you must have had a long day yesterday. I just want to say thank you for last night" James looked at her puzzled not quite understanding where thank you fitted.

"What's that for it should be me thanking you? I don't think anyone has ever made me feel like that before. I was very pleasantly surprised," Jeanie still blushing bit her lip half embarrassed and half intrigued.

"I just needed to say it anyway. What does pleasantly surprised mean," James took her hand and kissed her avidly, and as he pressed her against the door Jeanie wanted to stay.

"Please don't you're making this really difficult for me to go," Folding her hands around his waist James kissed her neck.

" I know you have work but just stay for a little bit longer."

She couldn't help but want him as his touch had been so gentle and now he was lavishing her with kisses her body had started to betray her once again. As he took his time to caress every part of her body resisting him proved tough.

"I've got to go! I have to go, I don't want to but my family and Eric." James pulled away and stood in the middle of the room.

"Ok keeping my hands to myself." Jeanie coiled her hair around the back of her ears and bit her lip again. As the sun streamed behind him it extenuated, his physic and Jeanie caught her breath thinking she was still in her fantasy.

"Are you ok." Jeanie still staring broke her glance.

"I'm sorry....sorry. Just you are attractive, and it seemed like a perfect moment I'm babbling...Ok time to go." Before she turned the handle his warm, smooth hands caressed her back and shoulders again, gulping the air down quickly, she counted to ten unable to move.

"Stay. Let's stay in bed and forget about the world." Jeanie closed her eyes as every touch created an image in her mind. In a tempting thought, her jacket fell to the floor, and his hands circled the nape of her neck. As his kisses penetrated her skin, every cell set alight. As he pressed her against the door, he lifted her hands and placed them into his forcing them above her head. As he gently caressed her skin with his mouth, Jeanie felt lost again in his embrace. "Let me make love to you."

"I should have gone when I said."

"You're late anyway what's another hour." His soft tone rumbled down her spine and with his body pressed firmly against her, she could feel how much he wanted her. Spinning her around James cupped her fingers again still pressing her firmly into the door, and as his lips grazed over hers, his tongue delved deeper. Jeanie breathlessly responded to every request not ever wanting to leave the room.

"James please stop. I can't" keeping her hands pressed against the door he stepped back halting at her request.

"Do you want me to stop."

"No but.." His fingers making light work of the buttons of her shirt dragged it from her body, and as he lifted her from the floor, she knew there was no going back.

"Wrap your legs around me." Doing as she was told Jeanie felt him enter her and as James's hot breath intensified on the nape of her neck his body pulsated around increasing the feelings from last night. His desire and ecstasy throbbed through her core, and as he carried her back to bed, he threw off her shirt and entangled himself in her embrace.

"Let it go Jea..." As she felt the rush of blood around her body the heat from her skin radiated causing the small beads of sweat to run down her back. As his whispers rippled against her skin once again, Jeanie closed her eyes feeling her breath escape from her lips, and as James's panted heavily, she wiped his brow still in the unknown state of how to react.

"I told you I wasn't going to let you go." As Jeanie bit, her lip James pulled her towards him feeling her heart race.

"James I have to go." As he grabbed her clothes and helped her dress, he escorted her once more to the door.

" I'm not going to try anything. I love you."
Grabbing her coat, Jeanie quickly slipped through, and as she leant on the opposite side, she wished she was still there.

"I love you." Hearing his whisper, Jeanie set off for work.

With both hands still firmly planted on the door frame he could still feel her and as his thoughts betrayed the anticipation of what was next was enough. As he took a cigarette from the bedside table, he made his way to the window and on hearing the side door of the pub open he watched Jeanie cross the street following the tracks she made in the newly laden snow.

"I love you!"

"You'll freeze." She could feel his eyes and his hands still on her body and as she moved and further away she felt the intensity melt the snow beneath her feet.

The embers of his cigarette looked like small clouds floating around the window gathering speed in the frosty air, and as he observed her, he couldn't help but hold his breath. Desperately wishing he had followed he tried to occupy his mind elsewhere. The problem was he could still smell the vague oily residue around the room and the smell of her skin on the bed. As he took the last drag, he breathed the smoke out longingly as nothing else was going to be able to take his mind away from her today. Standing at the fireplace he stubbed his cigarette out, and in doing so the room seemed cold and vacant, and without question he missed her. Unable to shake himself he sat on the bed reminiscent of the events from last night and this morning. As he smoothed his hand against her pillow, he started to imagine Jeanie's soft skin pressed against his body. Every moment ran through his memory as if he was sat watching a replay and he couldn't help but feel pleasure as every inch of him pricked with excitement. He had dreamed of this moment for so long that now it didn't seem real.

Jeanie was the one. She had to be.

He had walked away from a life that he had known just to be with her, and his family had begged him not to go, but they didn't know Jeanie as he did. He had also walked away from a six-year relationship, and when she had begged him to reconsider, he felt nothing. Catherine had never felt like Jeanie.

James had met Catherine at medical school, and she had supported him unquestionably even through his many infidelities. As his thoughts flicked from the past to present he found himself questioning his fidelity again except with Jeanie, he could never imagine any other woman, but with Catherine, any other woman who took his fancy was his game. The only woman to truly see him was Jeanie.

Staring at the ceiling, he remembered how sex felt with Catherine. However, that was it; it was just sex. For the first time in six years, he had made love. Catherine had never made him react the way Jeanie did and what he couldn't comprehend was that even now she played on his mind when no other woman had. Every other woman up to this point had been a conquest an assurance of his dominance and virility. Catherine was never enough to satisfy him however he liked her beauty and how she looked on his arm, but that's all she was a parade pleaser. His father used to scold him regularly telling him woman were not his toys and one day his looks would fade, and he would be left empty broken and alone.

With Jeanie, he had met his match. No matter how hard he tried to win her over, she was always one step ahead. She knew the game he was playing and never cowered when he tried to exert his dominance. Instead, she taunted him and scorned him genuinely exposing some of the inner insecurities he felt, and in all of this, she had somehow become his equal. She was the first and last thing on his thoughts.

Standing in the bathroom, he looked into the mirror examining his reflection, and in a way, everything felt different. He felt complete. Reaching for his shirt the damp collar smelt of her and as he breathed it in he felt alive, free, and she had liberated him. Putting on his jacket, he made his way downstairs, and as he reached the old doorway, he looked back not wanting to leave his memories behind. She was the gateway to his happiness, and all he had to do now was open the door.

Jim bumbled around the bar busying himself with the morning duties and on noticing Jeanie's scarf he picked it up waiting for the doctor's arrival.
"Good night was it. You know Doc she's a good girl. You don't lead girls like that astray." James took hold of his hand and shook it firmly knowing he meant well. On seeing the scarf, he took hold of it and wrapped it around him.
"I know Jim that's why I'm marrying her...." Jim still holding onto his hand smiled happy that hopefully this time she had met a good one.
"Good, she deserves a good bloke that one. She's a big presence around here. Heart of solid gold like her dad." James smiled back on hearing Jim's words. His sentiment seemed to echo his thoughts. She was the one.

Chapter 4

Jeanie arrived at the front gate of the factory, and as she slid through, she bit her lip and smiled ambiguously about her evening's activities. Sneaking through reception, she tried to pass the downstairs office without anyone spotting her. Seeing her antics, Eric finished his conversation and started on her almost right away.

"Half past four you were due in young lady, it's quarter past six, and you're due to service the General's car this morning!" His thick Glaswegian accent made any statement sound like a telling off. "You're up to something, I can tell!" With the passing comment, he turned and made his way into the downstairs office.

"Fucking great just what I need a poxy service to start my day with a smile!" Jeanie caught her words as she turned towards the workshop as her morning had been glorious, but it was nice to pretend for a change.

Turning to her toolbox, she started to throw things around taking out any unnecessary items she didn't need. Jeanie's distaste for services began when she was forced to do them by her father, and the only reason she continued to do them was that her dad had got the trust of the base and she couldn't let him down. He had worked so hard for the extra money Jeanie felt obliged to continue just out of courtesy.

Sitting down on the rickety stool which lay beside an old filing cabinet in the workshop made it easy for the memories to come back. Her dad used to stand pretending to tinker with bits and pieces so they could talk. They used to spend days locked away perfecting small pieces of equipment, so they worked beautifully and in some way it made Jeanie feel warm inside.

Leaning forward Jeanie felt a pinch in the top of her leg, and as she placed her hand in her pocket, she took out the engagement ring. It was beautiful, and as she slipped it on her finger, she shook her head in disgust as her fingers looked like two burnt chipolatas with a sparkly bit that had been thrown in.

"Mrs J Watson. Jeanie Rutherford Watson umm think I'll have to work on that..." Taking off the ring she placed it back in her pocket and as she gathered the bits and pieces together and closed the toolbox.

The old van beat and rusted looked like her old man before he died and as she flung the back door open the creaks and groans sounded like him too. Continuing to throw everything inside she continued to think about her married name. Lost in thought, she dropped one of the boxes on her hand, and as she danced around the back of the workshop, Jeanie looked at the snow. It was deep and treacherous, and the cold clung to Jeanie's clothes like a child to their mother's apron strings. Negotiating the roads would be difficult but reaching the base in one piece was an adventure she looked forward to.

The snow had been cleared from the front of the base as she arrived and the security staff looked like tin soldiers frozen to their post. Making her way through the precession, she remembered the engagement ring in her pocket, and there was no way to conceal it. Everything would be checked before she was allowed through and as she looked around frantically, she popped it into her mouth trying to act as natural as she could.

After the usual checks and being escorted over to the garage Jeanie paid lip service to the private who had escorted her. His constant gripes about her sister had become a regular conversation, and under the usual circumstances, Jeanie would forget to listen. This time he was pissed off, and Iris had blown him off over a petty argument. Jeanie couldn't speak in fear of swallowing the ring; wanting the one-way conversation to be over she nodded politely in all the right places.

"Will you talk to her Jeanie?" Jeanie turned sideways and spat the ring out into her hand.

"Yes Yes, course." As she smiled graciously to his request, the young soldier disappeared from view. Jeanie raced to her office sincerely happy that she was now on her own the next challenged was to look for an appropriate hiding place for the ring. Nowhere in the garage seemed to be adequate or do the gem any justice and as she thought out loud, she grabbed the chain tucked under the layers of clothing.

"St Chris…..you've saved me before time to do it again," her dad had bought the chain when she was confirmed and when he died she swore never to take it off. As she looked at both trinkets together, she felt assured that now she was doing the ring justice. Concealing it back under her clothes Jeanie started to feel bad that she had only half listened to the private and she had no idea what she was supposed to say to Iris.

Jeanie's mind wandered and unable concentrate the feelings from this morning sent shivers down her spine. Feeling the bump under her clothes felt strange compared to the flat St Chris and just knowing it was there was a constant distraction. Gazing at the ring she studied its intricate design, and for the first time she felt all over the place and unable to focus on one thing for more than five minutes.

As Jeanie walked through the yard, the wind had begun to howl around the open spaces and Jeanie had started to mumble to herself as she always did when she didn't want to do something she knew she had to. As she got to the car, her mumblings had begun to sound louder.

"Talking to yourself is a sign of madness!" As the voice boomed out from behind it rang with a vague familiarity but again not wanting to find another distraction she continued to open her toolbox. As each bolt turned she couldn't concentrate, and the questions had already started to circulate inside her head. "Where will we live?" Does he want children? What the fuck am I doing?????"

Taking off the oil filter the questions screamed louder and louder prominent within every thought. Everything was bubbling over, and as Jeanie placed her hand around, she moved it the wrong way. As the metal cut deep into her palm, Jeanie started to swear knowing it was her fault and as the blood dripped from the deep cut, she slid down the side of the car unable to comprehend her stupidity. Conceding defeat, Jeanie started to look for a first aid kit, but it was inevitable that a small dressing wasn't going to work. Releasing a groan she raised her head towards the sky as she knew the only option was making her way to the medical wing and the potential for more lectures than she cared.

The walk over seemed to take an infinite amount of time and as her hand throbbed the cold had started to creep in, and by this point, the mumblings had turned into swearing and cursing at anything and everything. As she walked through the cold corridors, Jeanie had noticed an influx of recruits and more Americans. The grunts lined the hallways awaiting medical examinations, and these poor raw young lads with nothing more than vests and boxers stood in the corridor waiting for a doctor to say, "Cough please." Lines of boys seemed to be misplaced all over, and it looked more like a boarding school than a base and as Jeanie past her curiosity started to creep forward. As she gazed at the different ends of the lines the worried pale faces at the start and the jovial almost flirtatious end she wondered how relaxed she would feel and whether her reaction would be the same knowing that there was a good possibility of death waiting at the end.

Jeanie had seen it all on the base and just being around men quite a lot made her familiar with the antics and tactics that most of them used. As she smiled again, she couldn't believe she had fallen for it.

"Jeanie, Jeanie, you ok?" Liz one of the nurses and a friend to one of her younger sisters had spotted her walking down the corridor. Jeanie didn't care for Liz but knowing her hand needed attention she took the action of being more friendly than obtuse knowing she was a means to an end.

"Yeah, okay jus a small cut on my hand. Did it while on a service; I don't think it's bad." Continuing to walk Liz checked Jeanie's palm.

"It seems quite deep I will get one of the doctors to check you out wait here in this room!" Liz took her in a small white office which in contrast to the corridors was bright and stark. Jeanie blinked in the light looking as if she had just emerged from a darkened cave after twenty years and discovered electricity. Everything was white, floor, walls, bed and curtains.

Liz drew the curtain and started clucking like a hen trying to be polite Jeanie tried to listen; however, with the speed, Liz was talking she found it hard to keep up. The only bit that Jeanie understood was that the wound would need to be cleaned and in the buzz, Jeanie started to take the first layer of clothing off. Liz instructed her to sit and obliging Jeanie did as she was told and subconsciously began to swing her legs feeling like she was going for a check up.

As Jeanie looked around the room, she knew she stuck out like a sore thumb, her dirty overalls and filthy coat sat on the bed black and grubby to the stark whiteness around. As Jeanie further glanced over the furnishings, she started to feel out of place. As Liz came back for a second time this time, she was pushing the contents of a medical tray.

"Right let's clean it up and shall we. You're going to have to be more careful. How are Ivy and the new baby? Iris was telling me all about her." Before Jeanie had time to speak Liz had already started a new conversation she could talk for Britain and more besides.

"Umm, it's quite deep. It looks like you will need stitches I will get the Doc, and you will be as right as rain." With that, she flitted out from the side of the curtain and disappeared down the hallway. Jeanie looked at her hand and shook her head in disbelief at how fast Liz could walk and talk.

Jeanie watched the clock starting to become obsessed with the time and unable to stop swinging her legs she counted the seconds by each swing. When fifteen minutes went by her impatience grew, and she just wanted to finish the service and go home. Without waiting Jeanie put her coat on.

"James Sorry??" stepping back he seemed shocked to see her.

"What are you doing here?"

"I'm here to service the General's car. Why are you here?"

"I'm the doctor on the barracks!"

"You enlisted then" James looked at her puzzled face knowing she could answer her question and already satisfying her demand he replied.

"I had no choice there's a war, and I'm needed. Are you ok?" Jeanie paused looking at her palm.

"Silly really I wasn't concentrating and cut my hand." Finishing the sentence, she began to blush knowing James would know the reason why.

"Not concentrating, umm can't think of any reason why?" James beamed at her response, and the fact he had thrown her off guard made her feel at ease. "No idea what it could have been. I hear it's a new disease called doctor springing out of the woodwork and asking a strange girl to marry them; I believe it's catching" James laughed looking into Jeanie's hand and as she winced he looked deeper at the cut. "Needs stitches and tetanus. So does this disease come with symptoms?" Giving a coy look, he kissed her on the cheek.

"I will be back in a minute don't move!" Jeanie saluted and smiled to herself again. James looked very handsome in his uniform, and she couldn't help but think about last night, this morning, and all the questions which had begun to circulate again and again.

Was he mine????? Am I that lucky??? Jeanie started to count the endless amounts of positives James threw at her; he's funny, charming, sensitive, really good at making me feel comfortable and able to find my sarcastic comments quite endearing.

As James arrived back, Liz had followed, and as he looked again at the cut, Liz had prepared the injection. Liz still incessantly talking seemed unable to see the chemistry which had started to build between doctor and patient. Jeanie has also taken an interest in how James stitched her hand back together and was impressed at how delicate he was something that was still in the back of her mind. Smiling to herself, James looked up, and as he smiled back, she knew he was thinking about the same thing. Unaware of the glances Liz began to interrupt the moment.

"Doctor I believe you're single and new in town, so I believe it's my duty to show you around and possibly look in on the local dance at the Parish rooms, so what do you say?" James didn't say a word or take his eyes off Jeanie, and by this time she was glowing with his advances, which was now visible to see.

"Her! You're seeing her! She's the fat unattractively disgusting engineer from a group of seven sluts for sisters, and you're turning down me for her!!" Liz instantly knew her outburst could have her reprimanded, but at that point, she couldn't keep it in.

"Nurse I suggest you take your deluded response and minor intellect out of my cubical before you do something you can't apologise for. Do not speak to her or me, in the same way, do you understand?" Before the door had closed on Liz's departure, James had already sat down and continued to patch up Jeanie's hand.

"James. Thank you for defending my family and me, but I also have to agree with Liz on some minor details about what you see in me? I know people say it's not just about looks its personality but I only have one is that going to be enough?" James continued to bandage Jeanie's hand without speaking a word.

"I need to give you the tetanus shot, please drop your trousers and bend over the bed" The flirtatious innuendo at the start of the conversation had dramatically disappeared as now he spoke, without a quiver of humour and Jeanie did as he said. After the injection, she fastened and adjusted herself and without conversation moved gingerly towards the door. James moved just as quickly, and before Jeanie could slide around the corner, he blocked her path.

"Where do you think you're going?" As he closed the door, he gently coaxed her back into the room. "Back to work" James looked at her unable to comprehend why she would agree to a petty minded nurse.

"Take a seat back on the bed I haven't finished." As he paused, he seemed to mull over his thoughts carefully.

"Listen to me now. I am a thirty-five-year-old man, and I have had sex with twenty-two women in my life, and I have had three long term relationships all ending in disaster. I have been engaged once before, and it fell through when I started working at Rutherford Metals."

"That's it! You think I don't know, and I'm flattered, but this is a mistake."

"Will you shut up! At that time I was an arrogant, insensitive pig with no real experience of what real life was. Not for the everyday man. My mentor told me a few home truths, and he refused to work with me until I knew how to appreciate a fellow working man. He sent me to your father who indeed taught me a lot and then it all changed. You know why? " Jeanie shook her head intent on listening,

"I met an amazing person who was more real, who had time, patience, respect and love for everything she did. She's intelligent, talented, ambitious and loyal and she has the biggest heart I have ever seen, and she frightens me to death. I didn't understand and couldn't believe that this woman was covered in grease and oil every day and loving it because of the gratitude and dedication she had for her family. From that point, nothing was the same my patients were brother, aunts, cousins to me and they needed to be treated the same. My relationship failed as I changed because realising I was marrying her because it was expected of me not because I wanted to or was that much in love with her. You changed me even though you never asked for anything in return and you were always willing to give more. I used to admire your confidence, especially with your people. With all these qualities you still have no idea of how beautiful you are." James paused, unfolding his arms which had been pinched tight. "Am I supposed just to say thank you. I believe everything that you've told me. Cause the truth is I don't. Last night, this morning was the most amazing experience of my life, but I just can't help thinking you're doing this because of pity. Cause you couldn't help my father." As he sat down on the chair, James looked up seeing that his words have little effect.

"Ok, Jeanie. So I left everything and had sex with you last night cause of pity. I thought you knew me!"

"You were a self-centered, condescending know it all."

"So why would I invite you into my bed if I didn't think you were worth it." Not able to answer his question Jeanie knew she'd been trapped into listening again.

"Right so you're going to listen to me. On the evening your father died, I went back to the factory. I saw you taking a shower, and I couldn't take my eyes off you. I'd never seen someone with so much devotion for her family, and you still had the passion for keeping everything going even if that meant you had to be there after your father died. You're the most beautiful woman I had set eyes on, and even in grief, you kept strong for everyone else. I needed so much to speak to you I couldn't get you out of my head or heart. I wanted you then like I want you now.

I made love to you, and I have never felt like this before. I cannot concentrate, I'm smiling uncontrollably. I never expected to be this close to you so soon, and I just want to love you. I would give my career, my life and everything just to have you.

I understood back then with the circumstances, but you insisted….you insisted I go and live if not for myself for you. I knew that, and that's why I'm here Jeanie, I'm here because I don't feel like a whole person unless you're with me, you are my dream, and it didn't take me long to realise it.

Catherine. I've talked to you about Catherine, and I understood that love shouldn't feel empty. Until you, I don't think I'd ever known what it was or how to give it." As her tears fell onto her jacket, Jeanie tried hard to push them back with her hands. "Why didn't you tell me? Why didn't you?" "Cause I didn't know how." As he stroked his thumb across her cheek, Jeanie knew he had more to say. "I can remember my first day at the factory. I remember you talking about something along the lines of my people are not as educated as you, but they have something I will never have. Until I learn that this is just a man and I am just a woman our lives will always be portrayed as futile and not important enough to save. We all bleed and feel just on different pay grades. In here it makes no difference if you fuck up, we don't kill people. If you fuck up, it's because you're an arsehole and not worth respecting. Do you remember that?" As Jeanie nodded, she gulped in the air feeling her lungs burn, and her cheeks flush once more.

"I remember those words like Shakespeare had written them because they were honest, decent and genuine. I did at first think who the hell are you to talk to me like that, but you pricked my conscience, and when I lay in bed that night I couldn't help but think about what you said. I love you for your honesty, and I love you for your grace. It is time to believe that in all my life I have never wanted anyone the way I want you…..." Jeanie looked at the floor unable to comprehend; she didn't realise those days had meant so much and when they kissed the burden of her family had just taken over everything.

"I love you, Jeanie Rutherford." Jeanie closed her eye's as she had dreamed about a knight in shining armour coming home to take her away and make her life better. However, something still seemed too good to be true. He wasn't running away, in fact, he was standing to defend her honour, and all she could do was doubt him.

"James I've never had anyone touch me the way you do. I have been so lonely, and I don't mind admitting it. I just don't want to get this confused with my loneliness I want this desperately to be real. We became close friends, but I always thought..."

" What did you think. That you weren't good enough for me?"

Jeanie nodded and took hold of his hand placing it on her chest,

" My heart is racing James this scares me. You're a doctor I was an engineer's daughter still am. I'm covered in grease, shit and god know what else to make ends meat but you, your this figure this incredibly handsome doctor with your black hair and deep blue eyes and you're just that fantasy icon. Girls like me dream about men like you but last night doesn't seem real this whole affair whatever you want to call it doesn't seem real. Listen I learnt that you came back for me. Why me of all things? I am what I am James. This, this to me just seems too good to be true you seem too good to be true…."

"What do I have to do to prove I love you, I sacrificed everything for you I don't….I don't want to lose you I can't and I won't.

I understand this is quick and rushed and possibly too much I just want you to love me as I love you.

   Also please stop putting me on a pedestal as I have done lots of things I regret especially to the people I'm supposed to have loved and I don't want to do that anymore. Let me prove to you please at least give me a chance." As Jeanie stepped down from the bed, she sat next to James trying to hear his words with sincerity.

"I've been in a toxic relationship, and I've never been in love...But I imagine it should feel like this. Please just give me some time...." As Jeanie walked away, James grabbed her hand pulling her onto him, kissing her he pulled at the loosely fastened shirt and as he kissed her collarbone, Jeanie closed her eyes. She didn't want him to stop. Kissing her fervently Jeanie held on tightly, and as the kiss reached her mouth, she rested her head on his.

"I love you. I'm not going to stop saying it, but I understand how quick everything has been. I don't seem to be able to keep my hands off you either. I'm sorry if you felt pushed. I just want this more than anything." Jeanie kissed him again and as a tear fell James caught the salty taste.

"Don't cry please don't cry..."

"You scare me just be patient." Escorting her to the door, she paused, "Promise me something, James..."

"Anything" Moving her hair away he smiled and as she looked into his eye's Jeanie wanted to believe him.

"When we next make love let me be the first to tell you I love you." James swallowed deeply holding her he felt scared to respond and as she slipped away he knew the more he pushed her to love him, the more she would run away. The last thing he wanted was her to leave.

The day seemed to have merged into one big event, and as she wearily made her way back home that evening, it felt like a long journey. Walking through the door for the first time in two days her senses were hit with the sounds and smell that seven women in one household can create. Jeanie paused at the living room door where her mother and aunt was sat listening to the radio. Jeanie breathed in her family as if she was breathing in the smells of a home cooked meal and as she walked tiredly towards the kitchen, she stood again at the door frame as the frivolities and silliness erupted in front of her.

He was right her family had become her life. They were scattered around the kitchen like chess pieces, dancing around to the music playing on the radio in the living room.

"Jea Jea come here. What time do you call this?" Rose winced with excitement looking more like a puppy that was trying not to pee on the carpet than one of her sisters.

"Iris has been in touch with Liz tell us everything." As Rose finished her sentence mum walked into the kitchen

"Busy Day you look dreadful and smell worse, Girls go and get the bath ready for your sister she looks as if she could drop."

A procession of "Yes mum" followed as they disappeared in a gaggle of noise and perfume.

"Two days, what is it can't stand being home?" Jeanie wearily took off her boots and placed them near the back door. She gazed onto the back garden which looked like a winter fairy tale and the noise from her mum faded in and out buzzing around the inside of her mind. As the noise started to re-enter back into the conversation, her mum jumped in first.

"What can't come home and can't answer me either!"

"It's been a whirlwind couple of days I'm tired, I'm hungry, and I've got to go to work in six and a half hours, I'm sorry if my conversation isn't sparkling enough for you, but that's how I feel." Wearily responding Jeanie didn't want to cause her any offence and started to undress from her blood smeared oil filled clothes. As she placed them in a bag, she tried to turn off her mother's scolding by doing what she was told.

Her head and her hand hurt, and she longed for sleep, and as she was ushered up the rickety stairway, every board creaked and cracked as if to welcome her home. The girls had placed the bath in Ivy's temporary bedroom and filled it to the top with hot water and soap. Iris stood behind the door unable to stand still anticipating the next juicy piece of gossip.

"Come on spill the beans, Lizzie is livid, and I'm glad, come on Jea," Jeanie stood in an old vest and pants shivering

"Can I at least get in the bath first before you start the Spanish Inquisition." Iris helped Jeanie into the bath, and as Jeanie lay in the warm soapy water, she waited for the bombardment of questions.

"Where did you meet?"

"No how long?" June was trying to settle the others but had to chip in because of all the excitement.

"Leave her alone she knackered, anyway sweet pea I'm happy if you're happy." Jeanie lay back and disappeared under the water and as she emerged Flora had her fingers in the bottom of the tub wanting to speak and not quite knowing how to go around it. She played with the water as a child played with sand contemplating her thoughts she spoke.

"Jeanie" her questioning tone aired her concern.

"You don't have to say anything about him I just want to know one thing. Do you love him?" Jeanie looked at the girl's inquisitive faces unrequited to Jeanie's new found romance.

She was usually the butt of her sister's jokes, the old cat lady and spinster type. However, on this occasion, Jeanie's life was more exciting, and for a change, their lives had taken a back seat.

"Go and get my coat from the door and look in the pocket."

Flora closed the door like a mouse prizing a small piece of cheese from a trap as not to disturb the cat which sat downstairs. Jeanie's cumbersome oil soaked coat both disgusted and intrigued her at the same time, and as she rummaged around in the many layers of pockets, she couldn't help but voice her disgust. As she raised the jacket, the St Christopher appeared first and then the blue sapphire ring.

"He proposed last night, and I accepted." A small yelp of happiness from the girls brought mum upstairs,

"What's going on?" The girls froze to the commander in chief as she stood at the foot of the bath.

"Nothing ...mum umm just a little fun that's all." the sound of her swearing profoundly under her breath could be heard as the door closed abruptly.

"That was close."

"Jeanie just be careful. I would hate anything horrid to happen to you?" Jeanie lay back in the water contemplating her sister's concerns. She had her own worries and the fact that James wanted to rush into a relationship and even marriage pricked Jeanie's conscious more.

"I will be. I think after what James said today he does mean it and that's good enough for me. Right, you lot bugger off I need to sleep!" Getting out of the bath she changed into her long johns, and as she sat in front of the fire, she tussled with her long auburn hair. The day replayed over and over again as if she was sat in a cinema and the thoughts of her and James together felt exciting, but Jeanie's scepticism couldn't be satisfied. Lying in bed unable to sleep all she could feel was James but the words of Iris echoed around inside. Jeanie was new to love, to sex, to life and she had sheltered herself away from any feelings after her dad died expecting her life to revolve around her mum and aunt solely. Never experiencing a sense like this before scared her and she didn't know what it was or how it was supposed to feel. Jeanie had an instinct specifically around people that never failed and being with James made her feel free, happy, loved. Questions circulated her mind and whether or not she was falling for him or whether it was lust didn't seem to matter. The general satisfaction that someone loved her back felt amazing.

Confused she lay in bed and looked out of the window at the frosty night sky. Her thoughts drifted back to the factory, and in a couple of hours, she would be back in the cold and on her way to work. Drifting unconsciously in and out of sleep a small smile rose to her lips, and pulling the cover's over her head she sighed deeply.

"At least he's better than John." After all of the events of the last two days she knew more answers would come in the morning, but for now, it was time to sleep.

Chapter 5

Jeanie couldn't wait for this day to come and with Ivy finally on her way home with the baby. Jeanie could not wait to tell her what had been happening. The whole house was alive with excitement and Irene was pounding around screaming at everyone as the panic took over like a rat infestation. Hot sweats and palpitations over a new baby were enough to send her into mild hysteria, and the rest of the girls were just about underperforming enough for her to blow a gasket.

Jeanie had borrowed the car from the barracks as bringing a new baby home in a dirty, rusty old van would have been punished by a penalty of death by her mother. She was fit to burst, and her heart jumped into her throat as she pulled up at the main entrance to the hospital. Ivy was waiting anxiously, and the thought of going home both filled her with excitement and dread.

"Can't wait to get home, that place was driving me insane!" Jeanie laughed as she helped her into the car. Jumping back into the front seat Ivy looked at Jeanie with purpose as she was glowing, she had never seen her sister so excited or happy over anything for such a long time. As Ivy studied her intensely, she stayed, silent until they reached the bottom of the hospital drive.

"You stayed, didn't you. I told you, Jayne."

"Who's Jayne?" Ivy scrunched her nose up unable to comprehend the outburst.

"The baby! I didn't think you would. What happened? I want all the details…" Jeanie held out her hand to display the sparkling blue rock which lay upon her finger.

"He proposed! When, how? Tell me." The excitement was too much, and Ivy gasped with delight at her sister's news.

"Well I had my usual I think you've got the wrong person episodes and he bent down on one knee told me I was incredible and proposed. I ended up staying the night, all night and you know. Anyway, I saw him the day after I had a bit of flap again about are you sure it's me he shouted at me and said again you're incredible and proposed again. See long story short. How am I going to broach this with mum!!!" Pulling up at the junction Jeanie lay her head on the steering wheel as if the sentence had taken every breath out of her body.

"She's going to kill me I'm going to get the speech again about being the sole earner for the family, and I have duties and responsibilities blah blah blah... I wouldn't desert any of you. You know that!!" Ivy leant over the seat and put her hand on her shoulder as if the reaction could take anyway any of the burdens her sister was feeling.

"Don't worry it will all be ok trust me." Within one sigh they drove through the centre of town, and the beautiful crisp white snow had made the place look like a Christmas postcard. Children played in the streets, and a thousand snowmen had appeared popping up at nearly every garden wall. Snowball fights become a village sport, and even through the cold, the streets felt alive with energy. As Ivy held the baby close, Jeanie could read her thoughts listening as they spilt from her lips.

"I miss your daddy I hope he's ok?" As she whispered under her breath to the infant who was sound asleep Jeanie smiled at her in the mirror and continued to take the pair home where an eager Grandmother and equally eager aunts were waiting.

Jeanie darted around the side of the car as she couldn't wait to unveil the beautiful new child to the family. Jeanie loved her family dearly, and the thought of a new edition and eight giggling women clucking around a baby excited her greatly. Ivy took exact steps as not to slip and Jeanie carried her sister's luggage just as carefully as the ice had created a shimmering path down to the gate. As they both arrived a man in a uniform was stood at the parlour door. Jeanie poked her head around her sister and held her breath.

"Jeanie should I be worried about George or is this one for you?" Jeanie tried to negotiate around her sister spitting as she moved.

"He's turned up; he's here what do I do!!!" Ivy laughed and pulled the infant closer.

"Calm down, it will be okay plus I need a wee, and she can't hit you if you're holding a baby." Before she knew it, Jeanie was holding Jayne in her arms, and Ivy had disappeared. Hearing her sister's screams arriving before their physical presence, Jeanie negotiated around the luggage awaiting the onslaught.

Pulling Jayne close, she softly whispered as if she was relaying an important secret.

"Just wait. My mother's going to explode, but yours will bounce."

A somewhat nervous Jeanie deflected the screeches of joy from all the women in the house. However, Jeanie had never seen Irene look so happy to have them home. Passing the infant to the gaggle, she began taking off her boots and jacket, and as she sauntered around to the parlour door she took a peek at the figure still stood in the room.

The tall, handsome figure stood next to the hearth, and as the newly lit fire was building into a smoulder, he brushed himself down and checked his appearance as if he was waiting for an inspection. James stood holding his cap under one arm smiling uncontrollably at a tentative Jeanie who by this point had tried to blend in with the wallpaper. As she moved into the parlour, Irene caught her almost off guard.

"Keep the doctor company for a minute while we are waiting for tea." Irene scurried away into the kitchen closing the door behind her. Jeanie was aware that all her sisters were observing her next move and as she sat at the table close to the window all eyes were still directly focused on her.

"Hello. I couldn't tell you." James paused awaiting Jeanie's interruption.

"It's ok don't worry, do you need to see Ivy?" James shook his head and walked briskly over to the table.

"I want to set a date for the wedding, and I've spoken to the vicar at the church in town, and the closest they have is the 22 July, so I've booked it." The door parted, and Jeanie saw Irene's face knowing she had heard every single word

" Jeanie you're seeing the doctor. The same doctor that delivered your niece?" Jeanie placed her hands over her eyes as she didn't want a fight today all she wanted to do was coo over a baby however she was now facing a new fiancé pre-occupied on setting a date and a mother scolding him for his lack of involvement.

"Can we all just sit down this is very sudden, and I know how this looks," Irene purple with rage looked attentively at Jeanie.

"You better not be pregnant girl" James outraged by Irene's comments couldn't believe what he was hearing.

"She isn't pregnant. Why would you not want your daughter to get married I don't understand…." Jeanie closed the parlour door as the congregation of people gathered.

"Sorry doctor, she isn't the marrying kind, and you will be putting a family out on the streets if you take away their sole income, would you like that holding over you!" James turned around to Jeanie; her head

57

by this point had bypassed her hands and headed straight for the table.

"I'm sorry Jeanie, but she's wrong. She wouldn't allow me to put you on the streets Madam, but someone needs to put you on your arse now sit down." The parlour seemed to fill with people intrigued by the noise and the response James had given their mother. Irene was harsh and sometimes insensitive but no matter what she spoke her mind and for the first time she seemed to do as she was told and sat at once as if a dog was obeying its master.

"I am in love with your daughter, I will be marrying her, you will not interfere, and I am here out of common courtesy and you madam should respect that an intelligent, strong, independent and beautiful woman such as your daughter has been able to put up with you for so long. Now take the flowers as they are for you and Jeanie will be back at six." Ivy mouthed the words GO, and Jeanie no sooner had walked in had walked straight back out again and this time with James on her arm. Getting back into the car and without a word, she started to drive and as they approached a lay by James placed his hand on the steering wheel.

"Stop the car." As he opened the door and as Jeanie got out he pulled her close and kissed her at the side of the road.

" James not that I mind being kissed. Where are we going." Still, furious Jeanie knew Irene had gotten under his skin. The thought of a mother not wanting her daughter to be settled and happy exasperated him even more.

"I'm so sorry your ......and I just don't understand what she's going to achieve....." His outburst was sweet, and Jeanie smirked reaching for his hand.

"I didn't ask that I asked where we are going?" James looked at her and kissed her softly on the hand she didn't mind his intrusion; in fact, she liked that another person was going to argue with her mother instead of her having to do it all the time. "Church James after the conversation we had in the medical wing. I thought we agreed to take things slowly…" Wiping away the steam on the window James took off his hat.

"I had some leave, and I got impatient. I went for a walk and found myself at your local church I told him who I was marrying and he opened up a small space in July." Placing her hand over his mouth, Jeanie contemplated her thoughts.

"I know you like to think what's best cause you are a Doctor… I remember having this conversation with you at the factory hold on," James sighed knowing his interruption wasn't received graciously.

"We were arguing, and I shouted at you, and you were wrong, and you didn't like it and sulked for a week. James, please learn something for God sake….."

"I apologised remember, and this isn't the same thing..."

Jeanie pursed her lips and smirked.

"You didn't apologise you sulked," playfully James pushed her arm.

"I do remember cause I fell over the chair in your workshop and you picked me up, and I accidentally touched your breast, and you shouted at me again, and I apologised again." Jeanie laughed, trying to keep her look serious.

"Sorry. Yes, I remember you grabbing my boob not that I minded, but that's another story..."

"You're playing with me this isn't funny, and you're making it a big joke. Come here." Jeanie shook her head wanting to make her point and trying to stop him leaning over James pressed against her shoulder.

"I'm not sorry for booking it….." Taking his hand, she stroked his palm with her fingers.

"I mean it, James, this is all too quick, and I'm in shock. James if she knew I'd spent the night with you…..just let's see how it goes…". As they turned the corner, Jeanie realised they were at Silloth Bay; she used to go to the beach with her dad and watch the boats sail between Scotland and England. As a little girl, she had played for hours in the sand until the sun disappeared. Those memories had imprinted into her mind which Jeanie referred to when she missed him the most, and as James got out of the car and lit a cigarette, Jeanie followed.

"I love the beach; dad used to take me down here when I was younger. I had my first kiss at this beach, by a boy who used to live next door to us. I fell in love with him a little too. You may have seen him at the plant a few times. I had my heartbroken though and from that point, I never really loved again." James took hold of her hand leading her down to the sea wall.

"What was his name?" Jeanie flicked James's cigarette away and playfully looked back to see his response.

"John Stanton. If you want to know about any man in my life, it would be him. He left me for another girl. What about you? You mentioned your fiance," James fastened his coat as the sea breeze ran through his clothes.

"I did. Catherine, I was with her a while. We met at medical school to my parent's approval. I don't know it wasn't right she wanted to live a life that I never felt comfortable with, and she wanted the accolade of being the wife of a surgeon. That I could give her, but nothing else I didn't like who I was when I was with her. Then I met you, and you shouted, screamed and swore at me, and then you cared for me and put me back together. It was strange as in my world I was right all of the time. I was supposed to play God, but with you, there was no edge no superficial meaning you meant what you said, and you kept your word and people respected you and loved you for it.

My dad is a doctor, and my mother was a nurse I don't think I ever talked about them while working with you. That was my life then though, a circulation of contrite no it all's whose job it was to be right, and according to you, everything I did was wrong, so it knocked me down off my pedestal. I never disliked you for it. In fact, I think I welcomed it. That's when I knew my relationship with Catherine was all wrong.

"You mean I showed you a different path!"

"You're making fun of me again aren't you." As she smiled playfully, Jeanie stepped down off the wall hoping he would continue with his story.

"I was unfaithful Jeanie, I had relationships with other women, and she knew, and as long as I kept up appearances nothing mattered, sex was a game I liked to play. I'm not going to lie getting what I wanted came easily. You, on the other hand, I didn't understand, love wasn't a game to the people in your life. No matter how trivial the part they played and all I wanted to know was why?"

"James you don't have to..." Lighting another cigarette, he sat on the steps of the sea wall.

"I'm an arsehole I know it, and I come from a long line of arrogant, self-righteous arseholes. I was told it in medical school, but without you, I wouldn't be a surgeon, without you, I couldn't have changed my life around, and without you, I don't think I would have ever felt love. I believe that." Taking him by the hand, she led him down to the beach. His warm palm filled her with possibilities and inside she hoped that a future with him would be worth it.

"Come with me" Jeanie stood on the beach bear footed and waded into the cold sea water she loved the outdoors and always seemed at peace listening to waves crashing along the shoreline. The cold sand trickled between her toes reminding her of visits she had there with her father.

"We all make mistakes, that's the fun part of life, sometimes we get to change them and sometimes we have to live with them. I'm no angel."

"How can you do this it's freezing! You will end up with hypothermia" As she ran through the small ripples of the tide enjoying the free time James stood watching her enjoying her freedom, and in a way felt privileged to be part of something special. Racing up to him she grabbed his hand dragging him towards the waves, and as the water followed behind, he picked her up and flung her around as if she was on a merry-go-round. The laughter echoed through the cold as if spring had taken a glimpse at winter.

Sitting on the sand, she buried her feet trying to keep them warm, and as she lay down, her hair became unravelled and filled with mustard coloured grains which entangled the strands together. James lay down next to her watching the grey coloured sky slowly block out the frosty winter sun and as the white flakes began to fall James placed Jeanie's hand in his.

The tranquil placing of snow outlined around them, and as the cold touches brushed against their skin, Jeanie closed her eyes and breathed in the quiet air. She needed to soak up the madness which had been the last week of her life, and as the sound of the waves soothed them both, they lay together on the beach neither one wanting to disturb each other in fear their precious moments may be over. As Jeanie sat up the sand spilt down her back like a river and as she looked across the water she clutched at James's hand as if to save herself from falling. "Come on time for a brew I think." Walking up the beach, Jeanie sat back on the steps which graced the sea wall, and as she brushed off, the sand James helped her with her shoes.

"There's a hotel at the bottom" Jeanie bit her lip and laughed playing on the unintentional innuendo.

"Sorry I thought you were suggesting a different way of warming up." Rubbing her cold feet, he breathed into his hands.

"Is that an offer or a suggestion." Jeanie cocked her head to one side and looked into his eyes as their previous conversation opened up more avenues she couldn't wait to walk down. He had made her remember their friendship he had also made her remember that there was more to life. Rubbing her shoulders, he looked at his watch.

"I think we better make tracks. Plus we've still got to face the music with your mum." The hours just lying on the beach had spoken volumes and as they made their way home the picturesque images of small farm dwellings covered in ice and snow unearthed themselves through the scenery. The warm comfort of knowing that she was happy and content was enough for Jeanie to realise that she was looking forward to becoming Mrs James Watson.

Darkness had fallen before arriving home, and as they pulled up, Jeanie was expecting the worst. The house was alive with every room lit and the fiery glow penetrating through the dark curtains. Pushing the door open and half expecting a barrage of abuse Jeanie found the house in practical serenity greeted by the usual family chaos. Her mum was waiting at the kitchen door, and with her apron tightly pulled around her waist and as she clenched her fists around a small jug in one hand and a dishcloth in the other Jeanie counted to ten.

"Tea's on. Go and warm up you both look froze." Jeanie shocked expected arguments and pandemonium, and as she entered the parlour, James was made to take a seat next to her aunt as Iris played the piano and May sang a medley of songs.

"She's different that one, special, she worries me always has done, she looks after all of us and in some way, I don't know what I would do without her. Make her happy she's the glue that binds us together, and she deserves the best. Don't tell her mind; she would never hear of it from me." As Irene patted James on the shoulder, she returned to her seat next to the hearth, and as Jeanie saw the interaction, she felt uneasy and waited with baited breath what her mum would do next. James looked over at Jeanie stood against the door, and as she leant on the frame, she felt lucky to know he wanted to be with her. Catching his stare, she nodded not just to acknowledge him but to allow his contentment and consent to his comfort. At the end of the concert, her aunt's snores filled the living room and deciding it was time to take her to bed Irene insisted some of her daughters helped.

Jeanie sloped around the corner and sat beside James. The cosy warm fire was burned intensely spitting and hissing in the dimming light and as James teased Jeanie's hand and she became fascinated with his touch.

"It's been a long time since I've felt like this...." Pulling her closer, he ran his fingers across her lips. "I promise I will make you happy." Irene stood at the door and watched the pair through the smoked glass, sighing she knew she had to let her go. "What you doing?"

"Don't do that." May had suddenly arrived as Irene lost herself in Jeanie's moment.

"Leave them alone. He seems ok?" Irene patted May's hand gently as to reassure her and as May made her way upstairs, she sighed again under her breath.

"I hope so, I really hope so."

The drive back to the barracks seemed too short, and as she stopped just before the gate, James leant forward wanting to take her with him.

"I want you to have this" Taking a small envelope out of his jacket pocket James passed it over.

"Don't read it now but tonight. Thank you for today and say thank you to your mum again for me." Jeanie clung onto the letter in her hand, and as it started to scrunch under her clasp, she couldn't leave the night at that.

"James, wait," Pulling him close she kissed him ardently. He held her so tight she didn't want him to go.

"I've been thinking about us. I mean. Oh god, here I go again mumbling. Here I go just bear with me. I feel you when I sleep, every touch, every kiss. But today, today was different it wasn't about what we did the other night. We have a real friendship well we had, and today we just enjoyed each other's company, but tonight I don't want to let you go so if July is booked then that's ok with me that's all I'm trying to say.." Jeanie bit her lip waiting for the anticipation of an answer; instead, James nodded his head and held her close.

"Is that it? After everything?" Confused Jeanie saw what looked like a tear form in his eye.

"If I don't go now Jea..." Kissing her again he left the car, he turned and waved, and as he disappeared through the gate, she wanted him desperately. As her stomach played nervous knots, she would have done anything to make him stay. Instead, driven away by barred gates, guards and dogs she felt a desperate longing to see him. In the lay-by, she clutched the letter to her chest not able to concentrate much on anything else. As she looked up at the window, a face peered through the car and a voice she had heard a thousand times echoed around her. Slowly coming to her senses, Jeanie got out of the car, and as she stood in the middle of the lane, she desperately looked around the soldiers. Unable to see the ghost and the thought that it was a figment of her imagination she couldn't help the sound of his voice violently penetrate her mind. As she walked back to the car, she played the scene over and over again making her believe that James's sudden arrival had sparked some underlying insecurities.

"I could have sworn it was him it couldn't be it was ten years ago the last time we met." As she put the keys in the ignition, she stalled as the voice appeared again in the dark.

"John Stanton."

Chapter 6

Walking around the back of the house and through the kitchen, Jeanie stopped unable to get the voice of her past out of her head. Questions surrounding how the thought of that murmuring, in particular, had caused such an uncontrollable reaction made her body shudder and her mind spin and as she sat alone, she remembered the cruelty and pain which John had left behind.

As Jeanie sat in the dark, she replayed her past as if she sat in a movie theatre. His drinking and violence had left deep scares some which she thought would never heal. Jeanie had forgiven him, again and again, unable to understand that she was the doormat to his feet. Maybe now after ten years, James was to be the cure. Jeanie realised that the short journey home had made her feel more out of control than ever and even though she was never irrational she felt she couldn't seem to find any logic to solve this particular problem.

Locking the door, she made her way upstairs and crept into bed. It was another busy day tomorrow, and she had to be up at 3.00 am. As she graced her bed, the blanket felt warm and safe, and as she curled up with her knees tucked tightly against her she watched the embers die in the fire. Her eyes felt heavy and sore, and she could hear the hail start to rattle the window. Suddenly remembering James's letter, she raised her hand to the bedside cabinet and slowly tore the seal.

"Jeanie I started to write this letter while still at the factory. I went to post it several times and couldn't. Then your father died, and I didn't know what to do. I wanted you to know I love you and you're the only woman that I have ever truly been in love with." As she turned the page, the crumpled soiled remains of a piece of paper fell from the envelope.

Noticing a mark, Jeanie realised that this letter had been dated, posted and returned over two years ago.

"Jeanie, I have started this letter a thousand times never knowing what to say or whether you would take the content seriously. The impact that you have had on me has been immense, and there is no other way of saying this.

I have left my fiancé. I am currently writing this letter in a disgusting dank hotel room in the middle of nowhere, and if I'm honest, I'm slightly drunk not knowing if this is the right thing to do.

I am sorry I could not do more to help your father, he was a good man, and I respected him greatly. It's the only time in my career where the guilt of losing someone has punished me more, and everything that I tried should have worked, and I don't know why it didn't. That day still haunts me more than I could ever tell you. I felt like I failed you. I know what you would say, and I can hear your voice in my head, but it's how I feel and in someway I know I seek your forgiveness.

However, seeing you the day after the funeral at work took me by surprise. I suppose life still goes on, but I did not expect you back so soon. You seemed to wander through the workshop as if you were looking for clues; you looked like a detective hunting for something which, in some way I never really understood. Jeanie, all I wanted to do was hold you and tell you that I would look after you.

I have one confession though, and on my last day, I walked into the locker room and noticed that the door was open. I didn't mean to pry, but you stood there still and silent under the water I couldn't drop my gaze. As the droplets of water cascaded down your body, I wished that my fingers were the water following each intricate curve caressing every inch of your body. You're so beautiful Jeanie that just the thought of being close to you makes my heart

68

skip a beat. I wanted to take you away. I wanted to wrap you in my arms and tell you everything would be ok but I couldn't.

I remember standing in your garden watching you comfort everyone else, and as you walked through your pain, you made sure those around you were at peace. Your patience and time for their needs astonished me. You were hurting, but they came first. Your selflessness makes me ashamed. It makes me question my insecurities and my foolish pride. We managed to sneak away after the wake, and as we sat in your office drinking our sorrows away, I wished the night would never end. We talked for hours, and I could see the conflict somewhere within and desperate to hear you I sat on the edge of my seat willing it to rise to the surface. I knew you were keeping something back but when I woke up with you in my arms, I watched the sun rise tinge your auburn hair, and I dreaded the thought of letting you go.

I can't forget that kiss, Jeanie. The way your soft lip met mine and the way that every cell and nerve ending electrified me with your touch. But I can't forget what you made me promise either.
Without realising the consequences of my actions I have hurt the people I care about the most, my mum doesn't understand neither does my father.
However, my mentor, can't believe the change in me and I wouldn't have been able to make this realisation without you.

This letter won't make any sense, the way I feel about you makes no sense to me. All I know is that I am in love with you Jeanie Rutherford and I have never felt this way about anyone. You have taken my heart, and I never want to escape the way I feel about you, and I am not going to stop until I make you my wife.

I will be starting my residency soon, and my new address is on the back of the letter. I would love to see you, and I know we need to talk. Just promise me you will come.

Yours always, James. " Jeanie's heart sank James was standing right in front of her, loving her and she hadn't noticed. As she pulled the quilt tight around her, she remembered his kiss. In fact in the months that followed Jeanie had dreamed about it. She had always felt it was out of pity only now to realise it had meant so much more. As she folded the letter up tight, she placed it into the top drawer sliding the drawer closed; this was her first ever love letter. It seemed ironic that James was the first of everything. As she slowly drifted off to sleep, Jeanie knew the sounds of her clock would be chiming soon and knowing it would beckon her out into the cold once again she turned off her light and tried to make the most of the hours which were left. After a couple of hours, Jeanie wearily arose unable to stand the noise which had been filling the house for most of the night. Jayne had been screaming for hours and as the cries had rung out loud and clear down the hallway and no matter how much Jeanie tried to block it out she was awake. As she made her way downstairs, she saw an exhausted and sore Ivy nursing the baby close to tears.

"She's been feeding every hour, and I don't know what to do. She won't sleep and I can't." Jeanie could see the guilt she felt making the child a bottle, but with the incessant screaming, it seemed to bring Ivy closer to breaking point.

"Stop it you're tired. Don't be stupid go and get some rest. Give her to me." Ivy wiped the tears away feeling more useless with every passing second.

"I don't know if I should. I mean that just makes me useless doesn't it?"

"Ivy you need help stop it and go back to bed. She will be all right with me." Jeanie stood at the kitchen window feeding Jayne's vivacious appetite and as the baby drank Jeanie began to sing a series of lullabies to quieten the infant for sleep. Rocking Jayne gently from side to side she felt completely at ease, but as she continued to work her magic, Jeanie could help the longing for a child of her own.

"Sorry I just I can't think straight."

"It's ok she's settling down now. Get into bed."

"I don't deserve this after everything I've...doesn't matter." Jeanie smiled knowing a little rest and reassurance would put her right. Swaddling her tight in her crib and ushering Ivy back into bed Jeanie sat for a while making sure both mother and baby were comfortable. Not saying a word she stroked Jayne's blanket mesmerised by how small and precious she felt. As Jeanie crept around the door smiling to herself at the sight of them both sleeping soundly and as she stepped cautiously down the old staircase she sat on the bottom step, putting on her boots.

" That was a good thing you did for your sister."

"Jesus mother just announce yourself before you do that! You frightened me to death." Irene handed her a hat and scarf and a wry smile.

"I was just saying that was a good thing you did for your sister, but I just wanted a quick word about James." Wincing at the door step Jeanie turned to face her waiting for the backlash.

"Ok...go on."

"Don't take that tone. You don't know what I'm going to say. I have had a good talk with your Aunt and sisters, and I like him, he will be good for you, and I appreciate what you've done for us. You look after us, and we need to stop relying on you. You need to live your life, and as a mother, I have held you back, and I'm sorry. We've decided as a family we need to do a lot more so starting from tomorrow

I will be working down at the factory, I can't do what you do, but your sisters can learn and we are all ready." Flabbergasted Jeanie for once felt stuck to warrant a response and as she tried to contemplate the words she looked into her mother's eyes feeling like she'd stepped into the wrong household.

"Right then off you go, and don't forget tonight you have got the dance at the parish rooms tonight and you need to be there to pick all of them up so be sharpish." Not only had she been forced out the door she had been given a speech by a woman who had openly detested any relationship she had.

"She appreciates what I've done; they have to stand on their own two feet, live my life" It was too much for her to comprehend and regurgitating it wasn't going to make it taste any better.

The journey to work gave Jeanie the opportunity think about the past, and her reminiscing had nearly caught her out at some junctions. James had been such a residual link to her dad's death that blocking both of them out had always been easier. She had always felt guilty for not grieving over her father the way she thought she had too and was expected to. Her only concern had been keeping the factory open, and her family fed, and it had covered up her emotions well, so well that even she had started to believe it. The thing was James's letter had brought back so many memories both good and bad and that day in the locker room was the only day she had cried and felt able to cry. Jeanie felt the sense of loss not just for her dad but her own life, and James had emulated a position she wasn't allowed to achieve. Jeanie longed to spread her wings and had been offered a scholarship education before he'd died. Before that, she had dared to dream of another life and turning it down had been the hardest decision she had to make. She was bound to the commitment of the business and the promise she had made her father. Watching her dad die on the factory floor had taken her youth and her freedom. James had offered an independence she wasn't allowed to have and something she had wanted him to experience and not give up because of circumstances.

Jeanie sat and thought about the last hours they had spent together and how he had asked her to go with him seeking new adventures. He had provided her with a starting point one of which she had refused for the sanctity of her family, and as she sat outside the factory gates, Jeanie felt their cold icy grip around her throat. The burden of it all had made her lose her way, and now James was back to release her from its grip.

"He was always there, and I never saw him. I didn't see him cause I couldn't.." Clenching her fists, she felt the anger build inside, and as her tears flooded down her cheeks, for the first time instead of guilt, she felt grief. Jeanie had held him while he was dying and James had tried to keep him alive. Now she realised that his tears had emulated her own.

Looking into the cold dark office, Jeanie felt as if it was a tombstone, a constant reminder of pain and loss weighing her down at every obstacle. As she gazed out across the hills and into the distance, the cold black air was thick with frost, and the tension brewing outside depicted the conflict Jeanie felt inside. As the marks appeared against the window pane, they stood lonely and sharp on the glass. Reminiscent of the past Jeanie visualised James, his spirit had been so inviting that she had held onto it as if she had been clinging to life. Jeanie had tried to suppress those feeling for nearly two years. However as she closed her eyes the distant reminder of her burden was ever present, and on hearing the wear and tear of the machinery in the distance, the factory still stood, and her responsibilities had grown bigger.

Jeanie knew she couldn't run away.

Reality amounted to the opposite end of every room and the fantasy of what it could be needed to be put on hold for another day. As she rested her head on the back of the door, Jeanie tried to build up the courage to walk out. She had to be strong after all everyone still relied on her for the factory to work and that wasn't going to dissipate because of a new relationship.

Making her morning brew didn't usually take long but as motivation dwindled, time seemed to elapse. A cold chill filled her body and Jeanie shuddered she stood at the Forman's office cup in hand.

"Eric," the inquisitive tone of her voice automatically sparking his suspicion.

"Has my mother been in touch with you about starting work at the plant?" Eric turned pale at the thought of Irene even stepping foot on sight. She had never seen eye to eye with Eric, and the relationship had become strained even before dad had started to become ill.

"NO, please don't tell me she's coming down here?" Knowing Irene would just turn up unannounced made Jeanie smile.

"That's what she said. She said I had to go and live my life and be happy I think someone had slipped her some narcotics."

Jeanie glanced at Eric as he started to laugh and Jeanie knew it wouldn't be long until his sarcasm kicked in. She heard the words before he spoke them and knowing his response was due Jeanie started to count backwards from ten.

"Fucking hell Jea go and live your life what did you do? Tell her you were getting married!" Jeanie smiled and lifted the cup to her lips before taking a sip.

"Yes." Unsure of her response he asked again.
"Did you say yes?" Jeanie nodded without explanation.
"Lass, what the fuck are you playing at? You're getting married when?" Jeanie continued to drink her rapidly cooling cup of tea ignoring the content.
"He's a doctor, he's worked here before, and he said he loves me so why not." Eric knew her nonchalant response was only to get on his nerves and ignoring the sarcasm he started running through names under his breath.
"James Fucking Watson the so called doctor with the rapport of a leper." Waiting for Jeanie to bite back he lifted his gaze as the sound of the wind howled through the central apex of the building. As he followed the noise, it led him back to a distant and distracted Jeanie. Putting his arm around her shoulder's, he pulled her close.
"Well suppose you could have done worse, it could have been John then you would have been in trouble." Still focusing on her drink, Jeanie smirked as she sipped.
"Tell your mum she can fuck off cause if she thinks I'm taking crap off another Rutherford woman she's got another thing coming!!!" Eric knew she was just like her father and if something were on his mind her father would lean on the same spot and Jeanie would join him. Side by side with no noise, no conversation and just silence remarkably they would work it out, and both of them would always come to the same conclusion. Eric could see she needed reassurance as she had the same pained look in her eye her father did when faced with a tough decision. Jeanie always required to know she was doing the right thing.

As Jeanie made her way down to the workshop, she concentrated on a valve that she needed to alter for one of the pressing machines, and as the quietness of the studio fitted with her mood, Jeanie knew she could lock herself away with minimal disturbances. As Jeanie put her brew on the small stool at the side of her tool box, she could still smell her father and the way she used to tease him about the stench of sweat, oil and grease. As Jeanie started to manoeuvre the metal through the lathe, she began to smile knowing that even though escape sounded right, this was where she was meant to be. Jeanie was the girl that fixed things and whether life had made her this way or the influence of circumstance she no longer cared. As Jeanie rolled the metal around her fingers, she heard Eric bellowing in the background.

"This is going to be a long day!"

Closing the workshop, she felt grateful for having a short time to think and put perspective back into her life. It had made her realise that the responsibility of a large family hadn't been a bad thing. She had seven friends, and now she was going to have a husband which her mother approved of so things could be a lot worse. As she left work, she wrapped herself back in the oversized scarf her mum had thrown at her earlier and counted the success of the day. Eight arguments with Eric over staff, two broken and now repaired pieces of machinery and two incidents with a soldering iron which meant in the scheme of things her day had been relatively quiet.

Tired and longing for sleep she remembered that she had promised to pick the girls up and wished one of the others knew how to drive. Having spent fifteen hours in work and dreading the evening's events, Jeanie put on a brave face as not to show her discontent at having to be the taxi. Reaching home the idea of a quiet night thrilled her however instead Jeanie was greeted by a screaming baby, a pile of clothes, makeup, curling irons and the complete desecration of a house. Skipping over the piles of crap she was glad she'd walked in at the end of the rampage rather than the beginning. Without hesitating, Ivy rushed towards her throwing Jayne into her arms.

"Grab her I need a wee!" disappearing up the stairs Jeanie was again left with a screaming infant.

"Good evening Jeanie, how are you Jeanie, tired Jeanie!" Muttering to herself as she made her way into the kitchen Jeanie glanced down at Jayne who by this time had turned purple and stunk to high heaven.

"Ok Jayne I get it, life is not fair! Come on!" Laying her on a folded towel on top of the kitchen table she started to undress both herself and the baby, as Jeanie dropped her coat on the floor, she began to take the rather full and discoloured nappy off the child. After cleaning her down and disposing of the offending items, she wrapped Jayne in the towel and started the juggling act between making milk and calming her. Remembering the success of the lullabies, Jeanie began to sing, and the once purple child started to calm to a better shade of pink. As the milk warmed in the pan, Jeanie rocked and swayed from side to side in the hope that she would calm her down enough to eat and as Ivy looked on Jeanie saw the small tinge of jealousy that rose underneath her sullen exterior. As Jeanie continued to sway the baby around the kitchen, Ivy removed the bottle albeit amazed and confused at the sight of her sister and her daughter bonding so well.

"I think she likes you better than me." Ivy seemed to choke on her words however still singing she handed her over.

"Nah she just knows who's boss. You ok?" Ivy swung her head from side to side trying to find the right words to say.

"Tired, lonely, you know." Kissing her sister's forehead, she began stripping off the remainder of her work clothes.

"Mum at bingo with Auntie Mabel?" Ivy started to imitate Jeanie's swaying synchronising the rhythm between the verses of nursery rhymes.

"Yes, she also said she would need picking up on the way home too!" Jeanie scrunched her face knowing that one trip had now just turned into two or three and again that nice comfortable peaceful and relaxing night had indeed disappeared. Making her way upstairs the night's activities seemed to unfold like a book only to reveal more devastation with each step she took. Hopping through the obstacle course of clothes, shoes and makeup Jeanie opened May's wardrobe trying to find something suitable for the evening's frivolities.

Her sisters had made her a list of what she could and couldn't wear, as her taste never seemed to fit in with the appearance of her other darling siblings, and as Jeanie grumbled again, she found a pair of trousers and cream blouse and proceeded to try to squeeze into them. As she stood in the mirror, she felt constricted. She was used to overalls, big jumpers and work boots anything that accentuated her body made her feel awkward and self-conscious. Now doubting her choice she started to rummage around in the piles of clothes left by her sisters and bending over the chest of drawers she looked like a duck tipping up in a pond.

"What's up?" Jeanie lifted her head and curled one lip

"You look beautiful let me do your hair. You know you should wear these types of clothes more often." Jeanie didn't respond but wriggled around uncomfortably as Ivy paraded her to the chair in front of the full-length mirror. Ivy tugged at Jeanie's thick hair and coerced it up into a relatively neat style. To say that Ivy was in her element was an understatement as Jeanie had now become a project and finishing her off gave her a sense of accomplishment.

Borrowing her sister Rose's coat, Jeanie walked awkwardly towards the car. Opening the door, it seemed to bulge at the seams with perfume, suspenders and patterned dresses. Pulling up carefully at the entrance the music was loud, and it flooded out of every door spilling an array of young soldiers with equally more adolescent girls attached. Ordering the exit Jeanie couldn't wait for the cloud of women to disappear. Resting her head on the steering wheel, she hoped this was going to be a quick and painless job, and as they exited with relative ease, Jeanie sped off without much time for any to coax her into the club. Returning home Jeanie settled down on the couch and curled up with Jayne and Ivy, and within no time she was asleep. Feeling a tug on her arm, Jeanie awoke to Ivy nudging her.

"You're going to be late. Jesus Christ girl you need to sleep more, it's just taken me twenty minutes to wake you up!" Once again ushered back into the car and still not fully awake she set off on the relatively short journey back to the social club. The loud and exuberant music seemed to pour through the walls sieving the ten piece band through every crevice, and as she stood in the doorway, Jeanie started to look for her sisters. Feeling awkward and out of place encased along with not having much luck at spotting them, she proceeded to find any redeeming features. How hard could it be there are five of them! Now scanning the room, Jeanie spotted Iris's bright red hair and immediately made a beeline for the table.

"Jeanie!!! This is my sister she fixes stuff and does messy stuff, but she's lovely!" Feeling slightly embarrassed for her sister Jeanie smiled politely. "Do you know where the others are?" Iris sloshed her drink around stumbling towards the knee of the soldier she had been pleasantly keeping company.

"Nope I've been with this sweet man here most of the evening, plus dance time come on." Pushing Jeanie out of the way the soldier accompanied by Iris waded through the sea of people to the floor. Admitting defeat, Jeanie turned and pushed her way through the masses to the bar. Seeing a small corner which hadn't been populated, she moved quickly before the hoards seised control. Taking off her coat gingerly she was pushed from behind falling forward over the stool, and as she dropped her coat and nearly herself on the floor, Jeanie felt a presence and then heard the voice.

"Do you need help with that?" pulling the jacket from the floor, Jeanie gritted her teeth.
"No I'm fine I'm sure I will…manage" In shock, Jeanie gripped her coat fisting the material within her grip.
"John. I don't know. Sorry."
"Is that all I get." Taking her hand, he kissed it seductively Jeanie still clutching at her coat gripped harder.
"John. Why? Well…..Sorry, let me start again. How are you?" Jeanie pushing the words through her lips began to feel the whirlwind in her stomach.
"Anyone would have thought your not please to see me."
"I'm sorry John, just in shock," As he took her hand and started to pull her towards the dance floor Jeanie pulled back not wanting to take the conversation any further.
"No. I'm….I don't think so!" Leaning into her shoulder, he grabbed her hand again.

"What's one dance going to do!" Jeanie's heart pounded in her chest, and she wished for the ground to open up and swallow her. Instead, the music played louder and faster contradicting everything she felt. As he placed his hand on her waist, she couldn't help but be intrigued as to why he had turned up.

"One dance John and after that, I'm off home." Still clutching at her coat, John prized it from her fingers and breathed her in.

"You look beautiful, as ever." Jeanie shook her head, remembering the last conversation they had. "I'd like to say thank you, but I can't help but remember someone saying a stupid little girl like me needs to grow up. What was it now, I was never one of your strong points."

John smiled revelling her smouldering anger. "That's because I am a complete dunce and I never realised what I had until you built up the courage. I must admit Jeanie you have improved with age." Feeling enraged by his arrogant and callous tone, Jeanie felt her anger grow, and she couldn't help but spit with venom.

"How would you know you arrogant bastard? You let me humiliate myself, and now you come back and ask me to dance, and all's forgiven, fuck you!" As Jeanie wiped off his embrace, she pushed him back into the crowd with force. John always had a tendency turning up like a bad penny, and Jeanie knew it more than most.

"Jeanie… Jeanie can't we be civil about this" grappling with the bodies he chased her down through the crowd. Jeanie knew she wasn't going to get away easily and hearing his footsteps behind she stopped waiting for the next episode.

"What do you want from me?"

"I was wrong, and I'm sorry, and I shouldn't have treated you the way I did. Everything from that point was my biggest mistake, and I miss you. I'm sorry I lied and cheated but Jeanie I have been miserable since you left and I need you. Let me make it up to you. Marry me, and I promise I'll change!" As the song came to its end and the red, white and blue balloons started to fall Jeanie stepped back from John as if he was holding a weapon.

Without a word she walked away, there wasn't a word to describe what he had done and as her tears fell hard with anger a ring, or a promise was never going to change the past.

"Jeanie are you ok? I saw everything." Flora now pushed aside, Jeanie ignored her callings, and as the sound of her footsteps pounded the street, she greeted the car.

"Please, Jeanie. Think about it I wouldn't come back if I wasn't ready for you." Jeanie took the ring out of the case pausing to take a look at the memento, and as she walked to the drain, she dropped it straight down.

"I wouldn't take you back if you, were the last man on earth. My father always tried to defend you, and I never knew why? Even until he died, he insisted you were a good man, and all you ever brought me was trouble and pain. As far as I'm concerned why don't you go back to that other slut, she might need you now!"

John placed his hand on her shoulder trying to make his point. Jeanie in her anger and her disgust hit him hard and as he fell to the floor blood poured from his nose, and for the third occasion, Jeanie walked away.

"Flora get the girls we are going." Within minutes her sisters appeared, and as an upset Flora coaxed them dutifully through the door, Jeanie sat shaking in the car. Having never hit someone before Jeanie tensed up with the adrenaline coursing through her veins. As she shuddered uncontrollably, she counted to ten waiting for the guilt of her actions to pray on her conscience, but somehow knowing her first hit was John felt made everything seem better.

As John stood at the side of the car Jeanie felt the weight of his stare through the glass and as Iris, May, Rosie, Flora and Daisy half drunk started to load back into the car Daisy immediately recognised John and in her drunken haze couldn't help but acknowledge him.

"Johnny how the devils are you!!" As she banged on the car window trying to get Jeanie's attention and completely unaware of the events that had just happened Jeanie looked straight ahead trying not to acknowledge her.

"Jeanie, Jeanie look it's Johnny, let's take him home!"

Flora still trying to squeeze them into the vehicle saw Jeanie's pain.

"Leave it, girls. Come on! Listen Jea just needs to go home."

As Iris and Daisy bundled John into the front of the car Daisy drunk fell into the seat amused at her find.

"Come on driver we got Johnny lets go now. Who did you fight again she said something about it!!!" Jeanie didn't say a word just swallowed deeply and started to drive the car. As she pulled up to the bingo hall, her sisters exploded once again in a sea of drink, shoes and sickness. Flora sat in the back of the car snivelling as none of her coaxings had made any difference to the drunken rabble.

"I'm sorry Jea, you know what they are like." Feeling very uncomfortable she got out and disappeared in search of her mum and aunt.

Noticing the blood on John's jacket, she handed him a box of tissues, and as it had started to drip all over the front seat and feeling responsible, she felt it was the most civil action. Mopping up his face,

John seemed more self-assured that he had been able to provoke a response at all.

"Jea..."

"Don't John I'm telling you now just don't. I forgot to say before that I've met someone, and he's asked me to Marry him, and I've accepted so whatever you have to say just don't." As John slid closer, he bent over her chest to grab some more tissues. Jeanie closed her eyes knowing he was doing his best to make her feel uncomfortable.

"You're getting married do I know the lucky fella,"

"Just move to other side of the car. I don't want to argue with you..." John bit his lip sliding back to his original position knowing if he pushed it too much he might receive something worse than a bloodied nose.

" So is it serious or was it no one else could pop your cork." Jeanie tried to bite her lip knowing he wanted to upset her on purpose.

"Why? Why are you here? I invited you to dad's funeral, and you didn't even turn up, and before you think I need an explanation, I don't. And I know you got caught fucking that waitress on the train back to London. Which is strange cause come to think of it you would screw anything else but me! Peculiar that don't you think."

"It wasn't strange by my standards Jeanie. I just couldn't bring myself to do it. There was something about you that just makes me want to better before I could."

"You're a smug, arrogant bastard! You never held me on a pedestal!"

"So now you've popped your cherry, and you're getting married is there anything else for Jeanie Rutherford." His sarcasm dragged Jeanie back to being a child and how he used to tease her over the fence to make her cry however the way he was making her feel now was something completely different. His tone made her feel useless, ugly and wrong and she could feel herself wanting to hit him again.

"What the fuck has it got to do with you anyway! You left me, and you didn't want anything to do with me remember! And you made it quite clear in front of everyone to see at St Pancs train station. What was the line oh yes I was a mistake you were never going to repeat? So let me see now who is the snivelling grunt sat in my car asking to have me back. So again who looks the bigger prick now you or me…" John pulled the tissues out of the box and spat the blood out of the window Raising the tissue back to his now swollen nostril he seemed unrequited by Jeanie's response.

"I can't leave Jeanie, and I don't care who this guy is I made a mistake, and I've paid for that mistake. I just want you, and I realise that now, I'm not giving you up and I mean that."

As a gathering started to appear, her sisters seemed to emerge from the hall in a puff of smoke and as Irene followed he knew the inquisition was to follow. Waddling through the girls and coaxing them with warmth and smiles suddenly Irene realised who the familiar face seated next to Jeanie.

"Why is he here?" Jeanie put her head on the steering wheel, and with her mum now spitting venom she knew John would react with his usual sarcastic charm.

"Girls get in this car now, and you move!"

"Mrs Rutherford so charmed to meet your acquaintance again as usual. Jeanie tells me she's getting married; I bet that shit you up didn't it?" Irene screwed up her face in disgust pushing her daughters out of the way she couldn't hold her tongue any longer.

"Jeanie drive the car. Listen to me you lack lustre piece of shit leave my daughter alone, or you won't just end up with a broken nose you will be picking your balls and teeth up out of the gutter. So why don't you just fuck off back to that cunt you married." John didn't reply but instead sat with a coy smile knowing it would annoy everyone.

As the group arrived home, Irene dragged all but Jeanie out of the car. Jeanie didn't need to two words however the two words were spoken: "Sort it." He didn't seem to move, and he wasn't fazed by any responses they had given. Jeanie slammed the car door and started to walk around the back of the house, and as John equally followed with a confident swagger he placed his head on the glass of the back door

"You could at least let me in for a brew now you've splattered my nose." Jeanie opened the door and walked through into the kitchen, however, she didn't stop walking. Instead, she ran straight upstairs pulling off her clothes in a temper. Hunting around the bedroom for pyjamas and throwing her dressing gown on the muttering's under her breath had increased to full out talking. Anger, hatred and disgust had been spitting from her lips as she ran back down the stairs.

"Ok fuckwit if you want a brew well you know where the fucking pot is don't you!" Jeanie slammed the teapot down onto the kitchen table and stood in front of it with her arms folded. Seeing her frustrations, John didn't say a word instead he took off his jacket and washed his hands before nonchalantly undoing his collar button.

Jeanie stood feeling the venom pulsating through her body. Knowing how powerless she felt at his responses, he filled up the kettle and lit the stove. Taking her actions in his stride, he crossed his arms and stood staring at her seemingly unaware of the tensions his visit had caused. He treated the kitchen as if it was his own and didn't care about the torture and turmoil Jeanie felt just being in his presence. Taking the kettle off the stove, he walked towards Jeanie. Standing nose to nose with her and as he placed it on the table, he put his hand on Jeanie's waist and pulled her close.

"Remember Jeanie; remember our unique way of making drinks." He pressed his body close to her and held her hand gently behind her back placing the leaves in the pot. Jeanie froze as she felt his breath on her neck and his leg resting between hers and as he moved closer, she could feel his intentions pulsating through his body and the heat which radiated from him. No matter how she had tried to resist he had her exactly where he wanted, and with her sisters watching in anticipation Jeanie knew every one of them wanted to take her place. As he slid his hand further down Jeanie's back, she broke free from his hold and pushed him out the way making her way through her sisters. He sat on the corner of the table drinking his tea as if it was a normal occurrence providing a cover for his ungentlemanly behaviour.

"Ladies I bid a fond farewell." As he quietly sipped the liquid, he seemed to drift away deep in thought, and without a care, John placed the cup back onto the neatly quaffed cloth. Gathering his hat John and fixing his jacket he proceeded to leave through the back door and with that he disappeared out of view.

Contemplating the evening events, he casually walked around the corner and down the pretty garden path and on hearing the front door slam shut he watched as Jeanie raced into the night. Jeanie's mutterings expelled their way into the evening air, and he had made her so angry and confused it frightened her to think that he could still make her react. Unaware that he had left she jumped back into the car and sped off. Seeing how agitated she was John couldn't help but feel like his efforts had not been in vain.

As Jeanie arrived back at work, Eric watched from the upstairs office with some concern. She seemed like a puppet, and someone was pulling her strings, unable to understand and after seeing her kick the flower pot over he made his way to the front of the building. Jeanie stood talking to herself at the front gate her arms exaggerated by her temper and her patience well and truly worn to the core. Eric stood in the doorway drinking his coffee waiting for the opportune moment to step in.

"Feel better now do we?"

"Don't you ever fucking go home" Again Eric breathed in and asked the question again.

"Feel better now?" Looking at the courtyard devastation and throwing her head back in disgust she calmed down enough to respond civilly.

"No, No I don't." Eric smiled back as she had been telling him how to control his temper and now the boot was on the other foot.

"Ok. What's up?" Jeanie sighed heavily and put her head in her hands; Dad was gone, and Eric was the next best thing and feeling no other choice she exhaled his name.

"John Stanton" Her head was facing the floor, and her heart felt like it was about to explode.

"He's back in town and reared his ugly head and has the nerve to think that all he needs to do is apologise and I will take him back and MARRY HIM!" Eric walked over and sat beside the bedraggled looking Jeanie.

"So what are you going to do?"

"It's ludicrous. John cheated on me, he hit me then he asked me to meet him in London and then tells me he's got married, and I'm a stupid little girl. Weeks later he comes back and wants me again, and I stood up I told him. You have made your bed, go back and lie in it without me" Eric placed his hand on Jeanie's back lovingly.

"Who do you want Jeanie?" Jeanie lifted her head with tears still staining her cheeks.

"Not him, the only thing I feel now is regret, regret that I wasted so much time chasing him around. James offers something different; I don't want him, Eric. I don't want JOHN." As Jeanie finished her sentence, John stood at the porch window, and for the first time, this seemed to hurt. Over the name calling and fighting this appeared to wound him more than any argument. Pale and lonely he stood on the opposite side of the glass waiting for some hope as Jeanie responded again.

"I don't want John." Watching him walk away it was like a light bulb switching on. John vanished like a puff of smoke, the blackness had provided him with an escape, and as she looked out into the night, he had gone and with it her first love. It was the right time and the right decision to say to Goodbye John Stanton.

Chapter 7

As winter turned into spring, more troops had started to arrive at the base and with increased volume Jeanie's presence was needed more and more. Traffic had begun to move through both the factory and the garage, and the amount of work at both ends had started to become significantly more challenging than anyone expected. Irene had stuck to her word, and as promised she turned up to do her bit with both Iris and Rose in the toe. Both of them had become a permanent feature within the office, and Eric was taking full advantage of their flirtatious natures.

Jeanie appreciated the all hands on deck nature of her family but as 1942 ended, and 1943 began Jeanie was racing towards her 30th year and time seemed to be more limited than ever.

Working at the base had caused an unprecedented amount of problems, one of which had been sleeping at the garage office. It had isolated Jeanie from the outside world and her day's circulated machinery and breakdowns and any quality time she had disintegrated into a barrel of grease and oil.

American soldiers had also started to infiltrate every part of the base and even though her sisters saw that as a new hunt Jeanie contemplated the amount of work they brought. Every part of her seemed to be covered in grease and oil, and Jeanie longed for a long relaxing bath and a good night's sleep.

Rising from her make shift bed she rubbed her face and tried to make a weak effort to become motivated for the day. Making her way to the garage door, she looked like a coal miner emerging from the rubble, and as she squinted at the sun, she looked as if she'd found her way out of a hole for the first time in days. The ritual good mornings were passed, and after contemplating running for the gate, she made her way back down the pit and continued to fix another broken axle. After several beatings with a hammer, Jeanie sat on the steps as tired and broke as the vehicle which was above.

Jeanie was usually frequented by the drill sergeant to speak about the morning's updates, however, instead of hobnail boots and hairy legs she saw a skirt and some highly shined shoes. The lady stood above Jeanie coughing loudly expressing the desire for her attention, and as Jeanie poked her head out, she had just started to shout out her demands for the second time.

"J Rutherford? I am looking for a J Rutherford," knowing the lady hadn't seen her Jeanie prised herself from underneath looking like a hobbit emerging from a mud bath. Dragging herself up she raised her body to all fours, and with the last effort, she rose from the ground.

"J Rutherford again I am looking for a J Rutherford," as she moved around the garage Jeanie knew she wasn't expecting a woman.

"Ok keep your knickers on love, that will be me," Jeanie sounded wounded and forlorn, and as the lady replied with some confusion, Jeanie waited for the usual look.

"Your J Rutherford, well then clean yourself up and make your way around to the Generals Office." A piece of paper fell into Jeanie's hands and before she could reply the smart official looking lady had disappeared around the corner of the garage door. Jeanie looked at her overalls and back again at the paper. Just getting out of the pit had been an effort and getting washed and changed as well seemed like a chore.

"Fuck it take me as I am or not at all that's what I say." As Jeanie wiped her chest with a cloth, she threw it down on the oil drum. Passing the window,

Jeanie saw the bags under her eyes, and as she tried to wipe the sleep, Jeanie hoped it would improve a small part of her appearance. Concentrating cleaning up, another voice which appeared from around the corner.

"You know talking to yourself in medical terms is not considered a good thing." James looked like a complete contrast to Jeanie's filthy exterior, and his starched white coat sparkled in the sunlight.

"Anyway you look tired, and you seem to have lost weight? Let me have a look at you. Are you ok?" Jeanie tried to present a smile but instead cocked her head from side to side. Taking that as her response James concern continued with his conversation.

"I was told to come and get you since I'm on the way to the General as well." Jeanie felt too tired to respond, and in the end, she was just pleased to see a friendly face. Wiping some of the grease from her cheek and smoothing some of the grime away from her tired skin he starred into her eyes seeing a distance he remembered well. As he kissed her forehead sweetly, he took hold of her hand and pulled her into his hold.

"Have you missed me?"

"Umm. What if I said no? Anyway, I'll get you filthy if you hold on too tight." Jeanie again tried to force a smile thinking about the turmoil another individual had put her through.

"So do you know what I am being summoned for? I mean if I'm in trouble surely still being a civilian should I run for the hills."

"I honestly don't know and don't care. It's given me an excuse to see you, and I'm not going to squander it. Besides I'm on leave soon, and I've been thinking about re-enacting a certain moment from not too long ago." Jeanie breathed in his response and laughed timidly.

"I thought we were waiting until the wedding night! Come on we had better get going I don't need anymore cavalry around here. My garage will be filling up with soldiers, and I will never get anything done." As James led the way to the main building, she realised she had never been permitted anywhere near it before.

Entering through the massive main door, she felt like Alice in Wonderland, except without the dress or the bath. The picturesque staircase and a ceiling which seemed to rise forever graced the wooden staircase which was highly polished and beautifully maintained. Jeanie instantly felt guilty at even putting her work boots anywhere near it, and all she could think about was the hour's someone must have spent cleaning it. Feeling very under dressed and out of place she felt like a naughty school girl going to the head master's office.

Following James, to the second floor, the opulence suddenly gave way to a sea of dust noise and chaos. From the large open spaces and grandeur of downstairs, it was a complete contrast. The only thing in common was the amount of activity, Jeanie stepped back at the noise of typewriters and the hoards of people deafening the air. James coaxed her along the corridor until she met another huge wooden door.

"I'm further down the hallway. Come and see me after." As James turned around, he winked at a nervous looking Jeanie contemplating the enormous door in front of her. As she tugged at her sleeves and bit her lip, she wondered what was on the other side, and as she took a deep breath, she knocked hard. On hearing a small voice, she entered to find the general stood in front of an enormous oak table and as he looked over his shoulder he saw Jeanie peering from behind the door.

"Come on my dear," he paused as she walked precariously along the rim of the carpet.

"I need you to meet a couple of people, and there's some other business we need to take care of as well, Sit down my dear, sit down." As Jeanie sat down on the very expensive looking chair she became very self-conscious again. Not over her appearance but over the fact she was leaving stains on the carpet and furniture. The only alternative was to sit on her hands and hope not too much grease was being transferred.

Hearing another groan and a few squeaks from the door Jeanie realised that two men had entered the huge room. As the gentlemen carried on their conversation, Jeanie could make out that one of the gentlemen was American and the other British. They seemed locked together in a debate, and as their footsteps got ever closer the General signalled for Jeanie to arise from her seat.

"Jeanie I need to introduce you to a couple of people first our new LC John, please meet my godsend, Jeanie Rutherford," Jeanie felt her heart sink as she turned to face the man

"John?"

"Jeanie pleased to meet you. Jeanie this is Lieutenant Frank Signthorpe."

"Please to meet you, my dear, I have heard lot's of good things about you." His hand was cold and clammy and his stare intense, and something about him gave an unnatural air. Jeanie still silenced at the diplomacy John had shown and stunned by how civil everything had become tried to keep the façade going. However, the puzzled look on her face said it all.

Jeanie always knew he had high ambitions and John had told her on many occasions that he needed to succeed for them to be together. She didn't understand his reasons why and it always was a source of conflict for them both. However, he was now an LC she did not quite understand how it worked, however, secretly she was proud to know he had made it.

The General continued to talk but Jeanie only heard the noise and found it difficult to concentrate, and as he put a piece of paper in front of her he indicated where her signature was needed and did it blindly. As the General left hastily, John continued the briefing.

"Thank you for your cooperation today Jeanie I know this must seem rushed, but we have some serious business we need to attend to. I also know you're very busy with what we are giving you at the moment so I will keep it brief. As you know, the war has stepped up a little recently, and our American counterparts are now on board. We have some of my co Lieutenants equipment and vehicles being shipped in, and I need you to bring his men up to speed." Lieutenant Signthorpe's stare weighted heavily on Jeanie and his manner intense. His behaviour fed his thoughts, and every muscle seemed to scream repulsion at the very thought of her going anywhere near his precious vehicles. "John, your not considering a woman do this, are you? This is highly irregular, and I don't know how you people work it around here, but this is not something which sits comfortably with me." The Lieutenant snarled at Jeanie as his comment aired into the room. Jeanie had already experienced this reaction on a number of occasions especially when she had to deal with the business at the plant. He reminded her so much of the men that used to frequent the boardroom offering her dad money and expensive gifts to off load the business. She also knew her job seemed highly irregular for most men to comprehend but something about this man made it ever more prevalent to bring up. John gazed at her willing her speak. Taking another deep breath as to hide her frustrations Jeanie sat up in her chair contemplating her response.

"Lieutenant thank you for your insightful comments. However, I have seen some of the carrying vehicles already. It came in a few days ago with the first of the American influx. If you look at the bearings on all the right axles they have been put on wrong and have split these all need to be stripped down and replaced, now I know I can't do this on my own but I assure you that if you suggest someone to help oversee my work you will be happy with the results." As she sat back in her chair, she felt her response was more eloquent and more dignified than usual however underneath Jeanie wanted a reaction. As John stepped closer he sat on the corner of the desk propping his leg up on the side of Jeanie's chair he seemed to have taken sides and chosen his team mate when he spoke.

"I assure you and trust me Lieutenant I do assure that this decision has not been taken lightly. Jeanie happens to be one of the best Engineers on the base and not to consider her for this delicate task would be ridiculous because of her being, of course, a woman and with your finest Engineer Lieutenant, I find this matter taken care of. Jeanie, we have a sight walk around arranged, please this way. Again thank you for you time Lieutenant." Offering out his hand Jeanie felt like she was the lady of the manor and the irony and expression of John's actions and speech made the Jeanie puzzled to who and where this person had come from. Taking his hand, he lead her towards the big mahogany door which now seemed smaller walking away from it, and as they made their way past the rows of make shift typing desks, Jeanie looked around at the opulence of the old house with a wondering of how it used to be before the war.

John had not spoken a word since exiting the office, and the deafening noise from the typist restricted conversation. Jeanie still felt underdressed, and self-conscious as the smartly dressed uniform personnel graced every corner, and somehow the oil and grease didn't feel thick enough. As they proceeded out of the manor house, Jeanie squinted in the sun and turned to say her goodbye's however before a word slipped from her lips John again interrupted.

"Jeanie, let me apologise for my behaviour the other night it was impertinent and rude, and I truly am sorry. The thing is when I saw you bent over a car the other day to be fair it felt as if I had never left. It was a lovely feeling knowing that you were still here. I made it the first thing on my agenda to find you." Jeanie looked at him with wide eyes as if to hang on every word.

"Let's just say I have made huge mistakes in my life and I'm sorry." Looking up at the sky the sun began to warm up the day, and Jeanie breathed in the paleness of the blue which had started to drift over. The overwhelming feeling of nostalgia appealed to her, and in his eloquence, John did seem appealing.

"John, you said something about a tour." Grappling with his hat, and trying to look official he stuttered at Jeanie's answer, and as the awkward Lieutenant began to regain his control, Jeanie wasn't going to tell him that she had walked around the base a thousand times. She knew she wasn't supposed to, but natural curiosity always got the better of her.

Jeanie forever polite looked on with intent as John described the different buildings and as they entered the medical block John was still describing architecture and dates. As they stepped into the medical bay, John spotted her rolling her eye's in between the pieces of benign information he had been spilling and as he finished his sentence he waited for the next opportune moment.

"And this is where I get the piss taken out of me by a contemptuous little shit!" Jeanie smirked and started to laugh knowing he would have to lose all of his graces to finish his sentence.

"You're a fucking witch sometimes how many times….. don't tell me I really don't want to know." John saw the funny side to Jeanie's amusement, and as he took her by the arm, he pulled her closer to him and with Jeanie still laughing she obliged unquestionably.

"I'm sorry I couldn't help it you got so carried away." John dropped his hat on the floor losing his calm composure.

"Well, you can find your own way back then!" as he turned to walk the other way he fixed his jacket and hat again and pulled on his tie. Jeanie playfully smiled back saluted and turned in the opposite direction.

As she made her way back to the garage, Jeanie remembered all the fun they had as kids. Fixated on the fact that all those memories contained John she realised they might be able to become friends after all.

As the day closed and night opened the sky was ablaze. The red fire sunset made a dramatic background to the rolling hills that surrounded the base, and as Jeanie sat on a chair taking in the energy of the fiery sky, she realised this was the most relaxed she had felt in a while.

As children, John and Jeanie used to gaze at the stars and John couldn't stop himself from interrupting her stare. She used to get lost for hours pretending she could walk within the atmosphere leapfrogging from one to the next. As John walked towards the garage, he could see the smile which had crept into Jeanie's thoughts and feeling he may have had an influence he couldn't wait to find out. "Penny for them."

"Jesus you scared me to death. For fuck sake don't creep up on people like that!" Dabbing her overall's she made her way to the small office. John noticed the garage office had been turned into her studio and he knew the increased commitment to the base would have been a struggle. However looking deeper he could see how it had become her living and sleeping space and Jeanie had used the two sets of lockers to provide her with food, clothing and reading material. She had made herself a bed which she folded away into the cupboard, and as Jeanie threw the soggy jumper into the corner, John stood amazed at the small flat she had created. She was always resourceful, and this could indeed be said by the handmade furniture now spread all over the garage.

"Turn around." Jeanie aware of his presence started to undress quickly. John's back was turned, but he couldn't help but watch her reflection in the window. With his stare fixated on her smooth pale skin, and perfect shoulders he didn't understand how she still made his body immediately react. He had dreamed about taking her a thousand times and even though he could never bring himself to the chance to take her even though she was older intrigued him more.

As she folded the bed back into the cupboard, Jeanie straightened herself out ready for round two. "Right ready, what can I do you for anyway?"

"I have a surprise, come on." Still contrite to his previous attempts she hovered in the office.

"You are always up to no good John Stanton. I know that look." Taking her by the hand, he pushed her into the car.

"Where are we going?" John winked and continued to drive out of the gate. Stopping the car on the dirt track at the back of Jeanie's factory, no questions where needed. The big oak tree at the spread over into the field and its prominence nearly as large as the factory. Jeanie had built her hideaway space in its branches years ago. A tree house to most but it had been modified over the years creating more of a cabin or lodge rather than a play space. As she built the foundations in her teens, it was a place to escape and a chance to relax to read and contemplate her future, and as they rose, Jeanie saw that the log burner had been lit and a plaid blanket had been placed on the roof. Reaching up to take John's hand she negotiated the steps and proceeded to sit on the neatly placed blanket.

"Well lie down!"

"John I know what you're doing. I have played these games before remember." As John patted the blanket, she knew her protests were falling on deaf ears, and as she lay next to him, she looked up, and through the trees, she could see thousands and thousands of stars.

There was no doubt that this was her favourite place in the world and remembering how she used to lay up there for hours and sometimes stay over when her dad had been working made her see how long it had been since her father had passed. It was only when she missed him the most that she would venture up for time to think. Jeanie imagined her dad as one of the stars looking down on her helping with the question or problem she couldn't answer.

John on the otherhand lay motionless looking at the stars. Jeanie knew what he was up to but couldn't help but play along, he'd been the best and worst of Jeanie's past and somehow even though she wanted to let go she was pulled back.

"I never told you this before." As he moved closer, his breath created smoke signals in the frosty night air.

"When you were sixteen do you remember that long hot summer? We chased the girls into the field at the back of your house. You asked me a question that day, and I kept silent, and I should have screamed aloud. You asked me something, and I didn't respond, and I just wanted you to know that I wanted to more than you could imagine. I felt powerless. I loved you so much you have to understand that

"John please this isn't...."

"Just hear me out. As I stood at the window that night, I saw you running around Mrs Morias back garden after that stupid pig in nothing but a pair of shorts and a camisole. I'd never seen you in the moonlight before, and you were mesmerising. I saw how the sweat beads made you glisten and how your clothes showed off every curve. You were always beautiful Jeanie." Jeanie sat up and curled her legs into her body resting her chin on her knees for comfort.

"John, we settled this the other night, I don't want anything more it's not right. We are not right for each other, and it just doesn't work. I can't make it work." Jeanie took hold of the ladder placed it at the side of the house her strength had grown with age and responsibility, and now it was easy to finish what she needed to say.

"I saw you watching me John. I saw you stare at me from your bedroom window and that night and you still did nothing. But its different now and we are not children anymore it's just not the same. We live in a different world, and I've made my choice. I just want you to know that I loved you more than anything you just didn't love me back in the way I needed."

"Jeanie please just hear me out." Jeanie bowed her head feeling that if she was going to work at the base, she at least needed to know they could be civil.

"I was a stupid, scared boy. I made decisions which I thought would change my life and make it better for us. Instead, I hurt you and caused you more pain. I didn't feel…I can't defend what I have done. I married a woman I didn't love and ended up creating a monster. I just want you to know that I have never loved anyone the way I love you and I regret every stupid mistake, and all I want to do is spend the rest of my life making it up to you because I'm in love with you." As the lump rose to her throat, Jeanie realised that her tears had dried. He was her past, and now she had to concentrate on the future.

"Thank you for being honest John, but it's too late." Jumping off the last two runs, she looked up at the house as he stood unable to admit defeat. Jeanie held her head high proud to know that she had done the right thing and this time she didn't have to argue, scream or shout to get her point across. As she looked back she felt her past as she turned to go back to the base it was time to leave it well and truly behind.

Watching her walk away hurt and he was now experiencing something he had done to Jeanie several times. The emptiness he felt was hard to swallow and the strength of her conviction even harder to take. As she walked up the road, she didn't look back, and he knew he had to fight for her there was no other way to prove that he had learnt his lesson. Knowing he was in competition with another man meant the first work he had to do was find him.

Walking back onto the base her hands had slumped in her pocket, and she felt exhausted from the drama which had unfolded. She couldn't wait to occupy her mind with the night's work ahead. Jeanie rubbed her face with her hands and stretched as she reached for the office door. Yawning she gasped aloud.

"Well, another night!" Gaining her bearings, she saw a figure stood in the corner of the room watching every movement.

"Hello, can I help you?" the figure moved again. Jeanie froze not knowing whether to jump into the pit or lock herself in the office. Moving around the garage the shadow seemed to leave through the back door. Thinking it was a figment of her imagination Jeanie continued to rummage around for the rest of her tools. Hearing another noise, Jeanie jumped to attention her senses now heightened at the intrusion.

"Hello! Hello! HELLO!" As Jeanie moved gingerly back up the steps, she noticed a man sat on her stool, cautiously she walked towards him and saw it was James.

"Are you ok? Has something happened?" James lifted his head and took another sip from the brown bag which sat on his lap.

"I don't know. Why don't you ask your new friend?" Jeanie looked at him and stepped back confused at his answer.

"I don't understand."

"Well like I said why you don't ask your new friend or should I just call him John. Well, are you going to deny it?" Surprised by his outburst, she knew she had nothing to be ashamed.

"No, I'm not. Yes, I have spent the last couple of hours reminiscing but at the end of the night I walked back to base on my own so why do you have a problem." James staggered and laid against the wall his dishevelled appearance a complete contrast to his usual impeccable exterior.

"So nothing happened. All good friendly banter because the way I saw it in the hospital ward this afternoon and in the courtyard earlier looked more than a friendly let's talk gesture."

James fell to the floor and doing so smashed the bottle he had been drinking. Jeanie sighed and shook her head understanding how the events could have been misconstrued.

"James. He's our superior officer, please don't do this. Everything has been going so well." Placing her hand on his chest, Jeanie tried to assess how drunk he was.

"Listen to me I meant what I said the other night. Please don't worry this afternoon may have looked different but it wasn't I can assure you." James made his way back up the wall, and towards Jeanie, as he reached for her he grabbed her arms and pulled her towards him.

"Do you know what my problem is! I fell for a fucking useless engineer's daughter and her fucking seven slut sisters and do you know the worst thing the one I got is only a half fucking sister to all of them because her bitch mother couldn't keep her legs fucking closed either."

"How dare you! How dare you even say those things to me." Feeling the past suddenly bite back Jeanie tried to move away thinking back to her arguments with John. Wriggling out of his hold James fell forward, and as James hit the floor, the realisation of what he had done sobered his thoughts. Blood poured from Jeanie's nose and cheek, and as she took a cloth and moved towards the door, she was greeted by her new apprentice. His cheery grin soon turned serious after realising what had happened. James now brushing himself down and trying to apologise moved swiftly towards the scene of his assault.

"Jeanie, I'm sorry, I got jealous, Jeanie look at me."
Forcibly turning her head around James could see
the blood still trickling from the cut on her cheek.
"I'm sorry Jea...I fell I didn't mean."
"I think you better go." Jeanie sat on the stool not
knowing why he had become so jealous and as the
alcohol drained his body, he fell to his knees in
front of her.
"Jeanie let me look. I just. I can't explain it. I heard
your sister earlier telling one of the nurses about
what had happened the other night and when I saw
you together I just. Jeanie, I love you, please believe
me."
"I think it's time to leave I don't feel you have
anything else to say to me James which could make
this any better, so please go." The new apprentice
escorted the doctor through the door and closed it
behind him. James took off his coat and threw it in
the bin lighting a cigarette he noticed John walking
back through the gate, and as he passed, he nodded
to the doctor.
James boiled inside knowing that this man wanted
more and now he had given him the opportunity to
take her. Knowing how stupid he had been he
wanted to run back inside the garage and make it
right instead he turned and walked away knowing
venturing back in would only make the situation
worse.
    Inside the garage, Jeanie's nose had stopped
bleeding feeling the embarrassment grow Jeanie
stood and held out her hand.
"OK I don't know what went on in here, but my
name is Mike Kowalski, Lieutenant Signthorpe said
you were expecting me."
Shaking Mikes hand timidly Jeanie sat down and
took in a deep breath. Regardless of how she felt
she had a job to do and as she wiped her face on her

sleeve she pulled herself together as professionally as she could.

"Yes, I am, Jeanie Rutherford. Suppose you can call me chief engineer I'm the only one on sight anyway."

"Listen no offence you can tell me to mind my own business but, what is a da…woman like you doing in a shop like this."

Jeanie laughed uncomfortably remembering the conversation with Signthrope earlier.

"I've been saying that for years!" Walking away with her new sidekick she showed him around the garage, and as she smiled politely and spoke, Jeanie felt sick.

"Welcome aboard and thank you, not so many people are as gracious about…you know." Mike nodded back seeing that she felt uncomfortable enough without him adding to it.

"0400 in the morning then Boss lady." As Jeanie held out her hand again, Mike shook it and left quickly knowing what he'd seen had naturally caused some upset. Jeanie hadn't been able to speak and the evening's events had taken such a turn that even Jeanie questioned whether they had happened.

    James had acted out of character, and he was even cruel, and as Jeanie sat at her desk, she pulled out the paperwork for the vehicles trying to forget. As the small droplets of blood started to fall from her nose again she looked across the workshop and felt safe in the reality that this was all she had ever known, and how could she ever be anything different. Taking her sleeve, she wiped away the blood away and continued to do what she did best. Work.

Chapter 8

The cut on Jeanie's cheek had left a small scar, and as she looked at her reflection, it made Jeanie feel like the past had risen from its grave. The scars were something she had gotten used to over the years with John however this felt more real than any betrayal of John's. Her now swollen hand was also overdue for her stitches and whether she liked it or not she knew she had to see James.

As Jeanie walked over to the medical wing, she could feel the knots inside her stomach tighten and churn.
Did he still love her? Did he still want to be with her?
The medical unit had an eerie silence to, and the quiet made Jeanie feel even more uneasy. The ghost town qualities of the corridor sent chills down Jeanie's spine. No matter how much she was dreading seeing James the silence of the halls seemed worse and as she desperately looked for any signs of life Jeanie searched through doors and curtains to see if there was anyone to take out the stitches. Hearing raised voices from the examination room, she followed the sound hoping someone other than him would be there.

The uncomfortable silent grey corridors seem to emphasise the noise within, and as she stopped at the door, Jeanie took a deep breath to gather her thoughts. Turning the corner, she could see the shadows of two people through the crisp white cloth. James's voice echoed through loud and clear. His velvet tones and his smooth manner were unmistakable. Wanting to leave and intrigued to see Jeanie peeked through a slit in the curtain. As the nurse climbed James's body the carnal nature of the affair played out for Jeanie to see as she watched his hands touch her and the way he slammed her hard against the hospital bed both revolted and repulsed her.

James had talked to her quite openly about his love affairs but watching his aggression and the way he treated her body made her look more like his plaything for sexual satisfaction rather than a human being. As he moved her body, Jeanie didn't recognise him. The soft, smooth touches of his hands and understanding character seemed to have been eradicated and replaced as the passion escalated.

Jeanie couldn't step forward or back she was caught up in the whirlwind of watching him have sex with another woman, and she was unable to understand how he had lost his way so quickly. Everything she had felt being with him that night seemed to disappear on seeing his treatment of the nurse made it feel so false. His actions appeared clinical, almost as if it was to satisfy an appetite than to express love. Jeanie couldn't help but stand there watch until he reached climax.

Climbing down from the bed the nurse started to fix her uniform, and James never spoke a word. Opening the curtain the nurse stepped back in fright as Jeanie just stood with her eyes hooked on both of them. Liz hurried past unable to say a word knowing full well how she would react.

Jeanie wanted to see his reaction she couldn't wait for his explanation, but instead, he slouched in the chair with his head in his hands. His cold hard expression never wavered he didn't even seem to care where this girl had gone. He just sat in the chair staring at the floor. As Jeanie took a small step, she hoped he would notice and understand what she had seen

"Hold on one minute I will be…." As he wiped his face and placed on a false smile, he ventured out of the cubicle.

"How long have you been their……" Jeanie just stood and looked at him, not knowing what to say. "Jeanie please how long have you been stood there?" Jeanie took off her St Christopher and slid the ring down the necklace laying it down on the bed.

"I need my stitches taken out, and I have come to give you this." Finishing her sentence Jeanie lay the ring on the ruffled linen moving quickly away she no longer wanted to be in his company. James punched the wall knowing she'd seen everything fastening himself he screamed after her.

"Jeanie wait! Jeanie wait …for fuck sake wait."

"Why what are you going to tell me."

"Jeanie just let me explain!"

"Just answer me this. Am I so much different to Catherine! Or am I just another quest except for this time you had to put up a fight." Feeling the hurt in her voice and condemnation of her words James could do nothing knowing she was right.

"Jeanie it wasn't like that."

"So tell me James…tell me what it's like cause I'd like to understand." As he stuttered, Jeanie shook her head knowing she'd already come to the right conclusion.

"You treat people this way because you think your special you still believe that you can do what you like to anyone you please just to satisfy that overblown ego of yours. Well let me tell you, James Watson, you are an insecure child! You need to feel something, so you use sex with anyone just to pander to your insecurities, and my worst mistake was letting you into my life and my bed." As Jeanie ran down the corridor her stomach churned and the overwhelming feeling to be sick was too much. Hiding behind the garage, Jeanie threw up feeling disgusted with herself that she'd let him fool her. Of the men, she had ever found a connection with both had pushed their way into her life, and they had also found their way into other women's beds.

Brushing her hands through her hair, she stood tall; this wasn't her humiliation it was his. Jeanie was numb, but the decision to stand tall and walk away was the only clarity she had.

"Jeanie please we need to talk."

"I have nothing to say to you."

"Your right Jeanie...everything you told me in the medical ward is true."

"And you think that makes a difference. I trusted you I had started to think that you were different that you loved me." Jeanie gulped down her tears unable to let them show and to make James understand that she was a lot tougher than he thought.

"No...but I hit you...I hit you, and I thought that you would never forgive me. I figured I had lost you for good and instead of coming to make this right I fucked another woman because that's the kind of screwed up degenerate I am. I feel dirty Jeanie. I feel used and unclean because what I did. What I have done is inexcusable, and I let my ego and my pride stand between us when I should have begged you to forgive me."

"Go tell it to that nurse." The rain had started to pour heavily, and as they stood together, Jeanie knew they were at an impasse.

"So what now Jea....Tell me how I can make this right. Jea..." As James gulped hard, Jeanie heard the crack in his voice. However, the hurt and pain inside swelled as if to emulate the grids which had started to overflow in the yard.

"You can never make this right." As she reached the garage, Jeanie was soaked to the bone, and as she sat in her office, she took out the Stanley knife and started to cut away at the stitches in her palm. Pealing them out one by one she sat and watched the rain feeling like her heart had just been ripped out of her chest. Her mind replayed over and over the scenes in the hospital, and everything that James had promised had been eroded in six weeks. "How fucking stupid am I to fall for another man who is so self-involved that he thinks of no one else but himself." As the storm grew stronger, thunder started to sound in the distance. The loud claps and bangs echoed around the empty spaces of the garage, and the puddles and swells had begun to form outside her door. The leak from the roof looked more like a shower, and as Jeanie looked at her palm, the emptiness surged inside like a swollen river bursting its banks. Jeanie knew immediately it was time to pack away her things and for the first time in three months, she had made the right decision. It was time to go home. James had been a fantasy and now what he depicted wasn't real. Inside her mind, she had placed him above every other man who had treated her like crap in hopes that this time, it would be different. Jeanie had nothing to lose, and as she entered back into the garage, she turned off the light and rolled down the shutter doors. This last action had given her a clear realisation that she had been in solitude without realising it and she had distanced herself from everyone who actually cared for her and for the first time in ages she couldn't wait to see her family.

Jeanie jumped through the puddles and tried to hide the disappointment her life had been so far. Consumed by the base and the factory she knew it had always taken control of her and as she walked in the rain, it gave Jeanie comfort. As the droplets soothed her, they dripped down her face washing tears and frustration away. Reaching home felt right.

Irene stood by the cooker scolding her for leaving oily marks on her walls and table, and instead of biting back Jeanie remained silent and happy that normality still existed inside these walls.

Jeanie needed to reach back out to her family, and her presence in the house had been sorely missed. As her sisters gathered around her clucking and fusing, as usual, Jeanie was just grateful for the support. She couldn't wait to slip back into her old way of life, and at least for now routine, normal and uneventful seemed very appealing.

As dawn broke, Jeanie had already gone to the factory, and even though most of her family were now involved, she felt she needed the security they had to offer. Ivy knew something was wrong from the moment she came home. Jeanie was like dad, and she hated the silence when something was on their mind.

Wandering around the kitchen Ivy impatiently waited for the kettle to boil. Jayne at least was asleep, and in part, most of the house surrounded itself in silence. Making the tea Ivy saw a shadow appear at the door and a soft wrap. The gentle noise startled her more than the kettle and seeing it was official she immediately thought of George.

"John what a pleasant surprise..." Her sarcastic tones echoed around the footwell, and as he stepped through the door, he was sodden as the rain had started to fall hard and fast. The cold droplets surrounded his feet like miniature ponds.
"This is an unexpected. How can I help you?" John had started to unbutton his jacket and take off his gloves.
"She in when I mean she I mean Jeanie not the other she-devil you call your mother." Ivy slammed the door shut and walked back into the kitchen
"What do want John?"
"Come on Ivy I know you're usually a lot more hospitable than this." Ivy slammed the drawer shut

as his sarcasm, and his quick wit made it hard for her to respond.

"Nice to see that things change." John sat down at the kitchen table expecting tea to be served. Ivy sat at the other end not moving or wanting to accommodate any request he had.

"She won't talk to me Ivy she won't even respond to any letter's I have sent. I want her back."

"I think you're probably a bit late plus after everything you have done to her do you think she would even contemplate taking you back." John knew this would be a stalemate; he also knew if he were ever going to get to Jeanie, Ivy would be the perfect ally to have.

"Ivy. Let me start again. Our relationship has been complicated in the past with my brother and all, but she needs to know I have changed," Ivy dropped her cup on the floor, and as the segments flew around her feet, she couldn't help but feel her temper boil.

"Shit. John do not ask me to put a good word in for you. I don't understand you. Mind you I never did. You've used and abused so many people that even the ones who thought they saw good in you have lost hope."

"I understand how you feel and I know the last conversation…Let me just say that I'm, sorry for dragging you into this but I need help."

"It's not just that John. There's something I need…forget about it." Getting out of his chair John bent down and started to pick up the fragments of the shattered cup off the floor.

"There's what Ivy?" Throwing the last few pieces in the bin Ivy rested her hands on the sink, and as she stared out of the window, she hoped she could find some courage.

"You know I thought you were here to tell me something had happened to George. Things ended not as I expected and I assumed you were here to say.....Oh, John, this is just all fucked up." Holding her head in her hands, she couldn't help but feel tearful, and as John offered his handkerchief, he placed his hand softly on her shoulder.

"The night I had Jayne she met a doctor at the hospital she hasn't seen him in a few months, and she's been really distant from all of us. I know he asked her to marry him cause I saw the ring come to think it was the first time I'd seen her smile in years. I mean properly smile. Not that fake I'm alright thing she does." John huffed under his breath remembering the last time he saw the same reaction.

"John she's changed so much since dad died. We all have, please don't do anything to hurt her she's had to deal with so much I don't think she could bear it."

"I don't want to hurt her anymore Ivy. I want to love her, and I want her to see that I've changed and that all the lies and deceit has gone." Ivy moved away from his grasp feeling too involved.

"What about your wife?"

"What about her she's not here or in my life Ivy and to be honest she's the reason I'm here. I've never loved anyone in my life, and instead of bringing Jeanie with me I forced her away until.... You know the story. You know I never loved my wife.
I found Olivia in bed with another man, and it serves me right, but it gave me the excuse I needed to get out. I wasn't there long enough to take details but I know he was an American and I know she was seeing him for some months before I left. I've been selfish and cruel to all of you, but that's over, and things are different, and I need to make this up to her." Ivy looked at the storm outside not able to swallow or believe a word he said and as Jayne started to cry it gave her the perfect get out clause to end the conversation.

"I have to get her she's due for a feed." as Ivy pushed passed John he caught hold of her hand. "Can I see her? I mean she's my niece." Biting the edges of her fingernails Ivy nodded nervously. John stood at the back door cigarette in hand, and as Ivy graced the kitchen, she pulled the bottle from the pan. Jayne had snuggled into Ivy's arms as she started to feed the contentment she exhumed being close to her mother was evident.

"She's beautiful Ivy. What's wrong with her arm?" Ivy kissed the infants head and started to sway.

"They had to break it to get her out if it wasn't for Jeanie both of us might have died." John smoothed his hand over the infant's head playing with the soft strawberry blonde tuffs as his fingers wiggled through.

"Do you want to hold her?"

"Another time maybe. Ivy Jeanie is special I know that now" Ivy's lip quivered trying to hold back tears.

"She's special to all of us John, but I'm not saying a word. If you want her it's up to you to prove it don't ask me to get involved cause I'm not. I'm not going to do it." John nodded understanding that the conversation had started to get more emotional. Saying his goodbye's John replaced his coat, gloves and hat which were still sodden from the torrential rain and before he slipped out the door he kissed Ivy gently on her cheek.

"Thank you. I'm sorry Ivy for everything I did I mean that." Ivy slammed the door again, and as she rested on the back of it, she closed her eyes.

"Not as much as I am John Stanton."

Chapter 9

It didn't stop raining for over a week, and when
Jeanie eventually dragged herself out of the door,
Ivy had noticed a significant change. The routine
was the same, but Jeanie was different. Her give it a
go nature seemed to be struggling under pressure,
and she was reluctant to talk about what was
causing the issue. Seeing Jeanie leave and needing
to know if she was ok Ivy ran after her.
"Jeanie stop," Through the huge coat two eyes
appeared and turned around reluctantly.
"Jeanie talk to me. I know something's wrong your
never this quiet. I'm your sister tell me it's breaking
my heart to see you like this."
"I'm all right, go back to Jayne before you catch
your death." Jeanie waved as she walked away
desperate to put her sister's mind at ease. She was
heartbroken, and as much as she tried, she couldn't
suppress the feelings she had.
   The thought that James was different was almost
tearing her apart. Unable to swallow Jeanie's
response Ivy stood in the cold drowned by the
droplets which by this time looked more like a
tropical monsoon than a rainy day in England.
Watching her sister walk away she couldn't help but
feel powerless to her plight, and now her head faced
the floor, and it made it look as if the weight of the
rain was holding her down.
   Jeanie's head swam with questions in which most
of them surrounded James's. Jeanie hoped home
was to be a cure however she now found it too
difficult to tolerate, and she was too hurt to respond.
The fact was, she detested her lies and knowing she
had never lied before made the truth harder to
swallow. She had created speeches in her head over
and over again about how he was no longer her

future. However, nothing seemed palpable. After all, how can you politely put:

"By the way, the man who said he was in love with me and proposed after the first four hours has now decided to sleep with a nurse and now it's all over." It sounded ridiculous. It felt ridiculous and to even be this upset after so little time didn't feel justified.

Jeanie's usual trip to work seemed to long and arduous, and as army carriers passed her, she tried to dodge the waves of sludge and water. Jeanie felt the puddle wash over her like a tidal wave, and even though she screamed at the passing trucks, not one stopped to help her on her way. Arriving at the base, Jeanie looked more like the swamp creature turning up to reek havoc rather than the chief engineer ready to start another day in the garage. Opening the door, she saw the fire was already lit in the workshop and Mike had left a series of notes around.

"Thought you would need this." The arrow pointed to the wood burning stove inside Jeanie's office, and as she began to take her sodden clothes off and hang them over a makeshift washing line, she shuddered at the thought of making the same trip home. Stripping down to her vest and pants the warmth from the stove made her feel sleepy. The dark skies made the day feel more like early evening, and the big oil soaked chair reeked of comfort. Settling down to drink her brew, Jeanie heard a knock at the door making her spring to attention.

"Sorry, I didn't want to scare you,"

"What is it John," Jeanie was abrupt if somewhat obtuse at his calling.

"I have to take the general down to the Grand Hotel. Can you give me the figures and vehicles completed and not completed I need them for a meeting in the morning."

"I have a couple of outstanding notes, but I'm sure I can have things ready for you within an hour." John nodded his head, but before closing the door, he turned.

"By the way cute washing line." As the door slammed shut, Jeanie saw the line fall to the floor, spilling her soggy damp things all over the room. Mumbling under her breath, Jeanie got re-dressed and started to gather the information John required. On opening the shutter, the rain poured through, and it was still torrential. Rivers washed down the gullies, and the grids had started to overflow in the yard. Deep puddles had sprung up all over the base, and even the narrow bridge had become swamped by the bursting river, everything seemed to buckle under the weight of water and army personnel.

Making her way to the Main building and cursing John for making her venture out again she reached the main reception. The receptionist looked perfect with no sign that the weather had even touched her and as Jeanie glimpsed at her reflection in the large gothic mirror her feelings of self-consciousness started to rise.

"I'm sorry Jeanie you might be able to catch him at the main gate, but he's already left." Swearing under her breath, Jeanie placed the documents inside her coat, and as she waded through the streams, she eventually reached the private on duty.

"Are there any more cars going to the Grand tonight?" The private stuck his head out of the gatehouse trying to avoid the torrents that had started to beat down.

"Not that I know of think you just missed the last one. It's about five miles over that hill if you fancy a shortcut." Jeanie smiled sarcastically muttering death threats to John as she made her way. Walking in the wet and cold she couldn't help but curse as the climb up the hill felt hard, and the mud beds had deepened due to the extra water. Reaching the top gave her a glimpse of the Solway Firth with its dense clouds surrounding the hills into Scotland, and as the stormy waters crashed out, she watched in awe at the violence of the storm.

As Jeanie made her way down to the road at the bottom, she descended carefully feeling the earth slide beneath her feet. Her large coat inhibited most of her movement, and the last thing she wanted to do was fall as she was wet enough, and she didn't want to add mud and cow shit to the equation as well. Reaching the gate at the bottom, she felt a sense of achievement and as she climbed over the rain poured harder and faster than before making her feel like her ordeal was never going to end. The only thing she wished, for now, was a nice hot bath and a warm, cosy bed. Throwing herself over the fence and onto the road Jeanie found herself in a puddle which resembled a small lake and trying to shake off the water she smiled under her breath. "Well, it can't get any worse…." Waddling through the puddle, she heard a car from behind and as she tried to hurry Jeanie got her boot, stuck in the mud. Dislodging her foot from her boot Jeanie fell backwards into the puddle and as the car passed the wave submerged her in the cold, dirty water. "Thank you, dick head!" The car slowed and stopped and seeing it back up the lane Jeanie waited for the abuse.
"Come back to have another look have you." John's face scrunched up in laughter, and with Jeanie still murmuring under her breath she finally looked up.
"Might have known it was you."
"Jesus Christ who let the swamp monster out! Get in the car I was coming back to pick you up." Jeanie sloshed her way around to the passenger side and waded in through the door. She was black, dripping and smelly.

"You stink, I'm sorry Jeanie but phew." Jeanie sarcastically smiled and pulled the document John had been waiting for out of her jacket and placed it carefully on the seat at the side of them. As John drove them down to the seafront, Jeanie couldn't believe how many people had descended on this small town. RAF personnel filled the streets, and the rumble of Lancaster bombers rippled through the skyline. Wrens lined up at the front of the hotel, and as John leant over, he signalled to Jeanie that it was time to go.

"I can't go in there like this look at me I'm a mess," John shook his head and routed around in his pockets, taking a key out he threw it over to the passenger side.

"I've got a room at the side of fire escape make your way up and get changed. Oh and wash because you smell like a cow's arse." Jeanie snatched the key from him agreeing with his observation.

Hiding in between cars she made her way up and onto the fire escape feeling like a criminal with every step she took. On the other hand, the place was swarming with RAF personnel and knowing most of them she didn't fancy any of them taking the piss out of the unfortunate situation. Wandering up the fire escape, she crept through the door and into the corridor which in contrast to her was painted a soft yellow. Whispering under her breath, she hurried through the door and into the room. An open fire was lit in the bedroom, and a balcony looked over the seafront. She could see the waves crashing against the shoreline in the storm, and as she took off her clothes, she felt trapped as everything stuck to her as if it was made of glue. Standing naked in the bedroom she hunted around for something to wear and finding John's bathrobe hung on the back of the door she covered herself.

As her bath beckoned she knew she might be recognised and wearing John's robe was only going to get her in more trouble. Negotiating the hallways and quickening her pace she searched for a relatively adjacent bathroom. Knocking politely and hearing no answer she ran through and locked the door behind her. Jeanie's eyes lit up as the steam warmed through her bones and as she lay in the hot soapy water, her thoughts drifted back to having to renegotiate the hallways as not to stir up suspicion.

Creeping back into the bedroom she changed into John's pyjamas and sat on the floor, she could hear the water outside and buzz of people downstairs, however, she was just glad to be warm. As Jeanie dried her hair in front of the fire, she remembered her kiss with James and the warm glow of the embers on her back. Feeling the warmth, Jeanie lay down and watched the fire burn. James felt distant and the happiness she felt for that brief moment seemed like a lifetime ago. As Jeanie drew up the blanket, she curled up in front of the fire feeling the loss of what could have been. The only thing she had left was the memory of that night, and as she listened with intent to the storm outside, she felt it wash her pain away.

As John entered the room, he found Jeanie asleep on the floor at the front of the fire. Her hair had grown long and had started to curl down her back, and the fiery red tint made it look as if the flames were dancing around her head. As he placed the blanket back, over her, he walked over to the window and watched the storm. It had been a long night, and as he looked back he revelled in how peaceful she looked. Underneath his breath the words," if only" spluttered out as he took another sip of his brandy he rubbed his temple. John looked out to sea and in some way, he seemed as defeated as the shoreline. The evening had been long and drawn out, and the fight was still raging overseas however the burden of his responsibility had started to become overwhelming. As he leant on the windowsill, he gazed into the night searching for answers.

"What's why if only." As he turned Jeanie stood at his side and moved the hair away from her face. As John led her back to bed, he placed her under the covers.

"Go to sleep it doesn't matter." Jeanie lay looking at his gaze, his sadness and loss seemed to emulate her feelings. Jeanie couldn't help but be inquisitive, and as she watched him loosen his collar and take off, his tie off she tried to understand his thoughts. Picking up his glass he sat down on the chair with his back towards her, Jeanie felt for him and in a lot of ways growing up hadn't changed him. When something was on his mind or when he was trying to be a gentleman he would never look at her. John would pretend everything was ok by blanking her out and she knew he was putting in the effort to make her feel comfortable.

As Jeanie got out of bed, she knew the consequences of her actions, and as she walked over to the window, she took his hand.

"I know what if only means and I know you want me; I'm here John why not show me." Before Jeanie had time to finish her sentence John picked her up and threw her against the wall. Ripping at her shirt, he kissed her ardently, and as she smoothed his hands over her thighs and hips, he started to undo the buttons on the shirt. Her eyes blazed with the desire of his touch, and even though she knew it was wrong, she couldn't help herself. Without a word, he carried her over to the bed. He'd longed for this moment, he'd dreamed about her wanting him, and now she was his present to cherish and undress.

Jeanie felt his body react as the intensity between them grew. He made every button seem like an eternity, and as he took his shirt off, he started to kiss her neck and continued his way down, drinking in every curve as they began to make love. Jeanie felt his heart beating with exhilaration, and as she slid her body over his thighs, he moved her hair away from her neck. As she moved closer, he kissed every inch of her collarbone and as he made his way down Jeanie hissed with satisfaction.

"I love you Jea" as the slow movement of his body made Jeanie climax he wanted more. Her body screamed out again wanting more of him inside her, and as he moved his hand slowly over her back and down to her thighs, he held on tight and couldn't let go. There bodies moved in perfect synchronicity, and every motion seemed to spring excitement.

"Please don't stop."

"I'm never letting you go." As her whisper electrified breathlessly on his kiss, he had to taste more. John moaned as he went deeper into her experiencing everything she had to give. Wrapping her hands around his neck, she nuzzled into his jawline as she rocked gently up and down every nerve ending seemed to explode in rapture. Feeling John climax Jeanie's body reacted to his ecstasy falling beneath a tidal wave of pleasure.

With Jeanie still in his arms, he didn't want to move just in case it was a dream. Everything he had ever felt had led him to this perfect point, and as he kissed every finger, he never wanted to let go. Jeanie stared into his intense gaze knowing that from the moment she got out of bed this was what he wanted and what she expected. He had felt so right but underneath the nag of doubt inside shrouded what should have been the perfect moment.

"What are you thinking? I know you're thinking about something cause of the line in your brow."

"I'm thinking you're going to be the death of me John Stanton." As John laughed timidly, he ran his nose over her forehead and kissed it sweetly.

"I love you so much." Turning on her side, Jeanie felt his warm hand caress her stomach, and as he circled her hip, she closed her eyes remembering his promise.

"I need to know something."

"Anything"

"Maybe it's morbid curiosity John but how do I compare to everyone else." Taking a large drag of breath, he sat up pulling her into him so he could face her.

"Nothing has ever compared to you. Ever. I have been in love with you my whole life and tonight I have realised what I have missed. I have lost a lifetime of making love with Jea, and I'm not going to lose you again. So trust me when I say that there has only ever been you and from this point on that's how I want it to stay." Placing her hand on his cheek, Jeanie pulled him close and kissed him softly, and as she ran her thumb along his lip, he kissed her palm.

"Why do you do this to me, John Stanton? Why do I let you in?"

"Because you love me. You always have, and I've been a fool."

Jeanie pulled the sheet around him, and as he settled in beside her, she could feel the sleep pull on her heavy eyelids. Unable to lift his gaze John watched her sleep, he wanted to scream out loud that she was his and how this was their new start. John had longed for his life to include her, and as he watched the wind sweep the rain around the building and the sea break over the defences he knew at least for tonight, she was his.

Chapter 10

As dawn broke Jeanie arose feeling John's hand making snake-like patterns on her stomach. As he kissed her neck and collarbone, he leant over checking the time on his watch.

"Times against us as always." As he kissed again, Jeanie grabbed hold of his hand studying each finger.

"I'm sorry my darling I have to go." Gathering his clothes from the bedroom floor, Jeanie watched him dress.

"Where are you going?"

"Breakfast you wore me out last night and I'm starving I will bring you something back stay here."

"No really where are you going?" Kissing her again Jeanie straightened his tie and pulled down his collar, and as her fingers grappled with the starched cloth he cupped her hand lovingly

"I love you" Jeanie kissed him softly again feeling his heartbeat pick up the pace again.

"I know." Moving the hair away from her shoulders he smiled softly in complete satisfaction; he never imagined a reconciliation after all he didn't deserve one. As he smoothed his hands around her shoulders, he pulled her into his chest feeling the familiarity of her hold.

"I promise I will make you happy. I don't ever want to lose you again. My life hasn't been complete and now…" Jeanie placed her finger on his lip, and as a lone tear stained her cheek, he wiped it away.

"Please don't cry. I hate it when you cry."

Wrapping his hands around her, he pulled her close. The stale, musty smell of his uniform jacket invaded her nostrils, and as the prickles dug into her cheek, she wanted to believe him. Running his hand over his cheek, he kissed her softly, and as the taste of her salty tears ran down his throat, it made him gasp in pain.

"I'll be back in an hour don't move. I love you." Dropping her hand as he left Jeanie watched reverently as the door closed. Knowing she was in his room would have disgraced both of them, and that was a risk even she wasn't going to take.

After an hour and a half of waiting Jeanie's patience had worn thin and as she put on his shirt and spare trousers she carefully stepped out. After hiding around a few corners and sneaking through reception, Jeanie made her way into a small conservatory room. Breakfast seemed to have been and gone and just like John it was nowhere in sight. Moulding her way into the corner of the room and trying to stay unnoticed she desperately looked out for him.

Making eye contact with a glamorous young woman who walked past Jeanie tried to remain as inconspicuous as possible.

The woman looked at Jeanie with contempt, and as she leaned in to get the waiter's attention, she looked decidedly confused about Jeanie's ambiguous position.

"Can you tell my husband I will wait for him in here he's late?" Slipping money into the waiter's pocket, she oozed grace and sophistication.

"Apologies madam who is your husband?" Jeanie couldn't help but stare she was stunning. Her wide blue eyes and golden skin distracted Jeanie from her goal of finding John. Edging back into the corner the woman continued to look confused about Jeanie but continued her conversation with the waiter.

"I'm looking for Colonel Stanton." Jeanie's heart sank, and in her bemusement, she fell over the pot she was standing beside.

Running back towards the main lobby the same thought repeated over and over again

What have I done? What have I done?

Slamming the door shut she hurried to take off John's clothes. After a few minutes of panic, she noticed John's drink still lurking on the small coffee table and as she gulped it down the, she pulled her face in distaste. As the voices moved closer to the door, Jeanie tried to increase her dressing speed and as the lock switched John appeared. Jeanie still tussling with dressing looked distressed.

"What's wrong you look like you've seen a ghost," Jeanie still half dressed, flustered and feeling guilty looked straight at John.

"Ghost, a fucking ghost." Still trying to find items of clothing Jeanie ran on the spot.

"No John I haven't seen a fucking ghost, just your wife!" John turned pale dropping the plate of food, and as it scattered on the bed, it made the quilt look more like an extravagant picnic.

"I can explain."

"You're still married, John. You said it was over. I have slept with a married man, and his wife is downstairs, how are you going to explain that." Jeanie tided herself up, and as she grappled with the laces she heard a knock at the door. With no time to explain John jumped to attention not knowing and not wanting to find out who was on the outside. As the door tapped again, a muffled voice was heard from the outside. Jeanie wide-eyed turned the door handle and tried to hide. Olivia Stanton stood at the door in all her perfect glory and as Jeanie picked herself up off the floor as Olivia spoke.

"Oh right breakfast, I didn't realise you'd ordered darling, oh sweetie can you bring me a cup of coffee and be a treasure thank you." John's face angered as his wife pointed towards Jeanie who by this time was trying to slip around the door inconspicuously. Olivia stood in silence feeling the tension she spoke again.

"Apologies have I interrupted something she is your maid isn't she John?" Olivia had given Jeanie the perfect excuse to leave, and she didn't need any formal requests.

"No, but I will see where your coffee is madam." Folding her arms, Jeanie closed the door, and as she made her way down to reception, she spoke to the concierge at the front desk and ordered the coffee John's wife had so desperately needed.

As Jeanie sat on the steps of the bay, she tried to figure out her next move. John had pursued her so consistently she didn't ask about Olivia. She was as much to blame as he was. The guilt wrapped her body and Jeanie couldn't comprehend how stupid she had been.

The suns rays beamed through the white clouds beautiful and bright on the horizon. The puddles sparkled in the light of day, and the warmth and calm reflection of the weather were nothing towards the turmoil Jeanie felt inside. She promised herself she was never going to do this again and she had promised herself that John Stanton was out of the picture for good. Now she had just left his bed with his wife still clearly in the picture.

Her long walk didn't provide any comfort it had only given time for her to reflect on the wrong decision she had made. No amount of self-reasoning, however, made her feel any better. As she passed the factory, the gates beckoned her through as an old friend and Eric watched from the office as her sullen, sunken expression passed through. These days every passing second seemed like a weight bearing down on her shoulders.

Eric had seen the same look on her father when he had problems he couldn't solve at home. The factory used to give Jeanie's dad a place to hide and a chance to contemplate what was needed to be done, and in this respect, Jeanie wasn't any different. Her footsteps echoed around the factory, and her presence was felt immediately. Eric diverting her sisters from the gantry made his way to the office where a defeated Jeanie sat in silence. Watching her, he didn't want to break her concentration. Jeanie never looked up from the papers she was so desperately trying to organise and on seeing the intensity of Jeanie's glare Eric decided to break the ice.

"Hello stranger," Jeanie didn't move or respond her head buzzed around the chaos of her life and she needed order and routine. The guilt of last night and the disgust she felt emanated throughout her whole body, and as she gazed out of the office window, she looked more lost than usual.

"I can't rewind the clock, I have made a massive mess of things, and everything is falling apart." Jeanie's response felt calculated. However, there didn't seem to be an emotion left for her to feel.

"We all make mistakes it's a part of life. We have to experience so much pain before we can appreciate the pleasure and whatever happens, you will make the right decision you always do. I know you." He kissed her head softly and walked towards the door.

"I spent the night with John Stanton. I let him in again and now. Now I've given myself away so freely. Olivia is still in his life, and I foolishly believed him."

"Jea I love you as if you were my own bairn. I will tell this now I don't care that you spent the night. You're a grown woman and giving away love is what happens. Love can be the hardest and easiest thing to do. What I care about is you and you alone. And I will love you no matter what." Tears ran down her cheeks and fell onto her hands as she gripped the window bottom.

"I'm sorry Eric. I'm so sorry."

"Now lass you have nothing to be sorry for. That man, that man makes damage no matter what he does. Look what he did with your dad. We all make mistakes. You haven't made as many as most so this is hard. It's not easy being perfect." Laughing through her tears, Eric placed his finger under her chin.

"Head up pride high kid. He's lost something more precious than he realises. You are one hundred percent worth more than that man, and you've always been my shining star. I love you, and so does your family. Now pick up your chin and walk high." As he pressed her chin together with his fingers, Jeanie nodded in agreement and swallowed back her tears. No act of kindness could wash away the disappointment she held for herself.

As the clouds drifted back across the horizon, another storm brewed in the distance and as Jeanie watched the dark sky without her knowing the storm inside was not yet over.

Chapter 11

John stood at the opposite side of the glass begging to be let through. Jeanie's office door was locked, and the wrappings of his fist echoed around the workshop.

"Jeanie let me in. I need to talk to you. You don't understand…." Jeanie faced the window unable to rise to his plight. Hearing John's constant calls, she felt the sound of his heartbreak, and she knew he would eventually get through the locked door. Jeanie knew an opportunity would walk his way sooner rather than later and with his foot now lodged firmly in the door Jeanie calmly turned her head and nodded at her sister.

"Jeanie I just didn't think..." As Jeanie stroked her sister's arm, she moved the latch and stepped aside. "Rose can you give me a minute please I need to speak to John as this can't carry on..." Ushering Rose through the door Jeanie was still almost tranquil in the chaos.

"Jea this has all been a big misunderstanding. I love you." Jeanie seemed emotionless in fact; her official stance made her look like the owner and director of her business.

"John I don't doubt that there has been a misunderstanding, but I have to say the fault is all mine I led you into something which I had no intention of finishing it was my mistake, and I'm sorry." John seemed perplexed at her demeanour, and as she sat down at the table, Jeanie looked as if she was taking a business meeting rather than dealing with her personal life.

"What are you saying that the night at the hotel was a mistake! It didn't mean anything! Because the way it felt.... We made love for the first time, doesn't that mean something." Jeanie took a deep breath and turned the pages of her notebook; she looked as if she needed to write down a set of instructions.

"I wish it did. I wish I could stand here and tell you I love you John but I can't. It was nothing more than a need to feel close to someone, and I know that I made a mistake and just because I feel lonely doesn't give me the right to jump into bed with any man including you. I'm sorry, but I have nothing more to say." John threw his jacket and gloves on the desk extenuating his dissatisfaction at her answer. The cold tone of her voice and the business like demeanour seemed to infuriate him more, but as he shook in temper, he knew he had to play on her terms.

"You're lying, and I know it."

"Prove it."

"I don't have to prove it I felt it. I knew it when I took you in my arms. You knew what you were doing the minute you got out of bed. " As John took a seat across from Jeanie, he realised how much toll the last two weeks had taken. Her sunken dark black eyes and sullen expression made it easy for him to understand that Jeanie hadn't concluded lightly.

"I need you to leave John; I can't.."

"Then don't. I can make you happy, and I can be a good husband to you, everything in my life has brought me to that conclusion."

"You don't understand."

"The thing is I do. I see it all over your face, and I know it's been eating you up inside." John held her hands pleading for any sign that he was getting through and as she pushed him away, Jeanie tried to find her sanctity at the corner of her desk. John's thoughts pushed around his brain hampered by the desperation to try to make her understand.

"Don't you know how I feel? In all these years I've never been able to prove myself worthy of you. I'm standing here Jeanie wanting…waiting to love you.

I know my past, and I know how bad I was. I've changed more than you realise and if you could just understand and let me in, I could make you happy I really could." Jeanie stood equalling his stillness as the contemplation of words spun around like a tornado.

"I can't turn back time John, and you keep telling me how you've changed, but I can't see it. I need to forgive myself, the guilt I have for even staying with you that night is eating me alive, and I can't carry on. Whatever you think we've had is over. "

"Then why did you let me in Jea? If I'm so bad and you've never actually trusted me why? And don't say loneliness cause its bullshit!"

"I don't know!" John slammed his hand on the table frustrated by the fact that he was aware that she wasn't telling him the truth.

"Bullshit! You let me in cause you needed to feel whether or not something was there. "

"That's not true!"

"Lier. You can shake your head as many times as you want and blame it on some simple self-sanctified guilt mechanism. But you forget that I know you. Sometimes better than you know yourself and trust me, Jeanie, I know how your body felt, and I know that was more than just sex. I felt every inch of you want me I felt your body give into me and I also know the only regret you have is not doing it earlier. So I'm asking you again why?"

Her silence hung in the air, and as he waited for her answer, John knew she wasn't going to give him one, and as he kept eye contact, he saw the glassy waters build within. As John took his coat and adjusted his tie, he felt like he was choking on his words.

"Olivia was here because I filed for divorce make your decision based on that....." and as he kicked the adjoining door his animation emulated defeat and as he jumped into his car. Jeanie heard the scream, knowing he wasn't going to give up.

Chapter 12

As days turned into weeks before Jeanie knew it two month's had passed and she had circulated her life between the factory, the garage and home. Without knowing she had crept silently back into her old life without a hitch. Ivy, on the other hand, had grown increasingly worried about Jeanie's reclusive behaviour as Jeanie had stopped all contact with the outside world. Other than work Jeanie didn't want to know or even care about anything else, and Ivy wanted to ask her a thousand times what went on between her and James, but she couldn't. Jeanie had become so withdrawn that even fun had become second nature.

Jayne, on the other hand, had blossomed and was the picture of her mother. Her golden hair and bright blue eyes were enchanting, and Jeanie adored being around her and as Jeanie lay on the couch engulfed in her engineering manual Ivy sat playing with her daughter. Ivy couldn't help but look at the intensity of Jeanie's concentration and wondered what possibly could be going on under the facade she was so gallantly playing.

"Why don't we go out Jea? You look lost in that book, and I think it would do both of us some good to get out?"

"No thanks got too much on, and I've got a problem on number two line, so I'm heading back to work soon."

"Right I'm sick of this melancholy we are going out." as Ivy stormed across the room she grabbed Jeanie's coat from the stand parading it until Jeanie took notice.

"Mum I'm taking Jeanie out we won't be long will you be ok with Jayne" As Irene's voice bellowed from the kitchen Jeanie lifted her gaze unimpressed at being forced out of her hole.

"Ok love yep no problem be careful." Jeanie shook her head and picked up her book and continuing to read Ivy stood impatiently waiting for another response.

"Jeanie get your arse off that settee and come on." Sighing Jeanie heavily, wearily and easily defeated placed the book on the couch and taking her coat she waded towards the door.

"See you in a bit." As they walked along the garden path, Ivy linked her arm with Jeanie's.

"So what now pictures, pub?" Jeanie was silent knowing her sister had spoken to Rose weeks earlier she knew it wouldn't be long until the Spanish Inquisition started.

"Can we walk for a bit first?" Ivy held onto her sister tight, questioning Jeanie seemed to clam her up more and as they walked the silence grew, and Ivy became uncomfortable. As Ivy clambered up the steps to the Old Cock pub, Jeanie seemed to labour behind.

"Come on you can buy me a drink and tell me all your worries." Jeanie's reluctance even on the walk grew as she dragged herself from step to step. On entering together, Jeanie headed for a quiet spot in the corner to hide. As Ivy sat down with the drinks and before being given a chance to use her interrogation techniques Jeanie looked as if she had something to say.

"What's wrong, come on you can tell me you always used to tell me everything, don't bottle it up come on." Jeanie looked at the ceiling and sighed again knowing she wasn't going to able to get on with her melancholic existence, and as the hours passed Jeanie relayed her troubles in detail and laid her heart on the table for Ivy to help mend. Ivy listened with intent occasionally comforting her sister.

"Well I don't know what you did to that doctor, but he's been in here twice looking for you. Last time I saw him, he was as anxious as a cat having kittens. I believe he's been sat outside the parish rooms for an hour." Ivy turned towards Jeanie still holding her hand from the heart to heart.

"Listen let's go home. Thanks, Jim." Rising from their seats, Jeanie began to feel quite sick, and everything spun around so quickly that nausea rose and sank with every step. Ivy held her tight knowing how much tonight had meant and knowing how hard it was for Jeanie to relay her mistakes for judgement. Even though the silence was still evident, Ivy couldn't help but notice how lovely Jeanie looked in the moonlight. Her hair glistened and sparkled as the rays hit from above and as much of the turmoil she had inside on the outside she glowed.

As they turned the corner close to home, Jeanie noticed a familiar car at the front of the house and as Jeanie's stomach turned again, she squeezed Ivy's hand so tight that finger marks had started to appear on her skin. Two gentlemen stood inside the cottage porch and intrigued as to why an army car was visiting so late Ivy walked through the door first "What's happening here?" Jeanie realised immediately, and as she stepped into the hallway, the atmosphere shifted heavily.

"Ivy go and sit down in the living room I will be in shortly. Gentlemen just give me the telegram and go away." Irene stood firmly behind Jeanie for support "I can't madam I've got to give it to Mrs I Stanton." Jeanie stood toe to toe with the private and stated her case again.

"Again, I will deliver the message just leave." Ivy opened the door on hearing the commotion and inquisitively stepped back out towards the porch,

"What message, Jeanie what message." Ivy paused as tears began to well.

"Its George isn't it," Ivy screamed again at Jeanie. However, this time panic had gripped Ivy's body. "Its George isn't it." As the telegram passed into Ivy's hand, Jeanie in anger pushed both of the men back through the door, and as Irene took the message, she read it back.

"Dear Mrs Stanton, I regret to announce that your husband George Stanton has been killed in action." Her sisters couldn't help but acknowledge the chaos and one by one they started to appear as the news spread through the household like a plague. Jeanie felt powerless, and she knew nothing would take the pain away now her niece would never meet her father. Taking Jayne out of her crib she placed her in Ivy's arms and as she lay there Jeanie's heart sank as all her problems seemed futile. Her self-loathing and pity had made her lose sight of the importance of her family.

Kissing the infant, she brushed her hair away from her eyes and started towards the kitchen. Standing at the door, Jeanie watched the rain roll down the glass and as she closed her eyes as the sickness returned. Watching the moon disappear behind the thick dark cloud she knew nothing else mattered except the need to look after her family.

Taking deep breaths and waiting for the nausea to subside she re-joined the group. Jeanie whispered to the infant and as the waves of disbelief crossed each sibling face she held onto Irene's hand.

"As long as we've got each other, we can do anything, and I promise no matter what I will love and support you until the end."

Chapter 13

Jeanie moved Ivy and the baby back into her bedroom knowing they needed more security now George wasn't coming home. Ivy had put on a brave face for her family and the incessant "are you ok?" questions had become more of an annoyance as she started the grieving process. The comfort of having Jayne gave her purpose and Jeanie saw the reliance Ivy felt towards her. The house had also been turned upside down by the news and Jayne had not slept in days. However, when Jeanie left for the base both infant and mother were sleeping soundly, and in all of its turmoil, at least peace had reigned for a few small hours. As she reached the garage, Jeanie called Mike into the office trying to get to grips with where they now stood.

"How many left."

"We've got 260 out of the 500 done, but hey you've still got me boss lady." He smiled cheekily and sat on Jeanie's desk waiting for a response. Jeanie laid her head on the desk and put her hands on the back of her neck adjusting the hours worked and units fixed to try to surmise an end date.

"OK another ten done tonight and we need to get that new lathe bit to create that secondary bearing. Other than that let's push on, and hopefully, we can get these completed sometime this century."

"No prob's boss. Just as a warning your Lieutenant on the prowl wants figures. It's been non-stop in here with visitors just looking for you." Jeanie had grown to love Mike like a brother. Even though Mike was brash, cheeky and always up for causing mischief, he made the days pass quicker and at least he was trying helping unlike some of the other higher ranking officers.

"Boss lady don't take this the wrong way, but you look like shit."

"I don't need a secondary opinion Mike I know what I look like." As she organised the pieces of paper and parts manifest, Jeanie seemed perplexed even taken aback by what had been left.

"Mike has there been anyone else in after me today?"

"I had some guy here before asking after you. Some crazy looking fella he looked like shit as well. Seemed concerned about you though and he liked asking a lot of questions as well. Why? You ok?"

As Jeanie disappeared in the rolls of her jumper, her muffled response faded as she became lost in the note.

"And? Is there anything else I should know?" Mike got off the desk, looking like a schoolboy who had given an impertinent response.

"Nothing just told him you were taking care of business at home. Oh, by the way, I'm sorry to hear about,"

"It's fine. Will you drive the next one in, and I'll start stripping number 261 down." Mike saluted in agreement and made his way out whistling in the background. She knew it was going to be another long day and with hour feeling like a lifetime her body seemed to give up quicker.

As the night drew in Jeanie's arms and shoulders ached, and as she sat on the edge of the pit looking across the courtyard she couldn't help but feel part of something more. Movements had increased, and more carriers had been brought into the base. Flights had also increased and as she heard the thunders of traffic overhead, the buzz occupied her mind.

Jeanie climbed back into the pit and continued to check the rear axle of the carrier. Everything she did was to help protect their freedom, and every vehicle that made its way out of her garage was a step forward. More and more men were fighting for their lives and when Jeanie looked at the bigger picture the pandemonium over the last couple of months began to feel inconsequential. She wished things had turned out different; she also wished that Jayne and Ivy had been spared the pain of losing someone close that they loved. Deep inside, however, Jeanie felt somewhat relieved that she had at least lived something of which had been a fantasy for nearly thirty years of her life. Wondering where Mike had disappeared to, she started to make her way through the yard and placing on her gloves she tucked her clipboard underneath her arm. As Jeanie gazed into the clear night sky, it was full of stars. Jeanie couldn't remember the last time she had seen so many together, and as she turned around to get a better look, she started to walk back to gain a better view. The clusters gleamed brighter than usual, and the constellations were lucid, and as she stared in amazement, she suddenly slipped backwards and as she rolled Jeanie tried to regain her composure.

"I'm really sorry. It was my fault day dreaming!James! Sorry I didn't realise....excuse me."

"Jeanie wait. Jeanie, please hold on."

"What am I doing?" Catching his breath, Jeanie could see him try to muster the words he needed to say; she could see he felt just as awkward.

"Oh for God sake right come on brew time. You coming?"

"Love one thank you." Surprised by her response, he followed still wondering why she was attempting the conversation. As James caught her up he pulled at her arm redirecting her course.

"No this way."

"Where are we going?"

"I think this one is on me." Following mainly out of courtesy and due to the fact she had just squashed him, she wondered why he so urgently wanted to speak and as the kettle boiled silence filled the air with James often sighing without mustering any words. As he passed the tea over, she decided it was her turn to speak.

"How have you been not seen much of you?"

"Fine I've been ok, but I think you've avoided me?" Jeanie chuckled a little and nodded.

"Any surprise. Listen I'm ok sometimes it feel's embarrassing but whatever will be!" James looked at her seeing the small scar situated on her cheek and the thought of the things he had done sent shivers down his spine.

"Jeanie I don't think you understand and I'm not making excuses because I knew what I did. I can't believe I hit you, but worse of all I can't justify any of my behaviour afterwards."

"James you don't have to its gone."

"I do cause its only right you know the truth. After walking away from you that night, I made it back here into the medical centre. Liz found me and sorted me out, and over the next few weeks, she proceeded to find me in a similar condition. After the fourth or fifth time of finding me passed out on the floor, I spent the next ten hours telling her about you and what I did to you and as she started to undress me well you know the rest." Jeanie sat uncomfortably in her chair listening to his demise, she had also experienced a moment of weakness, and she couldn't help but empathise with his situation.

"Jeanie the guilt is excruciating, and I'm so sorry for hurting you, and I would do anything to take it back but I can't. I'm a complete arse, and I know it." Jeanie leaned over and took the cup from him trying to ease both of their conscience.

"I've recently done a couple of things which were stupid and irrational which has hurt me a lot. I can't believe I'm going to say this but I've had a big lesson to learn recently and that in this day and age life is too short and too tough. You see Ivy lost George, and now I understand all the fighting and the arguing may seem harsh but what she wouldn't give to have all the petty squabbles back now!

So I made a packed that I'm better off on my own not to be selfish but to dedicate it to the people that love me unconditionally. So far it's working, it's boring, but its working."

"Sounds like you have a plan." James smiled into his tea feeling like Jeanie's self-confessed isolation was his doing.

"James this wasn't just you, and you're very naïve just to think that. We both have skeletons hiding, and maybe we needed to take into account that some of us had a life before you proposed."

"I get why you're trying to be nice and thanks for the cheap swipe." Jeanie felt just as guilty and knowing how lonely and desperate she felt was still no excuse for sleeping with John but, at least having the experience had made her understand James's point of view.

"You're welcome Mr Watson, and at any time you want to go through this self confessional diatribe I am happy to be at your service." As Jeanie sat back in her chair, she felt comfortable in his company not wanting more than a friend she was happy that the awkwardness was a building block. As James took her cup, he wrapped his hand around her fingers.

"Does this mean we are at least friends Jeanie Rutherford?" As she looked up and stared into his deep eyes, her body remembered his warm hands and the feel of his finger tips.

"For now Mr Watson. For now."

Sliding around the door, she smiled coyly. She had put James too far up on a pedestal to understand that even someone as perfect as him would to have his own set of flaws. She also had to take into account that she hadn't acted like an angel and knowing John wasn't going to stop the sanctity of at least having James's friendship felt like an added piece of security.

Walking over to vehicle 261 Jeanie realised she had left her clipboard, as she turned she saw James running out.

"I think you forgot this." Handing it back his fingers lingered on the edge of the board

"Thank you...I was just on my way back." As Jeanie took the clipboard, he kissed her softly on the cheek.

"Your place next time for tea then Miss Rutherford." As he walked away, she felt a cold chill down her spine and the small pricks of electric shock breathing life back into her heart.

Biting her lip and slumping her hands back into her pockets her mind wandered over the course of the evening's events. Feeling perplexed Jeanie jumped in the driver's seat and took the vehicle over to the garage. She contemplated their conversation and a small glimpse of wondering in each other's eyes. Shaking her head, she heard Mike rambling to himself and remembered that he was just in time to be scolded about his disappearance

"Oh, boss lady come on what are you waiting for?" As he stood at the foot of the door, he pointed to his watch.

"Where the fuck have you been?"

"Mike you're a cheeky bastard, but I have to love you." His playful nature and cheeky smile automatically made Jeanie snap to her senses.

Walking home the next morning Jeanie leant over the wall at the church yard and took an apple off the tree, and as she bit into it, Ivy appeared with Jayne.

"I saw you! Scrumping apples Miss Rutherford, what kind of a role model is that for your niece?"

"How are you doing?" Ivy straightened Jayne's blanket trying not to look at her sister, and after shrugging her shoulders, she changed the subject. "Anyway, how was your day?"

"Unusual... busy but unusual." Jeanie bit her lip again thinking of James rolling on the floor and the tender kiss afterwards.

"Saw James today did we"

"Umm... well, men aren't my thing so celibacy and looking after your kids will be my next job." Ivy giggled at Jeanie's sarcastic remark.

"Tired now time for sleep me thinks. I bid you a fond adieu Mrs and Miss Stanton." Jeanie bowed as she opened the door and Ivy couldn't help but smile again at her lightened humour.

Sitting on the bench on the front porch the sun warmed her face, and as she took in a deep sigh, she thought of George. Noticing Jayne had gone to sleep Ivy soaked up the peace of the morning air and as she gazed at her daughter she couldn't help but see how different she was to George. She didn't look like him, and she didn't smell like him, and as her eyes welled with tears, she couldn't help but feel her guilt.

"George if you can hear me you made me happy. I was selfish, and I appreciate you, and for what it's worth I was wrong I'm so sorry. Maybe I need to forgive myself before I can say goodbye. So be patient I just need some more time." Pulling a glistening white handkerchief out of her sleeve, Ivy wiped away her tears.

As she took Jayne back inside the house, Jeanie was still sat in the kitchen having her ear chewed off by Irene. Hearing the door close, Jeanie turned her head around and watched Ivy enter the hallway with the pram, smiling and rolling her eyes at Irene's comments Ivy relaxed feeling a small piece of her heart at least had some closure.

Chapter 14

James had started to stop by the garage for a chat and a brew with Mike and Jeanie, in fact, it had become a routine and before she knew it, the two cups had now become three. Mike sat in between them sharing stories and talking about his childhood which was considerably different from both James and Jeanie's put together and as he spoke of the vast cities and string of high-rise buildings both parties seemed captivated in his audience. His large family and the anguish he had felt as a child when his father left intrigued Jeanie feeling as they had shared similar circumstance.

Jeanie felt as if her existence had stopped being interesting at sixteen and the most she had to talk about was lots of children and a pig incident. "Right fellas, please excuse me your company is captivating but not as captivating as that girl's legs, and there's the dance on Friday, so I need a date..." As he climbed over the makeshift table, the weak, tasteless tea sloshed on the floor and the cup along with it.

"Don't worry I'll get it. I spend most of the time cleaning up after him anyway." Picking up the pieces James knelt down to help and as they bumped heads on the way back up Jeanie sat on the floor and laughed again.

"Are you always this accident prone?"

"Come on that's the second time in over a month you have tried to knock me out."

"Watch this now. It wouldn't surprise me if she slapped him and sent him on his way." Watching Mike make his move made great amusement for the pair and seeing the girl take no notice made the laugh linger longer.

"So there is a dance on Friday and as we are good friend's maybe you might want to go with me?"

Jeanie smiled trying to brush herself down as she stood.

"Do you think that's a good idea?"

"Why not? We like being in each others company, and if you're uncomfortable at the dance maybe we can do something else?" Jeanie looked at the floor feeling like she was on the edge of another mistake.

"I know you drop the girls off so I will pick you around 8.30?" James handed the pieces of the broken cup back to Jeanie and kissed her softly on the cheek again, and as he did she frowned unable to hide her concern.

"James is this good idea we've done this before. I don't want either of us getting hurt again…." James took hold of her hand and played with her fingertips. He knew if he pushed her anymore she would run.

"Just as friends Jea I don't want either of us to get hurt. I just want to enjoy your company if that's ok?" Nervous knots tumbled over inside her stomach, and as she nodded, she couldn't help but feel anxious. Jeanie started to bite her nails again considering the whole affair started to unravel. Mike buoyantly jumped back into work happy with himself that his mischievous temperament and his cheeky smile had got him a date. Jeanie perplexed smiled and thought of Ivy.

"Ok, just friends why not."

Friday came around too quick for Jeanie, and after dropping the girls off and being late home from work, she began the rampage through her clothes. Petrified of looking like she had been squeezed and squashed into most of them Ivy sat on the step and watched in amusement.

"Not that one Jeanie listen. Jeanie calm down. Jeanie!" Ivy had stood up and shouted at the chaos laughing as she dragged her into the bedroom.

"Sit I will help, just relax. It's a friend remember."
Jeanie screwed up her face at Ivy's response.
"Not funny". Ivy giggled as the rollers and curling
irons singed through Jeanie's thick unruly hair and
on hearing a knock at the door Ivy ran downstairs
impatiently waiting to see James reaction to her
protégé.

James stood at the door pristine in his uniform and
not expecting his splendour Ivy bit her lip as he was
without question a very handsome looking man. As
he took off his hat, he placed it under his arm and
waited patiently for Jeanie. Jeanie put her head in
her hands feeling like Ivy had made her into a
porcelain doll, and as she started to wipe some of
the makeup off her face, Jeanie tossed her hair into
position and took the broad steps downstairs.

James now distracted by Irene and Ivy's
conversation and trying to be polite didn't notice
Jeanie's entrance, and on turning around, he was
greeted by the smartly presented Jeanie who looked
unrecognisable in her flowered blouse. Thanking
both Irene and Ivy he couldn't believe how
beautiful she looked and as they made their way out
of the door he whispered in Jeanie's ear.
"I thought we were only friends." Jeanie smiled and
waved goodbye to her mum and sister who had
planted themselves in the living room window
spying and plotting what would happen next.
"You look very good…I mean handsome tonight.
Sorry."
"So what do you want to do?" Jeanie bit her lip not
wanting to share him with anyone else and trying
desperately to fend off any feelings for him she
hesitated.
"I thought we could walk around the block and wait
for my mum and sister to disappear to bed and go
back home for a bit if that's ok with you?"

"So... we are staying in?" Jeanie smiled and looked
back as not to make more of the gesture.
"I thought it could give us a chance to talk you
know without anyone else."

Walking back to the house took forever, and every
member of the parish seemed to greet them on their
way. James had helped out in the medical centres,
and the majority of town were interested in the new
doctor. After so many pleasantries Jeanie's feet
ached and wanting desperately to speak to him and
trying to fend off the nervous knots she had started
wondering what the hell she was doing. The closer
they got to the cottage the more it seemed to repeat
over and over again. The confusion swam around
her brain until reaching the back door of the house.
Trying to be quiet and masking James's stumble
over the back step Jeanie laughed.
"Do...do you want a drink?"
"Whatever you have." As the pair crept into the
parlour, the fire was burning down slowly and
placing the whiskey glass on the small table next to
the chair Jeanie set out to play cards on the floor in
front of the fire. James closed the door trying to
blanket out the creaks and groans of the wood
against the frame. Sitting down opposite from
Jeanie it was quite noticeable she was
uncomfortable.
"You look like you've swallowed a flea... what's
up?" Jeanie stood up without excusing herself she
crept back out into the hallway.
James shook his head and proceeded to take off his
jacket and tie bemused about why he had made such
an effort. Undoing his top button and getting
comfortable Jeanie crept back in this time sporting
her pyjama bottoms and what looked like her dad's
cardigan.
"Right, better now." Jeanie swept her hair back of
her shoulders and dealt the pack of playing cards.

Taking a drink of scotch, she pulled her face as it warmed her throat.

"You going first or me?" whispering the responses as not for anyone to hear James sat up.

"Ok, you go first." Turning the cards Jeanie bit her lip and sighed deeply in thought, not only did she not know what move to make, she didn't know which way this night was going to end.

Watching her play with the strands of hair James could see how deep in thought she was.

"I wish you wouldn't do that." Jeanie lifted her head as he broke her concentration.

"Do what?"

"Do that lip biting, sighing thing." Confused again at his response, Jeanie was still biting her lip, half concentrating on cards and trying desperately not to look at James. However, with Jeanie's natural curiosity she could not let the conversation lie.

"I do that all the time why is it such a problem now!" Leaning back against the couch and raising his cards James nonchalantly answered under the pretence of concentration on his cards.

"It reminds me of when you stayed over. It's a slightly different sigh, but the action is still the same. I'm up, by the way, oh and I enjoy it." Jeanie tried not to smile, look offended or be self-conscious and trying not to bite her lip she sighed again placing her cards on the floor.

"That's not fair you know it's a…a… Self-conscious reaction. I could bring up faces you pull, but I'm not going to. Plus that's that night leave it there…." Jeanie started to deal the cards again as James stood up to bring the scotch bottle closer to there private party.

"Sorry…." Confused as to why she was apologising he sat in front of her waiting for the second part of her response.

"I… just feel very comfortable doing this, and it's a bit frightening, and I just feel so out of my depth from the last time we did this. Let's face facts it didn't go well, did it? I'm scared of hurting you and in that case me, and I don't want to do that," "I've made some huge mistakes, and it's me that needs to be sorry. When I saw you with John, and after the conversation, we had about him on the beach I don't know what came over me. I thought I had lost you and my actions……plus the nurse I regret every single step I took after that day, and it was wrong, and I want you to know it would never happen again. I love you too much ever to want to hurt you have to know that." Jeanie sighed again, and in the efforts, she tried not to bite her lip.

"Please don't stop. It's one of the parts of you I love the most. I'm sorry I know friends. I apologise." Jeanie shuffled the deck on the floor trying to gain composure.

"Listen I have recently done some things I'm not proud of it. It was quite stupid, and I still regret some of my actions. We weren't together, and you had nothing to lose. I'm scared of disappointing you and not being enough. I'm afraid of just being that engineer's daughter with nothing else to offer. I'm afraid it won't work and being heartbroken do you understand?"

"If we never did anything because we are scared and we missed out on the adventure of a lifetime wouldn't we both have more regrets? I'm in love with you, and it's killed me not to touch you. I hate walking away, and I hate saying goodbye and not knowing whether you want me as much as I want you. All I'm asking for is a chance. An opportunity to prove that I can make you happy for the rest of your life please Jeanie," Ivy and Irene stood at the parlour door listening intently, and as Ivy pressed her hands together in prayer, she rested them against her lips willing her sister to make the right decision.

"Mum they will hear you shhh." Ivy felt just as nervous and as the intensity grew they heard nothing from Jeanie.

"Jeanie…..Jeanie.." Rising to her knees, she placed his hand on her chest to feel her heartbeat and as the seconds past her tears had started to fall.

"I missed you. I did. I didn't realise how much until you started coming back around to the garage and I have looked forward to seeing you. I've done something, and I don't think you would like what I've done,"

"It doesn't matter. I don't care, Jeanie, I said I promised I'd never hurt you and I did. I don't care about anything else that has happened I just want another chance." Curling her hair around her ear, he wiped away her tears with his thumb.

"Jeanie I don't care I promise,"

"James all I know is that when I'm with you, I like who I am, and we have a real friendship. I know I don't want you to leave when you're with me and if that's love, then I love you."

"I want to marry you, Jeanie. I want to love honour and protect you, but I need to know if you want the same." Reaching up to her he placed his hand gently on the nape of her neck, and as he fumbled with her hair, he pulled her closer to him.

"This war takes everything we have away from us, but if I don't have you with me Jeanie I have nothing left to fight for. You have always been my guiding light, and I want you at my side for always. When this war is over, I want to come home and spend the rest of my days making every single mistake up to you because without you I'm nothing." Jeanie rested her head on his she closed her eyes as his words were like poetry and his sentiment heart-wrenching. Kissing him, she could taste the salt of his tears and passion of his words, and as he cupped his hands around her face, she stroked her fingers through his hair deep in thought.

"I used to dream my life would be simple. A small cottage with a plot of land to grow a few veg and my little garage to make a few more pennies but I didn't realise that with all that simplicity was the complication of love." Running her fingers across his lips, he kissed them as each one passed

"You see in my head I still believe in happy ever after and fairy tales and what we got was something very different."

"What are you trying to say?"

"I don't want happy ever after James cause I know it's not real. But what I want is far better. I want everything you can throw at me. I want the dark days, and the bitterness I want to feel the fear and the unknown and the only person I want to experience them with is you. So if you will have me on this understanding, I will marry you. I'm sick of being a passerby, and I now want to live and have a very ordinary life, and I want that everyday life with you." Taking her in his arms, he lay her down gently in front of the hearth, delving into her embrace. As he kissed her he traced the outline of her face and taking back her hand he lay it against his heart knowing they were both taking a chance. "I love you." Hearing noises outside of the door James stood to attention, and as he took Jeanie by the hand, they opened it revealing a jubilant Ivy and Irene hugging in the hall. Ivy screamed in her ear excited to know that finally, her life was back on track.

"It's about time you two got this sorted." Ivy and Irene skipped into the kitchen and as Jeanie followed James grabbed hold of her hand and pulled her close.

"Jea there's something else, and before you ask, I didn't presume tonight would end up like this. I have kept this in my pocket since you gave it back to me." James pulled the ring out of his pocket, and he also produced a piece of paper with a date on it. As he passed it over, she opened it up reading under her breath.

"Jeanie Rutherford and James Watson have at this moment given notice to be married on July 22……."

"I didn't cancel it, and it wasn't until tonight that I found it stuffed in my jacket pocket. Jeanie, it's in two weeks…" Placing the ring on her finger, Jeanie took a deep breath and kissed him softly again.

"Two weeks. Ok, two weeks it is. Mum……Mum, I'm getting married in two weeks!"

Chapter 15

The wedding day had arrived, and with the house
was a hive of activity. Ivy and May were putting the
finishing touches on Jeanie's dress and as they
fussed over the last alterations Jeanie's mind seemed
to be elsewhere. James's parents had arrived at the
cottage, and unbeknown to her family Jeanie felt
under pressure to make a good impression. Standing
in her bedroom, she looked out of the window into
the garden. The urge to vomit had increased, and the
anxiety she felt had made Jeanie lose weight, which
had made things difficult especially for the dress
fittings.

"Hi, love are you coming for a brew?" Jeanie
nodded and followed her sister to the stairs. Placing
her hand on Ivy's shoulder, the nerves had become
increasingly evident

"What if..."

"Everything will be ok don't worry." Ivy patted her
hand comfortingly knowing how traumatic the
build-up to the wedding had been. On the contrary,
the house looked beautiful, and the garden was in
full bloom with the smells of summer wafting
through the house on the light breeze. The flowers
her sisters had picked to decorate filled the rooms
with the light perfume of petals and in all
everything was as it should be. James's mum
Florence helped Irene prepare the sandwiches while
his dad Robert busied himself tidying the garden.
Everyone seemed joyful and upbeat, except for
Jeanie. She felt like something unpleasant would
happen and she couldn't get away from the feeling
that something was going to go wrong.

   Feeling sick again she sat on the bottom step of
the stair.

"You don't look well." Jeanie's queasiness was for
all to see and the smell of the tea made her feel

worse, trying to stand up Ivy started to rub her shoulders.

"Listen everything will be perfect it's because it's been a rush. You will feel better once the ceremony is over I promise. Let's have something to eat and then quickly back upstairs cause I need to get you in your frock!" As Ivy watched Jeanie finish her sandwich and the glass of milk Jeanie was pushed to make haste up the steps. None of her sisters or her mother had seen Jeanie in her dress, and as Ivy gently buttoned Jeanie into her gown, she turned to look in the mirror, feeling unrecognisable.

"Thank you for this."

"It's the least I could do. After all look at the trouble I've caused this year."

As the buzz of people came and went from the house, it was time for Jeanie to make her way to the Church. Her mum and sisters beamed as they had never seen Jeanie look so beautiful. The cream coloured silk flowed like water, and the empress line dress flattered every one of Jeanie's curves. Jeanie's hair reddened by the sunlight had been pleated and put into a beautiful bun which supported her veil and to all who looked on she was unrecognisable. As they reached the Church door, Jeanie paused as her mum gripped her arm

"You ok love?" Jeanie looked as if she was about to cry and nodded placing her hand over Jeanie's she reassured her daughter.

"We will be ok!" As the door opened and the congregation beamed from every pew, she gasped at the people spread out in front of her. Jeanie didn't expect the large gathering which had assembled, and she certainly wasn't used to being the centre of attention and with eyes on her as she ambled down the aisle. Every step made the nervous swirls and nausea increase, and as she tried to control her breathing, it seemed to help only momentarily.

Reaching the alter James could hardly recognise the beautiful woman that stood before him. Lifting her veil her doll-like complexion and wild eyes sparkled under the stain glass windows.

"You look beautiful." Jeanie smiled still with an underlying feeling that the day was just too perfect to imagine. Taking their vows, James couldn't take his eyes off her and as rings were exchanged and the vicar pronounced they were man and wife Jeanie felt a small wave of relief that at least the first part had gone to plan. James kissed his new wife unable to mask his jubilation, and as they climbed into the carriage, the pair seemed inseparable. Wrapping his arm around her side, he pulled her close.

"I haven't been able to take my eyes off you."

"Well, no going back now!" James took the veil out of her hair and tussled at some of the auburn strands.

"I can see you now....I can't believe this is real Jea..."

"I guess I scrubbed up well then" Placing her hand in his he kissed her palm not able to take the smile off his face.

As everyone started to descend on the newly decorated cottage, Rose and May fussed over the house and garden which had become their pride and joy. The house looked like a grand palace, and the much-civilised affair was a long way from the screaming and swearing which usually filled the air on most days. James and Jeanie stood in the garden and admired how quickly the families had pulled together.

"Thank you all for this it's magical."

"I think you should do without your overall's on more occasions." As James kissed Jeanie softly on the cheek, he took hold of her hand raising it gently to his lips. His smile beamed from ear to ear and no matter how confused she felt Jeanie could feel James's contentment.

"I'm just going to Mum and Dad be back in a minute." Making her way into the kitchen, she placed the veil on the table and neatly began to tease out the folds.

"What are you smiling at?" Ivy had appeared from the living room and surprised Jeanie jumped back seeing Dr Frost stood at the side of her.

"Doctor I didn't see you there, thank you for coming," Jeanie's politeness made Ivy smile as she knew her sister's airs and grace usually stemmed to a screwdriver and an oil bucket.

"It was a lovely wedding my dear, and you look beautiful, I need to speak to you though." As the doctor took a deep breath, Jeanie teased the veil feeling like her bubble was just about to burst.

"When you came and saw me last week, we did a few test, and it looks like the wedding came just in time if you ask me."

"Just in time for what?"

"Well, my dear you're pregnant, congratulations." The doctor placed his cup carefully on the kitchen table and the other hand on her shoulder as he walked out into the garden Jeanie looked at Ivy unable to comprehend what she had just been told. Stunned Jeanie dropped to the floor unable to process the doctor's words.

"Jea I'm sorry I thought oh shit."

"I'm pregnant with John's baby Ivy how am I going to tell that to James!"

"I don't know how you tell James something like that." John closed the door behind him and strolled into the kitchen.

"I didn't even know you were getting married until I saw James's leave request. I came over before, but you had already left for the church." Jeanie unable to take in the news sat on the kitchen floor retracing the events of the last few months.

"John the doctor must have got this wrong."

"John please don't make a scene." John moved around the kitchen table looking more like a predator with every step.

"You look unbelievable in that dress. I'm sorry Jeanie I meant what I said. I'm not willing to give up, and now you're carrying my baby this changes everything." Placing both of her hands to her temples the room slipped from side to side around her. "John…I told you this is just a big mistake."

"I'm getting divorced Jeanie, she's here because she wants money, I tried....but you wouldn't listen and that night. I felt the connection between us that night Jea, and I know you love me. But it's different now you're having my baby we can be together now, don't you understand." Jeanie pushed John out of the way and walked back into the garden; she was pregnant, not nervous, not ill but pregnant. John stood at the back door waiting for a reaction, Jeanie felt sick again, and the confusion was emulating her nausea. James heard the commotion and on seeing his wife distressed he made his way over to her.

"Are you ok?" Jeanie pale and close to tears began to fall.

"I need to tell you something. James, we need to talk." Her voice was broken and troubled, and as James looked over her shoulder, he saw John stood at the door.

"What have you done?" Jeanie placed her hand on his shoulder and pleaded with her new husband "James we need to talk, please."

"It will never happen, not with her, you will see." As John's voice broke the frivolities, James marched to where he stood and punched him and as he fell to the floor blood trickled out of his nose.

"Get out of my house now." Jeanie pulled on James' shoulder and teased him away

"You've done enough John. Leave" John still wiping away the blood peered over Ivy's shoulder to take a glimpse at Jeanie.

"It's not over Ivy, and you know it, she belongs to me, she has my baby inside her, and I'm not giving that up!" Ivy using all her might forced him through the front door.

"John, don't come back." As the chaos in the garden began to settle, Rose and May had started to play the piano, and as Ivy gathered the rest of the guests, she tried to dispel John's intrusion. James held tight onto Jeanie, and as they reached the bench at the back of the garden, Jeanie looked pale and upset. One night of stupidity had now thrown the happiest day of her life into the worst, and the worst part of all was John knew she was pregnant.

"James I need to talk."

"I don't care. I love you, and I'm not going to lose you now, I love you too much Jeanie, and I want you more than I ever have done. This is our wedding day." Jeanie pleaded with James to listen feeling her heart and her mind pound in unison.

"You don't understand...I"

"It's our wedding day Jeanie, I have something for you, something for tonight I'm not supposed to tell you but I don't care, I've got you this for dinner this evening." James pulled out a small box from his pocket; the brushed velvet case was bright and opulent.

"It's my grandmother's, and it's tradition in our family, and I want you to have it." Jeanie opened the box to a beautiful pearl, emerald and diamond bracelet. James took it out and placed it on Jeanie's wrist, her clear pale skin made the colours of the bracelet sparkle in the daylight, and as James got down on his knees, he pulled Jeanie's hand towards his chest.

"I've never been happier than today Jeanie."

Jeanie's head rested in the nape of James's neck, and as the tears began to fall, she couldn't muster the words to tell him.

Throughout the day Jeanie was never alone enough to try to tell him why John reacted the way he did. Her strength dwindled in the moonlight and the confusion of the best and worst day of her life made Jeanie want to crawl under a rock. Knowing there was nowhere to run she had to stand and face him. As the evening began to draw in Jeanie needed to get dressed for the officer's dinner. During the goodbyes she still couldn't get the words out she needed to say, and as Jeanie hung her dress on the back of the door, she sat on the floor in front of Ivy.

"What am I going to do?"

"I don't know." Jeanie's tears hit the floor like raindrops filling a pond. She knew John was trouble how could she have let this happen As she rested her head on her knees, Ivy finished off her hair. Jeanie knew she had to go tonight and as she placed a long coat over the top of her new dress, she made her way through the sunset alone with her thoughts. Jeanie was pregnant with another man's child and on the same day as her wedding to another.

Thoughts flew through her mind, but as Jeanie needed to rationalise every situation, she needed to pull it together.

"No point wondering….until you tell you will never know."

James stood on the steps of Georgian house looking the picture of the seigniorial man. As Jeanie got closer to James, she could see the anxious look on his face, and as he rechecked the time Jeanie knew she needed to quicken the pace. As she placed her hands in the large coat pockets, she made her way up the steps.

"Waiting for me." James threw away the stub and buttoned up his jacket.

"Come on." He took her hand and nearly dragged her through the main doors at his distaste of tardiness. The building was beautiful, and the marble floors shone in the dim lighting. The ceilings seemed to appear to go on forever, as they graced the staircase they made her way up to the ballroom. Nearly forgetting she was still wearing her coat, Jeanie started to make the necessary adjustments.

"You go ahead I will check my coat in." James nodded and made his way inside the hustle of people congregating around tables.

Jeanie stood in silence as she gave the girl her coat her inner self-consciousness developing further as the dress again clung to every curve. The weight of the dress pulled the neckline down further than anticipated however even through sickness, anxiety and worry she looked beautiful.

As she walked into the room, no one recognised the ugly girl from the garage, and as she made her way over to James who by this time was clasping at drinks, he didn't again recognise her.

"Sorry bit of queue."

"Where did you get that from?" James looked Jeanie up and down and suddenly felt eyes descending on them from every corner of the room.

"Ivy made it for me why do I not look right." Jeanie's self-conscious nature arose again, and as she looked at the front of her dress, James knocked back his drink.

"Nope nothing wrong with it just never seen you look so.......but sexual, attractive, I don't know. People dancing let's go." James stuttered as he finished as Jeanie tended to have that effect on him but this time instead of replying with a sarcastic comment she giggled and for a moment forgot about what she needed to tell him. James placed his hand on Jeanie's waist and pulled her close. "Sexual nothing else came to mind." James moved his hand down Jeanie's back and bent in close. "You threw me off guard, and yes you look amazing." The compliment made Jeanie feel special as people were only used to the oil filled dungaree's and baggy jumpers, not a figure-hugging cleavage-bearing dress which fit perfectly.

As they made their way to the large round tables for dinner Jeanie's anxiety began to build as she knew one dinner wasn't going to make the problem disappear no matter how good she felt. James couldn't take his hands off her. He held her close all the way through the dinner and refused to let her go after the speeches and as the General made his way over to the table Jeanie's urge to be sick increased. As she leant forward and rested her chin on her clasped hands, she tried to dispel her nausea. "Good evening everyone, James isn't it I have heard a lot about you sir." As the General held out his hand, James stood and shook it masterfully. "And who is this delightful creature?" "I believe you two are already acquainted sir this is my wife, Jeanie Rutherford Watson, " "Jeanie good gracious girl so this is what you look like out of oil and grease." Jeanie nodded her head as the nausea felt like a weight around her throat and every time Jeanie tried to speak it rose again. Excusing herself, she made her way to the bathroom, and as she sat in the cubicle, she clicked her shoes together not knowing what to do for the best. As the chains flushed in sequence Jeanie's thoughts washed away in time with the flushes and unable to come to any rational conclusion she repeated the same action.

Standing at the large mirror, she smoothed her dress flat over her stomach and cringed at the thought of telling James the truth. As she placed Rose's lipstick back in her purse, her head faced the floor as the guilt, pain and anguish filled her heart. Trying to lift herself once more John stood in front her.

"Told him yet." Jeanie shook her head and tried to walk past. As he grabbed her arm, he seemed desperate.

"We are having a baby together Jeanie that's not something you can walk away from."

"Why can't you just leave me alone."

"You wanted me that night, and I know deep down Jeanie you want me still. This marriage means nothing; you have my child inside you doesn't that mean anything to you!" As Jeanie pushed past she knew John would follow and as she felt his breath and footsteps closing behind Jeanie sighed with relief as the General had caused a needed distraction. The thing was John was right she couldn't walk away from it as much as she wanted to James needed to know and as the music started, she couldn't bear the guilt any longer.

"May I have the pleasure, Mrs Watson?" Jeanie trembled in his grasp, and as she looked back, John was still at least occupied with the General.

"Yes as long as we can talk later." James led Jeanie back to the floor, and as the music played he removed a couple of Jeanie's hairpins and as her hair fell onto her shoulders and curled around he smiled

"There you are you don't seem real without oil and grease." Jeanie smiled and placed her hand on his arm; she didn't want the moment to end. Jeanie felt his breath on her neck as he held her tightly and the kiss behind her ear made her tremble.

"Jeanie, you're shaking is everything ok? What is it that you need to talk to me about?" Feeling a tap on his shoulder, John stood behind waiting patiently for his turn.

"James, gentleman's choice and my turn I believe." John stood to the side of him as James clenched his fists

"Not in here it's ok." James moved over and handed John, his wife.

"Five minutes Sir." Jeanie's heart leapt out of her chest as John placed his hands around her waist. John could feel every muscle tremble uncontrollably, but as she shook in his arms, her voice still was confident.

"What do you want?"

"You and my baby. Jeanie, you know what I want. You are carrying my child, and I want to make this work."

"I don't want you, John, this baby was a mistake just like you, but unlike you, I live up to my responsibilities. I married James because there is one thing you would never do."

"What can he give you that I can't?" Jeanie moved away and started to walk from the dance floor.

"Love." Watching her walk away was unbearable, and he longed for her to realise how much he wanted the baby,

"Come on let's go I need to speak to you." As they made their way down the staircase, Jeanie could see John was still in tow. Clinging to James' hand, they started to make their way down the front steps.

"You can't hide it forever Jeanie." Jeanie couldn't help but reply she needed time and he denied her that privilege.

"Not now John if you feel anything for me not now."

"He needs to know."

"What is it…..what do I need to know" She shook from head to toe and in her visible trembling her new husband placed his hands on hers.

"We talked two weeks ago about my mistake." With James still, hold of her hands he squeezed them tight. Looking back at John and at Jeanie he knew.

"You slept with him after everything you said… "

"James please."

"Why didn't you tell me? Doesn't matter the past is the past that's what you said?" John took another drink and walked down the steps towards Jeanie.

"There's something else though isn't there Jeanie."

"What does he mean?" Jeanie stepped away pulling her coat around her there was no point delaying it any further.

"What does he mean Jeanie!"

"I'm pregnant."

"No NO NO this can't be happening. Not now. Not NOW. .How does he know? How does he know before me?"

"The doctor, I went to last week, and he came to the wedding and told me in the kitchen. John stood at the back door as he told me. I tried to talk to you James in the garden, but the bracelet and I just didn't know…" James sat on the steps with his head in his hands unable to comprehend the enormity of the situation.

"It might be ours, Jeanie. What about our night."

"James look at me you're a doctor you know as well as I" Tears freely flowed from his eyes and his despair cried out to Jeanie's heart.

" Jea… No this can't be happening; this really can't be happening this is our wedding day."

"She's having my baby James, your wife is pregnant by me, and there is nothing you can do about It.!" James stood up and ran over to where he was standing.

"You're a fucking piece of shit Lieutenant you've fucked up your life her life and my life. I hope you're happy as this was supposed to be the best night of my life. Look at her she's one of the most beautiful women I've ever met, and you just fucked up everything."

Jeanie stood unable to comprehend the magnitude of the situation, and as John threw his glass into the verge at the side of the steps, she knew more was yet to come.

"Whether you like it or not I fucked her, and she enjoyed it, and that is my child. No matter what you do or say will ever take that away."

"If I were you I'd crawl back into that fucking cunt hole and die alone." John revelled in his disappointment and anger, and he couldn't help but enjoy James' frustration and pain, and as he slowly lost control, John knew he had James where he wanted.

"That baby is mine, and you can't-do a fucking thing about it." As James turned to walk away from the pain inside had started to eat away at his patience, and instead of walking away James threw John down the steps. As John regained composure, he stood up and hit him back.

"You had a fucking lucky shot before!" As the pair began to fall into full-scale warfare, Jeanie screamed at the both of them.

"I'm sorry to you both, but this isn't going to change anything. It's my fault!" James threw John to the ground picking up his jacket he took hold of Jeanie's hand and started to walk towards the main road.

"James let go. James, please let go."

"Why have you got something else you need to tell because my hearts already been ripped out, so I suggest you might as well do it now and save me any more heartache."

"Just leave. I'm no good for you. You can get today annulled, and you can start fresh. Please, James just let me go."

"No." Silence descended on the couple and as they hit the path outside James let go of Jeanie's hand and quickened his pace.

"James I need you to talk to me." James stopped in his tracks, his anger was evident and the chaos of the evening stomped deep into the earth.

"When did it happen?"

"Don't do this..." James placed his hands on his hips, his voice breaking every time he spoke. Jeanie felt disgusted with herself and worst of all she had let him down.

"Jeanie it matter's to me please just tell me."

"About eight weeks ago," James lifted his head knowing exactly when his indiscretion happened. "Just after I slept with Liz. Where?"

"James.....please," Her tears pierced every sentence, and as his patience faltered again, James shouted ferociously waiting to hear an answer.

"Fuck sake Jeanie Where..."

"The hotel on the front. James when I found out this afternoon I needed to tell you, but I just froze, I didn't want to lose you, but I understand if you need to go. I'm ashamed of what I have done, but I have to live with the consequences." James listened to her pain wanting to hold her but not knowing how to.

"Do you love him, Jeanie?"

"James please I can't...."

"We got married today, and it's been the most incredible day and when I saw you at the altar. You're beautiful and smart, and I don't know you make me feel something I've never felt before. But I can't stand the thought of someone touching you and now a baby. Do you love him?" Tears were streaming down Jeanie's cheeks and feeling the heartache spread from him to her Jeanie took a few seconds to regain composure.

"No, it was a mistake the biggest mistake of my life…."

"I just don't understand was this to get back at me."

"I made a mistake I was confused and angry with you, and I made an error of judgement. I have regretted my decision. What do you want me to say? I found out I was pregnant today.." James replayed the images of his own infidelity and how easy it was for him to walk away. Catching hold of her hand he understood her guilt, her pain.

"We've both made mistakes, and I can't judge anyone. Things have happened between both of us except this one resulted in you pregnant. You're still my wife, and I still love you…..we will just get through it together." Jeanie held his hand tightly as they walked back to the cottage and as he held the door and wished everybody a good evening, James escorted his new wife upstairs. They stood at opposite ends of the room and as James started to undress Jeanie starred out of the window. The whole incomprehensive nature of the events felt unreal. However, the sickness and pain were genuine, and unlike James, Jeanie found it hard to live with she had done.

"I will take the floor if you want the bed."

"You're my wife we both sleep in the same bed."

"I just feel…." James walked over holding her tight he ached with her pain and guilt.

"Eight weeks ago, you found me having sex with a nurse in the same cubicle I had professed my love to you. John took advantage, but instead of running home you spent the night and regretted your actions. Do you want me to tell you how many times I have done that very same thing I don't care Jea? Things haven't been easy for either of us, and it's going to take time for both of us to come to terms with this…we just." Sighing heavily and taking time to replace his words James rubbed her shoulders again knowing how tough the next few months would be. "We just have to figure out together what we are going to do with John. I blame him for this not you."

"Maybe it would be better if you leave." As she stood up and walked over to the window, she looked out onto the garden remembering how happy they had been for the few moments.

"I don't think it's fair for you to stay with me. I'm married to you and pregnant by someone else it's not right." James put his head in his hands and stroked his fingers through his thick dark hair.

"I'm staying Jeanie." As he stroked her neck and back, he tried to reassure her.

"I know how you feel. I've been feeling guilty and anxious for months after what I did. I would be a hypocrite to walk away now. I love you too much, and I meant what I said before in the garden, I'm not willing to lose you." As Jeanie turned around, she felt a lump appear in her throat, this was supposed to have been the happiest day of their lives, but instead, it had been marred by John Stanton. As James undid the blue dress, he ran his fingers down her spine and as she fought to hold back her tears he couldn't help but love her.

"You looked amazing tonight."

"Thank you."

"Jeanie you know I..."

"It's ok; I don't..." Catching her tears, she trailed off in mid-sentence, and as she moved towards the screen, she looked back in the hope that they could move past tonight. As Jeanie held up the nightdress, her sisters had bought she placed it back in the box and instead put her old pyjama's on. Seeing her appear he stood as she climbed into bed and as she distanced herself from him James held out his hand for comfort.

"I must be such a disappointment..." Stroking her hair, he pulled her close looking at the bunting still flying freely past the window.

"You're not. You never could be. But let's get through tonight and try to figure our way through this tomorrow."

Chapter 16

Over the forthcoming weeks, Jeanie blossomed into a very healthy pregnant woman however her sense of loneliness grew with each following week. She was still working long hours at the base, and for the time being she had taken a back seat at the factory. Only James, Jeanie and Ivy knew the truth about the baby, and as far as her mum and sisters were concerned, they didn't need to know.

Jeanie welcomed James's visits home and even counted down the days until his expected visits. However, he had grown more distant towards her as she entered her fifth month he had stopped frequenting the garage for their using tea and chat. The bigger she got, the more it reminded James that this wasn't his baby and it seemed that he was happier when they weren't alone together.

As Jeanie arrived home for the evening, she rested her head against the living room door and watched as he played with Jayne.

"Penny for them?" Jeanie smiled and made her way towards the kitchen.

"Jeanie is everything ok?" As she pushed for more information, Jeanie nodded and responded cautiously allowing room for her to hide her emotions.

"Umm yep everything ok."

"I don't believe you. Come on truth." Jeanie sat at the neatly laid table, and as she brushed her hands across the crisp cloth, she breathed deeply trying to hide the truth which was written all over her face.

"I know our wedding day was a shambles and I'm not exactly great to look at, but since our wedding day he hasn't kissed me, or touched me. He's even stopped saying I love you." Jeanie's bottom lip began to quiver as she started again.

"He loves me I know that, or he wouldn't be here, but I don't want to touch him just in case or try to hold him because it feels like I'm such a disappointment." James stood at the door listening avidly to the conversation. As he heard the pain and frustration on within her voice, James stepped forward needing to hear more.

"Even when he's here, he isn't, and that's because of me, and I knew three months ago I should have just let him go instead of going through this."

"Ivy can you give us a minute please, " James sat in Ivy's seat, and with Jeanie looking like a patient he started to assess his wife.

"You honestly feel like I'm treating you like a disappointment?"

"NO I feel like I'm a disappointment and that's why you're avoiding me!" As James stood, Jeanie saw the flash of temper and flare take a higher pitch in his voice. As the debate turned into an argument, she knew whatever he was trying to hide was now about to rear its head.

"How can I fucking avoid you when I see you most days at the base if I were avoiding you I wouldn't come home!"

"So why is it every time I come near you or try to touch you run away if I make you feel that bad James why in gods name are you here?"

"I'm here cause you are my wife and it's my duty.."

"I don't need your pity or your duty." As the argument grew, Jeanie stood mirroring his frustrations.

"I never forced you to stay I was the one pushing for you to leave!"

"That's it though, isn't it. Every time things get hard for you the easy option is to push me away even when I want to stay."

"How is that James when you avoid speaking to me, and you don't even look at me when you come home. I've been married to you for three months, and you won't even touch me If you couldn't cope with this situation why are here? I don't blame you I'm just confused." James unable to answer his wife lit a cigarette at the back door and tried to calm down.

"I don't want to say this because I know it's going to hurt, but I have to say it." Taking a long pause, he pondered how to word his concerns. The thing was Jeanie was right James had tried so hard to hide his feelings, and all that it had done had isolated her more.

"I look at you and it reminds me of him, it reminds me of him and I can't Jeanie." Jeanie nodded her head and swallowed deep.

"Then don't be here James, walk away and I won't blame you. I don't know why you didn't on our wedding day. I'm ashamed enough of myself that I slept with a married man who turns out to be the biggest mistake of my life, but I have to deal with the consequences because it's growing inside me. I don't need you to remind me every day because I'm living it. But don't treat me like a second class citizen either." Taking another pause, Jeanie wiped away her tears and stood straight making sure he heard what she had to say.

"You know through all of this I fell in love you, and it kills me when you're not here, but every time you're here I want you to leave because of the way you make me feel. Whether you think it or not I deserve more." As she changed back into her dungarees and old floppy jumper tears began to fall hard and fast. She wanted her relationship to work, she had also grown attached to her baby, and the choice between them split her heart. Running downstairs James didn't even say a word, and as she disappeared into the night, he remained at the back door and lit another cigarette, trying desperately to hold back the tears.

"I'm making her choose."

Hearing the commotion, Irene walked into the kitchen dropping her plates into the sink she made James aware that she had heard everything.

"You know Jeanie isn't her father's, and for a long time, I was ashamed to say it, but I had an affair a long time ago now which I deeply regret. It was my mistake, but never once did I regret Jeanie. Jeanie knows this as her dad told her, but you know Frank my husband loved her with all his heart, and she grew up exactly like him." As he listened intently, he wrapped his arms around his body expecting Irene to scold him.

"James, I never wanted to admit it but she's so special, she's only a half sister but she's the glue that sticks this family together, and in time I think after this war goes away you will understand the reasons again why you love her so much." James never responded he didn't need to Irene's words had resonated in his brain, and as he grabbed his coat, he ran out of the door before anyone could stop him. The baby would be half of Jeanie, and he loved that half more than anything else in the world. As he searched in the darkness, Jeanie was nowhere to be seen.

Lieutenant Signthorpe was rummaging through her desk as she arrived back at the base. Jeanie rolled her eyes as over the last few months he had been another pain in her side that she had to endure. As Jeanie approached him cautiously, Jeanie started to question his intentions.

"Anything I can do for you, Lieutenant." As stood abruptly he looked as if he had just been caught with his hands in the till.

"Pregnant now as well, so how are you going to get these done then in your condition?" Jeanie feeling a little more than pissed off didn't need another man with an attitude problem telling her what she could and couldn't do.

"All done. Just the final few checks to do SIR." Before he continued he spat on the floor and as the spit dripped down his chin she was repulsed at his actions.

"You're a pathetic little woman who apparently likes getting fucked. You have made me look ridiculous you insubordinate cunt. I fucking hate people like you who think they are better than anyone else."

"I believe you 're drunk and maybe it's time to leave sir." Before Jeanie finished, he threw her against the wall and as he lip burst on the concrete Jeanie began to feel the panic well inside and the uncertainty of what was to come.

"Well, little toy soldier I'm a fucking engineer make me leave." Jeanie pushed Signthorpe away and walked out of the door across the yard. Knowing Mike would be making checks Jeanie felt compelled to find him.

"I'm coming for you. You fucking toy soldier." He spat again and with it dripping off his arm as he wiped it away.

"What do you want from me?" Heading into the vehicle compound, she hoped to see a glimpse of Mike. As Signthorpe closed her down, he grabbed Jeanie by the throat pushing her into the side of the truck door. He draped his body over forcing her to gasp for breath, and as she started to fight, he seemed to revel in her distress.

"I'm going to fucking show you what a proper soldier feels like." As he punched Jeanie in the ribs, she fell to the floor feeling her breath escape violently, and as he lifted her towards him with her hair, Jeanie knew she had to do something. Vying

for her freedom, Jeanie head-butted him and crawled under the vehicle to look for safety.
"You fucking bitch. You are fucking going to pay for that." Jeanie still holding her side slipped around the back of the nearby truck. As she squeezed through the small gap between the back fence, she stood on the footplate of the truck wanting to scream out for Mike. Jeanie could feel her heart beat louder and louder in her ear the worst thing was she couldn't see or hear him.
"Where the fuck are you." As she moved slowly around the vehicle, she checked the side of the truck. She could smell him as his stagnant repulsive aftershave lingered in the air making her panic.

Signthorpe crawled underneath and grabbed her leg, and as he pulled her down, Jeanie's head hit the floor with a thud. Squinting and dazed blood poured from her brow, and as she fought to come to her senses, she felt him crawl over her body ripping the buttons off her dungarees. As Signthorpe lurched his body on top of her, he tore and pulled at the remainder of her clothes.
"Ready for a real soldier." Jeanie still trying to pull herself together felt the pain of him on top of her and as she started to kick and scream. Signthorpe placed a hand over her mouth and took off his belt, and she tried to bind her arms together Jeanie continued to struggle and kick. As the buckle end sliced her flesh, she grabbed his arm, trying to free her other hand from his grasp.
"Fucking hold still you bitch." Taking her opportunity, she hit him with her elbow, and as she felt the slight release, she knocked him sidewards. Dragging her body out from under the truck she made it to her feet, and as she ran away a noise shattered the silence, and within seconds Jeanie fell to the floor. Blood poured from her right shoulder, and as she gasped with the pain, she felt the hole

run deep. Jeanie cried out with the pain dragging herself to her knees.

"Fucking run bitch and I'll kill you where you stand."

"Help me please...someone help me."

"Fucking bitches like you need putting in their place." Jeanie desperate for help felt the blood drain from her left shoulder and as the rain poured it gathered around her like a red river.

Bullets fired again and again.

The pain intensified more as Jeanie lay struggling to breathe. Paralysed the blood ran from her body and on seeing Signthorpe standing over her, she knew she had to make one last stand if she was ever going to survive. As he rested his foot on her throat, he looked pleased with his masterpiece and saw amusement staring her bullet-ridden body

"Get out of this one bitch." Jeanie felt powerless as he licked the blood off the side of her cheek and in a way she knew she was dying. Running his fingers down her broken body, Jeanie saw her last attempt at life, and as she grabbed his gun, she refused to give up. Throwing him off balance Jeanie stretched up and placed the gun under his chin feeling his fingers take hold, she fired. Seeing his body twitch and jolt in the gutter Jeanie tried with all her might to drag her cold, wet, lifeless body towards the central compound. As she moved, the blood trail started to become more apparent, and as she lay face down on the floor, she could only muster a whisper. Hearing the commotion and desperately trying to find his way through the mass of vehicles Mike appeared from the side of the compound seeing two bodies he met the Lieutenant's body first.

"Fuck Jeanie. JEANIE!!. Help. Help someone help me." The disorder had sparked an early return for John and noticing the private screaming he stopped the car. On seeing Jeanie's body on the floor, the horror started to play out in front of him. Kneeling John checked her pulse, she was motionless, and the stillness of her actions frightened him more.

"Wake up baby come on Jea wake up. I know you fucking hate me but at least wake up to tell me." John held her in his arms and screamed to the private.

"Go and get a medic. Jeanie come on helps coming." John took his Jacket off and placed it over her trying to keep compression of the fluid which was now flowing out of her stomach. John held her tight trying to stop the stem of blood but as her skin was cold and clammy to touch he feared for the worst. Feeling his heartbeat in his throat, he couldn't let her die, and as his calls screamed out into the night, the seemed to float away on the pouring rain.

James had seen the gathering at the gatehouse thinking a fight had broken out he sauntered over to the crowd. As Mike frantically bellowed out his name he knew instantly something was wrong with Jeanie.

"John talk to me! Jeanie Jeanie, can you hear me?" As he reached out to her, the amniotic fluid had started to gush out of the open wound in her stomach, and as he stared at her body, he senses overwhelmed.

"James she needs you please."

"She needs surgery or she going to die. Keep compression on the wound, and we need to get her into a theatre." John took Jeanie's weight and picked her whole body up from the floor.

"James set it up; Mike make sure we get her there." Jeanie lay lifeless in John's arms, she looked more like a rag doll than a woman, and her pale skin translucent against the stark corridor lighting almost emphasised the lack of life she had left. John felt her heartbeat weaken until he felt nothing but his own.

Jeanie saw light after light as she lay unable to move and as John slid her body onto the table and Jeanie tried to speak. As her breath disappeared, James ushered John and Mike out of the room knowing it was a fight against time to save her. "Get her sisters and her mum we need blood." Without a second thought, both Mike and John disappeared down the corridor, James was grappling to save her life, and as he tried to repair her, he sought to forget this was his wife.

As John arrived at the cottage still covered in Jeanie's blood, he tried to wipe it away. He couldn't believe what had happened and as Irene flung open the door she spat with contempt at the sight of John "Why the hell are you here?" Noticing his coat covered with blood and the look on his face she knew this was no ordinary visit.

"Irene Jeanie." He didn't need to say more, and as she gathered her daughters within minutes, they were out the door and arriving at the base. As they all sat in rows, they waited their turn to be shouted, and as the blood flowed through into the clear glass bottles, she couldn't help but think of her beautiful, talented girl. Ivy couldn't sit still her agitation was written over every expression. John, held out his hand hoping to extend some comfort and as they sat together hand in hand, they both desperately waited for any news on Jeanie and the baby.

The claustrophobic waiting room seemed to squeeze any remnants of hope out of everyone and as Mike paced back and forth with his hands placed on the back of his head feeling every minute like an hour. Unable to comprehend the wait Mike had decided to follow John out into the yard and proceeded over to the place where she lay he stood next to his commanding officer.

"Sorry, sir but you're needed." John excused himself and soberly made his way to the courtyard. "Sir we need you to identify." Putting his hands in his pockets, he walked sombrely to the garage. Signthorpe's body was laid on a clean white board on the floor, and as John lifted the blanket, he could see Jeanie had killed him by a single bullet. As John sat on the chair at the side of the oil drum, he rested his head on his now crossed fingers needing to take another as if it would solve all of his questions. Lifting the cover John saw that Signthorpe had been beaten and saw the scratch marks deep in his chest John knew these where Jeanies last efforts to get away. As John wiped his brow, he didn't understand why this would happen. Questions had also started circulating as to why Signthorpe would want to kill a member of his unit and unable to concentrate any longer his thought's returned to Jeanie and his baby.

He loved her more than she realised and the idea of his child dying, and Jeanie along with it was something John couldn't comprehend. As the rain came down the whole base was sombre. Mike had returned to his side, and as John lifted his head, the pain and anguish were evident to see.

"Can I speak off the record Sir." John nodding his head sat back in the oil-soaked chair waiting for Mikes perspective.

"This piece of shit has been around here a couple of times scoping out the joint and asking after her. I never thought anything of it, but there you go. I didn't realise he intended to do this Sir. I just thought he was well you know after Jeanie, she's a bitch sorry sir but I love her as if she was my sister. But this is just fucked up." Pausing for thought, Mike continued

"Sorry if I've been out of turn, I just think it's fucked up beyond belief Sir…….." John stood up and walked outside in the rain Jeanie's blood still stained the compound, and even the rain seemed to avoid the spot where she had been laying. As he knelt to the floor something glinted in the corner of his eye and as he reached into the puddle of blood Jeanie's wedding ring sparkled in the rain.

"That will be all private."

"Yes sir" As Mike stood to attention, he started to make his way back to the barracks.

"Private."

"Yes, Sir?"

"Thank you." As Mike nodded his head, John put the ring into his pocket and made his way back towards the medical wing hoping for news. The room was silent, and the usual sound of seven women was nowhere evident. As John took back his seat at the side of Ivy, he leant in close hoping some new might have been delivered.

"Heard anything yet?" Ivy shook her head wearily, and as she leant back on the chair, she seemed to stare into space.

"Maybe you should go and take those clothes off John?"

"Not yet…..I can't."

Another couple of hours past before James appeared and behind him rolled Jeanie with an array of tubes and machines attached to her. As the family stood to receive Jeanie, James set himself ready for the questions knowing the bombardment would come thick and fast.

"I've done what I can. I didn't expect her..."

Breaking off mid sentenced James coughed trying to regain his composure.

"I know what you're all wondering. Jeanie had a little boy, but he wasn't able to…. I'm so sorry. Irene Jeanie needs you, and I need to go back. John can you follow me please." James swallowed his tears, and as he led John into the theatre, the baby was tiny and already struggling to breathe.

"John this is your son."

"Thank you, can I hold him before he ...." John sat in the chair at the side of the infant, and as the baby cradled in his arms, neither could comprehend the devastation. The inconsolable the pain and anguish was something that was too much to bear, and as John sat with his baby boy, James knew this changed everything. Both John and James had just experienced the worst thing for any parent, and there was still the possibility that Jeanie may not make the night.

As James left the room tears began to flow, and as he hid away in the store cupboard, he slid his back down the wall trying to gain composure. He couldn't lose both of them and as the questions circulated James' mind a tap on the shoulder brought him to his senses.

"Yes. Yes, Sir" James stumbled through his words unable to string the sentence together.

"Doctor if I might have a minute...." The General almost distant minded didn't look James up and down when he spoke.

"Yes, Sir of course." Exiting the cupboard, they walked into the hall, and the severe nature of the Generals stare hanging over them James wondered what was going to happen next.

"James I've known Jeanie for over fifteen years. Her father used to be the one who took care of all the vehicles on site, and when he died, I knew she was up to the job. On more than one occasion she came on her own and showed she was more than capable. What I'm trying to say is my condolences Doctor.

Now Lieutenant Stanton will be taking up the investigation, and I'm sure we will have all this cleared up and sorted in no time." James still in shock tried to be civil but all he could think about was the way she left and if he had only told her how much he loved her.

"All cleared up how can this be all cleared up my wife has been shot, in fact, she was shot three times. The last bullet resulted in the loss of our baby, and I could still lose my wife General, and you want it cleared up…" James paced around the room as if he had been caged, and intervening John knew emotions were still running high. James had given him his moment it was time for him to do the same.

"General this isn't the time James has to deal with his very sick wife, and he has a funeral to plan for his son maybe we should retake this conversation when it's not as sensitive." The rationality in John's voice was as calculated as his response. John knew James hadn't had time to comprehend the situation and the only thing he could do was buy him time. As John ushered the General politely outside the muttered voices disappeared from the doorway, and as John entered the consulting room, James sat down on the end of the table.

"Thank you. Let me apologise it just seemed…"

"No, I feel the same but thank you for my time with him."

The two men had more understanding between them, and instead of rivalry, they shared an essence of each others pain.

"You know James I was a bastard with her I cheated, hit her on several occasions and drank excessively, Jeanie even caught me in bed with one of her sisters. But in all my life I never met a woman like her, and when I saw her, I wanted her back desperately at any cost even at the expense of my marriage. It's hard to admit, but you're probably the best man for her.

You need to look after her, the way I never could"

"I don't think I was doing the best job, but I don't have to tell you how she makes you feel. Thank you, Lieutenant."

"Tell me if anything changes." Huffing out John folded down his lapel.

"Oh and by the way hurt her again and I'll break your fucking legs." He smiled as he slipped through the door and as James watched him leave he knew of his emptiness.

"John I am......If there is anything, we can do you will always be welcome." Striding down the corridor, he began to fix his uniform, and as he stopped at the window of Jeanie's room, he rested his hand against the glass. Tears appeared again as he did indeed love her and looking at her pale broken body John couldn't bear the thought of her not being there.

"You never realise until it's too late." James sat at her bedside, and on taking her hand, he kissed it softly trying to understand what kind of psychopath would want to do this sort of damage.

The white clinical room seemed to emphasise the bruising which had started to appear, and James knew the next twenty-four hours were crucial. In essence, he prayed for a miracle quietly.

As Irene entered the room, she saw James with his head in hir hand, and as she gathered her children, she knew no more could be done. For the first time, that evening silence fell over the wing and a strange melancholic calm distilled. James tried to relive what Jeanie must have gone through, and as he checked her wounds, he relived a small amount of the pain she must have endured. Placing his hands in his pockets, he rested his head on the door frame and reaching deep he pulled out Jeanie's wedding ring. As he put the sapphire gently on her finger, he finally answered Jeanie honestly for the first time since they had been married.

"I love you too much for you ever to be a disappointment."

Chapter 17

"James. James James! " Sweat poured off Jeanie like a river, and as she dragged the covers back, she pulled at the needles sticking out of her skin and tried to stand. Blood dripped from the marks making small droplet stains on the floor, and as she frantically began to feel for the bump, she felt confused and alone. Lifting her gown, she saw the bullet wounds and the lines which scared her body split her in half. Still dazed she placed her hands over her ears still able to hear the shatter as it ripped through her body. Signthorpe's voice pierced her dreams, and his breath still felt hot and putrid on her neck. Wiping her hands through her hair, she tried to move, and as she winced in pain, she called out again.

"Hello….Hello help me please…" blood dripped from her arm as she staggered down the corridor. Jeanie couldn't gather her thoughts, and she didn't know what was real and what wasn't. The pale bedraggled figure hesitantly moved down the corridor looking for any signs of life, and Jeanie felt like she was trapped in her nightmare. Reaching the end of the hallway, she saw the door ajar to a small windowed office, and as Jeanie stood watching James through the glass, she felt unable to speak. As she placed her blood smeared hand on the window, James heard the faint tap, and on turning to see what it was, he saw the figure of Jeanie stood watching him.

"Jeanie Jea…nurse you need to come now. Jeanie….." As she stared into his eyes, she seemed to fall unable to hold her weight and as she slumped into his arms the air around her seemed frantic. Her wide eye's asked all the questions her breath couldn't muster, and as the muffled voices bellowed in the background, she concentrated on James' musical tones.

"Jeanie, Jeanie talk to me baby come on… "James picked her up off the floor and screamed for the nurse who came running immediately.

"Yes Doctor," Seeing the ghostly figure in James's arms she froze.

"Fuck. Sorry doctor I just." James smiled at Jeanie trying to reassure her and as he carried her to her room he held her close making sure she felt safe.

"Doesn't matter I need fluid and gauze now." Jeanie didn't take her eyes off James; she didn't speak, she just gazed and blinked.

"Nice to have you back…Just wait for me, nurse. Sorry, my darling I need to look at your stomach and back." The words he had been planning on saying to her disappeared as the doctor inside took over. Examining Jeanie the words he dreaded announced themselves, and he knew no matter how sweetly he made it sound he wasn't going to help with the pain. James asked for privacy and as the nurse implicitly agreed to his request, James continued to examine her broken, beaten body.

"Please, I know the answer I just need to hear it." He was a trained doctor bad news was part of the job. However this time it was different. The woman who he loved more than life itself was asking him about her baby dying

"Jeanie, when you were shot the bullet, went through your abdomen, and you went into premature labour. Because of the internal bleeding, we had to operate, and a little boy was born the same night. Due to his injuries and the fact that he was born too early he passed away a couple of hours later." The explanation seemed clinical and calm as a doctor should be, but deep inside he wanted to scream and shout on her behalf.

"Thank you, James."

"You went through four hours worth of surgery just to stem the bleeding Jeanie you are fortunate to survive." Letting go of James's hand, she gripped her stomach processing the devastation that one man had left. All that was left was blood and scars and blinking him in she smiled and turned onto her side.

"I can give you pain relief Jea. If it hurts, you need to tell me."

Nodding her head, James administered the painkiller, and as her lids grew heavy, he stayed until she drifted back to sleep. Brushing her hair away from her face he lightly stroked her forehead softly kissing her hand, there was no way he was leaving not now she had come back to him. Pushing the chairs together at the corner of the room he settled in for the night. She was awake. She was alive. Nothing else mattered.

As daylight came news of Jeanie had spread across the base, and as John entered his office he looked out of the large Church window with some degree of relief. Anne, his secretary, had left a note on his desk telling him Jeanie was alive and as he lit a cigarette, he stood at the fireplace contemplating the last few week's events. As he bit through the corner of his lip, he tore through the skin, and as the blood trickled into his mouth, he sucked at the fissure trying to alleviate some of the pain.

Losing his son had been the worst experience of his life but knowing she was awake helped. He needed to find out what had happened and the thought of speaking to Jeanie brought shivers down his spine. Over the weeks the investigation around Signthorpe's life most of what he had found didn't surprise him. Damping the cigarette, he opened the drawer and pulled the file from the large oak desk. A handmade folder had been discovered in Signthorpe's office and the detailed drawings and pictures of Jeanie where protruding from every corner. He had planned the times and dates meticulously especially when she would be on her own, and the images had given John nightmares. Sections of the folder described her movements included pictures of her at home, and the anger of knowing such a dangerous man had hidden on site made John uneasy.

As he moved further through the pages a small piece of paper hung from one of the pictures. Detaching the note, it gave way to a drawing and wanting to know more John started to read:

"The night is nearly here, and that no it all bitch will suffer, she's a cockroach living in the shit I feed her on. Little Jeanie you think you are so fucking special you are nothing, and I'm going to prove to everyone when I fuck her to death that she's got the same bastard cunt of a whore.

Filthy fucking no good child doesn't deserve to be born to a cock sucking whore like her. Her fucking doctor husband can go and eat my shit as well. Maybe he should know what a no good bitch she is. Fucking a Lieutenant Colonel a damn LC he apparently likes dirty filthy sluts who begged to be fucked cause it's the only purpose they have.

Tomorrow bitch yours and the life of your cock sucking baby is mine, and when you beg for your fucking pathetic life, no mercy will be given as I will be sending you back to Satan where you belong. You will fucking learn your place in the gutter."

John put the letter on the table and rubbed his face. "She never had a chance." As his breath lingered on his lips, he saw a glint on the opposite side of the letter which made him sit up. On turning the letter over his heart sank as a cut of Jeanie's hair and a piece of the bed linen from the hotel along with name tag from James's coat had been stuck to the back of the letter and the words "this bitch dies tonight" written in the middle.

John felt sick knowing Signthorpe had been in the room as they slept. As he threw the rest of the letters onto the table, he couldn't read any more intimate details of that night. Her skin, her dress and the way she smelt confirming his obsession all played out in his words. Signthorpe hadn't left it there either he had also turned his attention to James cutting the label out of his jacket so concise that John realised how easy it was to access their intimate personal details.

Pushing himself to find more John noticed a drawing but this one was different. Raising it up to his eye line the intimacies of their relationship had also been photographed and then drawn. He knew to do the investigation justice no stone could remain unturned and these incredibly personal moments had turned into someone's sick gratification. The whole ledger spelt out in no uncertainty that all three of them had been chosen and all three had been deemed unworthy to survive.

The drawings and the disturbing nature of the journal made John feel dirty, and on turning to the last page, he realised Signthorpe had drawn a picture of Jeanie at work. Again this was different because unlike the other's it was beautiful. He hated to admit that he had captured her perfectly and every small detail hadn't been missed. John couldn't comprehend this man anymore, and the only thing that was definite was that he could prove beyond reasonable doubt that he had purposely gone to kill.

As he packed his case and moved the investigation notes into a large leather bound folder he placed on his jacket; he started to make his way to the medical wing. James stood outside with his cigarette, elated that she was awake and knackered as the chairs had been one of the most uncomfortable experiences of sleep he had encountered in a while. Seeing John make his way over he knew it was Jeanie's time to talk.

"So this is his folder." John nodded and clenched his hand tight around the binding.

"James is she ok to take a few questions; I just want to wrap things up it's just…"

"John she's stronger than us both. She a little tired so I suggest you need to be quick." As both gentlemen made their way down the hall the urgency of their steps seemed to ring out with each stride. Nurses stopped as they heard them pass and as whispers echoed it was as if being both were playing parts in a gangster film. John hesitated as he reached the door and as he closed his eyes he took a deep breath as the enormity of it all seemed to overwhelm him. James smiled uneasily as the pale, fragile-looking Jeanie was wide awake and no longer confused. She stared intently at both of them not faltering or saying a word to ease the tension. As the nurse stood, she placed her hand on James' shoulder.

"Doctor Can I have a word please."

"Doctor she…I'm sorry James but she just will not cooperate she is just a bit well impossible, to be honest…she has I can't explain it but she doesn't seem like Jeanie." Jeanie followed every movement and every word ignoring John who was patiently waiting. He noticed the differences too, and she did indeed seem strange and distant. John didn't muster a note.

"Nice to have you with us. You frightened us for a while." No reply came from Jeanie.

"I need to go through what happened with you, and if you can remember anything, we need to know for your statement."

No words came again.

"Jeanie I know this is difficult, but we need.."
"I remember everything, the way he smelt, his hands on my skin even his breath on my back. I remember his eyes and every nightmare ends with them glaring at me and I wait to hear the final shot." Jeanie bit her lip and pulled her mouth tight together. John looked directly at her unable to read how she felt for the very first time.

"Jea, look I was there I saw you, James …. Well without James you wouldn't be alive and trust me, but that night we all lost something, but James was determined not to lose you. Just like now I'm determined not to let some bureaucrat cover this up, I need your help, and I'm sorry. I'm sorry for hurting you; I'm sorry for being the biggest bastard on this planet. But I need you to tell me." Jeanie just gazed at the pair not purposely cooperating she relived that night every time she closed her eyes, and she didn't want to relive it during the day as well.

John placed the leather bound folder on the end of the bed and sat down with his head in his hands.

"Listen this isn't easy for all of us and for once I agree with John. We are all involved, and we just need your help. So Jea, please come on your tougher than the both of us in this room lets just finish this so we can all move on." Jeanie stared at the wall vacant, upset, frightened and angry.

"He approached me from the garage, and he threw me into a wall, and I knew. I knew from that moment what he was trying to do. I still feel him. I still feel him on top of me trying to undress me….. I just …..." Jeanie stuttered again reliving the agony and panic of that night.

"James can you give me some time with John….I just ….it's just uncomfortable, and I don't know it's hard….." James stood up and kissed her sweetly on the forehead.

"I understand its ok." James stood in the room opposite his glances never wavered as he paced the floor. His stomach began to turn and as the time dragged on his anxiety increased. Checking his watch, he realised forty minutes had passed and as he tried to relax his thoughts kept running over her first few sentences. He clenched his fists over and over again, and he could see Jeanie slump back into her bed exhausted by the recall of her experience. James saw her eyes fill and dry over again as the minutes laboured and unable to settle he arose again and placed his hands on the back of his head. His sickness was growing with each moment underpinned by jealousy and concern that the conversation was taking longer than anticipated.

The images Jeanie had conjured played on James's mind and compounded by the guilt for the way he had behaved that night he felt he had played a part in her demise. Jeanie's attack ran over and over again, and there was nothing he could do, and he felt powerless. Seeing John stand, James jumped to attention jealously growing as John's kiss lingered. James saw John clench his hands tightly around the leather bound file and as he opened the door John offered out his hand to James

"I appreciate your patience, James. I know everything thank you." John smiled and let go of the doctor's hand. He looked like a man on a mission, focused and determined John disappeared down the corridor. James, on the contrary, stood watching the door with his heart leaping out of his chest and after checking his stethoscope for the seventeenth time he had to make an excuse to walk into the room.

Jeanie lay on the bed looking half asleep and worn out and as he started to check her pulse he could feel his heartbeat thud heavily in his chest. Desperately needing to know what had been said, he couldn't concentrate.

"Why are you worried?" As she smiled, James sat on the side of the bed and kissed her, his guilty complex or his ruffled exterior had given his thoughts away cheaply.

"Why would you say that?" Jeanie shrugged her shoulder's rolling her head over the pillow.

"I know we argued before I left and I also know you didn't mean it." James held her hand, rubbing his fingers over hers. Fighting between the doctor and himself he needed her to understand.

"It wasn't like I was such…the night all this happened and I feel partly responsible."

"I don't blame you. I wanted my baby, but I don't blame you. I don't know why this has happened to any of us; I love you..." Placing his hand over hers he knew things couldn't be the same, and he was aware that an attack as vicious as this would change anyone. Jeanie also saw the lump appear in his throat and the sudden urge to force back the tears.

"I'm sorry…I just thought I was going to lose you and now I have tried to at least put you back together." Jeanie looked at her scars, he had produced them, but in doing so, she was alive and feeling his heartbeat slow Jeanie closed her eyes.

"Maybe we both can heal each other."

Chapter 18

Irene, Ivy, May, Rose, June, Iris, Daisy and Flora
stood at the window anticipating their sisters return.
Tensions were already running high in the house,
and with Irene trying to find her inner matriarch she
put her foot down for the first time in a while.
"Stop pissing about, change the covers and for
Christ sake put that kettle on." Bellowing at the
girls Irene's emotions flipped over within her
stomach, however, she couldn't let her daughters
know how she felt. She needed to be strong even if
it was until Jeanie got home. James brought the car
around the front of the cottage and opened the door,
and Irene sighed heavily at the sight of her
daughter. Jeanie looked pale, fragile and her
delicate condition upset her greatly.
"I have missed her so much, I never thought…."
May broke down in tears squeezing Ivy's arm for
comfort. Patting her lovingly Ivy couldn't bring
herself to respond just in case she was going to have
the same reaction.
"NO you're not carrying me in I can walk." Jeanie
still defiant couldn't let James pick her up. There
was no doubt she felt frail, but she knew the sight of
him carrying her would have worried her family
more. Stepping out of the car, Jeanie stood tall with
James by her side.
"Come here closer…" Jeanie kissed him on the
cheek trying to reassure him that she was ok.
"I never got to say it in hospital but Thank you."
James winced an unconvincing smiled while biting
his lip.
"Why do I not feel reassured?"
"Because you worry too much and you still think
you know what's best for me."
"I think I know whats best for you. I've been
looking after you in the hospital for the past six

weeks!" As Jeanie smiled again, James knew there was no point arguing. She had made up her mind, and wild horses weren't going to change that.

As the front door opened and before either of them got the chance to announce their arrival Irene stood proudly as her daughter and son in law where home and safe.

"My mum and dad have set off already so it'll be later tonight before they get here," Irene was grateful for the physical and moral support of another set of parents and James' though it would also help having another distraction within the house.

"May, Rose….tea she needs tea…" Irene was anxious, undoubtedly flustered and Jeanie as per usual just wanted to calm the situation.

"Mum…Mum." Jeanie tried to get Irene to settle without much luck.

"She needs a pillow as well. Flora upstairs get that big one from my bedroom…" Irene barked her orders as Jeanie smiled gingerly. Only being able to gain her mum's attention by grabbing her hand she tried to reassure her again.

"Mum I'm ok. I', I'm home.James sit down please both of you…." James had been pacing the floor quietly behind the settee unable to settle or relax, and as he sat beside her.

"I'm. We are just concerned for you. Today has been a big step for all of us." Jeanie held onto both of them as if it were the last moments together.

"Both of you listen I owe you both so much, and I'm sorry for putting you all through this. I'm where I want to be, and that's home... I need things to be as normal as possible…I can't…" Jeanie started to well with tears as she couldn't express how much she wanted normality. She wanted to move on, and more than anything wanted Signthorpe to be eradicated from her dreams and her memory.

"Sounds like things are back to normal in there any way…" Jeanie chuckled at the noise of raised voices and slamming cups from the kitchen. Irene at least wanted calm and some serenity for the first hours of her daughter being home. Instead, the bickering seemed to enrage her more than usual. James looked straightforward as if he was a judge and jury combined and Jeanie longed to know what was on his mind.

"Penny for them…." James wrapped his arm around her and began to settle a little.

"I'm sorry just I have to deal with…I'm struggling no one tells you how to cope when it's your wife. I don't know how …"

"Do you love me James?" closing his eyes he swallowed deep.

"Jeanie you know I do. What kind of a question is that?" James placed his hand on her cheek trying to comprehend everything that had happened.

"Then I'll be ok…."

"It's just a big jolt today, and I want….I want us to be a family, and I'm just grateful that your home. I love you." As he kissed her gently, James pulled her close stroking his thumb across her cheek knowing she was putting on a brave face just for him. As he gazed into her eyes, he saw the fire which burned so bright dim, and he realised how hard the journey back together could be. Irene stood at the door with the pot of tea in her hand and as the tears began to fall she watched as the pair clung together desperately trying to make it work. Noticing Irene at the door, James lept up offering his services.

"Irene is everything ok...Can I be of assistance." Placing the pot on the parlour table, she wiped away her tears with her apron.

 "No….No love I'm sure everything will be all right." As the family gathered around Jeanie slept as the comfort and security of her surroundings had given her the best gift. Carrying her upstairs, James rested his head on hers, and as he placed her gently down, he removed his shirt and got in beside her. As he put his hands on her back, he could feel her heartbeat and counted its rhythm making sure no irregularities had occurred.

The scars of her ordeal ran deeper than the superficial ones on her body and James still playing doctor could help but recheck her vitals. Unable to settle he kissed her shoulder and sat up on the end of the bed taking in the cold night air he walked towards the window and lit a cigarette.

"Do I make you feel so terrible?" Jeanie wished she could take everything they had been through away and as he stubbed his cigarette out he sat and ran his fingers over the scar on her shoulder and chest.

"I wasn't there for you. I wasn't there when you needed me and…I." Placing Jeanies fingers on his tears she felt his pain, she felt how close he was to losing her, and his vulnerability touched her deeply "I love you more than anything James Watson and without you…without you, I wouldn't be here. You're a good man and an excellent doctor, and I can't thank you enough. I'm alive James, and it's all because of you." Taking hold of her hand, he kissed it sweetly, and as his tears pierced Jeanie's translucent skin, as she moved forward she winced in pain.

"What is it? Where about does it hurt?"

"James I'm ok stop. Just lie down with me Please." Together in the dark James kissed her hand and again he couldn't get away from that night, and what he said.

Sharing the same pillow, he stared into her dark eyes, and as she stroked the hair around his ear, she ran her fingers down the line of his jaw.

"It's ok. Go to sleep…."

Chapter 19

Walking into John's office, James knew what he wanted.

"Where are we at John, I need to know whether she's going to get answer's of how a homicidal maniac was allowed onto the base." James protective over Jeanie and pissed off with getting nowhere confronted John. The sentiment of spending the night at home had pricked his conscious and it wasn't good enough anymore to be pacified that it was being looked into.

"Good Morning James, take a seat….. "

"Don't patronise me, John, I know things are a little different but you still can be a dick, and you know it. Have you seen her John? I have in a way I never want to have to again. I had to cut halfway around her body to stop the bleeding, and they want it washed away like a dirty secret. Well on behalf of myself and my wife tell them to go fuck themselves." John stood up and closed the big oak door, and as he smiled to his secretary, he knew she had heard every word. As John took his seat at his desk, he brought out his leather-bound folder.

"I have sat and read this file over and over again, every sordid little detail every misogynistic comment. Now I need you to calm the fuck down and let me deal with this. Do you understand?"

"I know you're keeping something from me…from us. What don't you want her to know John?"

Pushing the leather-bound folder over to James, John walked towards the window, and as he looked out, he wiped his hands across his face.

"This is Jeanie's hair there are pictures of her asleep…." John turned around sickened again by the predator that had pursued her so fiercely.

"He took pictures of us together at the hotel, and he also took clippings of her hair, the bed linen and the name tag are out of your jacket. James this wasn't just an incident it was planned, calculated merciless she didn't stand a chance. I'm supposed to burn this evidence, and the worst thing is I can't share my grief. I lost as well.......I lost my baby." John covered his mouth trying to swathe the break in his voice.

"You were going to cover this up. You were going to let them wash over this weren't you," John's silence angered him more and as his patience had already been worn down by Jeanie's recovery waiting any longer for answers played on his frustrations.

"John Answer ME! Weren't you!"

"I have no choice what do you want me to do James there's a fucking war on don't you think I have enough to contend without taking on the damn government as well. I have no choice."

"Give me something I can use John give me something which isn't going to implicate you. I haven't got a lot of time left and you know I leave soon let me do this for all of us." John ruffled through the file and found the letter Signthorpe had written to Jeanie pulling it out his head dropped "Listen to me no one knows about this letter, not even Jeanie. If she...take it to a bloke called Fred Tetherington, he is a correspondent in London I met him when I got married. He's an obnoxious twat, but he loves stuff like this. I can give you some time James, but it's not going to be much." John sat down in his chair and placed his head on clasped hands with emotions running high James nodded.

"I try to pretend I know what you're going through but I don't. He wasn't my child I never even touched that beautiful bump because it reminded me of you. My guilt of what I did will haunt me forever, but I pose this question to you. If Jeanie's was your wife and if you were in my position what would you be doing."

"I'd be fighting tooth and nail to protect her. You know I love her James you know I would do anything for her. I still am" As James smoothed down his tie he took a deep breath knowing John was still a risk.

"I know you do. That's why I have to prove to Jeanie now more than ever how much she means to me." As James shook John's hand, he left hoping that for now, he had some proof which would stop all the harassment from the secret service officials. John had protected her the best he could, but James had to watch as they had gathered around Jeanie's bed making the whole affair tainted. Jeanie had been forced to sign the official secrets act, gagging her from talking to anyone about her ordeal and only those closest to her knew the truth. But as far as the world was concerned she was some tramp who had sullied herself with another soldier, and the baby had died.

As James arrived back at the cottage, he made his way upstairs hoping that his news would help with her recovery. Jeanie was sat on the windowsill looking out into the garden watching May, Rose and Jayne play together and as Jeanie giggled James knew she was trying to move on.

Watching his family enjoy their time made him question his motives and more than he understood he wanted revenge, but he wasn't thinking about what Jeanie needed. The truth needed to be exhumed and the war had taken so much, that he didn't want the quest for justice misconstrued, and she already had to live with a lie. Their actions would be interpreted as selfish compared to the millions of soldiers losing their lives each day, and as a soldier, he couldn't allow his feelings for his wife cloud his judgement and his duty.

All the time James focused on Jeanie, her smile and her loving nature towards her family had never and faltered, and even with their father gone she had happily stepped forward even when they turned to her for guidance and being so loyal, she accepted without reproach. Feeling the enormity of the situation James hid the letter in his pocket and made his way downstairs. His foolhardiness of the morning made him feel as if he needed to apologise to John and now and only now he had started to understand John's position, but this wasn't going to be the end. The realisation and the truth felt unbearable and the fact that Jeanie had been carrying him all this time made him come to his senses quickly.

It was about time that he looked after her.

James sat at the bottom of the stairs lost in thought. On hearing the knock at the door, it startled him back to reality. Opening the gap tentatively his dad grabbed hold of his hand and hugged him assiduously trying to make up for some of the time he hadn't been there.

"Hello, Son we just had to when we heard……Irene, we came when we could…" his dad genuinely concerned couldn't let go of his hand, and as his mum stepped through the cottage she flung her arms around him.

"Where is she is she ok? Oh, James, I'm so sorry." James stepped back into the hallway as the reaction of his parents made the reality flood back.

"Where's Jeanie?" Robert stroked James arm as he whispered as not to disturb.

"She's upstairs dad; I will get her she would be thrilled to see you both. Why don't you go through to the garden the rest are outside?" Smiling his mum and dad made their way through the kitchen. James could still hear Jeanie's giggles, and as he stood at the bedroom door, he observed patiently.

"Can you only watch me from the doorway?"
Jeanie's playful response made James smile.
"I have a track record obviously….."
"Your mum and dad have arrived. I guess my mum
asked for the cavalry. You know when I first met
you, you used to hang around at my office door."
James walked towards the window and started to
lean into the pain.
"You know I was always cocky and self-confident
until I met you. Hanging around at your door was
the only way I got you to notice me."
"So kissing me after a shower in the locker room
wasn't enough." As she stood, Jeanie slowly walked
to the door placing her hand on the frame she
looked back.
"Are you coming?" Picking up Jayne's ball off the
window seat James threw it up and caught it with
one hand and as he placed his hand over the top of
hers he bent over he kissed her.
"I remember the first time you trapped me like
this."
"How can I forget? If it were up to me, you would
have never left." Jeanie's body betraying her
reacted as he leant in closer pressing her body
against the frame. As he stroked her hair, her deep
eyes told a thousand stories.
"Jeanie you're the best thing that has ever happened
to me, and I don't regret anything." Jeanie looked
perplexed.
"I don't understand. What do you mean?" James
kissed her again and held her tightly.
"I mean other than the fact that you nearly died. I
don't regret falling for you I'm who I want to be
when I'm with you." The safety of James's arms
felt comforting, and it was reassuring to know that
he had no regrets.
"I never wanted to leave that morning. I would have
stayed underneath that duvet with you forever. I

can't…" James rested his thumb against her magnificently soft lips.

"Forever is what I'm offering." As James kissed her again, he took her by the hand and led her down the stairs making sure she took her time. As he took her out into the garden, Jeanie sat in the shade of the large oak tree as they watched Jayne play she couldn't help but think what her little boy would have been doing. Crossing her hands over her stomach, she longed for her baby and the pain and realisation that he dead loomed over her. Jayne emphasised her loss.

James watched her intently from the gaggle of people surrounding the cottage grounds and seeing she had grown a little distant from her niece he too wondered how his son would have been. Jeanie gracious as ever offered refreshments and compelled not to leave her on her own he followed.

"Let me help you." James fussed over her and Jeanie knew it was his unrequited need to help and his way of loving her.

"James is everything ok. I have this feeling you need to tell me something. I mean you know I'm getting better now I'm home." Jeanie stood side by side and James couldn't help but look at her every move.

"James is there something you need to say,"

"I went to see John about what's been happening. I know you said not to, but I couldn't help myself. I needed him to realise that I'm not going to let this go Jea……" Jeanie picked up the tray and paused before exiting the door.

"Take these for me….." Seeing him disappear she realised his guilt of that night ran deeper than expected. Jeanie picked up her wedding photo and sitting at the kitchen table James saw her smile.

"You were the most beautiful woman I'd ever seen when you walked up to that altar I felt like the luckiest man on the planet."

"Fred Tetherington he said speak to him?"

"How do you know?"

"He doesn't exist. James, John knows that this will never have a resolution not now. The war has to be a priority, and a scandal now will undermine everything, and I'm a scandal." As James tried to interrupt Jeanie stood to make sure her point was heard.

"Please just listen I think it's the most admirable and honourable thing you have tried to do for me, and I love you for trying to protect me. I also appreciate what you're trying to do, but please don't. All I want to do now is live my life with you…" James stood at the table unable to understand how she knew.

"I see you coping with the pain and heartache, and I feel worthless that I can't-do anything to stop it. I'm a man Jeanie I need to feel like I could solve this. I apparently took it for granted that you wouldn't know."

"I'm smarter than you think. Plus it helps to have lots of sisters with boyfriends on the base…." James smiled seeing how her resolve shone through.

"So you have a sophisticated set of spy's watching my every move..."

"Depends whether you're in the shower then I only have photo's…." Her cheeky response made him blush, and Jeanie couldn't help but smile.

As the afternoon fell into early evening, the radio played softly in the background, and as she stood, he took her by the hand.

"You know Mrs Watson I think we've only danced once and I can't recall ever finishing it." Taking her hand, he softly placed his hands on her back, and as he pulled her close, she rested her head on his chest.

The soft swing of the music dipped and glided as they met together.

"What time do you leave?" James had rested his head on hers indulging himself in the brief moment of calm.

"Doesn't matter now…just being here now is all I need…" Jeanie sat in the chair brushing her hair, and as she watched James disappear back to the base, it seemed to pain her more than ever. Taking his bathrobe, she smothered it around her body and being surrounded by his smell it engulfed her senses.

"You know I remember Flori James's mother looking out of the window like that to me." Jeanie turned her head and smiled in kindness.

"You know my Son was a brilliant doctor before he met you but he was just too cold and forceful in his opinions. I thought it was a bad idea coming to work with you, but the Surgeon insisted he had to." As the conversation broke, Jeanie settled down to hear more about James' past.

"You know James had already spent time in France that's when he met the surgeon you know the one that told him he had no people skills." Robert paused again to dip his biscuit in his tea and Jeanie fixated by the conversation listened intently as this part of James life seemed to be a closely guarded secret.

"He spent around nine months with you and at Silloth Bay military hospital still as a soldier you know he had to keep that part secret of course, but you know that. He was with Catherine then oh been with her for years promised to marry her when the war was over. Do you know he never visited once when he was working for you and your father? He talked about you insistently. We didn't know it was you then, but he was different. Flori didn't understand him at all and Catherine. Catherine was so upset in fact furious I knew my son hadn't been faithful to her….

I always thought he would come to his senses sooner rather than later. Catherine had been on the scene so long we had made her part of the family, so when he said he'd met someone else, we thought it was another whim. The thing is I noticed he'd grown compassion and he started to understand fear and loss something he had never had to experience before. You did that…he told your mother the day after your father's funeral that he was going to Marry you.

What were the words he used? Oh, yes I'm the man I want to be when I'm with her. Or something like that. I knew then Catherine didn't have a chance." Jeanie sat in silence as Robert spoke, her heart felt as if it was going to burst as everything that James had said had been the truth. Jeanie had always felt his feelings were something out of fantasy but hearing it from his father's made Jeanie believe even more that James loved her.

Chapter 20

John sat in his office clutching a large bottle of whiskey and as he poured a large scotch he glanced at the advancement paperwork on his desk.

Daylight hovered over the distant hills and knowing that every member of staff under his remit would soon be shipped out elevated the level of responsibility he felt.

The cloud which had been hovering over the base since the Signthorpe attack had raised questions about his intensions and Jeanie's involvement in the whole affair.

The hundreds of vehicles lining up outside reminded John everyday that she had been such an integral part of everything he had ever done.

The fact he couldn't defend her innocence frustrated him more than anything and with questions surrounding his involvement and the fact that he was pushing for the authorities to release a statement he knew the pressure on his side of the desk had escalated three fold.

John threw his glass into the fire place. Leaning into the flames he placed both hands formally above the mantel, She was in his heart, his head and his life and like it or not she was his grief. Staring into the flames he knew he had to try to win her back. His life was tearing apart and thinking of her with James only made the feelings stronger.

Leaving his office he needed air he needed her family on his side but his relationship with her family was already fraught. The hours of negotiation and investigation had created distance and Irene had told him outright that he was to blame. The only empathy he had received was from Ivy.

He felt isolated, angry and not being able to talk to Jeanie about his grief was driving him insane.

Heading out into the night the thunder of aircraft over head drowned his screams. A job needed to be done and a war needed to be won. Duty bound he continued ahead to complete his 06:00 brief regardless of how he felt he now had his job to do.

Still slightly drunk John stood in front of his mirror, his usual calm professional and well groomed exterior looked haggard and dishevelled in comparison.

Standing at the back James faced the clock knowing this was countdown and as John entered the room the tension between them was obvious. As the men congregated into the room Mike poked his head around the door.

"Pst….Pst….James." James looked across at the signalling Mike, moving towards the doorway and shuffling around as not to cause an obvious disturbance he shuffled across to the door. Mike unfolded a piece of paper and passed it towards James. Opening the note he smiled and thanked Mike and as he made his way back John made it obvious that he had seen the exchange, "Doctor nice to know you're taking this seriously. Private shut the door please…Can I now proceed…"

James nodded and instead of making a scene he leant on the back wall and lit another cigarette. Clutching at the paper in his pocket, he knew he would need John's assistance and now was the last chance to show Jeanie once and for all that he was the right choice.

John packed up his papers trying to give the impression the next advancement was on his mind and as the last body disappeared James moved forward.

"I need your help…" John glared at him knowing full well he had bent over backwards giving James additional leave for Jeanie.

"What else would you like me to do Doctor because I'm hanging myself as it is…"

"I need her John." John slammed the door shut trying to cool down his temper, "You don't know what she needs. I'm listening but your going to have to make this quick..." James knew John was hurting, and he knew the fight for her had just begun.

"I'm shipping out John….I will be going for I don't know how long you are going to get your time I'm asking for now to let me have mine." "How long…."

"A few days four tops. At that point you will be throwing me on a plane." John stepped closer to James infuriated that he was asking the impossible again.

"I know she loves you I'm just not sure she's in love with you yet soldier. Let me see what I can do…." James smiled unconvincingly annoyed by John he tried to understand his pain.

"Thank you..."

"Don't ask for anything again I have nothing left to give." John slammed the door shut and with that James waited for his answer.

Two days later John paid James a visit and on handing over an envelope John walked directly past ignoring any signs of making amends. Looking inside James found he had been given a four day pass.

Running to the medical wing he changed his uniform and took the car John had left him. Arriving at the cottage he ran upstairs and routed around for a bag. Finding practically nothing he grabbed a few things and threw them in the boot of the car.

Hearing the commotion May ran into the hall, "James why are you here?" James still agitated he looked frantically for Jeanie, "Where is she?"

"She's outside with Flora and Rose." James flew out of the back door to find Jeanie huddled in a blanket, "Why are you here?" Jeanie looked as perplexed as her sister.

James was acting irrationally not knowing what was going on it scared her a little and as he shouted at her sisters he picked her up off the floor, "It's to cold for you to be sat outside. Tell your mum...she knows anyway but we will be back in four days." James raced to the car and dropped Jeanie carefully into the passenger seat. He seemed rattled, excited and zealous all at the same time. Jeanie smiled in amusement she hadn't seen him for nearly eight weeks and the fact that he was so pleased to see her thrilled her too. "Where are we going?" James leant over and kissed her on the cheek. The mystery of the situation made Jeanie's natural curiosity go into overdrive.

Jeanie fell asleep as the night drew in. The cold days and early evenings made her sleepy and the gentle rocking of the car seem to caress her to sleep without too much difficulty.

Hearing the engine stop she woke up to find they where parked at the back of a beautiful stone cottage. The picturesque double fronted windows and the small quaint doors made Jeanie gasp in delight.

James ran around to the passenger side and carefully picked her up out of the seat, "You know I haven't lost my ability to walk!" James smiled; as he opened the small green door. Carrying Jeanie over the threshold Jeanie surprised by his actions and in awe at how beautiful the cottage was delved into her curiosity, "What is this for?"

James twirled her around and smiled uncontrollably, "This is my confession I asked my parents to come up not just because they wanted to see you but because I needed them to help me get this."

Jeanie clasped her hands together and smiled back looking in every cupboard, "How long are we here for?"

"It's yours Jeanie this is my wedding present to you. Here are the keys and your name is on the deed. I love you and I want my life to be here with you!"

Jeanie stumbled and placed her hands on the kitchen table tucked in the corner next to the aga.

"You bought me a house. You bought us a house, why….when….James" as she sat on the chair unable to comprehend what had happened James planted himself in front of her on bended knee.

"This is for us. Our home our life. I wanted….No I needed to show you Jeanie and this house has been my dream for you for as long as I have loved you."

"Can I go and look around," James nodded as he started to fill the kettle.

There where two corridors running off the kitchen and one to the front porch. To the right hand side of the kitchen Jeanie wondered into the living room. The beautiful stone fire place set as a grand feature in the idle of the room and the double fronted windows lit up as the full moon streamed through the glass.

Jeanie noticed small details as their wedding photo had been placed pride of place on the mantel and pictures of Irene and the girls had been placed on the oak side board. The settee had been put in the centre of the room and Jeanie had to catch her breath at the realisation that this was her new home.

Closing the door Jeanie ventured out into the stone floor hallway, the stain glass window on the front porch streamed multi coloured pictures and Jeanie felt like Alice in wonderland.

Poking her head around into the kitchen James stood at the back door cigarette in hand, tiptoeing past she crept down into the other corridor, switching on the light Jeanie saw three rooms.

Wondering into the bedroom she immediately knew this was their room. The same fire placed greeted her and the huge oak bed practically filled the room. Standing at the door Jeanie bit her nails as the same double fronted windows with seats looked out into the garden.

Wanting to pinch herself James disturbed her. His warm hands wrapped around her waist. "Is it ok....I asked them to leave the furniture as we had nothing did I do the right thing."

"James It's such a surprise it's more than I ever imagined. Just a quick question though where does that door go?" James took her hand and smiled, "This is just for you I had to make sure it was completed before you arrived."

As he opened the door Jeanie bit her lip too scared to speak but to inquisitive not to go, looking into the room she held her breath.

"I have my own bathroom. I still don't know what can I say? I love all of it. I have a slight problem though what about clothes..."

"I'm sure we can figure something out." Hearing the kettle boil James disappeared out of the door whilst Jeanie continued her journey around her new home.

The bathroom intrigued Jeanie as another door led into another room, "Ok bedroom number two," her excitement increased with every door, this time it led her back into the dark corridor. Jeanie by this time had become very observant and as she came across a small hallway with yet another door she couldn't wait to look in. The door was ajar and the room seemed to be filled with boxes. Creeping inside the third room Jeanie saw it was much smaller and the window looked out over the vegetable patch at the rear of the house, Jeanie smiled and whispered under her breath, "My little project."

Sitting at the table in the kitchen she couldn't help but smile as James passed her a mug and winked. "You knew I would love this didn't you." Placing her mug on her lap James lovingly gazed at her amazement and felt content and relieved at how happy she was.

Starting the fire in the bedroom Jeanie pulled the two small arm chairs together and as she curled her feet up underneath her Jeanie and James sat and talked. After a while Jeanie rested her head on the wing of the chair, leaning over he took her cup "Come on bed….you need your rest…" Jeanie didn't need any persuasion the excitement of the day had worn her out.

"James I have nothing to wear for bed."

"And that's a problem because…"

"You know what I mean." Jeanie shook her head not minding James response and enjoying his company was something she missed.

"I've found this in one of the boxes in the spare room….." James held up an embroidered crisp white night dress, "I think it's a bit old but….. Better than nothing…."

Taking the dress she disappeared into the bathroom, looking at herself in the mirror Jeanie sighed as the nighty looked hideous.

Shutting down the light and closing the door James was already in bed, "Jean I forgot to close the other curtain." As she stretched over the window seat the moonlight streamed down over her and as the clear light glimmered through the dress it silhouetted every curve. The dark areola of her breast emphasised by the white material outlined Jeanie's elegant figure.

James couldn't help but stare as a few weeks before she was dying in a hospital bed and seeing her as his wife for the first time after that experience made him realise how lucky he was to have her back in his life.

Sliding between the sheets Jeanie rested her head on the pillow, taking hold of James's hand; she pulled it close to her chest

"You surprised me today thank you..." James moved her hair away and ran his other hand down her face and neck, "All...all I want to do is make you happy."

Tightly wrapping her up in his arms she felt his breath on her back and as he kissed her at the side of her ear and again on her neck tingles started to appear again. Feeling the warmth and comfort of his embrace Jeanie fell fast asleep.

Seeing how tranquil and peaceful she looked he slid his hand over her stomach, "I love you more than you know."

Jeanie awoke to James's head on her shoulder and his arm draped across her stomach. Seeing daylight she couldn't wait to see the outside of the house and the new surroundings. Sneaking out of bed Jeanie opened the curtains trying to take a glimpse at where she was.

Noticing she was missing he sat up and rubbed his eyes,

"Jea I really love you in that nighty and the dreams it's given me are the best I have had in years."

Wondering what he was talking about Jeanie looked down seeing her own naked silhouette. Grabbing James's jacket off the back of the chair her cheeks flushed with embarrassment.

"Why didn't you say something last night?"

"Why would I have wanted too...?" Picking up a robe he placed it around her dressing her with it. Jeanie could see he was watching every movement,

"I think I can dress myself by now" fastening the belt he pulled her forward and kissed her on the forehead, "Time for breakfast Mrs Watson…"

The normality of breakfast amused Jeanie as she had missed so much of the morning routine she had forgot that normal people started the day with food and not engine oil.

The enjoyment she took of just running a bath and being engulfed by sunlight pleased James. She had been through so much it was time to get simplistic.

Jeanie routed around in the spare room boxes hoping to find something to wear. The only thing that cropped up was an old flowered dress which was several sizes too big appeared but it seemed to be the only thing that fit the bill. Looking inside the big wardrobe Jeanie found a green cardigan and graced James's presence waiting for his reaction.

James who was trying to wait patiently had his arms folded as she entered the kitchen, "So what do you think…?" James laughed out loud and covered his mouth, "Beautiful as always…"
"You're not a convincing liar Mr Watson and I haven't found a coat…." James took off his jacket and passed it over.
"Your boots are at the door take this…"

Strolling out of the house arm in arm anyone passing by would never have known the trials and tribulations of the past few months. Jeanie seemed to glow and she shone in the daylight.

Walking out of the cottage led them straight to the wood and a small path had been chiselled out in the undergrowth.

Hearing a gun shot Jeanie froze, "James……" holding onto her tightly he could feel her tremble from head to foot and her heartbeat pounded in her chest. "Jea its ok I'm here." Placing his hand on top of her head he looked around to see where the shot had come from.

From the distance James heard a voice, "Mr Watson. Mr Watson……." As the man descended down the hill Jeanie still clung onto James "I'm really sorry my wife has only just told me and its rabbit's we're after. I'm so sorry Miss I really didn't mean to scare you."

Jeanie looked up at James still trembling she turned around and faced the man, "Jeanie this is Mr George Partridge they are good friends of the family and they are the people I bought the house off. Are you ok?" James shook the gentleman's hand and pulled Jeanie close. The sound of the shot had brought back the feelings of Signthorpe and the reality was he was with her whether she liked it or not.

"Just made me jump a little." George taking off his cloth cap held it to his chest, "I'm sorry I didn't realise you'd moved in or I would have let you know about the shoot this morning." Jeanie who was now facing him clasped her hand over his.

"It's ok. It's me loud noises make me jump..." George laughed and placed his hand over the top of hers, "As long as there is no harm done…James nice to see you settled down it was about time if you don't mind me saying you seem to have done very well she's a beautiful young lady."

Jeanie blushed and stood close to James and as they waved away the now pleasantries Jeanie sighed heavily.

"Jea let me have a look at you. You've gone very pale. Are you in pain anywhere?" Jeanie shook her head still trying to get herself together. Walking towards the end of the path Jeanie's silence worried him stopping he lifted her hands to his chest, "Talk to me."

"It …..It just brought everything back. I'm ok please don't worry. I was enjoying our time so much just give me a minute…."

Grabbing hold of her hand he pulled her down the hill and as they raced Jeanie's cheeks soon turned pink again.
"Come on I know what will get you sorted..."
Never leaving go of James hand they reached the bottom of the divot and as they walked across and old wooden bridge Jeanie strolled looking up to James contemplating there future.

Jeanie completely unaware didn't care where they where going but before reaching the end of the path he put his hands over her eyes
"What are you doing? James come on. I can't see"
Jeanie light-heartedly played along with his game,
"No peeking cause I want you to take this in at first glance ready....go"
As he moved away his hands the visions of the lake came flooding into focus. The hills rolling in the back white with frost looked as if the belonged in a fairy tale and as the calm still waters glistened and rippled in the breeze, the clouds in the sky looked like a perfect mirror reflecting back to heaven.
"I'm in Bassenthwaite. You brought me to Bassenthwaite......" Overwhelmed Jeanie hugged James tightly.

Making her way through the pebbles that scattered along the shore edge Jeanie took off her boots and socks.
"What are you doing it's freezing." Jeanie danced in the icy waters seemingly with no worries no cares. James picked her up from behind and swung her around in the waters. Their laughs and cries echoed around the still crisp lake.
"It's so beautiful and still here shame my feet are so cold." Picking her up he held her close and as she tiptoed from the waters edge her smile said everything. Jeanie was finally falling in love.

Making there way back to house no one could have separated them. The small touches, the glances and the laughter couldn't help but let him know how perfect it all felt.

"I've enjoyed today in fact I have loved today it's been a long time since I have felt like this."

"You need food come on." opening the latch Jeanie noticed a box, "What's that?" Opening it slightly she notice a rabbit, a few carrots and a couple of potatoes where inside.

"James there's a note, look" Picking it up out of the back of the box Jeanie read it out loud.

"To Doc, Sorry about before. Here's a little wedding present on us.
Mildred & George Partridge."

"Ok doc you on the bunny me on the other stuff... Stew tonight."

Standing at the kitchen sink James brought in the newly butchered bunny. Jeanie looked at the pieces and felt hungry for the first time in months, "You wash up and I'll have a go at playing wife for a change." Sliding his hands around her waist James kissed the back of her neck.

"I could get used to this Mrs Watson."

"I'm never going to get anything done if you carry on."

"Well I'm starving so you better crack on fast then." Feeling him let go of her waist Jeanie radiated happiness from every fibre

While dinner cooked Jeanie wondered around the living room. Everything was so neatly placed and organised just in the way she liked. The book case in the corner intrigued her the most and the old leather backed books tired and dusty cried out in desperation to be read.

Sitting on the settee in front of the fire she placed the old book on her knee. Hearing James's awful singing from the bathroom she realised that this is what she had been waiting for. This was normality.

James appeared with two bowls of the rabbit stew and sat beside her on the floor, "Shouldn't we use the table?"

"You seem comfortable why spoil it…eat."

Jeanie sat and read the book and as he listened attentively she stroked her fingers through his hair. As the pages turned and her words echoed out the whole routine slotted into place.

As James closed the house up for the night Jeanie had already crawled under the covers and this time getting to James close the curtains.

"Do you remember when we first met?" Jeanie nodded still lost in his stare listened attentively, "We talked about everything even my holidays as a child. I used to come to this cottage with my aunt. Do you remember? I told you about getting caught with no clothes on in the lake by Mildred. The more we talked the more you made me realise just how arrogant I was."

Jeanie brushed her hands through his hair, "I never thought you where just strong willed. You didn't have a clue about people. Oh you knew how they worked just not as people. We were the best of friends really. You know I did miss you a lot after you left."

"I'm glad we still are Jea before I left you told me about Bassenthwaite. Yow you used to take trips here as a kid and you told me your dreams of owning a cottage down here had gone because of your father's death.

I bought this place because it was your dream. My dream was you it's always been you and I brought you here for you to fall in love with me." Tears dripped down off her cheek onto the bed linen, "Do you not think I love you."

"I knew you loved me. I just wasn't certain of how deep that ran."

"I have never been this in love before and it's not because of the house…It's because of you."

Knowing she felt the same lifted a weight off his mind, no matter what happened she belonged to him and him to her.

"James I want to talk about something with you." Jeanie's concern made her body rigid and cold.

"What was he like? I mean I spent all that time not ever seeing him. I've been to the graveside and I've took flowers I.I just wondered what he was like." James kissed her softly stroking the hair away from her face."

"How long have you held that in for?"

"Honestly since you took me to see him before I came home from hospital."

"Don't ever be frightened of mentioning him. I mean that. He was a part of us and he was our baby as much as he was John's." The sincerity in his voice made Jeanie realise how much guilt he had felt about that night

"I'm sorry for everything I did that night and even now I feel like I could have stopped it from happening."

"You couldn't have done anything James. I've seen the folder remember. That day in hospital I realised this had been planned and if it wasn't that night it would have been some other time. I'm alive because of you and all these silvery lines on my body are where you fought for me and won.

I just never got to see him and I keep imagining what he looked like but I can't." A stray tear left James's eyes and as he breathed in deep he smiled at his beautifully courageous wife.

"He was just like you. He was absolutely perfect Jeanie. His crystal blue eyes just sparkled. He had John's strawberry blonde though." Choking slightly

James had to pull back the tears as every description only seemed to clip at his guilt.

"Jeanie he was sure pure and beautiful and if I'd have known how perfect he was I would have never, never made you feel the way I did. I'm so sorry I-I'm so so sorry. I wish I could have done more."

"Thank you. Please don't. I just needed to know and I know you fought for him as much as you fought for me and that's all I need."

Jeanie lay in his arms surrounded by the comfort of his embrace. James could feel her heartbeat fast and what seemed like hours passed in silence between them.

"I have a confession." James looked puzzled.

"Go on I'm intrigued to know…"

"I love you hands every time I imagine us together it's your hands that." Playing on her thought James ran his hand over her stomach, kissing her Jeanie closed her eyes.

"It's your hands that excite me. I just love the way you touch me."

Kissing her softly again, he leaned his head on his elbow and moved her hair away from her brow.

"I've been dreaming about you. I dreamt about how we would be when you come home from hospital and what I would say and do in fact everything I do with you starts as a dream. The reality is I thought I would loose you and I thought I would never be able to tell you I'm sorry. I used to sit beside you in that god awful room counting the hours until you wake up. Hating me for what I did. I would write speeches over and over in my head thinking of ways I could tell you I was wrong and how much I wanted you and our baby with me.

I used to think that you would be better off without me as I've brought you nothing but pain. The amount of times I repeated over and over what I would do better. But I always came to the same conclusion you are my life and my life is only better because of you. I learned the meaning of I'm sorry," "James please..." Placing his fingers on her lips he stroked the outline. As her tears stained her cheeks he could help but kiss her eye lids and wish he could take away the pain.

"Before I met you I had the inability to say sorry your mum. Jesus Christ your mum said something to me that night which I will never forget. She said half of the baby is part of Jeanie and no matter how hard you try that's the piece that you will love.

I wasted all our time on my own selfish inability and childish insecurity on John when I should have concentrated on loving you holding you. Making you happy and then a man tried to rape and kill you and it took that from me. It took everything from me and in that moment I had wronged you. That's my guilt that's why I need you to see how much I really love and will never hurt you again and I'll give my whole life to you just to make you understand….."
"I don't want you to be guilty you had every right to feel confused and upset I was carrying John's baby."
"No Jeanie our baby. He was all ours."
"Mum must have told you then. I wasn't my dad's daughter not in the biological sense. To be fair it made me realise how much I resented mum for cheating on him. I blamed her for years. I guess I found out the hard way. Loving someone and carrying someone else's child I fell into being my mum.

It made me realise how dirty and disgusting the whole affair is and you weren't selfish you where confused and upset and I wanted you to love me regardless. I understand that now. Funny how things change when everything you've been planning for gets suddenly ripped out from underneath you. Makes wishing so difficult.

You make me feel free you make me feel like I can spread my wings and be the person I really want to be. I just don't want you to feel guilty anymore. All of us including John have lost something so wonderful and special but I don't blame you. I love you James"

Stroking the scar on her shoulder he watched the peaceful tranquillity of her slumber. It made him almost feel invincible, he had repaired her body and she had repaired his mind. Feeling every breath he couldn't help but feel complete.

Chapter 21

The sun streamed through the window making shadows of them on the wall and as he lay stroking her neck he thought last night was a dream.
"If you want me to keep falling for you I suggest you get the fire started, its bloody freezing in here."

James jumped out of bed and grimaced with the cold as he looked out of the window snow had fallen overnight. Jeanie had wrapped herself tight within the blanket pausing in wonder why he was taking so long. "Jea do you fancy a snowball fight."
"It's snowed really." Frantically trying to find clothes and boots the pair looked like children fighting over presents at Christmas. The thought of snow made them return to adolescence.

Between the snowball fights and snowmen, Jeanie collapsed in a heap on the floor, "I forgot how much fun this was James." As he dropped at the side of her he was worn out by the all the fun.
"I'm here what's up?"
"Are you cold?"
"No but your shivering come on..." Lifting her up with a jolt the pair raced back into the house the same way they had raced out.

Standing in the bedroom James lit the fire. Jeanie fought with soggy snow soaked clothes stood in front of him and wrestled desperately with them to be free.
"I see the nighty's back." Jeanie shivered her lips were blue and her hair damp from snowballs.
Pulling her into his smooth skin he could feel the cold penetrating her body. "Jeanie this nighty is wet through its going to have to come off."

Closing her eye's James undressed hair and with her eyes still closed she tried to hide her body. The lines and scars ran like a map from one side to the other and Jeanie had never felt this self conscious with James. "Jea its ok you can open your eyes please don't feel bad." Jeanie opened one eye as he wrapped a blanket around both of them.

"I know you've seen me a thousand times it's just different now. I'm different now and I don't look the same and it scares me. It scares me to think you won't find me attractive anymore." Feeling her body on his skin he couldn't help think she was further from the truth. This break had been about finding each other again and as much as he wanted to keep sex out of the question being with her just made him want her more.

"How could I not be attracted to you I love you. From the moment you put on that see through night dress to standing in front of me in the most hideous flowered dress I've ever seen your one of the most intelligent, captivating, women I have ever met and I love you desperately for it." Jeanie stood on her tiptoes and kissed his cheek.

"Thank you maybe I just needed reassurance." As the fire roared James pulled the blanket off the bed," Sit down here I need to keep you warm." Jeanie shuffled to the fire place, curling up she lay in front of the hearth.

The warmth of the fire pierced the blanket and sank into her skin. James lay next to her worried she had done too much too soon. As the heat raised the folds of blanket opened up to display the soft curve of her breast, turning to face the fire her exposed shoulder sparkled in front of the flames

"Surprising that just looking into the fire makes you feel warmer," kissing her shoulder he folded himself around her and as she moved the blanket fell further. Her outstretched arm caressed the pillow he knew he was completely under her spell.

"Why are you looking at me like that?"

"Like what?"

"Like you want to say something." Jeanie bit her lip expectantly waiting for his answer. He couldn't put the words together as everything about her excited him. James smiled painfully as he was fighting a loosing battle to keep control. His body wanted her desperately and the electric shivers kept pulsating through every muscle. She lay glowing under the heat of the fire in pure radiance and his body was betraying him at every course.

"James I really want you to do something but I'm scared I'm scared because of what's happened between us that you might not want to." James stroked her back and neck line trying to keep himself composed. "Anything I would do anything for you."

"Touch me" her viscid whispers tore apart his restraint. Teasing the blanket the curve of her hip became exposed in the firelight and the warmth of his skin penetrated every curve of her body.

"Jea I want this I really do. I'm just not sure if you're not ready yet."

His soft hands still stroked the silver lines of her scars with every touch wanting more.

"I just want to close my eyes and feel you again. Instead of my dreams being haunted by monsters I just want to feel how you love me cause in all this I forgot. I forgot how it felt to be happy after being such a disappointment." James's finger stoked the line of her collar bone pulling the blanket around her he turned her towards him

"I thought I lost you and not because of Signthorpe. I pushed you back to John that was all my doing. We've both made mistakes, but my mistake was letting you go the first time and I not willing to loose you again. You're my wife for better of worse. I love you Jeanie….and touching you only makes me want you more. " James played with the blanket unable to look at her. Jeanie lifted his head

228

feeling his pain and discomfort. Kissing both palms he seemed lost in his remorse. "You've never been a disappointment you need to know that and believe it."

As he held her she felt his tears roll down her skin and as she held him tight she couldn't distinguish where she ended and he began.

As she leant back he kissed her passionately, her soft lips teased him into her more and as he lay her down in front of the fire the intensity built with every movement.

The touch of her hands down his spine sent shock waves through every muscle and as he caught his breath he lowered himself into her. Both could feel each other's heart pound and as Jeanie laid her hand on his chest, James couldn't help but do the same. Holding her in his arms, he trembled at the ecstasy of being united with her. Every sensation penetrated a new place where she had never been. Nothing had ever felt like her and nothing had felt as close. As she cried out into the dark he couldn't help but follow no words where needed and his plan had worked, the only difference being he'd fallen deeper.

Jeanie stood at the bathroom mirror and looked at her scars. Closing her eyes she breathed deep she had never wanted to be so loved and the door opened James stood in front of her

"Are you ok I was worried it…" He looked at floor as if the sentence was stuck. "Stop everything is ok I promise." Standing at the window he watched as the sun faded over the wood.

"I haven't got long left when I go back that's my time up. France was bad enough the first time. I don't think I told you how I got the scar on my back but France was bad enough,"

"What happened? It's ok if you don't want to tell me…" without him saying a word she felt his pain.

"? James look at me, " as he stood tall Jeanie wiped away his tears, "I love you and no amount of distance will ever take away these last four days I want you to promise you will come back to me. I want you to promise that no matter what you will come home to me."

"I'm going to find it hard to walk away from you…"

That night the book was left on the table. Sitting together Jeanie couldn't help but wrap her body around him and his around hers and as he stroked her face no words could describe how much love he had inside for her.

Four days James had to make Jeanie fall in love with him, every breath she took he exhaled, every tear she shed he would feel. This plan was for her, not realising the effect it would have on him.

No words had been spoken as they arrived at the base, Jeanie knew this would be the last time they would meet until his return and gulping at every breath she held him tight.

"Come home to me I love you too much now to let you go." James held onto her firm but he knew his time was up.

"Jea I thought I knew it all but I knew nothing till I met you. I will never stop loving you your every breath I take me love you so much…"

As the gates opened James grabbed his bag. Jeanie wiped away both of their tears and watching him disappear into the distance the thought of never seeing him again made her sick.

Closing her eye's she could still feel him, his heart beat, his warmth and his hands, getting back into the car she clenched her fists. How much more could this war take away from her.

Chapter 22

Dear Jeanie, 20/11/1943

I've arrived. I sat and thought for ours how to start
this letter, what to say and how to put my feelings
into pages of words, but I could only think of
wishes. I wish we had more time together; I wish I
was at home with you reading to me by the fire, I
wish I could take you to our bed and make love to
you. Then it hits me and I'm back from fantasy.

Reality is there is no time to settle, we are
constantly on the move and everywhere is covered
in undergrowth. The trees touch the sky and I wish I
could tell you it was beautiful and green but I can't
and again I'm straight back to wishing.

Maybe I should tell you that the rain hasn't
stopped for over a fortnight and the weight of the
water bears down heavy on you. There are some
good men here, I can't remember if I told you I had
served before?

The lack of sleep sometimes feels like torture but
when I do dream I dream of you. I always imagine
you in your father's workshop with your old
dungarees and big jumper just sitting and talking for
hours. I look in amazement as you throw together a
bit of wood for a chair and how you mould the most
beautiful things with your hands.

I don't think I have ever told you how proud you
make me feel to be your husband you're so talented.
Thinking about your hands makes me smile. I think
about how you stroke them through my hair when
you're reading and I could watch you work all day
long. I suppose I need to confess that I love your
hands in the same way.

Thinking of you makes me miss home, I often
dream of the cottage and our days there its odd

because I think of it of home and we have spent so little time there. I think of our first night and that old white night dress. As I am confessing I should tell you it has given me more pleasure than you would care to know.

Recently my dreams haven't been so comforting. Last nights dream was different I dreamt that you where stood waiting for me at the door but when I looked again you where waving goodbye and crying. It's only at that point I wake up. It scares me to think I may never see you again.

Waking up here gets harder day by day and it's hard to think about the future not knowing what's going to happen is exhausting. That's when I think about you, about us and all the stages we've yet to experience. I don't want to upset you and I know we've already lost one, but I would love to have children. I could have a son who would follow in my footsteps and be a doctor. He might follow his mum into engineering, that's if we have a son. We could have a daughter.

I know it seems presumptuous but I love the thought of spending my years getting to know you. You're the first and last thing I think about and the only thing that's getting me through. The comfort of knowing that I have a future with you makes me feel at peace. I love you Jeanie, more than I could ever show you.

Forever Yours

James

Dear James,   03/01/1944

 I too have been dreaming about our future and as a
result I have started packing a few boxes to move
out to the cottage. I can't tell you how excited I am I
just wish you where here to share it with me. Mum
came with me yesterday and I couldn't wait to show
her and for the first time she was speechless. She
loves the cottage. I didn't think her approval would
make it more real but it did.

 I'm eating more I don't know why I need to tell
you it just feels like it's something you would like
to know. Mum said she can't fill me and she thinks
I've put some weight on which is good.

 I have also been talking to your dad more and we
are planning a visit to Somerset when you get back.
I would love to see where you grew up. It's been
lovely having all of them around me in our home, I
even going to admit to singing in the bathroom,
badly I have to say but that's all because of you.

 I know I'm babbling inconsistently but I feel like
there's so much to tell you.
Is it wrong that I miss work? I have this
overwhelming urge to pick up tools and potter
around with our neighbour's motorcycle. I can hear
George insistently tinkering and it is starting to
drive me insane, I think I have finally lost the plot.

 I dream about the workshop. The fondness I feel
for Mike and the others floods through my dreams
and I just have the need to go back. I also miss Eric
I haven't seen him in such a long time surprisingly I
miss his constant bellowing and making young
woman cry maybe it is a sign I'm getting better.

 I decided after all this contemplation that I need a
project and I have started cleaning out the box room
at the back of the kitchen. The window looks across
the vegetable patch and the sun hits it beautifully in

the evening. It's a very peaceful room. Maybe even a nursery someday?

Changing the subject I can almost hear you telling me I should be relaxing and taking it easy but I am so board. I have invited Ivy and Jayne to stay with me. More people and noise keeps me occupied.

You need to see how big Jayne has got, she's so beautiful and the spitting image of her mother. The house just feels so alive with them here but I still wish you where here beside me.

I sat and read Jayne Eyre again last night reading it reminded me of you. It reminded me how I stroked your hair in front of the fire place and tried to put on a man's voice to play Edward Rochester. Jayne's character always intrigued me, with everything she went though she played her role so well always together and assured, it's only love that make's her courageous. Maybe that's what you have done for me?

I shouldn't keep telling you how much I miss you and how I have read you letter again and again imagining you here with me. I will always be here waiting for you please be safe and come home to me. I have so much I want to tell you...

Please don't give up I need you to come home so we can be a family. I don't know what I do if I lost you now.

Keep your chin up and remember I love you.

Yours always Jeanie

It feels a lifetime ago since I heard your voice and every time I receive any correspondence from you it makes my heart skip a beat. I just want you to know I'm ok I can't say I'm on top form but ok rounds things up.

The smell of your letter reminds me of your hair and the soft scent of lavender brings me back home to you. I have to say I don't mind your letters babbling, it makes me feel excited about our future.

I'm glad your mum approves, my only wish is that one day I can share all these moments with you.

I can't believe how well Dad has taken to you? He's usually the most difficult man to fathom out. I am going to admit that they did have reservations about me marrying you but I know my mum adores you now. She tells me in her letters how strong, kind and brave you are and that you could teach me a thing or too about family values. As much as I hate to admit I'm wrong I know she's right.

I have never met anyone who makes me feel at ease the way you do. You know me so well and don't mind my indiscretions and correct my selfishness without me realising. Lets face it I have said before I wouldn't be the doctor I am today if it wasn't for you.

Don't feel bad about work as you have gone from being out and about for twelve hours a day to being at home and resting. Emphasis on rest! I can imagine the cottage is driving you crazy and even though you know I would like you to relax I know you. If it makes you feel better pick up a spanner and help George out just remember to take it easy afterwards.

The box room project sounds interesting. Just don't do too much however a nursery sounds like a wonderful idea but that's something we will work on when I'm home.

I can never get tired of reading how much you miss me, or how much your thinking about me it makes me feel secure. I often think about how things would have been if I had told you I loved you before your father's funeral, as much as you are mine now the pain of what you have suffered would have never have happened if I had been courageous enough to stay. The guilt tears at me and I know these are just what ifs but I still feel the pain of nearly loosing you and our son.

Don't think ill of me but I often think about our reunion too. Being here has made me realise how special you are and it's made me realise how important your touch and love is and how you make me a better man. Your strength and independence make me understand that if anything did happen to me you would survive.

Jayne Eyre has nothing on. She could never have survived what you've been through, and your strength is amazing. It's one of the qualities I fell deeply in love with. And writing this letter I know you will disagree with me, but your humility is something I could never match. I love you Jeanie and I always will.

You're my star, my light and my guide.

Yours Forever James x

I'm wondering where you are as it feels like you have been away for a lifetime and the nights are so lonely without you. I wish this war would end for you to come home. Everything I hear on the wireless makes me numb and just thinking of you surrounded by chaos is too much to bear.

The factory has been overrun with army personnel and mum has been loosing her mind coping with the extra pressure. I've started back at the factory, I didn't know whether to tell you but she needed help. I feel more isolated here. At least while I was at the cottage you were with me.

I'm glad I'm occupied though and things have been in such a mess. If I had stayed away any longer Dad would have killed me!

I remember everything about the first night we spent together everything drifts back so clearly. The tentative look, the way you took my hand, the feel of your hands across my back. Parts of it just don't seem real. I jumped in with two feet not even knowing you. I'm glad I did. Looking back now I feel now everything has to happen for a reason. Maybe you're my reason.

I wasn't living before I met you, I existed and meeting you again made my heart skip a beat. I didn't want to admit it Doctor but you where the first and last chance I took. Everything before wasn't life and I was just kidding myself to make me feel better.

I'm sat on the roof of the tree house writing you this letter. There are millions of stars, and for the past half an hour I have stared up and started talking to one of them. Maybe I'm loosing my mind but it makes me feel like you can hear me, after all it's the same sky.

I feel like your closer to me and while you read this if you look up at those stars and do the same they could act as our own personal messengers. A romantic gesture but it's so hard. I hate not being able to see or talk to you and it's starting to hurt to miss you this much. On a different not my mother would kill me if she finds me here she keeps going on about my condition. I'm sure she thinks you have only put a plug in these holes as she is treating me like a leaky tap ready to explode

Changing to subject John came over to the house yesterday, I don't think he knew I was there but I heard raised voices and when I walked into the hall, Ivy and John where deep in argument. The last thing I heard was, "Don't you think you should have told me sooner, this is not about you it's about Jeanie." It seemed such an odd comment Ivy was in tears and when I confronted her she quickly dried her face and left. It just seemed strange.

I know why you took me to the cottage, and I know some of it was because of John. I'm not stupid you needed me to be totally head over heels for you before you disappeared for good. See there was one problem with your plan. I already was. John's part of a past that I'm going to be unable to forget. But he will never be a part of our future, and as I still stare at these stars, I'll count the days till you return.

You're my friend, my love and my life. I love you.
Forever yours
Jeanie xx

Jeanie pulled back the curtains at the cottage and started to dust around the kitchen surfaces. The damp cold kitchen breathed as Jeanie wiped life back into the room.

Letters from James had dried up and deep inside Jeanie had started to feel like she was loosing him.

"Shit…" Ivy bundled herself through the back door and as Jeanie turned she could see her sucking her thumb.

"Paper cut these darn things hurt more than slicing your finger off!"

Jeanie leant on the kitchen sink and watched the birds outside the window. This was the first time she had been home in two months and knowing it was only for a few days made her feel worse.

"Are you seeing John? I've often wondered what he meant that day in the parlour." Ivy fumbled and clasped her hands together; Jeanie could see her knuckles white as she clenched them together.

"What kind of a question is that?" Hurriedly Ivy started to clear the clutter off the kitchen table avoiding eye contact with her sister, hurrying Jayne into the living room Jeanie followed with more suspicions about her sister's movements.

"You seem distracted"

"Don't do this, he's just trying to get to you and he's being horrible to me instead. I'm just trying to protect your feelings, you've been through enough." Ivy wiped her hair away from her brow with her hand and as she hastily fluffed cushions Jeanie couldn't comprehend her answer.

"I don't understand why he would want to. He knows there's no going back and it doesn't make sense." Walking closer to her sister she placed her hand on top of the cushions that Ivy was so violently fluffing.

"Ivy I don't need protecting. He needs help and support but I just don't want him spoiling anything else in our lives."

Ivy squoze Jeanie's hand and smiled uneasily. Jeanie felt Ivy needed to talk more but seeing how uneasy the conversation had made she didn't push it any further. The last thing she needed was an argument spoiling the only time she had at home. "I'll start the stove and get a fire going." pulling her coat around her she went outside to collect some logs. The unease in Ivy's response intrigued Jeanie further and more than anything she felt Ivy knew more than she was letting on. Regardless Jeanie felt she had to know.

The living room looked as if life had never disappeared and even though the curtains where closed the room felt more alive as the flames danced around the mantel.

Ivy had settled Jayne down and Jeanie watched from the settee. Part intrigued to her behaviour and trying to mask her feelings Jeanie buried her head in her book.

Ivy sat on the floor next to Jayne stroking her hair. "What is there to do tomorrow?"
"All I can see is cobwebs so it looks like getting rid of them might be a start, I don't know lets see what it looks like in the morning, "
"I'm sorry, I shouldn't wrap you up as well, and I know you don't need it. Maybe we should talk after breakfast." With that Ivy scooped Jayne into her arms, "Night Jea Love you."

The uneasy feeling in Jeanie's stomach returned knowing something was going to happen, but not knowing till morning wasn't going to sedate her into a goodnights sleep.

The sun peered through the curtains in Jeanie's bedroom and as the rays illuminated the room with an orange glow Jeanie was already sat upright and counting down the minutes to when she could confront her sister. The suspense of not knowing what was wrong was too intense to bear.

Hearing stirrings from the corridor Jeanie opened the door and made her way to the kitchen. Jayne was sat on the kitchen floor playing with a wooden duck looking the picture of innocence.

"Auntie Jea is going to put the kettle on. Let's see if mummy is going to tell me what's going on." Jeanie paced whilst the kettle simmered and as it started to scream, Ivy poked her head around the corner.

"I'm just getting dressed," she yawned, "pour us one out..."

Peering out of the window Jeanie noticed a car moving into place at the bottom of the path. Looking outward the distinct colourings of the vehicle immediately made her heart sink,

"Jea what's up...?" peering over her sister's shoulder she noticed the base car pulling up on the farm track outside the back of the cottage.

"Jea it might not be what you think."

The panic could be heard in her voice and Jeanie knew this time there was no escaping from it. Throwing the tea pot into the sink she stood at the side of the stove in silence. Jeanie stood stern as the knock came to the door.

"Open it." Ivy looked for reassurance but Jeanie was severe, cold there didn't seem to be an emotion that would justify her look. As the gentleman walked into the room, Jeanie raised her head to greet him.

"Ivy Jeanie Ivy I need to talk to Jea."

"She can stay John get on with it." Jeanie glared heavily knowing there was only one reason John would make the trip. Angered by his presence she anticipated his words.

"Jeanie I'm sorry to have to say this but we have received communication that James is missing in action. I'm sorry to say presumed dead. I have the telegram here but I thought it would be better for me to deliver it." Jeanie stood unyielding with no reaction and her glare intensifying.

"You mean you thought you would drive up here and gloat." Jeanie spat her words out. John shocked at her reaction, didn't know what to do. He had expected her to fall to pieces and as she stood firm he seemed unsure how to continue.

"That wasn't my intension Jeanie I thought..."

"You never think John. The only thing you think about is what's best for you. What did you think I would do break down throw myself back into your bed so you could comfort me in my hour of need...." John stood tall placing his cap underneath his arm and stepping back into the doorway he felt the tension and tried to deflate her anger.

"You know that wasn't my intension Jeanie we've been through so much doesn't that count for anything..." Jeanie turned around to the stove; swallowing deep she took another huge breath adamant she wasn't going to cry and adamant that John would never manipulate the situation.

"The only thing that has ever counted was the baby we made and he's gone. But as for anything else no it never did." John replaced his cap knowing she was upset he tried to understand.

"You don't mean that I know you don't and I know you still feel for me Jeanie. I came up here to help because I appreciated what you did for me with our son. I though a friendly face, hell familiarity would help. I know you're in shock but......" Jeanie walked towards him and without hesitation she slapped him hard across the face, John held his head to one side unable to look at her.

"You only came here for yourself. Leave the telegram on the table and get the fuck out of my house."

"I did everything to get back to you and when you where lay cold and dying in my arms Jeanie I knew I could never love someone as much as I love you. I knew I'd lost so I let you go and burying our son whilst you were still fighting for your life just made me understand how wrong I had been.

I thought I meant something to you. I thought with you helping and understanding how isolated I had become that we had made a new connection. I thought maybe this time it would be different.

James loves you I get that but just maybe we have both found substitutes Jeanie. Here is your telegram. Oh and just in case your wondering what I mean why you don't ask your sister."

John slammed the door disappointed that he had lost his temper and disappointed that any chance he had of cementing a reunion had frayed a little more.

As the door closed behind him, Ivy stood petrified as Jeanie's heavy glare waited on her.

"What does he mean Ivy?" Ivy shook from head to toe and as she pressed her lips together she tired to move. Jeanie shouted again forcing an answer.

"Tell me what he means."

"Give me a minute to get Jayne sorted Jea please..." Jeanie sat at the kitchen table fixated on the unopened telegram however with her anger seething she could help but be impatient.

"Ok Jea you should know, you need to know.....Eighteen months ago George received a letter from John stating he was home on leave and at that point. Jesus at that point I knew that John's marriage had broken down and he needed a place to stay for a little while.

I didn't want to tell you. I didn't know how to tell you but with everything that happened. John moved in and George said he needed to sort a few things out for his new base and I swear to you now I didn't know he was going to be stationed up here he said he couldn't wait to meet up with an old friend and he was looking forward to getting away from London." Jeanie clenched her fists, wondering where all this was going to lead. Ivy stood up and walked over to the kitchen sink still unable to look at Jeanie she placed both her hands on the basin. "George got his papers and off he goes back to war and in the meantime John is still at the house. One night he opens his case and there is a bottle of brandy in it. I don't know how to tell you this….John and I been intimate before. George knew and I said some things before he left that I have regretted ever since.

John said he- he said he had spoke to a solicitor and Olivia was going to cost him a small fortune. Something about a business deal or something that went wrong so we start to drink.

Anyway one turns into two. I can remember falling over in the kitchen and as he picks me up he kisses me then apologises but I didn't stop……I suppose I didn't want him to stop see he wanted you and I've always been your substitute. I wanted him so I kissed him back and before I knew it we where making love in the kitchen and before I knew it I was having an affair with my brother in law.

Every time John was on leave, he was with me…..anyway a couple of months went by and George returned home for a while with injury. I told George then I was pregnant. But I knew Jayne wasn't his….." Jeanie sat motionless, closing her eye's she anticipated Ivy's conclusion, confused as to why she needed to know.

"Jeanie I don't have to tell you that Jayne isn't George's daughter, she's John's, you know it but just listen to me I know he's been in love with you forever and I was foolish to think that he loved me.

He would call me Jeanie and I would ignore it and I know he used me and I let him. See you weren't the only one in love with the wrong man and I'm just as guilty as John in fact I'm no different, I married George because he reminded me of John, not because I loved him. I used his brother as a substitute because I was in love with him but I know better now. I pleaded with George to stay but secretly I was happy he was going.

See when John turned up again our relationship all started again and I didn't feel guilty until the telegram arrived."

"What about the conversation I over heard, what was that about?"

"He visited, because he wanted to talk to you. I told him to leave you alone, he said I was jealous, I told him he wasn't going to use me again to get to you. "

"Does John know Jayne is his?" Ivy shook her head. "I couldn't I felt so ashamed and before James you where so squeaky clean. No exploits no illicit affairs. Jeanie I love you but at one point I couldn't I just couldn't relate to you. You could have never understood." "You could have made me understand, and you could have made me see. Is that why you said take a chance at the hospital is that it...?" Jeanie shook from head to toe as the anger took hold of her body.

" Ivy for Christ sake ANSWER ME!! Is that why you said you're a good girl you wanted me to fall in love with James so then you would have John all to yourself."

"Jea no…..no I could ever compete with you. That was my fault not you. I didn't expect you to be nearly killed by a raging psychopath I- I don't know how far."

"I know what you wanted Ivy. I know exactly what you wanted you thought I had a fucking moral pedestal that I needed to be taken down from. You thought sleeping with James was your answer and John would come running back to you once……once I'd lost my virginity and I was no longer a conquest for John but it didn't work did it DID IT!!
This is fucking unbelievable my own sister you wanted this…..you wanted me to fail at all of it didn't you so you could say I told you so" Jeanie had started to breath deeper trying to keep her emotions under control. The betrayal inside felt too much to comprehend.
"You don't understand I didn't want you to nearly die! I just wanted you to feel like me…I don't know Jeanie it's poisonous what I wanted"
"All your advice all your promises it was all lies and you did it on purpose why would you do that? If you wanted him so badly why didn't you tell him? I don't love him, or want him he's nothing to me anymore, but you…." Jeanie clutched the telegram in her hand and gritted her teeth, "Maybe I would have been in this position anyway without you. My husband may be dead or dying and all you can think of is how to fuck John Stanton and how to screw me over in the process. I don't think I know you anymore…"
"It's not like that. I was wrong. Please Jeanie I don't understand. What are you going to do?" Jeanie threw the telegram at her feet and as all the hurt and the hate started to rise she felt the bile rise in her throat.
"I am going to find him this time without you or your advice…."
   Grabbing her coat she ran down the hallway trying to escape the chaos that sat in her kitchen. Laying her hand on the glass the fog surrounded her

fingers and as the heat of her anger still raced through her veins it moulded her fingers around the etching in the glass.

Slamming the door behind her Jeanie swallowed her tears unable to comprehend that she could have lost him.

The actions of her sister had left a bad taste but underneath she was more alone now than what she had ever been. Walking through the forest didn't ease the situation and just the thought that her own sister had conspired against her made her sickness return.

Confused and alone Jeanie sat on the bank of the river looking for inspiration. "You look lost my dear, "Dorothy Partridge stood at the side of Jeanie her stern gaze and plad suit propped up her head mistress features.

She was a very petite smart lady and Jeanie instantly fell in love with her when they met, "If you don't mind me saying, it looks like you have been given bad news." Holding out her hand Jeanie took it and gently arose, "I was miles away, yes…yes I suppose it's not the best news Dotty." Smiling she wrapped Jeanie's arms around hers," I guess cause we are British it's time for tea…come along."

Jeanie clasped her arm tightly trying to hold onto to anything that felt safe. Tea and sympathy was never Jeanie's forte but this time she needed the comfort.

"I'm sorry Dotty James….." Jeanie coughed and cleared her throat determined to keep her emotions in check, "….He's been lost presumed…..dead..."

Dorothy sat cosily at the small kitchen table with her head slight cocked to one side she continued the conversation as if Jeanie had never uttered any words.

"I knew James as a child, peculiar little boy obsessed with pulling things apart and putting them back together…..never really connected well with children, no surprise he became a doctor, so young lady how do you feel?"

Jeanie looked puzzled, Dorothy had always been a direct woman but this sudden change took her by surprise, "Dotty what has this got to do with him going missing. I don't understand?"

Dorothy picked up the pot swilled the leaves around and placed it back down on the mat. Jeanie watched thinking she was going to read her fortune but instead she continued her direct line of questioning.

"And what do you feel about the gram?"

"I don't believe it…it doesn't feel right and I know it sounds ridiculous, but I know he's still alive. It feels calculated planned I don't know I have recently gotten this feeling that other people are pulling the strings and I'm stuck playing along.

You're probably going to tell me I'm stupid for feeling this way and thousands of other women in my position are going through the same thing but it just doesn't feel right." Dorothy smiled walked around the table and picked up Jeanie's coat.

"Well you're a resourceful girl you will know what to do. The first thing you have to do is get yourself sorted oh and don't forget to write."

With that Jeanie stepped outside feeling more pushed then ushered out of the door. Dorothy stood at the window waving as if she had given her the piece of mind she needed.

Looking back Jeanie felt more bemused by the whole conversation and as she peered at the light from the lantern that graced Dotty's door she felt uneasy knowing Ivy would still be at the cottage.

Contemplating Dorothy's words she made her way down the steep hill, and back to the cottage.

Weaving around the path Jeanie's thoughts, where constantly of James but as she reached the front door reality of dealing with this situation crept slowly from behind.

Closing her eyes, everything Ivy said had fallen into place. Jealousy, betrayal and hurt all because of a man. Her sister was still in love with him even though he had treated both of them despicably. The only problem was Jeanie's connection to John was dead and Ivy's was a living breathing wonderful little girl.

Entering the house the glow of the fire in the living room warmed the hallway. Hearing the latch Ivy raced to the doorway
"You had me worried. Jeanie I'm so so sorry." Jeanie took off her coat and as she hung it on the peg she wavered on the hook for a few moments.

Knowing Ivy would need an answer she contemplated her next move. Jeanie could see that her sister had been crying. The puffy red circles around her eyes and the look on her face felt enough to prove to Jeanie that she had just made a wrong decision.
"I love you and I love Jayne, as much as I could ever love anyone. Whatever has been done or not done doesn't matter all that matter's to me. It's about getting James home and I still believe he is out there lost and he just needs to be found.

You need to tell John he has a daughter. It's only fair and I don't want to discuss it anymore tonight. I'm really tired and I'm going to bed and I think you need to do the same." Jeanie hugged Ivy tightly and as she squoze Ivy's hand she disappeared down the corridor. Ivy's echo's of goodnight rung through the cottage.

The feelings of emptiness arose in Jeanie's heart. She hadn't felt this alone for a long time previously just knowing her family was there for support made everything seem bearable. This time knowing Ivy had deceived her made her feel very isolated.

As she closed the door to the bedroom she leant on the back of it and as the darkness filled the space quickly and she felt the fear creeping up on her as if she was a character in a horror show.

Placing her head in her hands she wiped them down her face and across her mouth unable to shake off the claustrophobia. Switching on the small lamp Jeanie closed her eye's confirming her irrational fear. She wanted to scream and she wanted to hit something hard to make it feel as bad as she did.

Trying to push the feelings away Jeanie followed the stream of light through the slit in the curtains. As the moonlight dripped in she noticed and old friend glowing in the rays.
"How did you get here?" Running her fingers over the lip of the old garage table she pulled a file from the draw. The repair schedules and sign offs on completed vehicles glistened in the stream and on noticing a familiar signature she pulled at the paper wedged in at the bottom of the drawer.

It had been signed by John and the general and the crest on the front gave it away as official war office papers. Racing her eyes through the content one word struck her immediately.
Enlistment.

Delving further Jeanie realised she had officially enlisted Jeanie into the RAF as an engineer. Sitting down in the chair at the side of the window she placed the signed document back in the file.

Maybe keeping away from John wasn't the answer, maybe now she needed him more than ever.

Chapter 24

Morning broke and silence took over the cottage and as Jeanie threw the last remaining bits and pieces into the car the lack of sleep hadn't aided her mood.

Staring at the folder that lay on top of her hand made table confused everything more and the underlying feeling that something was wrong conflicted with the facts in front of her.

Running her fingers over the cover thoughts of James raced through her mind. Something was definitely pushing her to make a decision but whether it was right or not preoccupied her mind.

Jeanie couldn't help but feel conflicted about John and Ivy had increased her suspicions that something was definitely wrong. As the door flew open Ivy stood waiting for her reaction.

"You scared the living daylights out of me…"

"I've got Jayne in the car and the last bits you wanted are you ok?

"How did this table get here?"

"I brought it here why?" Puzzled Jeanie couldn't help but feel she wasn't telling her the whole truth.

"Are you sure your ok you just looked deep in thought."

"No just…just got lots going through my mind come on then…"

Without hesitation she picked up the folder and placed it under her arm. Ivy couldn't help but notice how serious Jeanie looked as every thought seemed play out on her face.

"What's the folder for?"

"Things from the garage." Ivy still insecure couldn't help but notice the way Jeanie clung tight to it. It was as if her whole life was dependent on the content.

Jeanie closed her eyes and swallowed deep again, she couldn't let the tears fall and Ivy could never understand. Stepping into the car Jeanie opened the glove box and placed the file carefully inside. Before she was able to close it Ivy grabbed her arm. "I know your up to something and I know your thinking about doing something and I'm scared Jeanie." Jeanie moved Ivy's hand away and slammed the glove compartment shut. Moving the car around Jeanie still couldn't answer her sisters concerns.

"There is something you're not telling me Ivy and I'm being pushed in a direction I don't know whether or not is right. I don't care whether you tell me or not but I will find out eventually. Right now I need to do what I feel is right."

No other conversation was started by either of them on the way home. Ivy knew how serious Jeanie was and she knew once her mind had been made up there was no going back.

Dropping Ivy and Jayne at home Jeanie was adamant she wasn't seeing the rest of her family until she found out the truth.

"What are you going to do Jea you don't have control of this."

"No I don't but as much as I would like to trust you I can't. I also don't think you fully understand what's going on. So whatever you think you are in control of. You are sadly mistaken."

"You can't fix everything Jeanie it's not your place. Dad always thought the same and you just the same." Jeanie gripped the steering wheel in anger and as her temper flared the rub of the leather could be heard through her finger tips.

"No but I can get to the truth."

Ivy's heart sank as she raced away knowing the façade she had been hiding under had now been split completely open. She also was left to tell her mum and sisters the news about James.

Before the door had shut screams of despair filled the corridor as the news of James's disappearance was announced Irene raced out frantically looking her daughter. Inside her heart welled with pain as she knew Jeanie was once again coated in grief.

Jeanie sat at the lay by near the barracks gate looking at the glove box. She could hear her heart beating faster and as she clenched her fingers around the wheel she noticed John's car pulling onto the base.

Crawling up the gate she wound down the window and smiled sweetly, "Hello gents...long time no see" Jeanie cautious wanting to keep the conversation light kept smiling, "Jea what the fuck. Why are you back?"
"Meeting with the boss man you know how it is." The private without questioning anymore opened the gates.

Waving politely to the private she rolled the car along the side of the main building. Jeanie watched John converse with his staff and enter into the building and knowing he would be going to his office first she didn't make a move until he had entered the building.

No one questioned her reasons for being their as after all she was one of them and she was on indefinite leave. Still expecting someone to ask Jeanie started to mumble over excuses just in case.

Standing on the main corridor Jeanie felt her heart beat faster the noise of her heartbeat deafening her thoughts. Looking up at the ceiling she hoped for inspiration and as she clenched the folder tightly under her arm she knew it was now or never.

Loitering around the typist pool Jeanie waited for her chance and on seeing John's receptionist distracted she took her opportunity and slid through the gap in the large oak doors.

"Ah Jeanie now what do I owe the pleasure...." Walking to the large winged chairs at the front of the fire place Jeanie sat nonchalantly crossing her legs. Undoing the top button of her jacket John looked on in satisfaction that she may have come to her senses.

She looked as if she had all the time in the world with her act elegant and her demeanour coy she had perfected the swan like affect.

"I need your help John and lets just say I'm not exactly ecstatic about having to come to you for it." John already had a scotch glass in his hand and as he sat with it at his desk he mauled with it as if he was a cat playing with a mouse.

"My help Jeanie in the last twenty four hours what has changed?" You said you despised me and I was a part of your life you are only too willing to forget you. So let me ask again. Why now do you need my help?"

"I want some answers and unfortunately there is only you that can give them to me."

"I have to say Jeanie you've always been a piece of work but on this one I have to say why don't you go fuck yourself and whilst you're at it get out of my office." Jeanie ignoring him walked over to the drinks stand and poured herself a scotch and on walking back she sat in chair opposite the fire. Taking her coat off completely she exposed the purposely low cut purple wrap dress and as she crossed her legs she stared into the fire.

"Can you remember when we where kids John and you used to tease me a lot telling me how fat and stupid I was. I thought you where horrible. Then we grew up a little bit more and stupidly in my teens I thought I fell in love with you."

"Is there a point you're going to make or am I just going to be insulted again." Jeanie leant forward removed his glass and took hold of his hand. "We used to be inseparable. You where so beautiful and I didn't want to ever think of my life without you. Only I found out the hard way and when I caught you with that girl my world fell in pieces. What I didn't realise until now was that I saw you fucking my sister Ivy.

She's infatuated with you and even now I couldn't see it. She has loved you for a life time and I know now that I got in the way.

Olivia was just as much a pawn in all this; you ended up cheating on her with your own brother's wife. You see John secrets are great when they are just secrets but when the truth is revealed it's hard to be happy with the results." John stood up and walked back to his desk, taking his jacket off he faced the window

"How do you know all that?"

"I talk to my family John and they love me very much, I also love them dearly and hate them being hurt. I'm not doing this to be cruel…but you forget I know you John Robert Stanton and nothing you do seem to escapes me."

John lowered his head, knowing that all his secrets and been laid bare. He had kept everything hidden but in the end maybe if she had known the truth the disdain of his actions may have been forgivable.

"What else do I need to know Jeanie more mistakes, more wrong moves, I think you probably have enough dirt on me now to justify why I'm so bad for you "

"I know you love me and no matter what you where my first love and I will always have a place in my heart for you."

"I'm sorry for treating you the way I did and I'm sorry for never giving you the credit you deserve. James is a very lucky man." Jeanie placed her hand on his cheeks wiping away a tear which had started to fall.

"You know John wonderful things happen from horrible mistakes."

"You think our night together was a horrible mistake?"

"We have never fully discussed that night have we." Sitting back on the chair Jeanie grabbed the glass and tipped back the scotch in one.

"I felt like a catastrophe. Two men that had entered my life had both made their way into other women's beds and I felt like it had something to do with me. You looked just as lonely as me and as you stood in that room I wanted you. Just like I've always wanted you. You whispered regret John. You whispered two words of regret that made me feel like we could have had something and I let you take me the way I had always imagined you taking me and for that night it was right. Olivia gave me the excuse to run and I did. Not because you weren't sincere I know that. I ran because what we have is poisonous and not healthy and we hurt everyone around us just to satisfy something we can never have. But I don't regret our son. Our son was perfect in every way even though I never got to see him. But that wasn't your only failing John as there is another Rutherford woman part of that network of mistakes."

"Ivy what does she have to do with Jea."

Contemplating her next words Jeanie knew from this point on there was no way back.

"You have a daughter John"

"Is this a sick joke Jeanie, because this is cruel, "

"John Jayne is your daughter, Ivy fell pregnant with her after your separation from Livy I'd liked to say she spared me the details but I know exactly where she was consummated." Unable to comprehend he paced the room feeling the intensity of her words.

 "I have a daughter you're absolutely one hundred percent sure, because I don't think I could bare to loose another child Jeanie……"

"She is yours definitely."

"There's something else isn't their. I know you and you didn't come here just to tell me this. Did you?" Jeanie knew not matter how much she had tried to hide her intentions John knew her too well for her to ever bluff her real reasons.

"No - No I didn't."

"You said you needed my help and I have a feeling I'm not going to like what I'm about to hear. Spill Jeanie," taking the folder out of her coat she placed it on the corner of the desk.

"Ok John you want to know what this is about then you need to tale a look in the folder." John hurriedly rustled through the documents and as he glared at the paperwork he couldn't understand how calm she was and the enormity of what she was asking was intolerable.

   Rustling his fingers through his hair he slammed the folder down hard on his desk.

"I don't need to tell you what it is, I can possibly tell by your reaction." Looking into the fire the scares on her neck quivered in the light; still angered he tried to be reasonable.

"You signed it....I enlisted you." Clutching the document a lump appeared in his throat and seeing his reaction made it difficult for Jeanie to keep control.

"You enlisted me into a unit that hasn't been deployed yet and underneath that roll of paper is my signature. There is something not right with this affair. I need to get to the bottom of it and if I ever want to find out it means that I have to go to war."

Slamming the paper down hard again John shook his head violently.

"Are you fucking out of your mind, you are in no fit state to go to fucking War and you are a woman, do you know what would happen Jeanie. I would be fucking court marshalled so the answer is no."

Jeanie knew the seriousness of her request and she needed John to understand that she wasn't going to give up.

"I know what would happen John but with or without you I'm going. So you either do it and help me or don't and risk it it's your choice."

"I have no fucking choice you mean. Why can't you be like every fucking other woman and know your place?" Jeanie stood toe to toe with John and on taking both of his hands she breathed deeply to calm herself, she hated having to use him, but on this occasion she felt she had no choice.

"I know you love me and I know you care for me and I know why you have always done that and it's because I've never been like anyone else. You also know that there is something going on here that doesn't feel or sit right with either of us and I need to see and find out for myself whether he is alive or not."

"Why do you do this? Why do you always give me fucking reasons to want to punch you really want to say no Jeanie. For the reasons that I don't think I could take you getting hurt again." John stood with his hands firmly placed on his hips. Thinking it through was never going to be an option and he also had the same uneasy feelings that something just wasn't right.

"When are you going to be ready?"

"Give me 5 months, I will be ready and I won't let you down." Picking up the file she made her way to the door.

"When can I see Jayne? Tell me again why should I do this Jeanie?"

"Ivy will be waiting for you and for the second part cause if you don't I'll always make you miserable." Running to the door John placed his hand on the handle over Jeanie's. "I can't guarantee he's alive Jeanie……I…I don't want you getting hurt when he might not be alive….Please Jeanie please think about what you're asking me to do?"

"I have…I have thought of nothing else…see you soon Sir."

Unable to let go he rested his temple against hers and closed his eyes. Feeling her soft lips on his he couldn't help but pull her close feeling overwhelmed by her touch. As he pushed his body against hers Jeanie hurried quickly out of his embrace and down the stair case.

Hearing her footsteps disappear he sat next to the fire he running both hands through his hair. Picking up her empty glass he placed it back in the cabinet, "That fucking girl never changes."

Reaching home Jeanie knew the wheels had been set and all she needed to do was make them turn. Walking through the door Jeanie saw her family had gathered in the parlour. Wandering into the kitchen, Ivy ran in behind and slammed the door.

"What did you do Jeanie and don't give me any crap you are up to something and I know this involved John." Jeanie laughed under her breath and placed her coat on the back of the chair.

"You know I went for a drive today to clear my head because as you know my husbands missing in action and all you can do is question me about John. You're not exactly being supportive Ivy are you?"

"I should have never fucking told you anything. You've always been a snivelling know it all half breed. You've told him haven't you you've told him about Jayne cause that wasn't your place Jeanie."

Irene over hearing the commotion had wandered in unable to understand both of her daughter's outbursts. "What the hell is this about?" Jeanie filled the kettle with water and placed it on the stove, pinching her lip with her fingers, she answered her sister. "Yes I have told him, "

"Why Jeanie....why did you do that."

"I needed an excuse to get him on side and Jayne had to be that excuse, he's over the moon and wants to see his daughter, but I had to use her in order to gain his trust and win him around to the idea of me being enlisted." Irene pulled the chair back and sat heavily down.

"You did what?"

"I know he's alive, and they cannot confirm that he's dead, so I'm going to find him as Private Jack Rutherford engineering division." Ivy still in tears pulled on her sister's arm, "How can you in your condition? How long have you told him?"

"Five months, I have five months to get into a good physical condition and my mind won't be changed. I have seen death once and James brought me back so it's my turn to do the same for him. None of you can speak a word of this. It could have John court marshalled and me sent to prison for a very long time. Do you understand?" The room rang with silence. The muffled sobs where stifled and Irene sat in complete bemusement at her daughters outburst.

As Jeanie got up from her seat and began to walk past the crowd, Irene took her hand, "I know what it's like to lose a husband and if there is a chance he's alive and you can bring him home then do it and I will be behind you. I don't want to lose a daughter but I will help you with what I can." Patting her mum's hand Jeanie forced deeply to hold back tears. The following months where going to be difficult enough mentally, but her body had already been so much.

Chapter 25

Private Jack Rutherford stood in basic training covered in mud, bruised and battered. Jeanie looked unrecognisable, no longer a woman but a young man on the verge of War.

The mixture of British and US forces merged into the rainy background and as accents disappeared under cold breath Jeanie tried to take on the enormity of what she had gotten herself into.

As much as Jeanie had tried to blend in she still stuck out like a sore thumb and with her talent of course being undeniably mistakable Mick noticed the new recruit as soon as he opened his mouth and he knew it was her.

"Boss you look like shit and this is fucking stupid if you ask me, "Mick stood in the rain watching Jeanie force herself on patrol.

"I don't have a choice Mick, you know that." Blood pored from her nose and pain gripped her rib cage and as much as she would have loved to quit and go home she couldn't.

Wiping the blood away as quickly as possible and trying to hide how desperate she had become she couldn't help but feel helpless.

"I didn't say that. Listen I watched some fucked up piece of shit nearly kill you and it's something I haven't been able to get over, how can I take that to war?"

Jeanie wiped her face checking her nose again, she looked at his concern unable to sympathise as she had her end goal in mind and nothing and no one was ever going to change that.

"I don't think our units will be together unless you know something I don't?" Jeanie already had her suspicions and as he looked at the ground attempting to move away she grabbed his arm and pulled him backwards. "Mickey what have you said?"

"Nothing. There were a few official looking gents so I talked in the right places and just said you were a talented engineer and that our deployment into Burma could do with someone like you." As he brushed her arm away he sat on the cold soggy embankment,

Capturing a picture of herself in the puddle she sighed in disbelief at the pale distorted figure she had become and as the mud smeared her brow into her hair line she thought deep about Mick's last statement.

"Why would you do that?"

"Because it's the only way I can look after you." Looking at her feet she knew this was the opportunity she needed to try to get James home.

"Well shake it then, I can't exactly hug you here can I!" grasping her hand firmly he pulled her close and whispered lightly in her ear.

"I don't think you should be thanking me cause this thing is still fucked up." Jeanie smiled politely and as she dropped away she scanned the dark horizon.

In the distance she observed the vehicle movements in the compound. She felt like a part of this landscape and one she fiercely wanted to protect. On the other hand her heart raced in her chest and the overwhelming urge to be sick took control.

As she took on her watch the sudden realisation that this was really happening overwhelmed her senses. Throwing up at the side of the compound she tried to regain her composure. Jeanie felt the fear trickling inside her veins and taking over her senses.

Being escorted back to her old haunt she felt numb as this was the place where her life had started to change forever. Signthorpe had wiped out any good memories she had in the garage and any good recollections had been tainted by his attack.

Mick stood waiting in the workshop and as the introductions where made Private Jack Rutherford was dropped off at the garage. Mike had acted impeccably and he had played his part so well that even Jeanie believed they had only just met.

"Ok where do I start?" Mick closed the shutter doors and on walking back around slowly, he grabbed hold of Jeanie in his arms and held her tight.

"What are you doing?"

"This is more dangerous than what you realise Jeanie and if I'm ever going to feel comfortable…"

"I appreciate that you care Mike, but you have to promise me. You have to promise me that you're not going to put yourself in danger or do any heroics because of me. You have to look after yourself and I have to do the same."

"What if I can't Jeanie? What if I can't put you in danger?" Jeanie placed her hand on his shoulder and turned him to face her.

"That's not an option and if it makes you feel that bad then I need to go to another unit. Mike I can look after myself. I've been through enough. I need you to trust me. I also need you to promise me that this conversation is never going to happen again….." Lifting his head Mike's gaze had turned into a stern glance, "Then I will have to promise."

Turning around he walked away and disappeared into the back ground. Jeanie bent her head and pulled at the short tuffs of hair, she knew if anyone found out the situation would get immensely difficult. Not being able to keep it from Mickey had never made it any easier.

Walking into the office all her things where still neatly laid out as if she had never been away. Her diary and wall chart had been updated and the wood burner had been cleaned and polished in expectancy of her return. The comprehension that Mick had kept everything exactly the same sent shockwaves of guilt racing around her mind.

"Everything ok boss lady?"

"Thank you. But I need you to know that I'm going to war for one purpose and that is to find James." Placing her hands around his face she smiled, "Come on regardless we have a job to do."

Organising the numerous bits and pieces Jeanie instantly felt at home and the comfort and smell of the garage made her realise how much she had missed being a part of place.

As the day drew to a close Mick disappeared looking back Jeanie raised her hand as she always had done. The garage held so many memories for both of them, some too painful to look back, some too painful to let go. Watching him walk away Jeanie caught her breath as this was all for James. No matter what she had to endeavour it would mean it was one step closer to his return.

As the sounds echoed around the base Jeanie jumped falling back into character. She was a soldier and her freedom to come and go as she pleased was excessively restricted. The bellows of the sergeant could be heard ringing from the barracks. Grabbing her jacket she ran as quickly hoping to get back before she had been noticed and as she lined up at the bottom of her bed she knew she was out of luck.

"You decided to join us have you Private." Jeanie lowered her head awaiting the bleats, "Well for a little pretty boy like you, we have all the time in the fucking world for don't we gents.

Well you fucking little maggot, for holding me up I guess you will be up all night cleaning the shit houses won't you," Jeanie stood silent wanting to scream and as she held everything in the sergeant bellowed again, "Answer me puff won't you!" Jeanie screamed out with all the force she could, "Yes Sir."

It wasn't hard to notice that Jeanie still looked somewhat feminine and it hadn't gone unnoticed in the unit she had been assigned too. The rational explanation for the group of men together was that she was gay and a source of amusement. The abuse had started on her first day and whilst trying to ignore it the abuse had only become progressively worse.

Starring at her feet Jeanie noticed blood had started to poor from her nose and was dripping onto the floor. Using the back of her hand she wiped away what she could and stood motionless her brow errantly fixed on her boots.
"Sergeant Can you tell me why one of your privates is bleeding?" Turning around quickly the sergeant stood to attention, "No Sir" Jeanie felt a hand on her face as she looked up she gritted her teeth together again.
"I will take charge of this dismiss them sergeant inspection is over, follow me Private quickly." Jeanie jumped to attention and followed the Captain away from the barracks.
"Umm… you must be Private Rutherford. He said you'd be well…Lieutenant Colonel Stanton is looking for you and I really don't appreciate being used as an errand boy so I suggested you hop to it lad. Also next time you bleed on my foot Private I will make you clean my boots for a year. Understand…get off to the infirmary."
Captain Daniels spat the discontent at Jeanie as a cat spitting out a mouse, Jeanie sighed heavily, "How could this day get any better..."

Standing in the rain the blood had gone from a trickle to a gush and as the rain washed the blood over her boots and she was on borrowed time. Weaving around the barracks blood still poured heavily from her nose and as she reached the infirmary she began to feel dizzy.

As she swallowed deep the taste of tin engulfed the back of her throat and as Jeanie heaved the bile started to rise. Breathing deeply Jeanie could taste the ward as her nausea increased. Standing still in the corridor the lights buzzed over head and the ability to be rational was draining from her body. Frozen she heard a shout, "Good gracious what's been happening to you." Jeanie paused for breath. "Just a nose bleed I think." The sister dragged Jeanie by her arm led her into the examination room, Jeanie's legs felt weak and urge to sit rapidly took over her legs.

"Up, up up I will not have you messing up my clean chairs. Nurse bring some paper please." Forcing tissue into Jeanie's hand the sister left her stood pinching her nose and dabbing the blood away.

Great another feeling of being a leper.

"What the fuck has happened to you now?" John raced into the room lifting up her head and checking her face.

"Nose bleed nothing more" John tried to close the door as the sister re-entered the room. "Are we having a conference he must not sit on the chairs," "Sister….please can I have a word, " John closed the door behind them in the corridor and hearing the sisters clucking John entered the room clutching old newspapers, "Here sit on them I don't think I could take anymore noise.." John closed the door and pulled up the chair.

Jeanie's eye's where black and heavy and her smile had faded. The pale drained colour of her cheeks made John clench his fists wondering how far she was going to take this.

"Jea…….,"

"Don't. Please it's a nose bleed. We are all tired..."
"You know that's not true I've heard they think you
are ....I know they are giving you a hard time
because of it....you've been on more patrol duties
than anyone out of your watch and I can't stand and
see this happen anymore.....Jea you need out and
I'm pulling the plug." Squeezing John's hand Jeanie
looked into his eyes, "You know that's not why
you're pulling the plug. There's so much more to
this John and you know it. You also know that I'm
due to go to Burma in seventy two hours don't ask
how I know...I just do." John stood up and drew his
hands over his face cupping both of them over his
mouth.
"I know you're not stupid Jea...I've asked to be
redeployed as well." "John I'm going with Mick
and his unit and they have already approached you.
You have a job that needs to be done here and once
I'm off the barracks that's your job with me done
and I won't ask anymore of you...."
"Umm Mick."
"What's that supposed to mean? What are you not
telling me?"
Racing over to the door John stood close to her side,
"You don't get it do you. You must really love him
Jea but you just don't understand."
    In the rush John pressed himself into her trapping
her between the door and the chair.
"I love you so much and we are both in to deep to
back out of this and I know you can look after
yourself but I can't help it. I can't help bearing that
one day I'm going to loose you."
    Kissing her passionately he ran out of the room
and down the corridor. *He didn't look back, he
always looked back.*
    There was something he wasn't saying and
something she obviously needed to hear tugging at
her hair she sat listening to the rain. The sounds of

heavy droplets of the tin roof made her heart sink and John had pulled once again at her heart strings.

James needed her and she had to repay him for saving her life. Walking out of the infirmary Jeanie saw John stood at the doorway to main building. He seemed lost, sallow and alone, but she knew regardless of John this was the right thing to do. The pressure she had put John under was immense and second thoughts had already crossed her mind but if she was ever going to see James again this was the only way.

Standing tall John looked at the doorway and as she smiled politely and ventured out into the storm she couldn't help but feel the weight of his stare.

As he lit a cigarette John watched her every move whether it was her reasons or his reasons this fucked up situation was going to end when she disappeared. He was in deep and her family had more questions than answers he could give.

Holding her head high, she was petrified, in fact she was more than petrified because she had to be brave and she had to show both of them she could do it and no amount of persuasion was going to stop her.

John threw his cigarette into the drain and as he made his way back up to his office he couldn't help but throw his hat and jacket at his secretary before slamming the door shut. Sitting at the large desk he watched the fire burn fiercely and he knew his reaction in the infirmary would have pricked Jeanie's conscience. Something as happening he could feel the pulse of electricity in the air and hesitancy on her breath.

Hearing a tap on the door Anne Croston his secretary walked gingerly over to him. "Sir I have to report that Mary Conaghan in our telegram office has not reported for work again."

"Sorry Anne…Mary not turned in" confused to how this was his problem Anne's concern puzzled him even more, "I'm worried Sir she's been so reliable and it's been a week it's just not right…."taking a deep breath John waved her away, "I'll ask around Anne ok…."

As Anne left the room John sifted through the paperwork that she had dropped on his desk. Noticing an unopened file he began ripping it open still bemused at why Anne had been so distracted.

As the human hair and fingernails fell out with the photo he threw the file down and stepped back.

"What the fuck…Anne.Anne ANNE!" Running out of the room he accosted his secretary at the filing cabinet, "Did you see anyone in my room?" John had gripped hold of her arm tight Anne squirmed with discomfort, "No Sir you're hurting me."
"I'm sorry Anne please forgive me. Please can you call the Superintendent I need to speak to him urgently?"

John badly shaken went to the chest of draws and took out his gun. Walking around the room he proceeded to turn the lights on and in the dim glow he noticed the door leading into the back of his office was ajar "Sir…." She gasped as he raised his gun and as he pressed his fingers on his lips he coasted through the back door. Switching on the light nothing moved. "Anne what line" Anne flustered responded.
"Two Sir…on two."
"Go home Anne….don't speak of this…" Still holding his gun his eyes glanced wildly around the room.
"Matthew. Signthorpe wasn't on his own."

Chapter 26

Dripping wet, cold and thoroughly pissed off Jeanie arrived back at her barracks. As she stepped though the door she felt the atmosphere change as soon as she walked in.

"Oh look gents the little puff's back been cock sucking the Colonel again have we Jackie."

Walking to her bed and trying to ignore the comments Jeanie swayed her head from side to side. "Fuck stick I'm talking to you." Jeanie never turned but she felt him creeping closer. As his hand reached her shoulder she elbowed him in the stomach and as he fell she raised her knee into his face. The private fell to the ground spitting blood out of his mouth. Jeanie stood on his fingers grabbing hold of his hair she pulled his head back until his chin tipped. "The only cock sucking around her will be coming from you. SO if you don't want that to happen I suggest you fuck off"

As the crowd gathered one of the gents picked Private Danny Hargreaves up off the floor. Blood still pored from his mouth and nose and as he spat at her feet Jeanie was poised again.

"You're going to pay for this…"

"Do you want to try again then?" As Jeanie stepped forward she was greeted by another hand on her shoulder.

"What the fuck are you looking at" the private held his hands up in submission, "Listen for the record he's a prick and off the record I don't think you will be having that many problems anymore."

Lowering her fists the Private seemed almost compassionate to her plight and seeing he wasn't a threat Jeanie backed off and apologised. "Sorry just I can't stand….you know."

The other's seemed astonished at the violent outburst as she had been so quiet trying to divert any attention away. Her reaction was almost alien, "I'm Eric by the way…"

"Jack…I'm Jack" as they shook hands the crowd had started to move away seeing the excitement had come to an end. Danny on the other hand was still shouting jibes from the top corner of the room and Jeanie was very aware that he meant business.

"So I've seen you over at the garage, Sarge said it was some American."

"Yes…Yeah I studied to be an engineer and worked in my dad's garage for a long time so they thought I would be a safe pair of hands." Jeanie looked up and over Eric's shoulder, "I'd probably let it go now."

"We don't need a war in here. So why didn't you knock him out the first time would have saved you weeks of grief."

Jeanie wanted to cry cricking her neck from side to side and trying to calm down she replayed the question over in her head.

"I'm from a……a Methodist family."

Eric seemed to swallow her excuse without question and while he babbled on about his family and his finance Jeanie listened half heartedly as long as the attention had been diverted away from her.

John's reaction replayed over in her mind he was on edge and completely out of character and she knew he was up to something and the uneasy chill up and down her spine meant she was right.

The next day Jeanie made her way over to the garage where she was greeted by two Americans one of which was talking to Mick. Noticing Jeanie's presence the gentleman made there way over.

"Hello you must be Jack," noticing he was a Major Jeanie stood to attention, "At ease soldier….Mike come over here." Mike stood beside Jeanie and she could feel the nerves filtering through his body.

"Gentlemen, Mike you know me but I'm Major Sam McArthur and this is Lieutenant George Ripley. Mike has made us aware of your talents son and I've spoken to you LC and he's vouched for you. He also said you've been trained by the best so I'm inclined to believe him.

Now son you're going to be sent out with our troops in the next forty eight hours and I'm just scoping you out to see if a kid like you is up to what we need." Jeanie tried hard not to bight her lip. "Permission to speak sir," Jeanie waited as the pair colluded, "Go on son….." coughing Jeanie stepped forward," I can assure you both that I'm good at what I do and you just have to promise me that your team are up to my standards." Jeanie stepped back into formation as the two Americans smiled, "Well Mike you said he was full of shit welcome to the team your pass is waiting on the desk and say goodbye discretely what is it that you Brits say," "Loose lips Sir." McArthur nodded, "Yeah that's the shit 0400 Wednesday Private….carry on"

Mike turned around and walked into the office sitting in front of the wood burner he contemplated his thoughts as Jeanie followed.

"I need to go and gather my things," he didn't speak he didn't even gesture at her leaving. The cheeky spark, wit and the glib bullshit he used to annoy her with had all but disappeared, "Meet you at St Mary's tonight, I'll bring Iris she's about your type and you're buying."

Another teary episode would have sent her over the edge and right now she needed to keep her wits about her. Gathering her uniform and belongings together, Jeanie pulled out a picture of James, changing into her uniform Eric appeared from nowhere, "Who's this?"

"It's - It's my brother James he was a doctor lost in action..." Eric turned the picture over, "Has writing on the back of this. To my beloved Jeanie I'm sorry for leaving you at this time, remember me always your loving husband James" Jeanie swallowed deeply as she hated lying and she wasn't good at it but unfortunately in the circumstances she had to get accustomed to doing it.

"She gave it to me they where having problems she didn't want it so I took it with me only thing I have left of him now." Jeanie started to stuff her bag quicker, "Just seems odd that's all anyway where you going?" Jeanie rolled her eyes as she threw the sack on her back; "On Leave for a few days" Jeanie shook Eric's hand wished him all the best, disappearing before he had anymore questions.

The lane was swamped with mud and as Jeanie jiggled the pack on her back it reminded her of the night she ended up looking like something out a horror film. The rain started to pour again and Jeanie pulled the jacket around her for comfort.

That night had so many repercussions, Jeanie thought maybe if she had never ventured out the whole Signthorpe saga might never have happened.

Knowing that she was deluding herself, she found herself outside the pub. Looking up she could still she James at the arched window and she could still feel his hands running over her soft skin with the kisses hanging in the air as the passion intensified. It felt like a lifetime away from where she needed to be.

A million thoughts raced through her mind at a million miles an hour and as she ventured closer to the cottage the experience had now just become very real and knowing she would be soon on a ship going to Burma made her nausea return. As Jeanie heaved on the side of the road, she knew she had to pull it together as bring this home to her family was just going to make her departure worse. Being brave and stubborn wasn't going to keep her alive.

Walking down the garden path she knocked on the door as Irene appeared there was no gesture, no big welcome home. This was going to be the last time she walked though the door as a woman and this was the last time she was going to be able to be herself until the truth could be revealed.

Jeanie knew the next time she would step out of the cottage door she had to be Private Jack Rutherford, a soldier on the verge of war.

Chapter 27

John sat quietly waiting for Matthew.
Looking at the fire he rocked back and forth on his chair. The anxiety and tension of the situation was unbearable and no longer able to sit he paced up and down passing his desk and occasionally looking at the items which had been scattered. Tentatively he scratched his brow.
"For fuck sake….Matthew hurry up,"
   Unable to be patient John started to rummage in the top hand corner of his desk drawer, grabbing a pair of tweezers he began to sift through the blooded tangled hair and fingernails. Closing his eyes he took a deep breath before turning over the photo.
"What are you doing?" John fell to the floor in shock
"Don't fucking do that, "Matthew threw his coat over the corner of the table bemused at why he had been called out in such strange circumstances.
"So the three or four word conversion has made me turn up here at some god awful time because you feel that Signthorpe had an accomplice" John dragging himself off the floor handed the tweezers over.
"Well Matt you tell me what you think?" unaffected by John's anxiety he took the tweezers and placed himself in front of the desk.
"John you have full fingernails on your desk…have you touched any of this?"
"I was just about to look at the photo I just don't think…I don't know." Matthew now taking John's complaint seriously delved further into the envelope. "John I think you need to look at this…….."

Turning to face the desk he saw the photo and the note which was attached, "Do you know this woman?"

"Yes…Yes I do in fact I'd just had a conversation with my secretary about her not an hour ago she's an office girl…what's her fucking name…..Mary Conaghan…shit"

Delving further and trying not to touch the package Matt unpicked a note which had been attached to the bottom corner of the photo.

"Well sir I think you may be right with your conclusion. I also think you need to be worried as this is addressed to you do you want me to read?"

John poured himself a large scotch and lit a cigarette, taking a drag he he flicked his wrist at Matt "Be my guest."

Taking a pen out of his top pocket unfolded the note. "Here we go…"

"John I'm sure by now you've realised that Jeanie is going to be a long way from your reach and before now I thought all bitches only had one reason in life……but I think her purpose has changed she's more important to me alive at the moment.

Signthorpe was merely a puppet he was psychotic and ready to kill for a cause but a puppet. We had a pact but he became impatient and executed it before we where ready but now it shows me that we could have all three of you.

You see John you where a hick up and I understand that now even I have made mistakes. I thought you should know she wasn't the only one and she won't be the last.

So I thought I'd send you a reminder of what we can do to you. If you're lucky you might be able to save that fucking whore from a fate worse than death.

Mind you fucking her to death wouldn't be anything like Jeanie. So John you will have to pay as well. And when her cock sucking husband is dead she will run to me with open arms. And you you will die with her husband.

Just as a reminder I've sent you Jeanie's finger nails. I watched her claw at the ground to get away from death and as her nails ripped off I collected them one by one as a reminder.

John I'm in control not you and certainly not this war me. You've got 48 hours John what are you going to do. Save Jeanie or save this insignificant little bitch clock is ticking!"

Matt laughed nervously, "I think that's probably not just proved your theory but shot it to conclusive John…John."

John poured himself another scotch and threw it back. The thought of Jeanie dragging herself to save herself was too much to bear again.

"He's American…he's another American."

"You can't jump to that conclusion John, your going to have to set up interviews movements, times date you know the procedure," Slamming his glass down on the desk John didn't have the patience to listen. "Matt I'd love to indulge you but just take this from me that he's American and the reason why I know is that in forty eight hours he's off my fucking base and on his way to war.

That of which is fucking classified. You can't……he will know if you start interrupting those procedures it will put Jeanie at risk and I can't permit that. We will have to be subtle."

"I understand your concerns my friend but it's not just Jeanie he wants your involved with this. Listen I know……ask Anne some more questions but I need to take this it has to be formalised she could be dead and this is a potential murder enquiry. John you understand don't you?" "Yes...I do."

As Matt packed up the evidence John took hold of the photo. "Matt there is something attached to the back let me lay it straight. Look at the corner." Matt peered closely and grabbed the tweezers out of John's hand. "Hold on...Fuck John look at this..." As john looked over his shoulder a lump appeared in his throat.

"That's Jeanie...Matt that was the night she nearly died." John threw the glass at the wall. The fragments of glass exploded into shatters crumbling as they hit the floor. Standing in silence he didn't know which way to turn. Shuffling the extra photo and the papers into a folder Matt left without saying a word.

That night haunted him; he was living in a real life horror film. He lost her, he lost his baby and that night he lost hope. He was a broken man and this person knew it. Closing his eyes he raised his head to the ceiling in hopes the images of the photo would dissipate. The real in his mind replayed over and over again. The flashes of Jeanie being dragged under the vehicle blooded frightened with her hand outstretched dragging along the floor desperate disturbed his memory. It was meant to hurt, it was meant for him to take revenge, it was meant to mock.

"Anne Croston please." If he was going to start somewhere he had to start with Mary's friend.

As Anne entered the office John smiled politely, "Anne take a seat don't be worried I just need to know a few things about Mary just to see if I can help." Anne clutched at her bag as the earlier encounter had left her shaken. "Ok Sir.....I don't know what I can help with but I will try."

John took out his note book and opened his jotter he noticed that not all the fragments of hair had been taken. Brushing them away uncomfortably he tried to put Anne at ease.

" Ok. Would you like a drink?" Anne shook her head and clenched her bag even closer to her chest. John poured himself another scotch.

"Right Anne when was the last time you saw Mary?"

"Around ten days ago. I made her a cup of tea in the canteen and we talked for a while." John shuffled his chair forward and started to make some notes, "What did you chat about?" Anne still playing with the hem tentatively responded, "Well Sir it was ladies talk." Anne seemed coy. "Anne if I'm going to find her I need to know a little bit more than that." Anne lifted her gaze and pursed her lips together. "I'm sorry Sir it was rather frightening before…..," Pausing to gather her thoughts Anne continued anxiously, "Mary knew I was your secretary and she thought you where very handsome and that kind of conversation."

As much as John didn't want to admit Anne had pandered to his diminishing ego and as he raised his hand to cover his smile he felt a small spark of confidence return with her words.

"Anyway she said one of the soldiers had been sending her gifts and she had met him at a dance. She never said his name only that he was American and ten days ago they where supposed to meet. Sir" John snapped the pencil unable to keep his frustration within his cool exterior.

"American……did she say anything else?"

"I don't know Sir. I didn't think anything of it really I mean so many girls meet soldiers these days I didn't."

"Anne I'm sorry to drag you back up here but thank you. Why don't you take the morning off tomorrow? If there is anything you remember that you think may be important please just let me know."

"Sir sorry I've just remembered something. I don't know whether it's important but she said he was part of Ryland's men something like that...."

John escorted Anne to a car, scanning around the base John's concerns heightened. Watching for any unusual movements John knew if this man was still on the base anyone who had information could be targeted. Waving her off he lit a cigarette at the door he repeated the name. "Ryland I know Ryland...Ryland." Breathing in the smoke he stood to attention, "Ripley's unit!"

Throwing the cigarette he stormed upstairs and sieved through the filing cabinet. "Fuck Jack...Jack...Jack. There you are. Where's the fucking recommendation." Dropping the paperwork to the floor he found the signature George Ripley 1103 Engineer's division.

John backed up against the wall, he had signed off and recommended her to this brigade and he felt like he had just signed her death warrant. Underneath the recommendation was Jeanie's signature as Private J Rutherford.

He wanted to run, he wanted to get into the car and drive to her tell, plead, beg her not to go, but he knew if he did he would put all of them in danger. Helpless he screamed into the night as he knew the only way to save her was to find Mary and fast.

John watched from his chair as the daylight streamed through the window. The morning beckoned him out of his office and the uneasy helpless feeling of last night wandered around his body like lice. As the early morning noise filled the corridors he knew he had to start somewhere, the only place he knew of which was accessible to him onsite was Mary Conaghan typing desk.

John made his way to an empty desk, "Is this Mary Conaghan's desk?" the girl sat across nodded her head and continued to type. John started to tear at the desk, looking for anything he could. Reaching under the papers in the desk he realised he had found not just a clue but something that made his heart sink. Opening the box he knew exactly what it was it was Jeanie's St Christopher. John had taken it off her placing it in his pocket as she was lay on the floor. He had sent it to be cleaned and now it was in front of him sat in a box. As he turned it in his fingers he could see the blood had stained the back of the necklace and underneath the pocket of the box laid a note.

"From old friends come new beginnings, you will be part of my dream and the realisation of my future. Yours Truly COW x x"

John sat on the chair reading the note over and over again; these must have been musical, enchanting and even charming to Mary a man that was trying to sweep her off her feet.

Knowing differently the vile distaste of what laid in store for her made John's blood run cold. Leaning on Mary's desk he contemplated his next move and the complicated trilogy played out in his mind.

Looking blankly at the desk he longed for inspiration and as the air filled with smoke and the smell of ink the volume tapped precariously away in his mind.

"Anne said she was so methodical and reliable," John urged for any inspiration. The girl sat at the typewriter glanced over hearing the helplessness, "Anything I can help with?" John trying to be the picture of a perfect gentleman smiled politely, "Thank you. I'm just looking for a few of Mary's

things." The girl lit a cigarette and offered one to John, "Mary was lovely we've all been wondering what happened to her…you know she painted that picture hanging on the wall you know something nice for us ladies to look at other than the soldiers."
"Sorry. Apologies it's that picture over there."
"Yeah she painted it quite recently something about special time with her new bow." Racing over he took the painting off the wall and after excusing himself he ran back along the corridor to his office.
"Give me something I can work with Mary." The picture was beautiful it looked like a dense forest with streams of bluebells flooding the woodland floor and on the back it wrote *"Special place near home."*

John needed to know where this wood was and fast. Taking hold of Anne's arm he paraded her down the winding close boarded corridor.
"I just need a minute…..it's important."
"Sir sorry if you don't mind me saying you seem…….distracted?" John directing the orchestra of chairs ushered people out of a small side office, "I have a picture which Mary painted do you know where this is?"
"Wherever it is its beautiful but how has this got anything to do with Mary?" John exasperated started to loose his patience.
"Anne please just concentrate it says on the back near home do you know where that is?"
"Sir I think she said something about playing near the Solway as a child so maybe somewhere up there. I'm sorry."
"Anne can you get a map of the area around the Solway?" Anne still perplexed at John's manor nodded and quickened her pace.
"What does this have to do with Mary sir?"
"Just making sure she's not in trouble Anne that's all."

Maps, graphs and charts scattered around John's office in no particular order. He felt as if he was being mocked and the person involved had taken great care to do so. Taking his notes and the painting he needed help and the only friend he could turn too was Matt.

Arriving at the police station John caught a glimpse of himself in the black glass; he looked like a man on the edge. Trying not to draw attention John entered the station.

"I need to see Superintendent Matthew Lineage please."

The officer on reception raised one eye brow at a dishevelled John and how his obvious desperation had assaulted his cool charming façade that should have befitted his station. Instead his body was rigid with the anxiety that painstakingly ran through every contorted muscle and the constable felt the intensity within his presence.

Agreeing to the request he mumbled lightly down the telephone.

"Sir I know it's not my place but you don't look at all well."

John straightened his jacket and ran his fingers through his hair trying to smarten himself, "I'm fine thank you for asking."

John slipped back into his character trying to ease the situation and trying not to draw attention to the urgency he felt and as Matthew entered reception with an open hand John followed timidly.

"Through here please." Matt closed the door and ushered John into a small poky corridor.

"I told you I would come to you."

"Have you got something?" John pulled the picture out of his coat looking more like a dodgy salesman than a Lieutenant Colonel.

"I have this. I also have Jeanie's St Christopher but the picture. I've looked on all the local maps. Anne said she played on the Solway and the nearest place I found remotely close would be Kirkcudbright. The moor's are vast over their but the girl I spoke to said this picture is recent though look." John pointed to the back of the picture and to a faint pen mark situated at the bottom right of the picture. Matthew removed his glasses and put them closer to the picture.

"This is twelve weeks ago this could be a lead John when does....when does she leave. You know this can't carry on John you need to let her go."

"This is partly down to me I can't I love her Matt. It drives me insane thinking that she's with someone else but this is my penance for being an arsehole.

Can you look around, I need you to find Mary she holds the answers and if there is a possibility she's alive." John paused and placed an open palm on the door, "I need to go."

"Shake it…I will do my job just make sure you do yours."

John nodded to the constable who had been so inquisitive on his arrival. Lighting a cigarette at the door he buttoned his jacket questioning his own motives as he walked down the steps of the station. Time seemed to stand still and as he took a drag he stood back and glanced at the high street.

Children where still playing, women where still shopping and scolding their children and if it wasn't for the occasional army personnel nothing would be different.

Dropping the butt he pulled up his collar and as the afternoon started to turn into early evening the wind had started to increase biting into every crease and causing the occasional shudder for good merit.

Maybe Matt was right the fight for Jeanie had been so difficult and traumatic with him always at the centre. James had won her heart and she was willing to sacrifice herself in the proceedings. She searched for truth and honour whilst John realised his search was only to satisfy the guilt and not being good enough for her. John felt the chill again down his spine this time not from the cold or the predicament he was in.

Knowing her life was not just at risk by war but by another put John on the edge and he had to trust Matt as there was not other way. Taking the time to reflect and trying to calm and think rationally the walk back put his thoughts into perspective.

"Anne who is it?" placing her hand over the receiver she whispered, "Matthew quickly…." Signalling him over to the phone John placed the handset to his ear, "Hello its Galloway Forest I'm going up there now are you coming with me." John astonished at the speed of the findings felt a small fleck of relief, "Meet me out front in fifteen minutes."

The rain had started to poor heavily and the blackness had already started to draw in and as John dove into the car he was unable to comprehend the speed in which Matt had been able to work. "The painting was important John. I spoke to her Uncle he lives in Kirkcudbright her family are no longer there but she visited them with a man around ten to twelve weeks ago an American. Her Uncle said he seemed to be casing the place; too sure of himself apparently he also said they went for a walk through Galloway….the maps just down there." John leant between the seats lifting up the battered and torn paper, "There are several lochs and fishing lakes around there. Her Uncle also said she had been fond of going to Barrhill look at the bottom." "Did he ask any questions? Did he ask why?" Matt tilted his head and wiped the steam off his thick rimmed glasses, "I said she hadn't reported in and it was policy to ask family John…John if she's dead I have no choice..."

"I know…lets just get there."

The rain poured heavily and the weather seemed to be in direct conflict with the operation in hand. Both of them knew that tonight would be the difficult without the elements making it worse. The mood in car was tense and as they approached the wood the thickening tension increased. "According to the map we are at the top end of the wood." Matt pulled at the collar of his jacket and adjusting his hat shuddered in the floods.

"We will follow the path down keep to the main walkways looks like it's starting to flood…"

The ground squelched and gave way beneath there feet and the cold water trickled down there necks, it was like looking for a needle in a hay stack.

They had walked through the blackness for over an hour, looking for a sign, "Matt…..what's that?" John shone his torch through the dense forest leaves. The ferns gathered height in the darkness and the overbearing nature of there sprawl emphasised there helplessness.

"They look like bird watching huts…Look there's a clearing." Racing down the path John started to frantically look through the small huts, "Matt…they look like they are scattered across this brook you go up stream and I will look down if you find something shout."

The little black boxes where less than inviting and the sodden earth had started to seep through the sides as the water began to rise. After an hour of searching John's legs where covered in mud and instead of walking he had began to paddle.

"Matt….Matt have you found anything?" faintly in the distance he heard a No. Sodden and blackened Matt returned to find John frantic.

"John we need daylight. More people….."

"Matt you know this has to happen now if I have any chance of saving her it has to be tonight."

As the bank gave way John fell waste deep into the stream and as Matt bent down with a chuckle he welcomed the small reprieve.

"You ok?"

"Get me out." As Matt outstretched his arm he saw a twinkle in the distance, "John take a look over there there's something over there." As the torch shone the glint Matt had seen appeared again.

"John your on lower ground did you see that." John shouted back trying to raise his voice above the gushing of water.

"There's another dwelling across the water, look."

"Matt….there's another one hidden over there come on."

Not wanting to follow his companion Matt reluctantly stepped down the side of the brook submerging himself in the icy cold water letting out a whimper he waded through the swollen brook.

 "John I swear to god it's freezing."

"It's getting dangerous just hurry up or we will all end up dead."

John ran over to the den, it was covered in leaves and branches walking to the door John stopped, "What..?"

Looking at Matt he lifted his hand, "What don't the others have which this one does?" Matt following John's gaze saw the padlock.

  The water had risen violently and the rain had started to pour harder and as John started to smash at the lock with the end of his torch with a final slam it fell on the floor. Before opening the door John took his gun from his pocket.

"You ready…."

"As I'll ever be." Ankle deep they waded into the room, it was small, cold and the cabin was isolated John gasped in disbelief as a figure hung from the wall.

"Mary…Matt over here," naked gagged and half dead she hung like a violent portrait of Jesus. "Shit Matt get me your knife we need to get her down now." John took the gag from around her mouth and on hearing the sound of breath he proceeded to try to unchain her from the wall. "Matt…MATT for god sake help me." Matt stood and gazed at the walls, "John you need to look." Trying desperately to free her John shot the chains from her hands feet and waist. Taking his coat he wrapped her up trying to bring her around." Matt…I need you."
The walls where covered in photographs, detailing every torturous event which had happened to this poor girl. Looking closely at Mary the skin from her feet had been burnt away and placed like patchwork over the windows.

Matt started to drag some of the photo's down, it was like a living tomb and COW whoever he was revelled in her pain. Her hair had been shaven and small vials of tranquilisers where scattered around the small table which graced the corner of the hut. John frantic tried to wake her and all the time the water poured through the door.
"John we need to get her out of here."
"Matt look." Gathering the paperwork John moved as quickly as he could and as he carried her in his arms the walk to the car seemed endless. The violence of the air seemed to awaken her unconsciousness and without hesitation Matt jumped in the driver's seat and looked at the map in search of the nearest hospital.
"There's one in the centre of town…..John is she alive." Holding onto her John desperately looked for vital signs, "Matt get going we haven't time..."
John looked at the pale fragile girl with the reminiscence of Jeanie flooding back as the car jolted over bump and stone.
"Shh it's ok we are here to help."

"I thought I'd die in there, he said he would kill me." John pushed her tightly towards him, trying to warm her with his body heat.

"He forced me to do things…" John not wanting to acknowledge rubbed her small shoulders "Doesn't matter we need to get you to hospital."

"He came back last night he strapped me to the wall…he said I'd played my part…" John closed his eyes the car droned through the wind and the rain and every corner seemed to hold them back a little longer.

"Mary do you know who he is?" Mary folded the lapel of John's jacket around her face, "He said he was called Raymond Peterson but..." Mary coughed and drew her legs up close to her chest.

"I'm so cold. I know you…"

The car pulled up and stopped quickly, carrying Mary into the waiting room John placed her on the trolley, "Now you know me is there anything else I need to know."

"Sir he said someone called Jack was next he said lots." John held her hand tight squeezing it to reassure her that she was safe.

"Thank you Mary looks like the doctor's here, "as John let go of her hand and turned Mary yelled, "I remember."

John ran back to her side hoping for news and as Mary whispered in his ear her effort to shout him back had taken all her energy.

"Thank you." Running back to Matt John grabbed the keys out of his hand. "Stay here and look after her I need to go."

John leaped in the car looking at his watch he new the ship would be departing at 4.00am and he had two hours to make it back to Jeanie. Mary had given him the final clue the only thing to do now was race to stop him completing his plan.

The rain howled around the car, beating it from side to side and as he slid and skated all over the road John arrived at the dock.

Wiping his brow he knew he was too late.

As the boat sailed he spotted a man on deck. John lifted his gaze and as he waved catching his breath John clenched his fists.

"Hey Johnny boy guess what Your too late!"

John stood on the harbour side knowing he couldn't keep her safe, letting her go to face him alone was the toughest pill he'd ever had to swallow.

Chapter 28

Matt sat down with Mary's family and in trying to keep the information official Matt explained what she had gone through and how she was now safe in hospital.

Not being able to keep it together Mary's mum wept uncontrollably at the violation of her daughter. "Thank you for letting us know the main thing is she's alive." Mary's father was motionless unable to comprehend that there only daughter had been raped, tortured and nearly killed by a man who was abject on destruction and devastation. Lighting a cigarette he took to the door trying to escape the news.

"She's all alone down there I knew I should never have let her go…she's so pig headed exactly the same as her mother. Explain to me how I'm ever going to make this better for my daughter."

Matt's experience in dealing with difficult situations aided his reaction and as he rested his hand on his shoulder his words mustered themselves to the surface.

"I met a gentleman who introduced himself as Bill he said he was related."

"Eye that's right he's my brother…why?"

"He's visited Mary in hospital in fact he's been everyday so far even taken night clothes. I believe he's informed some of the family that there has been an incident and some have already commuted down from Glasgow. I also explained to him that I would see you in person as this is of a sensitive nature.

I can't take back what has happened Mr Conaghan I can only assure you that this will be dealt with severely." Throwing the cigarette butt Mary's father held out his hand, "I appreciate you coming sir please call me Pat. I'm taking your word as a gentleman please catch the bastard that's done this to my daughter." Matt shook his hand firmly reassuring Pat's concern and as Matt left Mary's home he couldn't help but dwell on the brutal cold hearted nature of the crime which now affected another family.

Climbing back into the car he threw his dark blue trilby into the back seat. Placing the keys into the ignition he rested both of his hands on the steering wheel in quiet contemplation.

"They know." John dipped his cap as the car pulled away. Tussling with his jacket he lent forward awaiting Matt's full debrief.

"You can't keep this name under wraps forever John this needs go further."

"You know as well as I do that this incident will be washed away just like Jeanie."

"You know since I've met you these favours seem to sprout legs and walk on there own. You promised he would be dealt with John!"

John emptied the packet of cigarettes and screwed the remains into a ball, taking a drag he wound the window down watching the smoke dissipate in the rain.

"When did you start smoking again?" John flicked the ash out of the window and looked hazily into the distance.

"The day I set foot in Cumbria…We need to see Mary."

Matt raised his hand mimicking a salute, "As you wish Sir of course." Glancing over to John Matt knew sarcasm would draw the conversation to a close.

Pulling up at Kirkcudbright Hospital the anxiety radiating from both gentlemen had reached an all time high. John pulled flowers from a vase which stood on a window ledge.

"What are you doing?"

"Relax you can't turn up and do what we need to do without a token."

Walking into the ward, the pale fragile looking girl looked so small in the bleak white sheets. Bandages graced her hands and feet and John found it difficult to look at her. The flash backs of Jeanie pained him dreadfully and the unease of his actions didn't sit comfortably. Everything else she had suffered could be hid, however John couldn't help but empathise that what was on show where the easy wounds.

Skirting around the end of the bed he placed the flowers in the empty vase already standing on her bedside cabinet. Not wanting to wake her John carefully placed two chairs at the side of the bed with minimal noise. As Matt sat down he took out his note book, Mary lay still and the awkwardness of the conversation in her home had instilled itself again in hospital.

"I don't like this John something just doesn't feel right…" John placing his large coat on the back of the chair and removing his cap had the same uneasy feelings, but he was committed to getting the truth. "We have no choice and before you say it I know how you feel. Let's just see how this goes shall we."

Mary awoke with a few small flicks of her eyes. She seemed like a child stirring from a good night sleep knowing it was probably medically induced didn't give any comfort to either of the gents.

"Good Morning Mary, "taking in the figure she seemed to jump as the two men appeared out of the mist.

"Sir sorry what are you doing here?" Mary pulled at the bed clothes seemingly ashamed of her appearance.

"Apologies, my colleague and I just wanted to finish off a getting your story if that's ok with you." Mary pulled the bed clothes tighter around her. She looked as if she was using the thin white cloth as a human shield, noticing her distress the nurse appeared around the curtain.

"You ok petal? I see you've got some odd looking company?" her Tyneside accent brought levity and Mary grabbed onto her friendly concern, "Please can you sit with me Sheila I…I just don't think," A tear welled as she tried to finish her sentence, "Don't worry pet if these likely lads cause you any trouble I'll give them the boot you can count on that."

Matt took off his trilby and placed it neat on the end of the bed, contemplating his thoughts and his next move he looked at Mary's broken existence. "I can understand this is difficult and I can't imagine what you have been through, but we have seen your family and explained our position. The man who did this to you is currently…well quite frankly my dear he's not in the country but I can assure you he will be dealt with most severely under the circumstances." Mary gazed at Matt, his kind round face and friendly disposition made the words, we haven't caught him seem easier to swallow. Sitting up straight she appeared to gain in confidence.

"So you're saying he's gone to war and he's going to be dealt with."

"Yes. He will be dealt with severely."

"I don't understand all I here is he's going to war and because he might die this will all go away!" John perplexed at Mary's outburst suddenly realised the frail little flower which lay in the bed only minutes before no longer was frail as the flower had grown thorns and teeth. Mary sat up patiently waiting for there next response.

"Mary you know me I'm Lieutenant Colonel John Stanton I found you remember?" Mary nodded tolerantly waiting to here his thoughts," I can assure you that I intend to make sure that this man is brought to justice and I can promise you that it will be personally dealt with by myself and that Ko…this man pays for what he has done to you and your family." Mary clutched at the sheets and looked at the brigade of people sat around her bed, smiling uneasily she let go of the nurses fingers; "Can I have a moment alone with the Captain please?" Matt glancing at John shook his head underneath the gatherings of his hat and as the nurse stood Matt smiled and politely let her past.

"John I think this is a bad idea."

"We don't have any choice I'll meet you in the car." Matt stood behind the curtain understanding that his first feelings where right. Worried about the next instalment Matt tentatively placed his hat and coat back on as he graced the corridor.

Hearing the curtain close behind John felt like he'd just placed a cat in a bag, he was trapped and no matter what happened now Mary was in control.

"The flowers are lovely. I'm sure I saw some in the hallway just like them yesterday. Know everyone has gone Lieutenant please don't insult my intelligence. I know why you're here and I know what they did to Jeanie. I worked in the offices you hear things."

"I can't change what happened Jea…I can't and I'm truly sorry. So the question I need to ask is what you want from me?" Mary bent forward and clenched both of her fists and as she did they seemed to coil with venom like a snake waiting to make an attack, "I want him dead John. I want him to suffer and then I want proof."

"Mary this is out of the question I can only assist you with military law this is preposterous." Mary sat back on the bed annoyed at John's response starring at the foot of the bed she took a deep breath and looked him directly in the eye.

"Then there is nothing you can do for me and I will be pursuing a more public approach."

"Ok Mary I get it I have seen the aftermath and I know the feelings I'm not going to lie to you, "John paced in the small space knowing Matt was right. His actions had made the situation even more difficult to handle and Mary had him trapped waiting for a response.

"I know who he is and I want to help but Mary this is ludicrous there's only so much I can do," moving her hair away from her temple she glared at the reaction.

"I saw you after Jeanie don't get me wrong she was a nice lass….but I'm not her and I'm not so forgiving. You're a distinguished soldier I'm sure something must spring to mind."

"Mary I can see you are a strong woman and I understand your position. I'm sure something can be arranged and I will get the confirmation myself I can't guarantee you understand."

Mary smiled, the kind of smile that girls make when they know they have got exactly what they want, "I know you will do your best John I just don't want anyone else going through what Jeanie and I have had to go through." John stood at the curtain and replaced his cap, after adjusting his tie he left through the wisps of clean white curtain.

Standing in the corridor he placed his hands on his hips unable to bear witness to what had just happened.

What have I just gotten myself into?

His time was running out and knowing that he wasn't just battling a war, propaganda and a raving lunatic Mary had just started to become the straw that broke the camels back.

Throwing his jacket into the rear of the car he proceeded to rummage around for another cigarette, slamming the door shut he opened the window knowing it would be long until Matt had his piece of mind to share.

"That good!" John stayed silent his brow pained by the thought that he now had to become and accomplice to murder in order to satisfy Mary's demands.

"I told you. I told you when we entered this one would be tricky don't tell me she wants revenge?" John dropped the butt out of the window and wiped the sleep out of his eyes.

"Oh yes and not just revenge proof."

"What are you going to do?" John sliding another cigarette from the packet turned towards the passenger side window hoping inspiration could be found on the moor.

"Nothing...Nothing until I've found Jeanie."

Matt arrived back at the base worried for his friend, but equally worried about the complex dilemma which had now started to unfold and as John waved goodbye the only thing either of them could do now was wait.

Walking into his quarters John took off his shoes and tie, undoing the top buttons of his pristine shirt he poured himself a drink and placed his weary body in the chair. The week's events played on John's mind like a Shakespearian tragedy.

Jeanie had nearly died in his arms and the baby he so desperately wanted had died and all through the events Jeanie had never asked for revenge. Mary on the other hand wanted revenge and wanted proof. Unable to settle his mind he gulped down the last drops feeling the relief as the alcohol hit his blood stream. As he undressed and showered, he couldn't get Jeanie off his mind, he remembered pleading with her in the infirmary and they way his jealousy and pride had took control because of James. His insecurity didn't count either as no matter what she wanted James.

Sitting on the edge of the bed he pulled a hand made box from the drawers of the bedside table and as he ran his fingers across the intricate wooden carvings Jeanie still played on his mind. Opening the hand made hinge photo's spilled out onto the floor and as he gathered them he stumbled on a rare find. A time when they where both happy together.

Lying on the bed thoughts of her kisses, her touch and the way her skin smelt beleaguered his senses and as he closed his eyes he could see her vividly. Her bright auburn hair and piercing brown eyes burned into his thoughts, he wanted to remember and he didn't want to forget. His memory's drifted through the fields of wheat that grew as children and the sounds of smiles and laughter filling the streets as they played innocently side by side.

His thoughts saw Jeanie disappear into the orchards which met the edge of the field and where the line of wheat broke and as they tumbled their innocence shone in the sun. As he lay her down on the blanket the kisses the touches of there adolescence filled his soul.
She was beautiful.
Happy.
Contented.

The feeling of her hair against his skin and the passion he felt overflowed in each passing moment and as Jeanie handed him the intricate box, the world in his memory spilled out into his dream

"I made this for you John Stanton...I made this for your memories..."
Her voice echoed around him as if she was in the room and as he took the gift he studied the detail. The rose carvings and swallows which had graced his parents back garden had been weaved into the wood.

Jeanie's talent had always astonished him and as he lay in her embrace he moved her hair away from her face remembering how inadequate he felt.
She deserved more
She needed someone to be proud of and that wasn't him.

Feeling his inadequacy again the dark clouds gathered in the bleakness and in his passing moment of bliss she had gone. The happiness together grew cold and the anger in the air intensified.

As he desperately tried to find her a figure under the tree at the edge of the field beckoned him closer. As he started to run the panic started to rise in his chest and stopping before he reached the tree he found Jeanie.

Only this time she was different, older. She stared into the sky as the violence of the night grew. As he ventured closer all the fears of losing her collated together in this one moment and there she stood, not moving. Her blackened filthy uniform and with her shirt ripped and torn, she looked fearful and isolated. The dried blood stained her shaven head and as he grew close he could see a noose wrapped around her neck.

Grabbing her arms Jeanie's gaze didn't falter she was still, no emotion, no comfort and no happiness. John began to try to release her from the rope, but everything he tried bound her further and tighter squeezing the life out of her.
She screamed, "He's here."

The rope snatched back around her throat and John awoke brutally from his sleep. Throwing back the covers he went to the sink splashing his face with water.

He had become the epitome of what she had needed and all it had done was push her away. Lying back down on the bed he picked up the picture which lay on his pillow, wiping his face for the final time he threw the towel to the floor.

The picture haunted him; his inadequacies drove him away from her especially when it should have been the happiest day of his life. She had asked him to marry her that day and she had wanted him to make love to her under the tree that had hanged her in his dream. Instead he felt like the noose strangling her from the tree. Starring into the smiles of the photo he knew all his regrets had been pin pointed into that one moment.

Matt was right this was more than being in love. She ran too deep in his veins and without him knowing she had been the voice pushing him further and further. His army career wasn't forged by lies and deception it was formed on the understanding that one day it would lead him back to her. He had stepped on numerous toes and even used his own wife and his future father in law to get what he wanted.

Lieutenant Colonel Stanton was still not good enough for Jeanie as it had made him into the type of man she loathed. Standing in front of the mirror he looked at the excuse he had become, egotistical, false and unfaithful, knowing she needed more had pushed him further away, but he knew if he had the chance now he would give it all up just for her.

Chapter 29

"This is my sixth month and I still haven't found anything to lead me back to James, all I find is death.

There are only six of us left, radio communications are non existent and trying to find a friendly in this god forsaken place is like looking for a needle in a hay stack. The men keep talking of home, I feel like I have forgotten the good memories of home. I keep feeling like this is a dream and I'm going to wake up with James beside me but all I have is the stench of death rising up from my feet.

I always thought there was hope; this place drains it out of you like a leach.

They seem to respect me now, far cry from what it was back in the dorms. We attacked a carrier yesterday, coordinating the attack has been something which I strangely enjoyed. How can that be when the only result is death?

We are still alive though. I keep thinking about my sisters and that I've left my family alone, the reliance on them is something that I now crave it was so simple.

I suppose taking care of these men and making sure we stay alive has become a priority.

My dreams have turned into nightmares, I'm haunted by the screams of my battalion dying, I'm haunted by the things I've done. This feels like murder. I feel like this is punishment. Staying alive, this is survival nothing else. This war is leaving me with more scars than what I care for. I still feel like this has a purpose and there is something more I'm going to face. Maybe I need to learn to survive!

I need to get these men back to a base camp, I'm lost and frightened I can't do it but if I don't that's all of us dead. James dead or alive I'm going to find you even if it's the last thing I do."

Putting her pocket journal away she closed her eyes and took a deep breath, after the decimation of there regiment she knew it wouldn't be long before they stumbled across someone on the same side. *Anyone from the same side please for god sake we need help!*

 "Mike stop hiding in corners it's your patrol tonight." Jeanie didn't lift her head; she didn't even change her glance.

"What you writing about?" Mick sat down at her side and lit a cigarette, the emphasis of him looking after her had become ironic and almost the butt of a bad joke.

"Nothing that would interest you I need you to stay on patrol. If you keep wandering off you're not looking after the group I can't...you know the plan we need to keep together."

"Jea...Sarge I do know the drill my turn your rules you've made that plain enough. But you know if I was at home..."

Jeanie looked up raising an eye brow and wrapping what was left of her jacket around her, "If you where at home go on I'm intrigued to know cause I'm sat in a fucking jungle with half of the squad dead and the other half wondering what the fuck is going on so enlighten me Kowalski please." Mick cricked his neck trying to respond calmly and trying to rephrase the meaning of what he said.

"I shouldn't have to take this bullshit from you. You're a fucking wo...pain in my arse."

Mick wandered about the camp like a child scorn she wished she could tell them everything would be ok she also couldn't say how much she wanted this nightmare to end for all of them.

"I wish I was back home Mick….I really do."
Huddling under her jacket, she attempted to sleep
and as she lay in the dark she listened to the rain
hitting the leaves in the trees. No matter how tall or
wide the leaved felt they didn't give you much
shelter and the fact that death was around every
corner made it even harder to relax.

Mick stood at the bottom end of the camp lighting
another cigarette, staring at her intently.
"Oh bozo got another smoke." Pete had seen his
glare and broke it to cut the tension, "Yeah…hold
on." Pulling the crumpled packet from his inside
jacket pocket he threw one down, "Thanks you
know he's only trying to do the best he can. You've
got to give him a break….some days I swear it's
like you want to kill each other and if I didn't know
any better I wouldn't think you where friends."
Smiling under his breath Mick bent down and lit his
cigarette grabbing Pete's collar his discontent at his
thoughts fell through the puffs of smoke.
"It's none of your fucking business what I talk
about especially to that over there are we clear."
"Listen Mike I think you need to take it easy the
wars out there not in here."

Throwing his cigarette away Mick disappeared
into the dark. Jeanie sat up and watched him from
the distance knowing that everybody was on edge.
The only thing she could control was letting him
walk off his anger. Jeanie nodded to Pete
acknowledging that she had seen the event. Pete
shrugged his shoulders as Mike's reaction had
become a usual daily occurrence.

The stress of survival had affected some more
than others and in Mick's case Jeanie put it down to
just that. Watching Pete settle back down in the
undergrowth Jeanie felt relieved that he hadn't
taken Mike's outburst too personally.

Watching the darkness Jeanie saw the shadow of Mike and she was pleased that he'd at least done as she said for one night. Trying to get comfortable she rested her head back against the tree Jeanie thought of her sisters in the parlour next to a warm fire. The comfort of at least knowing they were safe gave some relief.

Jeanie had been already been up a couple of hours as dawn had broken. Looking at the maps of the surrounding area Jeanie sought for points of reference. They had been isolated for so long that the lack of radio contact made it feel as if the where walking in circles. Sitting with Merle she hunted for the easiest trek and the safest route down to base camp. "Merle point us in the right direction. Eugene pack up the rest of the supplies and count what artillery we have left. Pete help Eugene. Billy find Mike,"

"Sarge…Mike's at the stream I found him down there before." #

"Thanks Billy go get him we leave in five."

As everyone dispersed Jeanie winced with pain throwing back her jacket she bent over counting to ten over and over again until it subsided.

Having to bind her breasts with dressings had created pressure sores and as she packed to leave it was noticeable she had a problem.

"You ok Boss?"

"Thank you." still sheepish from the disagreement he began to swallow his pride," You can't keep doing this, there going to turn bad and then what's going to happen.." Jeanie trying to ignore his concern started strapping the rest of the equipment around her.

"I appreciate that you're worried about me but you know as well as I. I have no where to go."

"So let me help?" Jeanie laughed uncomfortably at the thought of even showing her boobs to him.

"Can't do that soldier…fall in."

Wading through the under growth Jeanie couldn't help but admit to herself that things had started to get tough. Between the sores, the gun and the uniform the irritations of jungle life where starting to bring her down.

Though the rains had started to dry up the damp dark stench made her pray for a clearing of daylight. "Sarge look down there."
Hurrying from the side to the front of the group Jeanie took hold of the binoculars.
"Looks like POW's…shit looks like there digging…Fuck me."
Jeanie didn't want to look anymore, the emaciated bodies of the dead where being burnt and the rest of the POW's looked as if there on the brink of death. "So the rumours where right then. Those fucking men are being tortured." Jeanie slid down the tree and sat on the floor, kicking the dirt as the helplessness she felt was evident.
"This fucking war!"
"What can we do? We need a plan we can't leave them there Sarge." Jeanie starred into the overgrown mangled earth and as she shuffled her feet she started to dig her own hole. "With what Eu we are just about staying alive. We need to get over that ridge and we at least need to retain some fucking fire power." Eugene stood and looked at the silent crowd unable to comprehend what she was saying.
"So where just going to leave them to die?" Mike placed his hand his shoulder trying to reassure his concerns. "What the fuck do you want you're fucking preoccupied all the time you don't give a shit."
"Eugene that's enough. Sit the fuck down. Don't you think we all feel helpless spouting off is not going to do us any good it may even get us all

fucking killed and if anything happens to us they die any way so sit down and let us think."

"Sorry Sarge it's just fucking SNAFU!"

Pete tried to make out the acronym sounding words out to try to make out what he meant. Looking over his puzzled stare continued

"And where the fuck have you heard that." Eugene ruffled around in his pockets for something which resembled a cigarette.

"What never heard of situation normal all fucked up SNAFU!"

Jeanie curled the corner of her mouth in jest at the acronym She was please for the small light relief but she was just as angry and frustrated as the rest, after all James could be down there dying or even dead for all she knew.

Looking at the equipment she knew there was no possible way they could even make a successful attack.

"Right listen all of you I know how you feel but in order to make this any better we have to get supplies, artillery is down to shit and Eu thank you for your SNAFU but we need to be realistic, if we get caught both us and them are fucked.

If we make a stand we don't have the fire power to deal with it so we need to carry on down the ridge and hope that we hit a base by tomorrow morning. If anyone's religious pray for the poor bastards and if your not give it a go. Right round up everyone bayonets on everyone with full rounds lets keep going."

The only thing Jeanie could be was practical and the thought of James in one of those camps made her blood run cold, but she had to keep these men alive and she had given them her word and so far it was working.

Silence was easy, no sarcasm, smart comments or smut transferred across anyone's lips for the rest of the afternoon. Even Mick had decided that his usual aggressive bullshit needed to be put back on the back burner.

"Billy pssst Billy..." Merle grabbed his collar tight and dragged him into position.

"What the fuck man."

"Shut the fuck up and get down..." Merle signalled to the group and everyone dropped and took cover. Jeanie could feel her heat beat in her throat as the majority of what they had faced had been hand to hand combat.

Feeling the bayonet knife puncture the skin and spurt of blood in the air made her feel sick. Crawling through the undergrowth she signalled for Mike and Pete to go wide.

"What have you got?" Looking through the scope he whispered softly

"Two maybe three of the little bastards are in there holes." Signalling to the rest of the men Jeanie knew this was a chance to get away; making a move was now or never.

"Come on…come on come….there you are" The two shots rattled through the trees like thunder rolling over a hill and as the men fell Jeanie saw the third. "Got him. MOVE!"

Mike and Pete started to fire at the guard on top of the carrier and in the cover fire Merle, Jeanie and Bill had made the way to the side. Crouching at the wheel both gents waited for the next move.

"Grenades…the hut is at the back of this carrier get the grenade as close to the hut as possible, there are fuel drums at the front go."

The noise disappeared in the jungle mass and as the waves of heat washed over her Jeanie had made a run for the jeep. Looking for a key and grabbing the gun from the dashboard she fired as more men washed over the sight. Fumbling under the steering column Jeanie tried desperately to get it started.

Hearing the fire being drawn closer and hearing the cries, the emphasis on leaving immediately had become more than visible.

Seeing her men jump in one after the other she began to count.

"Where the fuck is Merle?" Pete still firing shots out of the back of the jeep looked around. "He's coming now."

Looking out of the mirror she heard the shot and Merle fall forward lying in a pool of blood.

"Mike get in the fucking seat...." Jeanie ran and picked him up as Bill followed behind.

Jeanie dragged with all her might.

"Get in the fucking jeep and don't say a word,"

"Move now!" Jeanie started to fire at the oncoming attack dropping each time to look at the bleeding dying soldier.

"Sarge.....he's." Jeanie took a breath trying to compose what was left of her nerves.

"He'll be fine just keep pressure on it."   Watching the trickles of blood fill the curved ridges of the jeep the group were once again reminded of how fragile every situation had become. Jeanie clutched at the gun in her hand feeling guilty that her actions had put them all in danger.

"Mike...Mike Does that radio work?" As she shouted back he could hear the change in Jeanie's voice. She had taken a chance and they weren't out of the woods yet.

"Should be able to find a frequency...give me a few minutes"

Three hours had past and nothing but static was reporting back, Merle was pale and drawn and Jeanie had started to blame herself.

Standing at the side of the vehicle, the anger and disappointment that she may have killed one of her own started to arise

"Give me anything Mike please. Come on" Smiling he dragged everyone to the front of the jeep. "I got through we are about seven miles off that ridge there," pointing to the map everyone focused intently as hope began to rise. "If we can keep going we can make it by dawn."

Huddled in the front seat she placed her feet on the dashboard and as she held her head in her hands she needed to know that she had made the right decision. The last few months, had left them desolate and the reliance upon her to get them back to camp safe had been the only plan she could stick to. More than ever she felt alone

"I'm sure he will be fine Sarge. You made a decision so far so good." "We aren't there yet. Don't count them to soon." looking back at Merle Jeanie feared the worst and as the blood started drip out of the back of the jeep no matter how much pressure they put on the wound it never seemed to be enough. Within the first three months they had lost twenty two men but loosing one especially one who you had become close too filled her with dread.

A blistering red sky met them as they continued towards base and Jeanie dreaded the repercussions. Seeing the solemn faces in the rear of the jeep she scoped the horizon for a glimmer of hope.

"There's someone on the ridge look. Stop the car..." Jeanie stepped out of the vehicle and held up her hands, friendly or not she wasn't going to risk any more casualties. "Private Jack Rutherford. We need help."

"On your knee's soldier" Doing as she was told Jeanie placed her hands on the back of her head.

"We need help Sarge I've got one injured."

"Out of the vehicle now." Jeanie still on her knees screamed back feeling the fear cross between the patrols.

"Friendlies sir we're friendlies" seeing the blood on Jeanie the two men looked at each other. "Someone hurt in there."

"That's what I said before…we need help he's lost a lot of blood and he needs a medic."

Scrambling back to the jeep they followed the guards down to the main base. Bill and Pete dragged Merle's lifeless body from the rear and as the stretcher scrambled around Jeanie closed her eyes waiting for the screams. The fuss just seemed to buzz past and the haziness around her swallowed her thoughts.

Walking through the camp there was too much noise and as she looked at her blood stained uniform she tried to wipe the dried patches clean without much success.

She was lost.

"Excuse me do we have anywhere I could get this off,"

"Yeah there's a pool bout half a mile down you ok." Jeanie just smiled and patted his shoulder. She wanted to cry, she wanted to laugh she wanted to scream, but knowing she couldn't do any of it was driving her insane.

Reaching the brook she found a large tree that stretched out leading to a small pool which lapped the shore. Jeanie took off her clothes and as she sat at the edge the water soft waves started to take the stains away and the dark ripples caressed her feet.

Jeanie lay with her head on her knees wondering when the nightmare was going to end. She felt that she had forgotten how to cry and as she looked into the dark water Jeanie tried to find clarity, she had no option and falling apart now wasn't going to take her home.

The war had only given her pain, suffering and misery but it had also given her the capability to survive and fight if she needed to. Watching the pool she willed her tears to fall instead she saw a flicker of a reflection. Feeling eye's burning into her she grabbed her clothes and pulled out her gun. From a distance it looked as if she was getting dressed but in reality Jeanie had started to watch and wait. She was now a fully fledged hunter with instincts to match and as the crack of a twig echoed in the distance she knew her survival senses were working.

Reapplying the blood stained bandages and bindings hastily she knew the first thing she had to hide was her identity and quickly. Luring her culprit into plain sight she waited patiently until she felt the presence behind her. Counting to ten she stood up and pointed the gun behind the tree.

"Out! Move now or I'll shoot,"

"Put your gun down it's only me." Jeanie lowered but did not let go feeling uneasy about his presence.

"Kowalski I have told you before about sneaking around,"

"You know you shouldn't be out here on your own, it's not safe" Mike circled her with his eyes piercing her dressings.

"I don't know what's going on with you Mike but you're starting to scare me"

"I didn't mean to I just admire you Jeanie your not like the others. It just makes me think why you where made so differently than the rest?"

"The rest of who?" Mike knew his comments would cause a reaction as her inquisitive nature had always worked to his advantage

"Women I've had my fair share even an officers lady. But you I just don't get you."

"Mike you know why I'm here...I'm here for James. We've had this conversation please don't make this difficult."

"What if I said I loved you? What would you say then?" Jeanie taking small steps didn't turn back to respond.

"I would have to say you're delusional and to get over yourself quickly!"

Hearing him close behind she hurried trying to return to a form of civilisation. Side stepping behind a medical tent she tried to get her bearings.

The awkwardness between her and Mike increased with each passing month. Every time he would snipe and jibe for her to react to anything he would do and Jeanie had made excuses for him. When she had tried to talk it out her would always come up with the same conclusions:

"Everyone has a plan Jeanie don't you know that! For some of us it's already written when we are going to live, when we are going to love and when we are going to die. Why should you be any different?"

Trying to avoid any conversation surrounding James had become a daily occurrence and rumours about their relationship had circulated between the close nit quarters of the men.

Taking a few seconds before moving out into the crowds she stirred her thoughts wondering where he could be. Feeling his hands around her waist and his breath bearing down on her neck he pulled her into a small quiet corner leaving Jeanie once again isolated.

"Just to make you aware or until you understand why I'm here Sarge as always it's been a pleasure."

Jeanie watched him walk through the crowds; his abhorrent air worried her greatly and reminded her of the same arrogance which had put her in this position. Shaking his grip and making more excuses for him the tides of tiredness washed over her tugging her into sleep. Flicking through her journal Jeanie realised that she had not slept properly in seventy two hours. Lying on the temporary bed, the past day played heavily on her mind and as she relived each episode and nearly killing one of her men she felt no closer to finding James. Seeing the rest of her men pile into the shelter she tried to regain a sense of perspective.

This is not the time to loose it; focus Mike is just being Mike stop looking into it……

"Any news? I asked before and they wouldn't tell me anything." Jeanie tried to be strong, after all five of them had survived even if by sheer dumb luck. "They've amputated his leg…" Bill threw the contents of his cup to the ground spitting the rest at Jeanie's feet.

"What the fuck! Bill it's not his fault he had to make a call or else we would all still be trapped possibly dead for fuck sake," Pete stood in front of Jeanie almost protecting her from Bill's actions. The last few days had been rough for them all but deep inside Jeanie felt as if she was to blame. "He's lost a lot of blood Sarge that's the main problem. We've also been told its touch and go."

"Sarge it's just fucked up!" Eugene sat still on the floor looking to Jeanie for solace the thing was she couldn't even find it in herself to dish it out. "I promised to get you all here. After seeing the rest of the guys slaughtered in front of us it was the only option we had. I'm sorry if it was the wrong one we weren't going to survive out their much longer and I had to make the call….."

Turning around to walk away Jeanie scratched heavily at her forehead, seeing the blood under her finger nails she felt as if she was slowly loosing her mind. Grabbing onto her arm Mick pulled her back into the group.

"Gents we've lost enough already without blaming each other. Sarge took the call; at least he had the balls to do that so take your fucking tins and let's just salute Merle. I couldn't fucking stand him but you set of hopeless bastards seem to have become sentimental." Forcing the cup into Jeanie's hand he rested his arm around her shoulders, lifting her cup Jeanie stepped out of his hold feeling the same unease return.

"To Merle may you still be the most boring piece of shit on the planet…" In chorus the group toasted his name, Jeanie played with the mark on her head unable to believe that she had made the right decision. "Sarge your heads bleeding."

"If that's all I've got to worry about after today I think I've done well." The corner of his mouth curled at Jeanie's feeble attempt at sarcasm but it was painstaking obvious that this war was taking its toll both mentally and physically.

"Sarge….looks like we've got company." As the officer approached Jeanie fastened her jacket trying to avoid another negative encounter.

"Come on you lot we don't need another excuse for a bollocking!" "Private Jack Rutherford….I was told a Private Jack Rutherford would be found over here." Jeanie rose to her feet and stood to attention.

"I'm Private Rutherford sir." the officer looked at her in disgust which in turn was made to sound even worse by his stifling British accent emulating his feelings without course.

"Walk this way." falling in behind Jeanie marched to the headquarters, "At ease private. Jim take this over to the chief medical officer. Ok lad. You where the one that led the five yanks into camp aren't you?" Jeanie puzzled expected more questioning or at the least a bollocking as to why a lowly private saw fit to lead a group of men.

"Yes sir....yesterday." The officer didn't look in her direction; he didn't even see fit to lift his head before continuing.

"Right I know what happened to their platoon unfortunate really as we could have done with the men. You've been missing for sometime private but I've been informed you will be staying here and going out with 4th in the morning the rest of your...your group will be going meeting up in the North."

"Sir sorry I don't quite understand what's going on?" This time as Jeanie questioned his method the officer saw fit to raze his gaze.

"I've just told you what's going on and that should be enough I don't stand for insubordination private. You're dismissed!" The officer returned his gaze to the course of paperwork which sat in front of him. Jeanie felt unable to move as she needed more of an explanation.

"Sorry private is their something more that I can help with."

"No Sir sorry sir." Whispers emulated around the room and as she was about to be dismissed again the whispers met the officer's ear.

"Ah yes forgot that...that's right?"

"Sir?" on interrupting Jeanie's sentence he continued as if she had never spoke

"Yes well we've heard some of what you have done and you've been brought up to the ranking of Sergeant. As you where soldier."

   The group stood at the bottom of the hill waiting to hear about their next move. Separation wouldn't be easy as these men had become family even brothers.

"Sarge what's next." grabbing Eugene's shoulder Jeanie looked at the floor.

"You will be joining the other Yanks in the North and I'm staying with the engineering unit"

315

"Sarge I'm sorry that's just," Jeanie interrupted Eugene's flow knowing there lives had been changed by every experience they had been through.

"I know SNAFU…it's just all SNAFU…"

Chapter 30

Ivy paced the floor as Jayne continued to scream and no amount of bobbing was pacifying her today. "Jayne please stop mummy is so tired. Please just stop," bobbing up and down in Ivy's arms Jayne's face was crimson. Ivy continued to rub her back in hopes the rocking and the condolence would pacify the toddler even though in her efforts that wasn't going to be any time imminent.

Peering out of the window Ivy waited on hopes for a word from Jeanie. "Mummy needs to know if Auntie Jea is ok because I have sent her letter and I need her reply back and now she is worrying me to death and I don't think I can take it any more. Nana is getting on my nerves about it as well and everyone needs answers and Auntie Jeanie is not supplying them!"

The window steamed with her breath and the anticipation of every visit brought on nervous butterflies. Seeing the postman Ivy still holding the now pink and whimpering child ran to the door. Before the gentleman even had time to knock Ivy had opened the door, "Thank you come Jaynee lets see what's happening." Before the postman had time to respond Ivy had already closed the door.

Dancing over to the kitchen table she started to sift through desperately anticipating Jeanie's reply. "Nothing hold on Jayne…Nothing shit….nothing" throwing the envelopes down in anger Ivy couldn't help but feel despair. It was difficult to hide her disappointment and as Irene past she waited for her to comment on her dismay
"What's up with you?" Irene barged past grabbing hold of Jayne smothering her in spidery finger tickles and kisses.
" Don't mind me I'm just invisible."

"You're beginning to sound like Jeanie talking to yourself like that. She sent anything?"

"No…Nothing…nothing at all."

Every day there was no response made it more unbearable and Ivy was desperate even if it was to appease her own conscience.

"Don't worry so much you know Jea she's tough a war won't slow her down and you know her she won't make any decisions until she comes home. Come on girl time for a pot of tea…..Come on Jaynee." Ivy didn't unfold her arms; she couldn't even take comfort from her mother's words.

The guilt felt painful.

Something was wrong and Ivy felt it.

"Mum I know something's wrong," Irene ruffled the living room curtains trying to stay positive as the thought of Jeanie at war made her sick and talking about something being wrong made it even more unbearable.

"You're being silly if something was wrong we would have heard something by now look at George. That girl….that girl never ceases to amaze me. She will be ok and we have to keep thinking that. I have no other choice and I don't think I can bear to loose anyone else." Ivy rested her head on the parlour door contemplating her mums new found positivity however in the pit of her stomach it felt like a washing machine churning.

"Guess your right no other choice." Jeanie had been the glue that kept them together living without her it was hard for everyone.

"Ivy your visitor is here and one word of advice watch him. No matter what he's done so far I still don't trust him."

The knock at the door was light and Ivy knew her day of reconciliation had come. Resting her head back on the door she counted to ten under her breath.

"Hello John come in."

"Ivy…Irene…" He seemed just as beaten as Ivy and as Irene gazed at the pair she couldn't help but feel their pain.

"John…." Irene coughed again to try to soften her voice.

"John you seem very distracted. Just as distracted as Ivy is there anything we should know." He smiled uneasy and adjusted his gloves several times in his cap, looking up he found it difficult to keep eye contact.

"No. No just a hard couple of days and I leave tomorrow so this scenario play's on your mind." Ivy escorted him through to the parlour where Jayne was still busy playing, closing the door Ivy sat in the chair next to the fire place wondering what the next move would be.

"You know something and you've have kept it from us for weeks. I can't stand this anymore" John sat on the floor at the side of Jayne, her smiles and gurgles lifting his spirits.

"If I did know anything Ivy do you honestly think I could tell you? It's hard enough that I…I love someone desperately that doesn't love me and I also have a child to her sister in regards to love complications I think we have reached the pinnacle don't you." Ivy sat back in her chair with her arms folded, knowing he was right didn't make it any easier and it hurt to hear that he still loved Jeanie. It hurt even more to see him with Jayne.

"Hello darling who's this. Who's this?"

"Just wondered if I could let her know you know," Ivy holding onto her daughters hand lifted her gaze.

"Yes…yes she's going to know anyway. Jaynee this is daddy dada dada," Jayne looked lovingly to Ivy and gargled her responses. John surprised at how soon it had happened appreciated what Ivy had done.

As the second hour past John gathered his things, "Thank you."

"What for it's all out in the open now we have nothing to hide," John took hold of his daughters hand playing with her delicate little fingers.

"I know but with everything even Irene has been gracious."

Opening the parlour door Irene stood at the foot of the stairs and as John put on his coat, gloves and cap Irene cocked her head to one side admiring her view.

"I'll say it for my daughter John you suit that uniform" Ivy blushed in agreement and embarrassment.

"Thank you I just wish I could have done more....for Jeanie." Irene heard the break in his voice. He was usually so sure of himself and Irene knew something must be breaking down his defences and Jeanie wasn't at home.

"Right I must go thank you again." Leaning forward he kissed Ivy on the cheek and held out his hand, Irene ignoring his request nodded in confirmation still studying his demeanour. John disappeared out of the large front door and Irene still not convinced leant to look through the porch window.

"He's hiding something I didn't believe you before but that boy is definitely hiding something."

"I told you before. So what can I do about that now?"

"Go after him he and do it quickly cause he's getting into his car." Grabbing her coat Ivy ran out to meet him

"John…John wait one minute." As she got to the car she took a minute to catch her breath and to think up a reason of her sudden arrival.

"Sorry phew ok. Listen I know you leave in the morning oh god this is awkward. Do you want to go for a drink nothing funny…I mean shit? Right here we go again….As friends would you like to go for a drink I think it would be good for both of us and help when Jeanie comes home." "Ivy we had something but I don't know whether it's such a good idea." Ivy bent down and looked at John hiding underneath the lip of his cap

"I don't want anything from you I just want to sort out for Jayne's sake." "Get in get in before I change my mind." John drove out of the village and headed out into the country.

"Are we going far?"

"No. We don't need any more rumours in this village."

Thirty minutes later they pulled up at a small country tavern and as they rushed through the door both of them looked windswept.

The fire roared in the centre of the room and the inglenook fire place glowed with the heat. Sitting at a table in the corner John ordered two drinks and Ivy felt the nervous butterflies return.

She was out of her depth and she knew it.

"I've got you what you used to drink. I hope that's ok." Ivy nodded as John pulled up a chair.

"So what do you want to talk to me about?"

"You just seem distant and I wanted to help."

"I knew it…your fucking mother put you up to this didn't she!" Ivy bit her lip trying not to agree but knowingly she had already given her position away.

"If I said no I would be lying she just knew something was wrong"

"Lets face it Ivy I lived next door to you for practically my whole life and there are only two other women that know me that well and one of them is my mother. I have nothing to say Ivy and I can't make up stuff just because your mum has a feeling." As his sentence finished his voiced raised in anger at Irene's actions.

"John I said right away something was wrong. We are not getting any mail from Jeanie and we're worried."

"I know why you are worried and trust me that place will be the last thing on her mind right now!" John picked up the glasses and put them on the bar and as he grabbed Ivy's hand he began to drag her out of the door.

"Where are we going?"

"You will see!"

Driving for hours the hills and moor land had rolled around every corner and every brow. Pulling up on the small cobbled street John stopped the car and violently and as he opened Ivy's door his mood had darkened.

"Get out. I know I've been cruel before Ivy but you need to see what's going on here for real. This fantasy situation that you have built up inside your mind doesn't exist and Jeanie is caught up in something that you could never be able to control" Grabbing her hand again he pulled her down the corridor and as they walked into a side room John closed the door.

"Mary meet Ivy this is Jeanie's sister. Now she doesn't know what's gone on and she doesn't need to know....but I think you may know where a few of Jeanie's belongings may be and I think today is the day you fancy enlightening us on the matter!" Ivy sat on the chair confused and dumfounded and the young woman sat in the hospital bed was just as dumbstruck as she was at his outburst.

"Sir I don't know what you are talking about." John sat on the side of the bed and smirked his hours of research had come back to Mary and now with Ivy in tow he wanted the truth.

"Come now Mary after your last outburst you didn't think I would just walk away without investigating you a little longer do you. You see a little birdie told

322

me that whilst in the midst of this relationship they caught you a couple of times lets just say in places where you shouldn't have been and playing with papers which weren't yours to play with." John folded his arms raising an eyebrow; Ivy just sat waiting for the event to take its course. Mary by this point had started to pull at the sheets and as her tears began to well she knew he held no sympathy for her this time.

"You don't understand."

"Make me understand cause this still says to me that you're working with him and against me."

"Fine I just want him doesn't matter."

Mary looked away disgusted at herself, "He used to meet me upstairs next to the filing room. I thought he loved me and he used to dare me to do things and I used to promise him intercourse. He said we had to keep it up so I started in the mail room first and I gave him the letters I took….." I'm not proud of doing it and I feel guilty all the time but he was very persuasive. I got caught up in something and did things I regret because I thought he loved me then look what he did!"

John raised himself up off the bed and as Ivy sat in wait of John's command, she was still confused and now distressed at the girls circumstances.

"Mary you should have told me sooner this is important. Thank you for being honest with me. Ivy its time to go." Ivy stood to attention as if she was one of his soldiers but she couldn't help but feel for this poor woman and as she took hold of Mary's hand she hoped her feelings would be transferred through her touch.

"We've all made those mistakes and I promise it will get better." John closed his eyes knowing Ivy was talking about their affair and after lighting another cigarette he paced fiercely down the corridor.

"What was that about John…John…JOHN you answer me now god dam it! I have had enough games."

"Not here outside now." Ivy threw her head back; she had been drove all over the country to meet a desperate girl in hospital and have riddles played out in front of her.

"Are you going to tell me now or do I have to guess?" Blowing the smoke out into the air he walked around the side and leant over the bonnet of his car. Ivy pulled her coat around her and waited in desperation. "I can't tell you everything but that girl has been involved in something terrible which affects Jeanie and I think she has been hiding or filtering letters telegram and who knows what else for someone who doesn't like me or James or Jeanie. The one thing I have found out is that someone wanted her out of the way and now Jeanie is at war and in small mercies at least she is away from all of this.

From the reports that I have received she is fine and this is where you come into it. I need help and I can point you in the right direction but I can't take you all the way…I'm not going to be here."

"Why couldn't you tell me? Why couldn't you let me know?" John run his hands through his hair and shook his head.

"Ivy on track record you haven't been the greatest when it comes to trust and let's face it would anything I have just said make you or your family feel any better?

I have a job to do Ivy and I have a war to fight. I have to do what's right not for her not for me….for my country my men and our way of life…..I took on this responsibility with or without her."

"So what now?" Stepping into the car he looked across Kirkcudbright's sleepy town and wished he could disappear in its quietness.

"Now I have to go and say my goodbyes." Ivy jumped back into the passenger seat unable to understand why he felt so defeated.

"What do I need to do John? You said you needed my help and I don't understand what use I'm going to be in all this."

"I need you to find out what shit that little girl in there has been hiding from all of us and you need to do it fast."

Reaching the cottage John looked a pale gaunt reminder of his former self and Ivy knew whatever information she was about to acquire wouldn't spell good news for any of them.

"How will I get on the base?"

"You're working with Anne and show this at the gate. I've authorise it. And before you say anything I knew this was going to happen. You're not the only ones who lives are predictable. Just make sure your discreet...please." Ivy pulled her coat around her again this time not because of the cold; his words didn't bring her any comfort and now she had been cast in riddles.

Not knowing the full circumstances made her more curious about what was really going on and the next challenge she had to face was walking back into the house and trying to pacify her mum.

"Where have you been till this hour you know I've got to go back to the factory," Ivy took off her coat and looked to the floor for inspiration

"Mum I know we had car trouble I'm sorry" Irene glanced a look at her daughter, the only look a mother could give when she's working out the truth. "She needs you and the others upstairs asleep. Tell Iris as well that if she doesn't turn up tonight on time there will be hell to pay."

Waking up the next morning she felt sick with anguish and the card which John had left sat on her dressing table mocking her at every glance and making her feel worse.

Running to the bathroom she vomited with the nerves, frustration and guilt. Hearing the commotion Daisy opened the bedroom door taunted by Ivy's sickness.

"Whoever's making the noise can they go and make it somewhere else? I'm not in the mood." Seeing Ivy's washed out complexion her annoyance soon turned to concern.

"You ok love you really don't look well. You're not pregnant again are you?" Ivy laughed and wiped her hand across her face trying to gain some composure. "No Daisy you have to have sex to be pregnant and that's not happened for a while. No I think I must have caught something off Jayne she's been cranky for the last couple of days." Daisy sat on the floor pulling her pretty pink dressing gown around her. "Tell you what then if you need a break it's my day off and I will take Jaynee out for a bit gives you a break." Ivy needed an excuse to get out of the house and Daisy had just walked straight into it.

"You're an angel if you could. Think I might nip down to the docs....you know just in case."

"Ok Dokey that's sorted come on chicken."
Grabbing the already awake toddler she started to mutter nonsense to her down the hall.

Ivy laying down on the bed closed her eye's and thought of Jeanie, she couldn't help but wonder whether it was courage or stupidity that made her give up her family and walk away from everything she had ever known.

Looking through her wardrobe she tried to find something that looked suitable for an office and as a glimmer distracted her search she excavated deeper into the depths of her wardrobe to find out what it was. *Jeanie's engagement ring not from James from John*.

Ivy placed the ring on her own finger and as she admired the clear cut simple diamond ring she knew it was Jeanie all over. Despondent Ivy placed it on the mantel and continued to dress as no matter how much she had tried John was too much in love with her sister to ever look at her again twice.

Feeling self conscious she realised other than looking after Jayne for the last two years, she hadn't really done anything important not even towards the war effort. Ivy still a little vein and selfish looked again at her appearance she was still beautiful and the spitting image of her mother. Her blonde hair curled and sparkled in just the right places and Jeanie always used to tell her how lucky she was to be that beautiful. Looking back at the mantel her beauty still wasn't enough to win the man she wanted and today she might have looked a picture of elegance but, deep inside she just felt sick and alone. Ivy placed the ring in her jacket pocket and headed out of the door, shouting her goodbyes to Daisy and Jayne her mind was set on finding out what was going on at the base.

Arriving at the front gates her stomach flipped over and the effort to stay calm was overwhelmed by the effort to throw up again. Anne graced the stair way as Ivy waited in reception and she couldn't help but notice Anne's contempt at her presence.

"Ivy Stanton. Jeanie's sister is that right?"

"Yes…Yes that's me."

"I can see follow me please." She didn't even hide the fact that she was doing it. Ivy felt uncomfortable; she was scared and this was the first situation she had ever encountered which she had been solely in control of. The thought of messing this up now felt unbearable.

Ivy knew of the rumours which had circulated the offices, Jeanie had told her already about the cruel nature of some people and by the sounds of it Mary had been one of them.

"Follow me please I've been told you're needed in the sorting room." Anne escorted her down a small corridor into a smoky dark dank room and instead of taking her all the way she pointed to the direction she had to follow.

"Thank you...oh and for the record I know what you have been saying about my sister and just so you know. So does John." Ivy made her way through the badly smelling room and as she reached the desk at the end she was greeted by a white haired gentleman.

"Ahh you're my new recruit...never had one before but walk this way." He scuffled his feet as he walked and Ivy couldn't help but smile at the curled pipe in his hand.

"My granddad used to smoke a pipe; the smell always reminds me of him... I'm Ivy by the way." Taking his time he sat on the chair at the end of the corridor," Jacob that's me. Jake sometimes but seen as you're a pretty one I'll let you make up your mind." Ivy took off her coat and placed her handbag on the desk behind the chair.

"So Jacob what do you need me to do?" as he smiled his little white moustache curled into his cheeks and he reminded Ivy of a little elf.

"John said you where going to sort out that stuff that had been held back or something. I do forget my dear...age and so on. The room at the back is for all those things that go missing a girl used to come down here before. Forgot her name and she had a Scottish accent. Another pretty little thing to."

"So it's in there. Am I on my own?" Jacob had started to shuffle back to his desk at the far end of the corridor; he hadn't heard Ivy's reply and as she wiped the sweat off her hands she opened the door not knowing what to expect.

"Shit for fuck sake girl gets a grip." Ivy stepped cautious into the room but as she did so she calmed in moments. It was tiny more like a broom cupboard than a room and as she slid around the door she immediately saw the bags of letter's thrown around. It was if someone had brought a whirlwind inside and blew them about.

"This could take me month's…come on Jeanie give me a clue." Sifting around she came across three pales, one was labelled unclaimed, the other no address and on the other POW. Realising quickly that all of the letters had been opened, read and the information stripped out she realised she had found her starting place.

"I'm missing something I've been here hours and I know there's something that I have to be missing." she rested herself against the wall folding her arms. Ivy looked up towards the ceiling hoping for inspiration.

"I'm talking to myself Jeanie this is all your fault and usually when I caught you doing it I though you where made. Well it just goes to show you that it runs in the family!" Stamping her foot down in temper something on the dresser caught her eye. Grabbing the chair she reached up and realised the paper on the end was the photo of James.

The same picture she had given to Jeanie before her internment. Ivy froze, recalling John's conversation whilst out on his trip. James and John had been some of the focus of this person's attention.

Stepping down Ivy placed the box on the table and as she searched the piles of letter's she noticed these were not from Jeanie, they where for Jeanie delving deeper Ivy jumped in fright as Jacob entered the room.

"Sorry my dear did I startle you I have brought you a cup of tea. You left your bag as well so I thought I would bring that down here," catching her breath she replaced the lid on the box.

"Thank you it's still a bit messy in here I'm afraid." Jacob looked around the room smiled and left without question.

Stuffing the contents into her bag she knew if she left immediately it would arouse suspicion and as she drank her tea she paced the floor counting down the clock. After twenty minutes she left the room and in a stroke of luck Jacob was no where to be seen, wanting to run down the corridor she tried to keep her emotions under control. As she reached the gates of the barracks Ivy set off home at pace nothing or no one was going to stop her finding out the truth.

The house was empty as she arrived home and as she ran upstairs she kicked off her shoes and coat tipping out the contents of her bag onto the bed. Frantically she started to search through the papers. They all said the same thing:

"I love you Write back....Write back......Write back."

Finding a telegram stuck to the bottom of the box Ivy tentatively pulled it from its envelope.

"We regret to inform that Private Jack Rutherford of the Engineering division has been lost presumed dead. Dr James Watson has been informed of his passing."

Ivy screamed hysterically, "John said she was fine, he said she was ok. I don't understand." James's letters screamed at her wanting to know what was going on and who Jack was. Ivy frenzied ran to the phone box and the panic of not getting to John welled inside like an unexploded bomb as they where all in danger.

Her hands shook as she requested the number from the exchange. "I need to speak to Lieutenant Colonel John Stanton please its urgent. I have clearance….I promise I have clearance."

"One moment please I'll just put you through."

"John….." Anne Coston's voice deflated Ivy immediately and her contemptuous tones continued through her introduction.

"No he's not here he's otherwise engaged."

"You don't understand Anne I need to get an urgent message to him it's important." Anne placed her hands on her hips unrequited at Ivy's melodrama.

"Well it couldn't have been that important when you ran out here this afternoon,"

"Now you listen to me good Anne Croston. You need to write this down and listen well tell John James is alive and they are all in danger." Anne screwed up the piece of paper unable to listen to the drivel any longer.

"This is bullshit Ivy what are you talking about,"

"For fuck sake. He sent me to see Mary." Anne paused shocked that she knew about her.

"My Mary. Mary Conaghan?"

"I don't fucking know some girl in hospital in some place that begins with Kirk. Please for the love of god listen. Tell John that James is alive. I found letters and his picture the name on the back of the picture was shit EC…..it just says EC…they are all in danger and the telegram that Jeanie received was a fake. I've checked Mary did it her signature is on the bottom. Anne I'm trusting you. Please get this message to him." Anne was silent on the other end of the phone Ivy screamed again.

"ANNE…ANNE!!,"

"I'm here I got it I'll go now I need you to wait." Anne dropped the phone and ran down the corridor, the carriers where all but gone but she knew John would only travel by car. Seeing John she raced out in front of the vehicle and as the car slammed to Holt. John stepped out.

"Anne what are you doing?" Still in shock Anne handed over the scribbled piece of paper. "Ivy...Ivy on the phone she said you would know she said it was important."

"Go back inside and tell her...tell her from me thank you and I will do my best."

Anne didn't stop to see the car leave and as she raced back up the stairway tears streamed down her face.

"I'm here Ivy...I've done it." Ivy cried with relief dropping the phone out of her hand. Taking a deep breath Ivy sobbed uncontrollably feeling the relief at having got to John just in time. Leaving the phone box she wrapped her jacket around herself.

Irene pacing the floor realising that the secret of the letters had started to be unravelled. Not able to comprehend what was going on she waited for Ivy's return.

"Mum?"

"You tell me this minute what's going on you said it was nothing these letters aren't nothing where's my girl tell me now Ivy. NOW!."

"I found these at the base this afternoon reading through them I realised that something wasn't right and I've told John."

"My girl is fighting a war for a husband that isn't dead and by the looks of it was never in danger she could be dead I could end up burying her because of him again. I can't cope with this anymore. I feel as if I'm loosing my mind." Ivy walked cautiously towards her, placing her hands over Irene's she pulled her close.

"We can't think like that Jeanie's strong. Jeanie's stronger than all of us put together and like you said before if anything had happened we would be the first to know Mum I promise."

Holding her close Ivy looked at the trees outside
the window, the violence of the wind lay heavy on
Ivy's heart. Knowing she had to be the strong one
was always a difficult role to play.

*John said she was fine so it must be true. He
would lie after all this.*

Stepping into Jeanie's spot she felt the burden, the
burden of what her sister had carried for so many
years and as she wiped Irene's tears away she
realised how selfish and cruel she had been.

"Come on Mum stiff upper lip. I think its time for a
cuppa…"

"Ivy Thank you." Ivy smiled back puzzled to her
mum's response.

"What for?"

"You've been through a lot as well and I don't think
I have given you enough praise….so thank you."

Ivy just hoped John knew what he was doing not
just for her sake but for his as well.

Chapter 31

John looked at his reflection in the broken mirror and as he washed away what little suds he had and replaced them with razor burn he knew the decision to shave had been a bad one.

Knowing he was addressing the troops he felt as if he needed to make an effort or at least look like it was important enough to. Reading through the telegram again he couldn't believe that part of the nightmare he'd been facing for the last six years was coming to an end.

"Gather what troops are left in camp get some water stations set up." John replaced his cap and trying to smooth down the now red marks under his collar; he couldn't help but think of Jeanie.

Standing on the embankment John took the telegram from his top pocket marking the momentous occasion.

"I have received a telegram today of great significance. The war in Europe is over." A small cheer erupted from the few that had gathered but in no way did it signify the event with the celebration it deserved.

"Ok settle down we know we still have some way to go here so as much as it is good news we need to keep focused and continue to push forward so this war can end for all of us. Please resume duties."

With that John undid his tie and loosened the top buttons of his shirt, it was short, sweet and at least it marked the occasion, however thoughts of Jeanie and finding her seemed to have more of significance.

Unaware of John's presence Jeanie had packed up her things and waited patiently in line for a new pair of boots, dragging her heals the thought of not knowing where she was going next exhausted her.

"Jack I remember you...your Jack." Jeanie vaguely remembered the voice and hardly lifted her head to acknowledge that someone had spoke. "The last time I saw you…yeah the last time I saw you where kicking someone's head in at the barracks."
Knowing the conversation wasn't going to end Jeanie looked around to see who was talking, "I remember you don't tell me….Eric bed at the side leant me shoe polish..." Eric nodded and shook her hand; juggling equipment on his back Jeanie walked his way happy to see a friendly face.
"Sorry bout before been a long few months just not what I expected…" Not being able to find James in the chaos made Jeanie feel like her mission had failed.
"So where bout's are you heading?" Eric was upbeat and Jeanie couldn't understand his happiness or his enthusiasm.
"I've got a few men which I have to meet at the far station. Be given orders at that point mind you I've heard rumours this war's winding down so hopefully it might end soon." Jeanie paused wanting to scream out. Eric waited for her as his blank expression said it all.
"I know what you mean. I'm heading over there now apparently we have a new Sarge let's hope he's not a bastard like the others!"

Gossip had already started about the end of the conflict in Europe, and how it must signify an end for them. If the conflicts had finished the next phase would be the liberation of the POW's and for Jeanie that meant there was still hope that James was alive. She had seen the conditions of POW and dreaded the thought of anyone putting up with the cruelty and brutality that had been dished out over this god awful conflict. The stories needless executions, dysentery and starvation made her anxiety heighten and whilst Jeanie hung onto hope she new it was the dangerous option.

"Sergeant are you with us today," Jeanie hung her head knowing the blank vacant stare would have to be eradicated.

"Apologies Sir."

"Ummm if I'm to believe your recommendations a blank look when I'm giving you orders isn't going to bode well with me. At ease soldier.

There are six of you altogether I will give you the names in a moment."

"Thank you Sir."

"There are several yank warehouse stations to the north and we need to start moving what we can. So come here…" Jeanie wandered over to the desk looking at the map placed in front of her; still self conscious of the previous look Jeanie dipped her head.

"There are a number of stranded vehicles which are going to be essential to get this stuff moved. So when you arrive you will need to report into Sergeant Kowalski understand."

"Yes Sir." As Jeanie was dismissed her heart sank knowing the war for her wasn't over yet and the thought of stranded possibly burnt out vehicles to get back on the road made the fight for James more distant.

Gathering the group Jeanie briefed out what was needed and double checking the munitions Jeanie placed another hand gun into her inside pocket just for good measure. The journey may have sounded simple but knowing the endeavours she had just faced made it all the more reason to be prepared.

Setting off Jeanie looked back at the sanctity of the camp, she longed to be home and to be with her family. Her feelings by no means any different than any other soldier she had met. The experience of war had changed her and the near death experience had become the crutch she leant on to keep her alive. Like before war had made her strong enough to fight and her will great enough to survive.

Eric started to whistle as the lads trundled down the road.

"Come on Sarge you know this one." Jeanie smiled as he confidently broke out into song and as the moral lifted if nothing else it took their minds off death.

As night fell John entered the camp head quarters, "At ease men as you were. We don't have as many men as I expected. I know we have had some casualties in these regions but I've just been made aware that group of men have been sent to recovery some of carriers…..how many in total again was it?" The group in front of him hurriedly looked through the remnants of paperwork scattered behind them.

"Six altogether sir and I believe the have gone to meet the yanks."

"What do you mean the Yanks? They where supposed to be heading up towards Rangoon?" The blank look on all of the faces made it easy for John to understand.

"There was a Private Jack Rutherford in that group…." Confused as to why John asked he handed the sheet over.

"You mean Sergeant Jack Rutherford Sir they moved out earlier this morning meeting an American Staff Sergeant Kowalski."

"Read out the names of who is with him…" Again confused as to why John would be interested he read them out.

"Fred Armstrong, Bill Kidderminster, Arthur Roberts, Joe Andrews, and Jack Rutherford…" John counted under his breath hoping not to hear a familiar name.

"That's only five you said there where six?"
Hearing the aggravation in John's voice he
desperately looked for the missing name.
"Sorry Sir bottom of the last sheet, Eric Cowley."
John screwed up the piece of paper in his hand.
"Cowley you said!" looking frantically at the sheet
he repeated the name again. "Yes Sir….Eric
Cowley."
Throwing the piece of paper on the floor John
clenched his fists.
"I need more details……find out where they are
going exactly where they are going and let me know
right away."
"Sir these orders came in from General Peterson."
"I know where they cam from I just need the details
of exactly which ridge they are going to."

   Walking away he couldn't believe that she'd been
in camp and he didn't notice. He could have been
with her saved her and as John paced unrequitedly
in camp Jeanie started to set up perimeters for the
night.
   Taking the first watch she took out her journal:

*"I'm back to sleepless nights again, I don't think I
can take anymore rain everything is drenched and
it makes it more difficult for me to keep up my
spirits in the rain.*

   *The new lads seem ok, everyone's a bit quiet but
I'm sure we will get to know each other before the
days out. Every time I think I may be closer to
finding you they send me in another direction, this
time its more carriers.*

   *I've lived in shit so long maybe it suits me. I met
an old friend today, we where in basic training
together. I don't look like a sergeant I look like a
scared young kid in charge of men who have been
here years.*

We have passed so much death on the way that it is just normality now every path you take is little with the stinking stench of death. Its make you want to vomit but instead you just step over them and carry on. If push comes to shove and its either me or them my gun is always poised. What does that now say about me?

People have been talking about the POW camps and I just can't stand the thought of you being persecuted. Maybe you're not being persecuted, maybe you've developed the taste of death and killing has become second nature. I don't know why but it doesn't even seem senseless anymore. It feels like a means to an end just another job.

Its pitch black, I like to say it was peaceful but the rain just keeps falling. I feel I'm truly on my own and for the first time in a while I'm not scared, just homesick. One day I will give you this journal, maybe our kids can read it about their mum's adventures trying to find dad in the jungle. But I don't think they would want to know how many people I've killed or what I have had to do to survive.

Wherever you are I hope you're thinking of me as I think of you, I miss you. Night Night may you be safe."

Jeanie popped the pencil back into her jacket pocket and placed her hand over the top of the book. Her thoughts had become her conscience and her notebook her guide back home.

The temporary shelter wasn't pretty but at least it was keeping some of the rain away and as Jeanie stoked the fire and walked the perimeters; the rest of them had tried to settle as much as they could. Eric still jovial started to reminisce back to the barracks and Jeanie still confused could recollect that he talked a lot but he was never this optimistic.

"Sarge we can't make out your accent where the fuck are you from?" Jeanie knelt beside the fire glad to be out of the rain.

"Originally Lancashire quite close to Chorley. We also did a stint in Manchester for a while and then when I was a teenager we moved further up to Cumbria so I suppose I'm a dolly mixture." Joes still trying to figure his new leader out looked intently at Jeanie as she warned herself by the fire.

"Listen Sarge I mean don't take this offensive but you look well different. You know what I mean..." Jeanie laughed, it was amusing to see so much attention about her looks and the fact that the same conversation had been regurgitated so many times prompted the story she had told over and over again.

"Sorry did I say something funny..."

"No nothing I haven't heard a million times over since I joined up but I'm sure you lot will make me a man. Well you can try. Ask Eric what I did to the last one who called me a puff."

"Jack put him in the infirmary apparently his nose has never been the same since!" Joe couldn't help but laugh and as no story needed to be told he felt at ease.

"Told you! Anyone who looks like that my old sunshine has to have a decent personality."

Jeanie chuckled the reminiscence of the situation was uncanny; she had the same conversation with the American soldiers she had been stationed with. In fact the de ja vue was implicit that every moment after had been embedded into her memory.

Jeanie watched the sun rise feeling something different hovering in the air. Te temper of the morning unnerved her and the aggression of the weather made her stomach turn. Doing the last checks, Jeanie looked at the violence of the sky, her gut feeling was never usually wrong and something really didn't feel right. Holding back Jeanie looked cautiously around her, feeling a tap on her shoulder she jumped.

"Fuck sake Eric don't do that" Eric still highly strung kept his hand on her shoulder. "Sorry Sarge just we're off and I didn't want you left too far behind."

The walk was arduous and Jeanie's legs throbbed, the pains in her knees made the terrain feel worse and as she reached the top of the clearing Joe slumped over her shoulder.

"Joe this isn't the time to dick about." Sseeing the blood drain from his body she fell to floor with him covering her legs.

"Incoming...Incoming. FUCKING INCOMING! GET DOWN AND LOOK SHARP!!"

The brigade dropped to the undergrowth on her request, rolling Joe off her legs she picked up the map.

"Bill you need to radio in our position Arthur...Arthur that's a sniper that was a precision shot scope around and look for anything suspicious Eric take the map we need to find which route to go."

Jeanie tried to wipe the blood off her hands; the stains ran down her legs like small rivers and again she was covered in someone else's blood

"Arthur 12 O'clock"

"He's at the top of the tree."

"Can you take the shot?" He didn't respond and within seconds Jeanie was down to four men.

"Sarge there is a warehouse something at the bottom of the ridge if we can make it back round...FUCK!" Eric fell to his knees gripping his knee.

"Shit where are you?" Jeanie felt out of control and she needed to make a decision. "Pull back...Pull back now all of you" Fred and Bill straggled the undergrowth fighting for survival. The small task of getting vehicles back up and ready had just turned into a blood bath.

"Scrap the route over the clearing we are going to the back of this ridge. Eric said there is a road down the ridge we need to fix him up and make radio contact." Bill and Fred took hold of Eric's arm and started to run towards the ridge. As they reached the ridge negotiating down the road wasn't going to be easy especially with Eric. Sliding down the rock face they hid behind a bolder at the bottom.

"Fred you in front scope around and cover us if necessary. Bill help me with Eric."

Walking out in the open wasn't something Jeanie wanted to face; the wooden structure seemed to drop into the side of the cliff face and dozens of burnt out personnel carriers littered the road. Jeanie felt the panic well inside.

Hiding behind one of the carriers Jeanie pushed open the wooden door, the boxes inside where stacked high and the smell of decay was highly present. Taking the gun from her pocket she scoped out the first door she came to.

"Right in here put him on the desk. Where's Fred?" Bill had started to bandage up Eric's leg wound and as he fumbled around with bandages and dressings Jeanie had started to venture back out.

"I'm going to see where he is stay here" Checking the small corridor Fred was no where to be seen.

"Where are you?" hearing two shots Jeanie ran to the front of the burnt out carrier and as he fell Jeanie looked up the roof. The masked man walked around the top looking for any signs of life, Jeanie pressed her body into the overhang and as she saw him walk by she grabbed Fred's shoulder and dragged him to the side of the compound.

"He I didn't cause......frie..." without another sound he seemed to take his last breath, she wanted to cry she wanted to scream but she needed to help protect who was left.

Going back inside the building Jeanie cautiously made her way back into the corridor, there was silence. Bill was sat on the chair and Eric was no where to be seen. Jeanie feared for the worst and as she spun the chair around, his head slumped and the blood filled his lap. Jeanie didn't want to look or breathe.

Hiding behind the door she heard voices counting the footsteps under her breath she mapped out their approximate location. Loading the gun she counted again.

Twelve steps to the door, five steps to the racking. Go Jeanie you need to go now!

Hiding between the stacked boxes she made her way down to the clearing. Eric stood in front of another man, fearing for his life she moved closer listening attentively to the conversation. "She's here I brought her." Jeanie needed to get closer and as she crawled through the slight gap she crouched down trying to hear more.

"You said we would be together…You said you'd love me…." Jeanie confused glanced over her shoulder; the man grabbed hold of Eric and kissed him passionately.

Jeanie gasped never experiencing anything like it before. Crawling further into the tetris of boxes she tried to make out the masked figure.

"I told you before I don't fuck degenerates…."

"I've done everything you said I took his picture like you asked and I even got that bitch to plant it. I even delivered what you needed to Peterson."

"My darling boy don't you understand there's a bigger picture and you are just a stepping stone in a long line of stepping stones and like I've just said. I don't fuck degenerates."

Jeanie closed her eyes hearing the gun explode and the thud of Eric's body hitting the floor, the realisation set in that this had been an elaborate ploy to lure her here.

Jeanie adamant to find out more kept the figure in sight and as she backed up along the short walk way, she felt a tight hand over her mouth. "Shhh" Jeanie held her gun tight and as he spun her around she froze to the spot John wiped the tears off her cheek.

"Are you ok?"

"What the fuck is going on…." John cocked his gun and pushed her against the wall of the crates.

"Can't explain now just stay here….." as he smiled Jeanie didn't feel at ease, watching him disappear around the side of the crate she knew this wasn't the end.

John walked around the compound, sliding around the office door towards the far end he saw a figure tied to a chair.

"Ahhhh the delightful John didn't know you'd even make it across….." John lifted his hands as the gun dug into his skull.

"Always a pleasure!"

"See I know she's here. I can smell her. Can't you? You've dipped in the delights of Jeanie before….Come out come out wherever you are…." Jeanie slid around the boxes out of sight; looking at the man in the chair she knew it was James.

"John I'm sure you're aware of your honoured guest."

"I know you don't I?"

"John we've met a number of times before and in some very altruistic positions." Throwing him to the floor he placed the gun against the man's head.

"Jeanie…Jeanie…..you need to come out and play now James really needs you and John well probably not so much." Firing a shot he hit John in shoulder and as she heard a thud John fell to the floor.

"You know I wouldn't think twice about killing him. Lets face it he's not important in the grand scheme of things. But James well he's needed elsewhere!" Jeanie still hiding she slid her body through a small gap, holding her gun high she quietly stepped towards him.

"Hello Mike long time no see." Mike held his hands in the air and as he smiled coyly he coaxed her anger.

"Are you going to shoot me Jeanie? Cause you know I've done all this for you!"

"For me you've done this for me! Don't be silly Mike we all know you've never been able to think for yourself. Well I tell you what else you can do for me…" Mike grabbed her hand the sound of the shot echoed around the warehouse. As he punched her, Jeanie retaliated, kicking him in the groin punching him in the kidneys. Running for the gun he threw himself in her path, Jeanie slid along the concrete floor connecting back with her gun

"Get the fuck off me. MOVE now you fucking piece of shit…" Jeanie kicked him in the face and as her boot connected the blood spilled out onto the pale grey floor. Still leaning upright off the floor she signalled which direction he should move to.

"Back off Mike now…Make another fucking move you piece of shit and I'll shoot!" Jeanie blooded rose to her feet.

"Stay on your knee's put your hands behind the back of your head," Mike spat away the blood in distaste at her getting the upper hand.

"You arresting me now Jeanie?" Placing the gun at his temple, Jeanie sneered

"Just tell me why? What did I ever do to you?" Mick spat again. "Jeanie…Jeanie don't do it." Holding his shoulder John stepped forward

"Let me take care of it…."

"Do whatever you must. I have more important things to take care of!" John started to tie his arms together cupping them behind his back Mike dug his elbow into John's shoulder. Lunging for Jeanie she placed her hand in her jacket. The shots fired and he fell to the floor, gasping for breath Jeanie stood over him with her boot on his throat. Mick squirmed as she squeezed the breath out of him and as the short gasps came and went. Mick reached for her hand.

"You know this isn't over don't you." Still with the gun in hand Jeanie pressed her finger tightly against the trigger.

"You know we will always be with you Jeanie….." as he lurched again Jeanie pressed harder against his throat.

"You know Signthorpe did this to me seems befitting you should have the same fate." John placed his hand over the top of her gun.

"Enough Jeanie that's enough…" John couldn't move her, she was killing him, squeezing every last breath out of him and John saw her intent

"Your better than this I know you." Mike began to claw at the concrete beneath him easing her boot up slight he gasped for breath

"Remember P is for Partridge…. Jeanie" John placed his hands over the barrel pleading with her inner moral compass.

"Move away he's nearly dead and your husband needs you Jeanie…" Stepping back she saw James still strapped to the chair, looking at Mike on the floor she couldn't walk away.

You don't understand." grabbing John's gun Jeanie stood over the top of him.

" I won't remember you…this is done now!" Shooting him point blank the blood washed over the floor in waves.

"I hope you can live with this….this needs to be the end Jea."

Brushing his hand away she ran towards James and started to undo the ropes, "I knew you where alive." No response came from James, checking his pulse she looked at John.

"He must have been drugged John you check him I saw a jeep outside I'll see if I can start it…" John sat on the floor throwing his head back desperately looking for a cigarette

".Is it done Jeanie?"

"I've done things in this war to another human being that didn't deserve it. What I did to him I don't regret." John watched her run confidently towards the exit. Sliding in at the side of James he lay on the floor taking his last cigarette he lit it and watched the circles disappear.

"I don't really blame you!"

Chapter 32

John lifted the lifeless body of James and dragged him across to the exit, hearing the jeep start filled both John and Jeanie with relief. Lying James down gently Jeanie checked his vital signs again.

"We need to get him back to camp we can't be more than twenty miles away."

"You know questions are going to be asked about the rest of your men you need a plan..." Jeanie wiped away John's grasped more concerned about getting James back to safety.

"Then I was ambushed." Jeanie stopped mid sentence, "Listen do you hear that..."

"Yes what's over there...?" Slopping around the side of the jeep she cautiously looked across the compound.

"Fred but I thought." Hearing the moan Jeanie went to the corner of the building still cautious in case it was another ambush. John following her lead stepped around her so he could see. The soldier was dragging himself towards the compound and from the pools of blood around him there wasn't much time to spare.

"For fuck sake we can't leave him," Jeanie gave John a look of stupidity, Jeanie still cautious looked around the roof and as she reached for Fred she started applying pressure to his wounds.

"He's got one in the shoulder and looks like one in his chest," Fred coughed, as blood spattered from his lips Jeanie applied what pressure she could to his wounds.

"Sarge...it was..."

"Don't talk I need to get you home quick...John on three..." as Jeanie counted John flinched in as much pain.

"I'll look after him. Can you drive?" John punched the side of the jeep, "We have to talk!

"Is this the time John. Look where we are."

"Just get him the fuck in so we can go….." The jeep started to bounce away from the compound and as she looked back Jeanie knew whatever she felt had to die with Mick.

Applying pressure to Fred's wounds she forgot herself, as he placed his hand over hers she smiled sweetly hoping to provide some comfort. John could hardly focus on the road the blood pored from his shoulder and his hand had started to become numb.

Reaching camp and throwing the vehicle to the side of the medic's tent, he fell out of the door already dazed and dizzy from the blood loss. Jeanie had already organised a stretcher to get Fred out of the back and as the next wave came for James he opened his eyes.

"What the fuck happened with this lot…" Snapping back into focus Jeanie tried hard to explain.

"We were ambushed we just didn't stand a chance. The private has been shot in the arm and chest and they took our medic we think he's been drugged. He's just not with it but he's just opened his eye's." Seeing John being helped by another soldier she took over trying to avert any more questions.

Seeing the injured and dying in front of them John lay himself down on the nearest stretcher, "Soldier…Soldier you need to take him to…sorry Sir I didn't see I thought."

"Where do I go I just need something for the pain?" Flustered he ushered John into the wash room.

"Can you take off your jacket and shirt…umm looks as it has it gone straight through pretty clean. Has he had any pain relief?" Jeanie helped him take his clothes off, seeing his pain she answered for him. "No sir. I took over as the other medic was needed."

"Don't move anywhere I'm going to need you. I'll get you some morphine"

"You owe me again Rutherford." Jeanie smiled not wanting to argue or correct him.

"OK lets have a good look. Bite down hard on this." Jeanie scrunched up her nose as the medic prodded and poked at the wound.

"Artery is in tacked looks as though it's mainly superficial." As the bullet fell in the pan, Jeanie kept pressure on the wound.

"Ok I've stitched you up right you…drop those I need you to wrap him up I haven't got time I have to go sir I'm sorry." Leaving Jeanie alone she could see John become docile as the miniscule amount of morphine kicked in. John was laboured and heavy eyed and almost the most compliant she had ever seen him be.

"Apparently I have to wrap you up tell me if it hurts." Taking off her jacket she lay out the dressings and as she started to wrap the bandages around him John rested his head on her shoulder.

"You can't do that John what if someone comes back"

"I don't care tell them it was a request from an officer they all think we are fucking interbred anyway..." Jeanie smirked knowing the drugs where doing there job.

"Ok sir you wounds are dressed your head is heavy and I need to check on James…." John caught her fingers and as he fumbled them between his own he contemplated his words carefully.

"I'm sorry I should have done better I tried to protect you."

"It should be me. I should be saying thank you. I have my family back because of you. Please don't apologise I understand…" John placed his hand around her waist pulling her back into him.

"Don't go yet please I just need," Jeanie stroked his hair around his ear

"You need a haircut…" Johns head still resting in the nape of her neck felt comforting and his words echoed sincerity. Feeling close to him felt right and wrong but finding James had also confused her more.

John stroked her hip drinking in her comfort feeling the kiss on her skin Jeanie had to catch her breath.

"John please someone could come back at any minute…" Resting his head on her chest he counted her heartbeat.

"I don't want to loose you again…" Jeanie swallowed deep, just as she had travelled to war to save James; John had done the same for her.

"Why do you make me so confused…?" There was no sarcasm, or smart comment and he knew he would never get this opportunity tell her how he felt and make her understand.

"After all this I've followed you half the way around the world just to make sure you where safe. It would have killed me knowing you where in danger and I couldn't help you. I've never fucked up as much as I did with you but I've never loved someone this much either and I know your going to walk away from me but I just want you to understand that I will always love. Even when you tell me I shouldn't I just want you to know that I'm always here for you whenever you need me."

"I appreciate everything you have done for me and I'd be lying if I didn't say I love you. I think I owe you that." Stroking her face she kissed his finger tips. Feeling his kiss on her cheek the sentiment of the moment pulled on her heart strings. Taking her jacket she slipped out of the side sheeting and as she stood outside in the chaos inside her own mind she felt at peace.

Walking past the next makeshift medical wing, a gentleman sat outside with a cold compress and a pained look

"Someone looks as if they have had a good night on the tiles," James lifted his head and looked at the soldier.

"What? Sorry do I know you...."

"That depends." James looked painfully at her face.

"You seem vaguely familiar."

"Glad to know." Taking a drink of the water canteen, James seemed more confused by the riddles.

"How's your head? Did they tell you what he had given you?" James still looking deeply at her was vacant.

"I don't understand."

"Ok I'll help I'm the soldier that found you. You where pickled on something and I just wondered if they knew what they gave you?" As her words clicked into the puzzle Jeanie took off her jacket, the unmistakeable scars which run around Jeanie's collar bone and shoulder jolted James like a bolt of lighting.

"What's you name?"

"Sergeant Jack Rutherford of the Engineering division at you service."

"How did you get that scar?"

"This one well not that long ago some crazed psychopath tried to kill me and doctor I knew saved my life. I suppose would have been dead if it wasn't for him."

Dropping the flannel to the floor James stood up.

"Can you follow me please? I just need to look at something." Jeanie jumped to attention catching her jacket and followed implicitly.

"I have heard that name before and I can't remember where. You see I know of a woman who had that scar and everything is just so…would you mind me taking a look."

"I've heard about your kind are you one of those doctors…" James taken aback and still confused on medication hesitated at her sarcasm

"You winked…Why?"

"Because I've been looking for you for nearly twelve months and I was told you where missing presumed dead but now I know it was all a lie." James startled by the response shook his head in disbelief.

"It can't be she's…" Jeanie undid her shirt, revealing the bandages and bindings she had worn to keep herself hidden and as James ran his fingers over her scars his disbelief continued.

"It is you it can't be." wiping away the tears Jeanie placed her hand on his cheek. "I came all this way for you for us because I was told you where dead and I didn't believe it" James wrapped his arms around her pulling her tightly around him.

"I can't say I like your hair cut." feeling James near her lifted the weight which had been sat on her shoulders.

    John's words on the other hand still played over and over in the back of her mind. Closing her eyes she tried to enjoy James's embrace and as the affects of the drugs wore off his legs seemed to buckle beneath him. "Come on sit down."

"I've dreamed about being close to you. I've dreamed about what I'd say and I can't remember a single word." Jeanie grabbed her shirt still conscious of her surroundings.

"I have too but not here. We're still at war and I'm still Sergeant Jack Rutherford Engineering division. I'm just glad that you're alive." Jeanie started to put her shirt back on as James caught her arm.

"You have sores under your arms and they need sorting Jeanie." placing her hand over his mouth

Jeanie frantically looked around to see if he had heard. "Jack remember to call me Jack. At the moment they aren't important but when we are away from this war and safe at home we will sort all this out. I have to go I love you." James breathed deeply unable to comprehend that she was there with him.

"I'm going to feel like this is a dream in the morning I love you….." Grabbing her hand he kissed her unable for her to disappear without proof. "I needed to steal one just to make sure."

"I really have to go. I love you…" Disappearing from sight she stood outside trying to pull back to Jack, she also knew that her evening infirmary trips were not over.

Jeanie sat on the chair at Fred's bedside all that night, knowing they needed blood Jeanie sat and gave what she could knowing he wasn't just a casualty of war but another victim. He had served his country and fought for freedom and the person to try to kill him was on the same side. Thinking of a logical explanation had become difficult; the fucked up nature of what had happened due to two American soldiers had devastated too many lives.

Sat in the darkened infirmary she watched the laboured breaths of her responsibility and she realised why Mike had wanted her to come to war. She now understood that death was so much easier to comprehend when it's your day job. She had killed, Mike had seen her do it but, what he hadn't seen was the guilt and anguish it caused and the tears she had cried the first time it happened. Death was inevitable everyday; happiness was hard to celebrate especially when you had blood on your conscious.

The blackened room with Fred befitted Jeanie's thoughts.

"You still here you know he's got to do it on his own now." Jeanie smiled and scratched her head pulling at her collar as she stretched.

"Doesn't matter Sir I owe it to him to be here." Clutching a clipboard the doctor bowed his head. "You're the lad that brought the other doctor back as well" Jeanie

"Yes Sir." Trying to discourage the conversation she looked at the floor just wanting to be left alone.

"Your not supposed to be in here you know…" The doctor could see the anguish on Jeanie's face; she just wanted to be their regardless of the outcome. "I suppose a few moments more won't do any harm." As the doctor left Jeanie sighed heavily resting her head on the bar on the bed feeling her sense of duty.

As the skyline filled black and red, the rains fell heavier and the winds howled around the camp. When Jeanie emerged from the medical wing another day was looming. Sitting on the embankment Jeanie clutched at Fred's tags.

"Tough night soldier?"

"Yes Sir." Jeanie didn't lift her head

"How's James." again Jeanie didn't raise her head

"James is ok still dopey but ok."

"You know it looks like you are disobeying an officer from where you are sat so I think you might want to jump to attention…" Brushing down her clothes she stood and saluted, "Sergeant Jack Rutherford reporting for duty Sir."

John threw away his cigarette and buried them in the sodden ground.

"Ok Sergeant at ease walk this way…" Jeanie dragged her feet, over everything that had happened she should have been elated that Frank Signthorpe and Mike Kowalski where out of the picture for good. All Jeanie felt was emptiness and alone in the feeling that she had let her men down and Fred had died with it.

"I need to get you out of here."

"John we've been over this before."

"Look at you…your men are dead. I'm sorry Je.Jack but that's war you look as if you've been shot yourself you need to rain this in and pull your shit together." Jeanie didn't raise an eyebrow she could because again he was right and after everything she didn't want to give him that satisfaction as well.

"What you can see John is disappointment. I kept a unit together and alive without food or radio communication for six months and yesterday I just feel like I let those boys down but your right I do need to pull my shit together. Sir."

"I need you out of here…Fuck did you just agree with me…"

"There's a first time for everything." John pulled the chair in front of her and as he took hold of her blackened hands he knew Jeanie had learnt the art of survival

"I was ready for our own war you've caught me off guard."

"All I want to do is go home." placing his hand over hers he clasped them together.

"I've …I've done nothing but think about you and its drove me crazy. Matt said I've been obsessed but even now I know your safe but I don't want to have to be the one to put you back in danger."

"I don't know what you've been through and I'm sorry I didn't realise…I don't see any other choice we have I'm not injured and I was part of the last group to come over. You don't have any choice…" As the door way opened Jeanie dropped her fingers and the awkward silence increased the tension.

"Yes…what is it.." the private embarrassed awkwardly stepped towards him," Sorry….sir this came through…." And as the private left Jeanie stood and buttoned her jacket.

"Please don't go we can sort this out." Facing the doorway Jeanie opened the slat really hoping he could.

"Let me know if you figure something out."

Jeanie ran her hands over her head and as the rain berated the earth like an angry parent she felt tired, frustrated and disappointed as she headed back into camp.

The last 24 hours had been a living nightmare and John's determination to find her had touched her deeply. Confused and alone she concentrated on the reason she had come to war in the first place. James.

Jeanie headed for the showers looking out for other personnel she contemplated her next move. Walking slowly through the showers she noticed the James on his own in a bottom stall. Checking again she tapped him on the shoulder.

"Can I talk…? I'm sorry I didn't mean to frighten you."

"Jeanie I thought… it doesn't matter."

"Can you watch whilst I take a quick shower I'm covered." James saw the blood stained uniform and how tired and forlorn she looked.

With James guarding the door Jeanie stood inside the cubicle trying to wash away the dirt and grime which Signthorpe and Mike had created. Jeanie shivered and hurriedly dressed back into her dirty clothes.

"You can't where that it's full of blood let me get you some spare clothes stay here…." On his return James brought spare shirt and trousers for Jeanie, seeing the sores he also brought with him spare dressings

"Before your shirt I need to look at those sores,"

"I'm…it's been so long I'm scared James." Placing his hand on her cheek he tried to reassure her.

"I love you your always beautiful to me and I can't continue to see you in pain with these." Wincing Jeanie turned around and took off the shirt, her pale milk like skin showed the scars of her ordeal. Cupping her hands and arm around her breast she turned around.

"I needed the bandages to be tight." James looked at the blisters and swabbed them with iodine. "I've got most of them the one under your left arm is the worst. Jeanie why?"

"Can you help me with the bandages...?" Seeing her desperation he didn't force any more questions, feeling his hands smooth around her back Jeanie closed her eyes.

"I used I used to dream about you touching me not like this though...not like this at all...." As he pinned her into the bind, James run his hands over her shoulders.

"Let me get you that shirt..."

"I love you very much and I don't understand what brought you here and I may never know but I'm glad you are." Jeanie kissed the back of his hand.

"I don't think I deserve you I don't think I deserve anything at the moment." Pulling her close, he kissed her forehead.

"John's here...isn't he?" She didn't have to confirm because he felt it. John couldn't leave her on her own and he would never have expected him to.

"I can remember seeing you last night, when you showed me the scars I knew it was you. I thought I dreamt it but days and nights blur so easy here...you should know that now."

"I'm not injured and I can't go home James I only knew John was here when I found you Mike Kowalski was working with Signthorpe...I shot him dead last night and brought you here with John. I lost five men....because of some sick elaborate plot to kill all of us and now...now I don't feel like a whole person anymore. I don't sleep, I don't eat...I'm sick to fucking death of being called a degenerate...but I did it all for you...I thought you where dead or dying but I couldn't contemplate loosing you...so I left our home, caught a boat and enlisted. Does that make me a fool or a hero James... cause at this very moment in time...I feel like a murderer." James swallowed deep, her words remorseful and sallow made him understand her actions

"I don't know any other person in this situation who would be as strong and determined as you are to see this through. I went to war thinking you where safe....and now your hear because someone wanted all of us gone...but I can't help but rejoice in the fact that you are the only person I have ever known who would give up her life for me and Jeanie I feel it.. I would give you anything and everything for you I want you....I want to love you forever just let me." Jeanie smiled as his words comforted her and before exiting the showers James kissed the palm of her hand.

"Let me love you." Looking into his eyes she felt the sincerity of his kiss, "James I'm broken in more ways than you could fix...loving you will never be the problem. My whole existence is the problem." Letting go of her hand he placed he watched her walk across the camp, heading back to his own quarters he turned around to gather another glimpse. "Let's mend each other..."

Watching the other soldiers play cards Jeanie lay on her bed thinking about James's words, let me love you rung through every pore. They had been apart for twelve months but some of the men had been away from home for years, Jeanie plucked at her bandages deep in thought. Not able to settle she walked around the camp trying to make sense of this complicated situation.

"Hey stranger. You not fucking left this place yet?"
Merle was sat in an old wheelchair taking a drag if
his cigarette.

"Jesus Christ Merle….how the fuck are you?"
Jeanie surprised to see how well he looked revelled
in the fact that he was alive.

"Lost my leg but there are worse things that could
have happened at least it means I get a free trip
home…" Jeanie looked under the tatty blanket
inquisitive at the sight of his stump.

"It's good to see you it really is." Merle offered
Jeanie a cigarette and knowing her refusal he looked
at her distant gaze.

"Eh Sarge come on you look like you've lost a
dollar and found a penny."

"Is it that obvious?"

"I heard about what happened I'm sorry. You know
Pete's saying tough. It's all SNAFU in here…"
Jeanie smiled nervously knowing the details of the
encounter where sketchy enough, rumours just
made her feel worse. "So what did you hear...?"
Merle took another drag of his cigarette and looked
out at the rain.

"That it was fucked up you had no chance just stuff
like that

"You don't know what you're walking into in this
place. So how long till the trip home?" Diverting
the conversation Merle perked up

"Yep two maybe three weeks back to old Blighty
first then off to Milwaukee. Virginia will be waiting
for me back home just can't wait to see them all
again you know. What about your family got
anybody special waiting for you?" Merle hung onto
every word intrigued to know about Jeanie's life
even the six months that they had spent together she
had been a mystery.

"I mean Sarge you practically know everything
about us. Jesus Christ even down to the fact of how

360

many nights Eugene had to piss." Jeanie dragged a chair up to the side of him.

"I know. I suppose I have been a little guarded. I do have someone special just hope I live up to expectations."

"Maybe it's your baby face do you think…"

"Or maybe looking at the bets you all had against me that it's because I'm a woman. Which odds where they again..." Merle flipped open his notebook counting through the pages the small element of light relief felt right.

"35/1 odds on that one Sarge. Let's face it though your not?" Jeanie smiled again not answering his question either way. These men had become part of her family and knowing they had started a book made Jeanie feel even more mysterious.

"So any plans set in stone for you Sarge…." Jeanie picked up a piece of twine and rolled it around her fingers.

"Not yet I believe the Japs are retreating out of China so probably be sent up there. But only time will tell Merle. For now all that I have is in this camp so that's got to be good enough for now."

Chapter 33

The preparations had already started in the cottage and Jeanie was finally coming home. John had been the first to be sent home and knowing her family would be waiting in anticipation he brought them the news that Jeanie would be home mid October 1945 and James would follow in early November.

Trying to hide her whereabouts had become a challenge to all of them and in the end Eric had to be told. As Irene ordered the banners to be raised, the rest of them congregated at the window.
"Mum the taxi is here what we do…"
"Just let's be as calm as we can be."
Jeanie had been instructed to burn her uniform and in that moment Jack Rutherford had officially died on the crossing back from Burma. In his place Jeanie Rutherford Watson was reborn.

John had left her a pale blue flowered dress and Jacket, not knowing what to do with her hair Jeanie wrapped her head in a scarf and bought a matching hat.

She didn't bare any physical scars from her experience however; deep inside everything about her had changed. Not knowing how her family would be able to cope made the journey home more apprehensive than exciting.

Stepping through the front door Eric was the first to grab hold of her. "You're braver lass than I give you credit for. Don't worry you mum let me know and I promised to keep a secret." Eric kissed her on the cheek and shook her hand as if she had been welcomed home a hero.
There was nothing heroic about her actions. Just death.
Nothing more.
"Welcome home pet." The brigade of girls clattered around Irene and as Jeanie flooded through the

crowd and as her watery gaze met Irene she froze to the spot.

"I'm home Mum." The array of kisses and hugs overwhelmed Jeanie to the point that they barged her back into the hallway, revelling in the noise Jeanie clung to them. As they all gathered together in the living room, Jeanie forgot the feeling of security that only home could give. Listening to the buzz of conversation and the delight that home comfort could bring Jeanie fell asleep.

Everything about coming home had been stressful, reinventing herself had been worse, at least as Jack she knew her job her role and her purpose, now as Jeanie everything was back to chaos.

Reaching her old room Ivy caught hold of her hand.

"We've missed you and there is so much I need to share with you." "I'm…I'm not the same person Ivy. I had to change to survive but as Jack those things where easy to accept as Jeanie I don't understand how I did them." Ivy kept hold of her hand trying to understand what she had been through. "Your home now maybe we can figure everything out together…"

Getting changed for bed Jeanie caught sight of herself in the mirror, looking at the floor she realised how long it had been since she could see herself as a woman. As she lay in bed she couldn't get comfortable, the ironic thing was she had been dreaming about a soft warm comfortable bed to sleep in and now it just felt like a coffin. Dragging the blanket onto the floor she lay under the bed, "It's over with. Got to let it go…"

"Mum….Mum MUM! Come now mum its Jeanie." Irene leaped to her feet Daisy hysterical by this point had started to run on the spot.

"Mum Jeanie's locked herself in my wardrobe."
Irene confused by her daughters outburst, stood at
her bedroom door.
"Daisy calm down. What happened?" Daisy still
running on the spot started to panic.
"Mum she's got a gun in there she says people are
trying to kill her….." Walking into the bedroom
May was stood at the wardrobe. "Jeanie…Jeanie
your safe now it's me open the door. Please open
the door," Jeanie crouched inside with her hands
over her head, all her experiences playing over and
over in her mind.
 "Come on love it's only me. I don't want to hurt
you sweetheart come on." Jeanie cowered in the
light her thoughts encasing her past and present
state. Her nightmares had felt so reel and even now
in her own home she didn't feel safe.
"I'm sorry…I'm sorry. I don't…" Irene sat inside
and held onto her daughter tight.
"I love you. You're my baby girl come on. It
doesn't matter what you've done you had to do it to
survive. Come on." Irene coaxed her out; Jeanie
dropped the gun on the floor and held onto her
mother tight.
"I didn't mean to I had no choice mum." The tears
stained her nightdress and the girls held onto every
word with baited breath.
"Girls go back to bed….Jeanie will be getting in
with me." Irene poured a large glass of Brandy and
sat Jeanie down on the bed.
 "Ok love I'm here shhh come on. Drink that and
let's get some rest..." Jeanie gulped down the
brandy pulling her face she dropped the glass and
placed her head in her hands.
"It's not over mum. I can feel it there is something
else and I just can't put my finger on it. These
dreams, nightmares are haunting me and they won't
go away. I've had to fight and kill to stay alive now

I'm home it just seems like it's not real. I'm still waiting for the ambush or death to jump up at me I….I can't explain it. He followed me into the jungle and he's followed me back out again and I swore I swore that was it when I killed him I swore to myself this wouldn't happen. Mum I'm so scared this isn't over." Irene wrapped her arms around her daughter, she felt powerless in her struggle. Knowing she had gone to war because someone else wanted her dead made the reasons far harder to justify. Lying in the dark Irene watched Jeanie sleep, Jeanie was still agitated but at least she was asleep, no matter how hard she tried she couldn't imagine what her daughter had been through.

Iris, Daisy and May sat in a circle on the floor of the bedroom.

"I don't understand what happened. Daisy tell me again…Iris can you get the door..." May huddled the group together and with Daisy still upset by the incident she tried hard to explain.

"It was awful I'd just turned over and saw Jeanie stood at the door of the wardrobe with the gun and as I sat up she disappeared almost eerily into the wardrobe. She looked at me and told me to shush and whoever it was where coming and I had to keep quiet. That's when she started to scream…It's awful I can't imagine what she's been through…."

May's sigh was heavy unable to comprehend what had happened, "I just hope things start to settle down…."

"The thing is Ivy desperate to discuss the plant and I don't think she will give her enough time to sort it. Lets face it girls this situation is fucked up. I heard her talking to Mum and she still feels there is someone out there trying to kill her and to be fair after everything that's gone on it feels justified."

Irene stood at the door and listened to what had happened; her heart sank as she had agreed that

Jeanie should go. As the girls dispersed Irene poked her head around the corner.

"Goodnight girls she's asleep now and that's what we need...love to you all," Watching the twitching slumber Irene hoped for now that she had settled.

Jeanie was up first the next morning self conscious about last night's incident she made breakfast as an apology. Laying the food out on the table Jeanie saw a familiar face at the window, opening the door Jeanie hugged him tightly.

"What's that for? Are you ok?" Feeling her tremble John held onto her tight. "No I did something last night I forgot where I was and I hid in the cupboard expecting him to come for me...I don't know what to do."

John moved away from the door, still holding onto her Irene came into the kitchen.

"Irene what's happened?"

"John it's my fault. I've done this to all of us." Irene took her daughters hand still reminiscent of her other daughters conversations.

"Don't worry love it will be sorted have a chat with John. A bit of fresh air might be a good thing. John?" Looking at Irene she seemed desperate for anyone to be able to help, placing her coat in her hand it was the first time she had given John permission to be with her daughter.

"A talk might help I know its John but James isn't due back for another couple of weeks and needs must." Jeanie started to cry she couldn't believe how excited everyone had been, and she felt like she had let them down.

"I'm so sorry mum I'm a mess aren't I..."

"No love just sometimes bad things happen to good people." Watching her mum from the kitchen window Jeanie could see the strain of last night's outburst.

"I want to go to the lake in the old wood. I want to lay some flowers on him. Funny really cause dad used to take me there fishing in summer."

"I thought of you I was bringing it around as a welcome home gift…" Undoing the wrappings the knitted hat and scarf fell open in her grasp. "There lovely thank you." wrapping herself up in the items Jeanie linked John's arm as they strolled. The cool crisp morning was sharp and clear and in some ways the frost seemed to clear her mind.

"It's funny we only go for walks in winter." John smiled and strolled casually alongside. Reaching the clearing there was a small skim of ice on the water and the tree's where bare. Isolated in the coldness the whole area was at peace in its woodland grace. Resting flowers below the small plaque she read out the words under her smoky breath.

To Our Dear Son Francis John Stanton.
Taken from us by tragic circumstance. Loved and
treasured for a lifetime. May the wings of heaven
collect our angel and may the tides of time heal
our wounds.
Forever in our hearts.

"I know you did all this because James told me. You know I love this spot and you also knew I would want his ashes scattered here. I just wish I could have seen him. But obviously it was never meant to be."

Jeanie sat on bench looking over the water; sitting beside her John lit his cigarette and placed his arm around the back of the chair

"So are we going to talk about what's really going on?" Jeanie shuffled away unnerved by his question.

"Mike Kowalski spoke to me before I shot him the words didn't make sense at first but I thought I

367

could escape all that by killing him and I can't. I promised you that I could leave it behind but when he said it wasn't over. I already felt it. It's easy to hide death when you're at war it's easy to kill without question the only question is can I live with myself…"

"Jeanie no body tells you how to deal with war. But on the other hand you haven't just had to deal with war you've had to deal with two raging psychopaths who kidnapped your husband and wanted you dead. Don't beat yourself up about it…" Jeanie stood and walked to the water looking at the ripples underneath the ice it symbolised how she was feeling

"John this just isn't about Signthorpe and Kawolski and you know it. Don't treat me like an idiot. This thing obviously runs deeper than either you or I have imagined. I needed to be sent out of the way. I don't know what for but my mind is racing at one hundred miles and hour and I can't catch up."

Learning forward on the bench he understood her concerns and watched the last few years take more toll on her already fragile state of mind.

"He thinks I'm torn John he thinks I still love you."

"And are you." Jeanie looked back into the water knowing she couldn't run from either of them.

"Would it make any difference?"

"It would to me." Looking

"He love's me John I know he does." Walking back along the river edge, Jeanie distance and isolation grew with every sentence.

"You're not a back up if anything goes on. You need to find someone to make you happy, "

"If your have second thought's about us Jeanie I need to know. You know how much I want you I just want to love you and I don't care about anything else and please don't tell me to love someone else when I don't want too." Jeanie tried to smile elevating some of the tension.

"I'm not torn because of you and it's not because of James. I love you both in very different ways. I don't think either one of you could be happy with me or sometimes I think I would be better if I didn't love either of you. I'm cursed and so far I think I've proved that. Deep in my heart I know I'm too broken to be fixed and no relationship no matter how much love anyone gives will ever change that…."

"No matter what you think I will never give up on you and if this wretched event isn't finished then we will see it through together" Jeanie starred back at the hopefulness in his gaze.

"I'm going to have to tell James that I went half way around the world to find out that all my problems are still back at home.

I don't want you living half of a life with me just like I don't want James to feel that because he said I do he's eternally stuck with me." John wrapped his arms around her waist and turned her around.

"Jea this all changed that night I got shot didn't it…didn't it! We've been through so much and I want you to understand one thing I helped you because I want you to happy. But for my own selfish reasons it's because I love you and would do anything for you. But I helped you because James was the reason that made you happy now if he isn't I need to know." Jeanie could pick her head up off the ground trying desperately to hold onto her coat for comfort. She felt cruel.

"Those moments after you where shot have confused me more…but you have to realise…I'm not yours anymore…and you have to stop waiting for me it's cruel and I don't want to be cruel anymore," Dragging his hands from her waist he placed them on either side of her cheeks. The pink rose shone through his gloves sparkling in the cold air.

"You couldn't be cruel if you tried and I understand what you're trying to say but you love me and no matter what happens from this point Jeanie I'm not going to be able to forget that.

But besides that what you're doing now isn't helping and blaming yourself or thinking that you're cursed is not going to solve how you feel. It's going to take time you or any of us don't just get over what you have been through in five minutes. I just want you to know that I'm here for you and I understand…" Placing her hand in his they began the walk back to the cottage. Reaching home Jeanie pushed on the window of the back door.

"I love you Jeanie Rutherford you'll get through this I know you and when you do…I will be right beside you…" Kissing her softly on the cheek John disappeared around the side of the house.

Jeanie didn't feel any better for telling him, she didn't feel any better coming home. Normality seemed further away now than before the war and knowing James was coming home made her feel worse.

Dropping Jeanie back at off at the cottage made Irene feel sick, the thought of leaving her on her own didn't sit comfortably.

"Are you sure your going to be ok I can stay with you for another couple of days…"

"You know I have to do this on my own I need routine, normality and James is due tomorrow." Irene nodded close to tears letting go of her daughters hand had been the hardest action she'd ever had to take.

Watching her family leave Jeanie felt a weight off her shoulders, the last couple of weeks had been tough and at least for now her every move wasn't being observed by every member of her family.

Jeanie sat on the settee watching the fire burn down; the anticipation of James being home made Jeanie feel sick. Wanting and not wanting him had sent her into turmoil on more than one occasion. Jeanie sat questioning why she put herself through a war to find him especially when it had all been lies.

Lying in bed Jeanie looked at his pillow, the last time they had been at home together had been magical now it just felt like someone else's life. Listening to the wind howl around the cottage Jeanie checked every window and door. "No point worrying now Jea you wanted him home this is what you did it for."

Standing at the kitchen sink she wiped the same plate several times over before putting it away. Jeanie felt nauseous and hearing the kitchen door open Jeanie nearly threw up.
"Morning my darling I've brought the left over from the shoot yesterday thought you might need them…What's wrong my dear you look white as a sheet, "Jeanie looked at George and then back at the door, "..Hello Jeanie…" James stood in full uniform with a box under his arm.
"I'll be off then give my love to the little un…nice to see you lad," George shook James hand at the back door and as it slammed shut Jeanie jumped. "Jeanie is Jayne here…" The noise grew louder and Jeanie just starred not knowing what to do. Snapping back into reality Jeanie ran into the box room. James stood at the back door just as nervous. "I tried to tell you I tried to write several times I didn't know what to do..." James placed his cap on the counter as Jeanie juggled the little girl. "Jeanie who's is the baby…." Jeanie clenched hold tightly of the baby girl who was dressed all in white, her little rosy cheeks red as she cried, "James this is Elizabeth Watson…she's your daughter…" James

staggered to the back door, "My daughter I have a daughter"

"The night before you left…I found out I was pregnant a few weeks after James I tried….I didn't know how to…" James hesitantly stepped forward, "Can I hold her. I mean will she let me." Jeanie nodded wiping the tears away on her sleeve.

"Hello Elizabeth…Jeanie she's beautiful..." Jeanie looked at the pair together, she looked so much like him and as she tried to regain composure James sat at the table, "Jeanie why didn't you tell me?"

"Because I received a telegram saying there was a possibility that you where dead." Elizabeth sat and gurgled happily on James's knee

"You left her for me…you left everything that was safe to find me. Jeanie look at me please I don't want to fight I just want you to tell me…tell me its ok for me to stay." Looking at James's sincerity again made her feel guilty, "I came to find you because I couldn't give up. I had to believe that there was a happily ever after if not for me for Elizabeth. I couldn't think about her because she broke my heart and every time I look at her I see you."

"There's more to this tale then what you're telling me isn't there." James clung onto the infant feeling like his soul had been handed back to him.

"I know you read my journal and I experienced some very dark days over there but I never stopped loving you. I stopped understanding who I was. I mean what kind of mother leaves their child…the guilt I feel the unquestionable amount of guilt I feel includes looking for you and my motives. I know you're going to ask about John and yes I do have feelings for him I can't help that.

I just feel there's something still hiding out there waiting for me and… and I feel like I am too broken…I'm too broken to be able to be loved by anyone not even Elizabeth. " Tears rolled down James's face, clinging to Elizabeth he stood and walked to Jeanie

"I want to love you forever Jeanie and I don't care if you feel broken I want to love you enough to take away the pain. Your actions everything you did to find me speaks volumes about the type of person you are. You've been through so much already that I wouldn't expect you to forget about it. But we have a baby, we could have a good life and if you just let me love you we could see if we can work this out together I've not come this far to loose you…..I can't." Jeanie took hold of Elizabeth and cradled her in her arms, his tears washed over her.

"I feel like I've let you and Elizabeth down." James run his fingers through her hair and kissed her forehead.

"Don't ever say that you have done more for me and Elizabeth than what you could know. I'm standing here with you now free and my daughter has a father. I have never been as proud of you as I am today."

"I feel like poison James, I feel like my whole life has been cursed and you and John are caught up in the nightmare it's become."

"Jeanie you are my world and by leaving you you're asking me to leave everything I love and hold dear to me. I hear because I want to spend the rest of my life making you happy. You deserve happiness Jeanie and I'm asking for you to let me provide it. John loves you. I have had to come to terms with that. But if you're asking what sets us apart. He could never love you the way I love you. He could never want you the way I want you and he could never loose himself completely in you the way I'm lost with you."

James and Jeanie sat on the kitchen floor watching Elizabeth play with James tie, Jeanie leant into his shoulder, lifting her head she kissed him softly. "I forgot to say Welcome home..." James kissed her back.

"Welcome home Jeanie..."

Chapter 34

Jeanie tossed and turned in her sleep, opening her eyes it was 2.00 am again and after blinking several times she froze as a pair of eyes leered at her through the window. She could feel them burning into her skin, and as she grabbed James's arm she shook it hard. "James…James there's someone at the window."

"Jeanie we've been through this before." getting out of bed, he put on his shirt and strolled around to the window.

"Jea….there's nothing there I promise you..."

"When you got up they moved…I know someone was there..." "Jea please this is scaring me now. I mean maybe we should see a doctor…" Jeanie got out of bed and put on her dressing gown horrified at his insinuation. "You think I'm loosing the plot don't you they moved around the side of the house James please just listen to me." James gritted his teeth as for over a month Jeanie had been walking him up at 2.00am and every morning she had said the same thing. She had convinced him on a number of occasions to walk around the house to check.

"Jeanie I really think you need help there is no one there." Loosing her temper she wanted to scream instead she slammed the door and walked into the kitchen, pacing the floor James followed.

"Jeanie I don't understand what you're going through and I'm concerned. Please let me help you…"

"You think I'm loosing my mind. I know what I saw and there is someone trying to get into my head James. There is someone playing with me. Kowalski said it wasn't over with."

"Jeanie he's dead you killed him. Baby please who else could it be." She sat in the middle of the kitchen floor with her head in her hands.

"You don't believe me." Wrapping his arms around her James sighed heavily. "Help me understand…"
"It's been every week for a month and the same thing happens. I don't know I here a sound a voice and when I wake I feel someone starring at me….then I look at the window and they are its strange. I don't want to scream I just want to know why? Why this is happening? I feel exhausted with it all." James felt her tremble in his arms, whatever was happening had hold of her and was relentless to not let go. Making her a warm drink Elizabeth started to cry, "I'll go you drink that. I love you."

Jeanie smiled cautiously; she felt there was something out there, waiting in the dark to make its move and as she sat drinking in the dark kitchen she played out Kowalski's death over and over again.
"Why partridge…I don't understand." Juggling Elizabeth James stood in amazement, every puzzle needed to have a fix that was just Jeanie. Except this one was playing havoc with her sanity, Jeanie stood at the nursery door as James put Elizabeth back down to sleep.
"I think she was cold I've wrapped her up..."
placing her hand on his chest Jeanie played with the button as if she had something to say.
"Back to bed before we freeze…come on." Taking her hand they slid between the sheets.
"Tell me what you're thinking," Jeanie took hold of the button again and started to rub it between her fingers, "Jea tell me. Talk to me I can't help you if you don't let me in." Jeanie still playing with his button looked directly at him. "That's the thing James no one can whatever is going on with me I need to sort…"

Watching the sun break over the horizon was nothing new for Jeanie, as dawn hit she was out of bed dressed and ready to start another day. She had already started back at the factory and Elizabeth was never too far behind. "I'm sorry it so early and you've got to see the hospital today remember. Elizabeth is with me she isn't awake yet. I've got all her things and I can pick you up on my way back if you like..." James squinted at the alarm clock, "Ok come here…" kissing her goodbye Jeanie tried to find a reassuring smile.

Looking out of her office window, the clouds had started to gather for another winter and Jeanie could not help but think about Kowalski.

"Maybe it's all in my head," Iris threw her coat and heels on the chair interrupting Jeanie's moment.

"What's in your head...?"

"What are you doing here?" Iris raised her legs onto the couch.

"Looking like I've been to work. You look pale maybe you should have that checked out. Anyway you're supposed to be coming over tonight for teas remember Mum's orders you know she's just checking up on you."

"You mean the business don't you!" Checking on Elizabeth Jeanie picked up her cup from the table and sat beside her sister, the smell of her strong perfume and glow of cigarettes made Jeanie smile.

"Remember when you stood on Me." smiling coyly Iris took hold of Jeanie's cup, "Yep that was a night out I really don't want to forget anyway you where talking to yourself again. You know you remind me of dad when you do that. So go on why is it all in your head?" leaning back into the chair Jeanie tried to find a diplomatic response.

"I'm seeing things well I don't know that I am cause I can feel it too." Iris looked puzzled. "Well go on there's no point telling a half a story. That's what you used to tell me…" Moving her legs Jeanie wriggled uncomfortably as if being question by the police.

"For the past four weeks every morning at 2.00am not everyday….just one day a week. I wake up and see someone looking at me through the window. It feels real and I can see the stare but I'm not afraid I just want to know why they are doing it. James thinks I need a trip to the doctor and I can understand why. My brain just doesn't seem wired that way..." Placing the cup on the floor Iris sat up looking Jeanie directly in the eye.

"You see I know when you lie everybody does and you believe every word your saying is true therefore my darling if you feel like your missing something do what you always do…" Jumping up Iris got her coat and made her way to the door, pausing for thought Jeanie looked blankly at her, "Oh come on stupid its obvious…find out how it works and fix it…" Smiling Iris waltzed out of the door and down to the locker room, Jeanie watched how she had no cares or worries in the world.

"Maybe she's right Lizi maybe mummy should go out and see if it's real……" The infant squirmed in her sleep as Jeanie spoke and looking back out the window she noticed her 12'Oclock had just arrived.
 "Maybe Auntie Iris is right."

   The factory had seemed slow compared to how Jeanie remembered it last she knew now the war was over the plant had to return to its small contractual duties, but knowing it wouldn't survive without changing its direction was going to be a difficult conversation with her Mum. They had already broached take over once and the only person who pushed for it was Ivy. Jeanie knew Ivy wasn't in favour of the plant when her dad had first bought it but Jeanie had a plan and selling the business was never going to part of that plan and attempts had been made whilst she had been indisposed. The only thing was nothing could happen without her say so and her say so at that point was in Burma.

As Jeanie arrived at the hospital James was already outside waiting for her, "You know we are at my mums for tea tonight don't you" James took off his hat and cooed at Elizabeth in the back seat of the car.

"Yes you told me last week. How's your day been, "Jeanie wrinkled her nose and smiled back not having to explain.

As dinner finished Jeanie started with her speech, pouring out her idea's over the family Jeanie expected the usually decent into chaos.

"If I get this contract Mum….it means at least we will be set up for the next five years and it's up to us to show them we can do it. Dad's not here anymore and we need to do this for all of our families. So what do you think…?" The silence held at the dinner table, Jeanie looked around the room until eventually Irene stood and grinned like a Cheshire cat. "Jeanie girls….I think she's done us proud and I know for a fact her father would be immensely proud of her and if you think we can do it we are right behind you..." Jeanie sat back in her chair and took a huge sigh of relief; James kissed her forehead seeing that at least one weight had been taken off her shoulders.

Helping with the dinner plates Jeanie took them into the kitchen, seeing Ivy at the back door she rested her hand on her shoulders.

"You look miles away…" throwing the butt of her cigarette Ivy took hold of her hand. "Sometimes I wish I was its nice to have you back you know…"

"I can't thank you enough for looking after Lizi you did a good job…." Letting go Ivy seemed distant.

"I'm sorry….I should have told you everything before and I didn't mean to hurt you…." Jeanie stood at the side and nudged her sister's shoulder.

"It's all done now anyway big sis how long is it since…" Jeanie pushed Ivy's shoulder. "Oh really that's not fair..." The pair started to roll around the kitchen like teenagers and as the noise progressively increased Irene and James entered the kitchen. "What the….You two stop it you're going to hurt someone…" the laughter of the pair echoed around the kitchen, Jeanie stood up and brushed down her trousers. "Decorum Ivy come on…" Jeanie giggled as Ivy nudged her shoulder again, "Yes of course Jea of course..."

As the pair squashed each other in the door, Irene let the giddiness continue as it was nice to see her daughters smile, never mind play and be silly.

Jeanie smiled all the way home, James revelled in her happiness it was nice to see Jeanie smile. "I'll get Elizabeth sorted won't be long…" Jeanie started to sing to sooth the infant to sleep and as the gurgles turned to yawns Jeanie put her daughter down for the evening. "Night Night angel sweet dreams…"

Making her way to the living room Jeanie could here the music, resting her head against the door she watched James run around trying to light the candles.

"Just a quick question what are you doing?" James unaware of her appearance blew out the last match. "What does it look like?" Jeanie sloped in and stood at the back of the settee, "It looks like you might be trying to seduce me."

James bit his lip holding out his hand. "You know I don't think we've ever danced properly have we." Taking his hand he held her against his chest and as they swayed in time with the music Jeanie played with the button on his shirt.

"Ella Fitzgerald this song always used to make me stop and listen….." James rested his head on hers. "I didn't think you would know her"

"You know me still full of surprises." Twisting her around Jeanie twirled in his arms.

"I have my own surprise for you here. I was discharged in London, and as I walked to the train station I thought of you I hope you like it."

The Harrods box sparkled in the candle light; Jeanie placed it in front of the now roaring fire and carefully undid the twine. Inside the cream satin slip twinkled and the crystal broach under the bust dazzled in the fire light. "It's beautiful James you shouldn't have. But it's beautiful." Sitting at the side of her he rubbed her shoulder.

"Why don't you try it on?" Kissing him on the cheek Jeanie raced to the bathroom, she'd never seen anything so luxurious. Slipping it over her skin Jeanie saw every scar in the mirror and as she ran her fingers over the bullet holes she forgot to revel in how beautiful she looked.

Standing at the sink she closed her eyes as the overwhelming feeling she was being watched came over her again. Wanting to look at the glass and see the eyes burning in towards her Jeanie stepped out of the bathroom, closing the door behind her. She almost felt teary at ignoring the stare.

Checking Elizabeth's window and closing the curtains she rested her hand on her chest. She was warm snug and fast asleep.

Catching a glimpse of herself in the gown, all Jeanie felt where the scars ripping her body apart. Wrapping her arm around her self consciously Jeanie entered the living room.

"Jea you ok?" Jeanie went and sat in front of the fireplace, holding a large cushion in front of her James felt concerned.

"Have I done something wrong," Jeanie shook her head furiously and placed her hand on his cheek. "No...No James it's beautiful and it fits perfectly thank you. But my scars you see everything…and…" James took away the pillow and ran his fingers over her collarbone.

"I created them without them you wouldn't be here and I don't care. You're the most beautiful person I have ever laid my eyes on" Kissing the mark on her collar bone Jeanie dropped her head.

"You know what I missed the most about you whilst I was away I missed everything. Talking to you, arguing with you missing your laughter and tonight you smiled….but smiled from the inside for the first time in I can't remember and that little spark that makes up you appeared again" Jeanie took hold of his hand wrapping her fingers in his grasp.

"You're everything I live for and that spark you have that infectious, incomprehensible spark makes up every reason why I married you."

"I don't know why I get like this." The dress showed every exit wound and every scar and as James stroked each silvery line he felt close to her for the first time since he had arrived home.

"When I first got to Burma it was like hell in fact it was worse than that, receiving your letters every month give me hope. And when I went to bed at night I used to read your words again and again and imagine you saying them. The the letters dried up and I didn't know what was going on but I thought I'd lost you. I thought you'd forgot that I loved you and I felt alone and afraid for the first time in years. Not being able to talk to you…to tell you that I loved you was harder still I'd never felt like that before even with Catherine? With Catherine I could be away for weeks or months at a time and I didn't care with you not hearing from you not having that solace not being able to escape made me feel like I didn't want to come home. Resting her head Jeanie closed her eyes.

"When John told me there was a possibility you where dead I felt like part of me had died I couldn't believe it now we are here and things seem so complicated. I really did feel like death followed me everywhere I went and it would be so much easier to be alone. I didn't realise how important having you and Elizabeth are."

Moving her close he wiped away her tears "You're a part of me Jeanie and the part I never knew and I can't live without you." Taking his hand Jeanie stood pulling him towards the parlour door. "I thought you said you where going to get me drunk so we could fool around." Smiling back he picked her up flinging her over his shoulder. "What about if we miss getting drunk and go straight to fooling around!"

Grabbing the dress Jeanie slipped it over herself, 2.00am was back and she was awake but this time no one seemed to be about. Feeling the cold Jeanie put on her cardigan and crept into the hallway. The house was quiet and still and standing at the kitchen sink Jeanie started to clear some of the evening's dishes away. Picking up the tea towel Jeanie heard the creak of the letter box and seeing the figure disappear she picked up the letters off the floor. They where addressed to James except they where all open. Jeanie sat at the kitchen table contemplating what to do next.

Feeling no other choice she dropped the letters out of their shells, and as she flicked through the content she started to read out loud.

"Dearest Catherine, I know I never treated our relationship with any reference but I'm hurting more than ever you wouldn't have done this I know that...Maybe I need to leave!
Dearest James my arms are always open and will be waiting for you with every baited breath. Leave her pass this off as lack of judgment and come home to me yours forever P"

Letter after letter had conversed between them, most of them before Signthorpe and as she scanned through them again, she also realised they had met on several occasions.

Standing at the bedroom door Jeanie through the letters onto the bed, "What's wrong.." clasping her hands over her mouth, James sat up suddenly seeing Catherine's handwriting, he knew she had read them. "Where did you get these Jeanie? This is not what you think please…" "Someone posted them through the door over an hour ago. James you lied to me. You met her and talked about me if I was some slut you met off the street and you lied to me. Why does she sign all her letter's P just answer me that..." James looked through the pile on the bed. "Jeanie it's not what you think." Still looking for answer's Jeanie repeated herself.

"Why does she sign her letter's P James all of them are signed with P…what does it mean…" James threw the covers back pacing the floor he put his hands on the back of his head.

"Fuck. Her name is Catherine Partridge I used to call her P because it's short for Partridge Jeanie. " Jeanie staggered at the door.

"Partridge as in Partridge in a pear tree."

"Jeanie this was before…before everything Jea please I swear to you…I haven't seen her since since Singthorpe"

"After everything we've talked about you don't know even now the reasons why I need to go."

Running out of the kitchen Jeanie grabbed the car keys. "Someone is looking through my window, and someone is trying to play with both of us". James ran out trying to follow but she was gone.

Jeanie folded her cardigan around her and as she climbed the dark stairway she reached Flat 615and knocked hard.

"Whoever it is I'm fucking busy…" as the door opened John saw Jeanie shivering in the corridor, "Fuck Jea just hold on a minute," John closed the door, Jeanie could hear muffled voices from the inside and as the door re-opened a woman exited. "I need to deal with this I'll call you…"

Jeanie bowed her head to the floor and listened to her footsteps as she clambered away. "I'm sorry John I had no where else….." taking her hand he gently coaxed her inside. "What are you doing here…?" Jeanie wrapped her cardigan around her even more.

"It's not over John someone is trying there best. I don't know how to explain…" Sitting her down in the chair John poured a large scotch and handed her the glass, "Jea it's 3.45am….your at my flat and as much as I have dreamt about this happening the state that you're in doesn't sit very comfortable start explaining…." Jeanie took a drink and explained how the evening's events unfolded.

"They just dropped through the letter box and you've been being watched for a month. I don't know what you want me to do."

"Catherine's signs her name P everything is P John and I think she's in either in trouble or we need to speak to Catherine. I just need your help." Taking his hand Jeanie hugged him tight.

"Thank you I didn't know who else to turn too and no one else believes me…" John held her tight; feeling her soft skin underneath the sheer satin reminded him of what he lost.

"Jea I can't you need to go and speak to James."

"John he won't….he doesn't believe me please."

"Every time you're here I don't want you to go and every time I hold you Jeanie."

Jeanie looked around the flat, the dreary tired wall paper blackened and stained signified a desperate man, "I understand I do….I'm sorry for asking so much of you all the time I even interrupted your evening." Jeanie rested her head on the large wooden mantel. "I can't apologies enough."

He wanted to hold her, he wanted to comfort her but he also knew he wouldn't want to stop. "Before I go please can I use your bathroom?" John showed her the way tidying his dirty clothes as he went. Jeanie ran the tap splashing her face with cold water realising how desperate she had become. John stood outside the door, lighting a cigarette he replaying the scene in his head, as she exited Jeanie couldn't look at him.

"Thank you again I'm sorry for interrupting..." Jeanie quickened her pace to leave feeling the embarrassment of her intrusion.

"Jea please just hold on" John rested his hand on the door.

"John please I've encroached on you enough..."

"I don't care anymore." Slipping out the door she ran to the car; the rain pored heavy and as the thunder rolled in Jeanie fumbled for her keys. John picked them up and as he kissed her he pressed her against the car.

"Tell me you don't love me Jeanie and I'll leave forever tell me....you don't need me and I'll walk away and never come back." still in his embrace she couldn't speak, shaking her head she needed help and he needed love. "Please don't ask me we've been over this" John stood in front her," Tell me you don't love me the way you love him Jeanie….." pushing him away Jeanie jumped into the car and as she started the engine John stood in front of the car. "I love you Jea. I just need to know how you feel," driving around him Jeanie sped off into the distance. John left standing saw her stop and get out of the car. As he stood at the driver's door Jeanie looked at his desperation through the glass, getting out he grabbed hold of her tightly. "I won't ask you again Jea…I won't ask you again…"

Chapter 35

"John. I wouldn't be here if I didn't need to be,"
John answered the door after James had been stood
outside over twenty minutes.

"What do you want?" James took his gloves off and
threw them on the coffee table. "I know she came
here that night John she told me. She's took
Elizabeth and I haven't seen either of them for over
a week. I've been to Irene's and she's refusing to
talk to me. I've even been to the factory. John it
pains me to say it but I'm desperate she thinks
something's going on." John lit a cigarette and
laughed at how the tables suddenly had turned.

"James there's nothing more satisfying to me than
to see you squirm but the God's honest truth is I
haven't seen her since the other night and trust me I
would tell you but only cause of Elizabeth. I'm not
that much of an arse..."

"Where is she John? I don't know how she has
these letters. They weren't for her that was my own
stupidity..." John stood at the opposite end of the
room pouring two drinks.

"She told you where the letter's came from James
you just didn't believe her...." James didn't
appreciate John's comments and he hated that he
was right but he needed his help.

"Some of the things she said just didn't make sense.
I walked around that house inside and out and I
couldn't see anything." Sitting down at the coffee
table John slid the glass downstream.

"You're not going to like what I have to say but
your going to listen to it. When she talks to you
when she looks into your eyes and speaks to you
what does she do? Now think about it..."

"Wide eyed, no quiver and stubborn about it" John
nodded his head and took a drink. "So when she lies
to you or tries to keep something from you what

does she do?" James gritted his teeth waiting for another glib comment, "She hides her face and hides her eyes."

John smirked at the state of James and seeing how uncomfortable he was gave him great pleasure.

"Your loving this isn't you I know what you're going to say and yes she looked at me direct and asked me to believe her and I didn't even though everything about her was telling the truth..." Sitting back in his seat John winked at him.

"So again I believed her straight away I just didn't want to help because of you."

"Did she stay with you John?" John picked up the glasses and placed them in the kitchen, unable to leave his question unanswered James followed.

"Please did she spend the night with you I just need to know..." throwing the glasses in the sink, John hung his head.

"No she didn't want to not for my want of asking...I love her as well James she wouldn't stay cause of you for the simple fact that she loves you more than me."

"I need her John. I need my wife and my daughter so if you know anything..." starring out of the kitchen window John didn't want to help but knowing she hadn't been home for over a week concerned him more.

"She asked me to see if Catherine was ok she felt the last words Kowalski said had a...I don't know had a connection. The thing is she never told me what Kowalski said" John noticed James's demeanour he seemed suddenly agitated like he had just hit a nerve.

"I know what he said we spoke about it that night Catherine's last name is Partridge. I used to call her P. The last thing Kowalski said was remember Partridge. She's gone looking for Catherine. John she's out there looking for Catherine."

"We need to speak to Matt if she is looking for Catherine and if this isn't finished she's in a lot of danger James..." John grabbed his coat, still feeling nervous about the conversation he asked James for reassurance.

"James are you positively sure about all of this."

"Finding out who P is has become her obsession John I'm just hoping she wrong. But I need to know where Elizabeth is she's got to be with Ivy Jeanie would never have put her in danger."

James felt the uncomfortable silence as they drove to the cottage; John was obviously involved deeply but no matter how much he protested Jeanie loved him more he knew she still had feelings for John. Spending time with a man who wanted his wife was never going to be easy, but having no other choice was even more difficult.

Banging hard at the door James saw Irene. Looking at his reflection through the door she chose to ignore him and walk away,

"I just need to know if Elizabeth is with you Irene please," John stood at the door shaking his head. He had been through similar scenarios in the past and he'd always admired the will power of all the Rutherford women. "She's not letting you in there's only one way of doing this stand back," John kicked at the door until it opened.

"Thanks for the lovely hospitality where the fuck is the kid."

Pushing him out of the way James ran to Elizabeth, holding her in his arms he kissed her head sweetly.

"Ivy where's Jeanie." Ivy ignored him, following in pursuit James anxiously trailed behind knowing that any more time could be putting Jeanie in more danger.

"James you should be ashamed of yourself. She's told us about the letters she told me everything,"

Not able to wait for Ivy to finish he needed her to listen.

"For fuck sake Ivy please just tell me when you saw her last."

"She's been here most of last week and this week she said she had a few things to sort out in London but I haven't heard from her since.

James what's going on?" kissing Elizabeth's head he grabbed John.

"She's gone to find Catherine. My last address was in Brentford....Ivy look after Elizabeth I'm going to find Jeanie ..."

Reaching the police station John and James barged through reception, "Matthew Lineage please..." seeing John Matt knew it was trouble.

"I guess you both better come through..." Sitting at his desk Matt started to take notes as James spoke.

"So let me get this straight after the whole Mary Conaghan incident Jeanie went to war, you where shot and he was drugged. Jeanie shot Kowalski dead and now she's seeing faces pushed up against the windows at your home. Then the other night letter's came through the door at 2.00 am. Gent's if I hadn't have lived through some of this I would say it was a joke," James sat back on his chair wiping his hands through his hair.

"I know how it sounds. I have even questioned some of this myself. I'm a doctor for Christ sake and at the beginning I couldn't believe some of it but she believes it and I've got the letters to prove that she can't be making this up. Matt...please we need all the help..." Matt sat back on his chair puzzled as to what happens next.

"I can make an enquiry possible get a house call on Catherine Partridge maybe they can take a look to see if she's ok but have we ever considered what we need to do if she isn't?" James looked over to John and vice versa. "James these letters aren't very

391

flattering towards her and in order for me to help you I need to know everything that happened that night."

"I've already told you Matt we came in from her mums we talked for a couple of hours and we went to bed." Matt looked at James and then John still at a quandary as to which one was finally going to tell the truth.

"James I'm not saying this is you quite the contrary but I think both of you are hiding things from each other. Above everything it's quite possible she's gone to complete this new business deal."

Matt needed the truth and he knew certain details where going to upset one if not both, looking back at his notes he tried to gather a picture and continued with his questioning.

"So which one is going to start first?" James swallowed deep looking at John he knew he had to take the first steps.

"I'm not good at this Matt in fact pointing out my infallibilities is very hard for me. OK listen we talked about what happened to both of us over there and I told her that night. Fuck why is this so hard! I told her that night she was the part of me I couldn't live without.

On my way home I had an overnight stay in London but I didn't see Catherine. I had a few drinks and got talking and realised half way through that even though this stunning blonde woman was available and willing she didn't compare to what I had waiting for me and when I turned her down flat I found it amusing how pissed off she got. I told her about my beautiful wife and how I couldn't wait to reach home. So the next day I went to Harrods and bought her a present something that would match how special she is.

These last few weeks have been so tough to the point that she told me to walk away and forget her. I know she has feelings for him cause she told me. She told me that you don't walk away from something like this and not appreciate what you did and how you helped. She even told me about the day you visited Francis and I can't say I'm not jealous. My wife is conflicted because she nearly dies twice and now I gave her the excuse she needed.

"And what about that night James. What happened that night she left?" James fumbled around with the stationary on Matt's desk unable to stay settled in one spot for more than a few seconds at a time.

"She caught me trying to set a romantic scene and we danced. You see since coming back from war she hasn't let me touch her or be near her to be honest and it was only in the last couple of days before the letters that I moved back into our bedroom.

I had an appointment at the hospital and she had a business meeting and I knew the results of both would need to be discussed at the family get together. She was different, I don't know seem to be coming back to herself and after that evening she had more clarity than what she had done in over a month and I thought...I thought she was coming back to me.

When I asked her to put the gown on she looked like a kid at Christmas and when she came back her whole demeanour had changed. She seemed agitated, nervous and just completely different.

Before getting changed she had a spark a glow it was very infectious and at that moment I told her how much I loved her. Matt I took my wife to bed I wanted her with me and when we where making love she didn't have any inhibitions it was almost as if for a moment something had scared her."

"Do you really have too? For fuck sake Matt what does this have to do with Catherine?" James looked heavy hearted at Matt for support.

"Someone was there you think she's seen someone when she's been changing and she's hid it from me because I didn't believe her the first time and the letter's where all part of that aren't they.." Matt nodded still face down in his notes. Before making a comment he looked at the pair down his spectacles.

"James you're probably a shit doctor but I think you would make a good detective. John we need your version of events now." John slammed the chair down obviously distressed.

"No we don't we've heard enough bullshit for one night what the fuck,"

"I know James's recollection of the evening hurt deeply and I also know you don't want to hear or feel anything but both of you need to face facts." Silence dropped between the men, waiting for John to continue he sat down.

"She came to me after she'd read the letters she was upset disjointed…it wasn't helped by the fact that I had another woman in my bed at the time. When she knew she couldn't even look at me not at first. The thing is I rarely feel guilt but that woman. Jeanie knows how to make you feel guilty. She was shivering so I sat her down by the fire the only other time I've seen her this upset was after we lost the baby. We talked about the letters come to think of it she wasn't upset about the content….not really…she mentioned that she'd been described as a common slut but she was more hurt by the fact that he'd met Catherine behind her back. She went on about P James calls her P and I asked her to leave and go back to him and he knows that's only cause of Elizabeth.

I didn't want her to go and when she held me and apologised I changed my mind. I had to tell her again how much….how much I love her…and that I would do anything for her," Finding it difficult to listen James clenched his fists and closed his eyes. "I stopped her at the car before she left and I kissed her….the thing was James she kissed me back and as she got in the car to leave I stupidly I ran to her.

I'd asked her if she loved me she didn't answer, she couldn't answer I know that. I asked her to stay with me and I told her I would make all this go away and I believed everything she said but she didn't stay." John faced the window looking out into the darkened alleyway and as Matt ran his fingers over the page looking at the tear between both gentlemen it was obvious how much one action had torn both their worlds apart.

"Why didn't she stay John?" Closing his eyes John pictured her standing in the rain. "Does it really matter…?"

"Why didn't she stay?" Throwing his head back in defeat he knew he had been caught out.

"She didn't stay because she was using me she needed to find out information about Catherine and by playing me off against him she knew she would get what she wanted. Once I told her where she lived she left and like that I was sat on my own. Ironic as it's the thing she has ever leant from me." James shook his head, not able to comprehend the truth. "You knew. If you knew then why all this."

"I thought she would cool off and come to her senses. I didn't know she would do this."

"You have both brought this on yourselves. I have known you for years and I've been telling you for years that what you where doing would end in disaster. I told you then she would hurt you more than you know. Whether she has any kind of feelings for you is not the question.

She has married James and whether you like it she feels compelled to do the right thing. For Christ sake John she even told you when she arrived home that you need to move on and be happy without her.

Then she has you James and when she needed belief, understanding and you to trust her all she got was lies and accusations. When she needed her husband to lovingly protect her you pushed her away in fear of your own ego. What did you both expect her to do? She has been so much and always on her own. So she left and I'm not surprised and then she turned to John and knowing you'd follow her like a blind fool she got what she needed to solve this mess on her own.

You both ought to be ashamed of yourself and James these letters are not just hurtful but derogatory and bitter and I don't care that these are dated whilst she was pregnant with his child but if you love her that much why say it in the first place. Both of you make me sick this woman is crying out for help and you isolate her even more.

What are both trying to prove or is this just point scoring. James I think you need to understand what love is because you told her that night that she was a part of your life that you couldn't live without but nothing what you have said or done has proved it. The only person that seems to be showing that is him and that's because he's an idiot.

Jeanie gave up her freedom, her family, her child and nearly her life to be with you. Too many lives have been marred by a thoughtless psychopath and his assistant and she now thinks someone is trying to ruin her marriage and her new life and she's probably right.

Excuse me gents if I'm not too sympathetic to your plight but I'm really finding it difficult to understand which psychopath I'm hunting for when I have two sociopaths in my own room. I going outside I need some air…" Matt placed the journal under his arm and closed the door firmly, seeing the pain shudder John sat back down on his seat next to James

"You love her a lot don't you...?"

"Yes and I would do absolutely anything for her if it made her happy even give her up." Glaring at each other, they felt each other's pain.

"Matt's not right about everything I'm not letting her go John. This last month…this last month I've been the happiest I've ever been. The one thing he has got right is that I have been thinking about me and not her and when she needed someone she turned to you. How do you think that makes me feel?" John threw his chair back angered that again her was thinking about himself.

"It's not all about you! I never had a chance because of you and now…now I don't sleep without her, I don't eat and I can't fucking breath because I don't have her and you treat her like shit because you can.

"I'm fucked off with hearing how you can't operate without my wife she's my wife and it's not a fucking competition. You can't give her what I can." John grabbed hold of James's collar,

"And what's that fucking lies and letters which tell her how much of a slut she is or sex on tap because she completes you." Punching John in the throat he fell back against the wall.

"I'm not doing this with you." John stood up and adjusted his collar not willing to give up the fight so easily.

"Why cause she isn't good enough or is it that you know if you fucked up she'd run to me in heartbeat…"

"You're such a fucking arsehole stop being a cock. I wasn't the one who left her at the train station John…Who was given chance after chance to marry her….love her be with her and you ran away and married the generals daughter cause it fucking benefited you."

"It wasn't like that."

"What was it like then John after asking her to marry you she found you in bed with Ivy or was it the fact that after a drink you used to use her like a punching bag. Well fuck me…I wrote a few letter's to a ex fiancé not very nice ones but I didn't trip up and stick my dick in her sister did I,"

"I never felt good enough for her."

"What? Don't give me that bullshit."

"It's true. I don't care whether you believe me, but its true I always thought she needed better than me. So you're right I did marry a general's daughter because it befitted me. But it was all in my fucked up plan to prove I was good enough." James paused, calming down quickly as the moment had pricked his conscious.

"Fuck…I know what's going on John get Matt we have to go now." John puzzled grabbed his hat. James leant on the car trying to be patient

"Can we hurry up please?" Matt jumped into the back seat and started to ruffle with some papers.

"Who's Mildred?" James turned around and looked at the paperwork Matt was holding. "Catherine's aunt…..why?"

Grabbing the paper from his hand and reading the contents he felt sick.

"John drive faster….I'll explain when we get there..."

 John pulled up at the side of the road, the long hours in the car had felt like an emotional prison trapped between Matt's conscious and James lucidity he felt like a puppet waiting for his strings to be pulled.

"Matt this isn't Brentwood. I'm going into the city."
 James grabbed the piece of paper from the dashboard and jumped out before the car come to a

stop. Throwing the car onto the curb John chased after. "Matt I don't understand why we are here?" "I'm sure everything will become clear. Let's just go." Running up the stairs the trio congregated at top of the landing between the conservative collections of front doors.

"Can someone start talking please this is becoming slightly fucked up and unnerving…." John panted heavily anxious about what he was going to see next. "John I know your carrying, I'll go next. James follow up at the back."

The door was slightly ajar and the decadent interior of the corridor cried opulence, John starring into the dark black space manoeuvred around the archway into the large living room. The stench of death emanated around the flat and as John counted to ten he could feel the blood pulse in his veins. "There's only one reason this place stinks. James check the bedroom. Matt stay in here I'll go and check the kitchen."

As the Gents separated John's apprehension increased, the smell grew stronger and as he moved closer to the kitchen he expected death. "Matt, James there's something definitely in here…" John stood frozen to the spot as the blood washed over the kitchen floor. "Whatever is here it's in that pantry!"

James hadn't moved from the bedroom, the large wardrobe in the corner had captured his attention and the small spots of blood which had been dripping out of the door made him go cold. Grabbing the poker from the hearth he took a deep breath before opening the door. Slowly unhinging the lock the large door swung open and as he stepped back he realised inside it was empty, except for a large pool of blood. Moving quickly he met the gents at the kitchen door.

"John, Matt it looks like…" The blood marks streaked along the kitchen floor marking there deathly course into the pantry.

"Moved…it looks as if someone has been moved…."

"There's bullet holes in the cabinet look. Whatever's happened they have had a fight…" John rubbed his fingers along the wall.

"Jeanie!" Reaching for the light anticipation grew between all of them, as to who or what had happened.

"James, Matt have you ever seen anything like this…." James checked her pulse knowing she was already dead, shaking his head he stood and wiped his hands.

The woman lay blooded on the floor, she had been strangled at first with barbed wire, and it had cut deep into her throat exposing her windpipe. Her wrists had also been slashed down to the tendons. Clothes lay around the floor where an attempt to save her had been made.

John switched off the light trying to at least give her some dignity.

"Do you know her?"

"She's Catherine's aunt she's the one I bought the cottage off for Jeanie." Matt leant on the kitchen door wiping his forehead with his handkerchief, looking at the art deco table in the hall way he noticed a photo. Taking it back to the gents in the kitchen, he was intrigued to know who the gathering was.

"Do either of you know these women…"

"Those two on the end….that's Catherine and her aunt. John?" John only glanced having see the picture a thousand times.

"That's Olivia this was taken at her bridge club that was before…before I left…shit…"

"You're ex wives knew each other! John when did you last see Olivia." "Just after I got back she still wanted closure on that stupid deal. Come to think of it she wasn't exactly…You don't think…" Matt grabbed the picture feeling he would need it later for evidence.

"We need to go." Before closing the door John looked around the hallway nostalgic at his former life.

"I remember buying this place and look at it now. I know your right James. I married Olivia to help me and I also did a lot of things just for me. We can't leave that woman in my pantry Matt. If anyone finds her including our maid were in deep shit."

"I'll make a call but if something's going to happen it looks like it will be soon and it looks as if Jeanie has disturbed someone…" James paced the corridor running through the scene over and over again.

"I know why we are here. I just don't get how Jeanie ended up here…" John placed his gun back in his pocket. "Catherine must have the same picture." James turned pale, looking at the photo still in his hands.

"The sideboard in Brentwood. In fact she's mentioned your wife on a couple of occasions I never thought…John both of them must know about Jeanie…"

Chapter 36

Jeanie arrived back at the cottage, clattering through the door she stripped off down to her vest and as she stood bare in the kitchen she tried to take small breaths.

"I think you better put something on." Jeanie closed her eyes as the gun dug deep into her ribs, trying to keep composed she raised her arms. "Why did you do it she only had a small part to play I don't understand." Binding her arms together Jeanie felt the rope pull tight.

"You don't go this far not to complete what you set out to do. I mean it now would be a tragedy saying that a mindless troglodyte like yourself wouldn't understand that. Stand up please." Jeanie felt the gun dig deeper into her rib cage. Feeling trapped she scoped the kitchen for a solution.

"So Jeanie Rutherford Watson tell me the story so far I'm intrigued to know how much you've found out already." Jeanie took the spare of pants from her hands and still in silence she started to dress.

"This isn't a game so you better start talking."

"You approached Signthorpe and Kowalski coinciding visits to check up on progress and recently you've been spying on me in my own home." Jeanie felt her hands being tied to the chair, being forced to sit down the rope burnt further into her skin.

"In summary I think you've done alright. You've missed a few things out but I'm sure I can forgive you for those minor indiscretions."

Her once white vest had started to turn a distasteful shade of brown and as it cracked with every discomfort shall flecks started to fall on the floor.

Jeanie stared into her eyes trying to figure out their next move. The war had taught her many things, but Jeanie's impatience for action spurred her to react further.

"What did I ever do to you?" Without question the blunt thud of the end of the gun split the top of her eye and as the blood ran down Jeanie's cheek it seemed to anger her visitor more than her question. "You don't have the right to ask any questions plus all good things come to those who wait..."

Hours seemed to pass and Jeanie watched the break of dawn rise through the kitchen window.

"I know this is about James and I know you couldn't care less about whether I live or John lives. Just tell me one thing. Who else other than Catherine is pulling the strings? Cause I know you couldn't do all this on your own."

"You think you're so fucking clever don't you. I had to finish this once and for all but you just couldn't follow a simple plan could you. I really don't understand why two men would even be interested never mind fight over you.

John seemed to have such good taste but this was all about you. Your right in one way I couldn't have done all this on my own but I haven't been on my own have I. Frank and my dear Mike helped. By the time we had finished with him he hated you and taking pieces of your hair and gathering your nails just made it more believable for John."

The sun had started to stream through the blackened kitchen and as the shadows hovered over the sink a car had started to pull up in the driveway.

"Oh look someone I need to kill! Jeanie I think your husband and lover are here," Feeling the gun raise to her temple Jeanie closed her eyes once more. Regaining her thoughts she followed the fire arms directory and cocked her head to one side. "Scream and they all die now...."

Jeanie sat still at the kitchen table as the three men entered the house, the door closed superfluously behind them revealing the unwanted guest. "Good morning gents I didn't think you'd be here this quick but I suppose I have to commend you for some things. Now if don't mind lowering to your knee's James is going to be a dear and tie you up, "Olivia please where's Catherine?"

"Just making her entrance now darling so I suggest you kneel." Kicking his feet from under him James fell to the floor.

"Hello darling missed me! And I see you've all been invited to our little soiree…." Looking at Jeanie James tried to move towards her.

"Catherine I don't understand." Catherine took hold of Olivia's gun and pointed it back at Jeanie's head. "That's a pity you see Jeanie has more of an understanding then all of you don't you…"

"Catherine it's me your angry at not her please don't do this," Catherine smirked and kissed Olivia tenderly on the cheeks.

"Tut tut tut see that's where you are wrong my darling and this runs much deeper than just a woman scorned. She's the cause of mine and my angel Olivia's pain and you two well you're just caught up in Jeanie's entrapment of lies. I mean James look at her if you where going to leave me for someone at least make them well in the same league." Jeanie gritted her teeth; the blood had started to crack as it had dried on her face, speckling dried droplets onto her lap.

"We saw the photograph Livy," Spitting violently at John Olivia rushed over to where he knelt.

"You don't have the right to call me Livy anymore you useless piece of crap. You left me with nothing you owe me and to be humiliated by her do you know how that felt. "John had never spared her feelings, and today was no different. "Olivia you where fucking a subordinate when I reached home what do you expect me to do get involved."

"I know everything John and I know all about your fucked up web of business deals but when you involved me as one of them and use me as a stepping stone I felt a little dejected. Especially when I thought you loved me."

"Baby come on he's teasing badly and revenge is so much sweeter when it's justified. James your very quiet in all this nothing to say," James glanced at Jeanie then over to Catherine her gun still pointing at Jeanie's temple.

"What if I did Catherine you would never listen you've only been interested in yourself and how far I could take you and I got tired of it of you. Jea…you've given me more love than I ever had from her in ten years,"

"Lovely James but the sentiment is well a little dull especially now she has read those lovely letters! Anyway let's have a little game shall we seeing as it's now a party. My game is called guess the reasons why we are both here. Let's see if you're wife gets it right." Olivia wiped her hand along the top of Jeanie's shoulders.

"If she understands what's going on she lives and if she doesn't she dies simple enough for everyone..." John tried to stand not able to put her in harms way again.

"Don't move John because I will shoot her and then you." lowering himself, John tried to keep control of his temper. Catherine shoved the gun further along Jeanie's temple. Jeanie pulled at the binds around her wrists, feeling the gun pressured further into her skull, she looked at the three gents knowing if they where ever going to make it out she would have to play their game.

"Is it my turn" sliding the gun down to her throat Jeanie looked directly into her eyes. "Don't make me kill you now tell the rest of the group the whole story as I'm sure they're dying to know."

Jeanie didn't drop her gaze, she wasn't frightened anymore knowing Catherine and Olivia had constructed this elaborate plot made her more determined to see it end.

"I suppose I better start with Mike. I know he had already been arrested a couple of time's in London he didn't exactly tell me the full details of his sentence but I knew he got off on a technicality. It must have been serious enough to have even got him to a technicality. He met Signthorpe just after his short stint in prison. I later realised that Mike had been blackmailing him to carry out the attack on me. If he didn't Mike said he would go public with what he had done to another girl. The problem was Mike didn't know how much of a psychopath he was. He was later introduced to Olivia and Catherine as a man that could sort out their problem. Me being the problem. He reported back on my relationship with James….he also experienced some of my relationship with John and which from reading the letter's caused James to run back to Catherine and John to seek out Olivia. That's why she turned up at the hotel. I've read Signthorpe's journal John didn't know until now that I stole it from him. I saw the the cloth and hair in the book could and piecing the puzzle together it could only have been taken by Olivia. How do I know this well there is an entry in his journal which would prove he was never at the hotel. Catherine instigated Mike's attempts at getting to Mary. Because I didn't die the first time and a new plan was needed. In fact it was a crucial part of killing me off they had to produce an official document for me to believe that James was missing. They needed me out of the way and the only way of doing that was getting to Mary.

Mildred was easy…all Mildred had to do was whisper a few words in my ear telling me I was a resourceful girl. Mike was James's babysitter and had to be there to make sure I didn't come back.

James was supposed to be comforted by Catherine and for Olivia John was supposed to die leaving his money, business and whatever else to you since you are still married.

I messed up their plans when arrived home safe as did John. The time away wasn't long enough to settle what business had been started. The only thing I don't understand is why kill Mildred?" Olivia slapped her across the face.
"You don't have the fucking right to question us" Catherine moved her to one side still trying to play the part of a graceful host.
"She has a question the least we can do is oblige before she dies. You see Mildred found out about our little plan and she came to confront me. She said she'd posted the letters but we needed to stop and well before she got to the police. You know the rest don't you."
"Catherine please don't do this. I was wrong...I was wrong about lots of things but please don't do this." Jeanie rose in her distraction and as she removed her final binds she snatched the gun out of her grip.
"You see Bitch going to war taught me a few things as well. Drop to the floor and place your hands on your head. Olivia why don't you give your gun to James and we can all have a good chat. In the meantime slowly move over there." Olivia stood tall not able to acquiesce her request.
"You fucking bitch let her go or James dies now." Jeanie walked around the front of Catherine looking more like the predator than the prey.
"I don't think your friend wants that do you."
"Not him Livy I only want her."
"You see I'm sick and tired of this bullshit and all I wanted to do was live a normal happy life and you two twisted fucks keep messing everything up. Now

I know you both know I killed Mike in fact I shot him point blank in the head so I suggest Livy you drop the fucking gun before I shoot her." Olivia lunged towards Jeanie pushing Catherine out of the way, defending herself Jeanie dropped the gun and started to grapple at the carving knife, Olivia held in her hand. James pounced towards the fallen gun and as Catherine stood he knew he was too late.

"All of you move now." Tying John and Matt's hand together she wrestled with James binding him to the radiator. Shooting Matt in the leg, she wiped away the blood which had splattered on her face. "That should keep you busy excuse me gents." Catherine shot twice into the ceiling trying to take back some control

"Now I'm going to tell you once before I shoot again I'm running this show. Livy drop the knife. Jeanie back against the wall…"

The room had descended into chaos and Olivia lunged again at Jeanie grabbing her hand. Jeanie pushing on her chest plunged the knife deeper feeling it tear through bone and sinew as forced it through.

James tugged at the bindings loosening them off he ran into the kitchen.

I heard two shots there was only two shots. Jeanie please.

Jeanie lay motionless on the kitchen floor Catherine had vanished and the blood swilled around the cottage like an abattoir.

"Jeanie baby hold on. Come on baby we can do this remember," Jeanie raised her arm up to James's face and as the blood poured from her mouth as she started to choke.

"Baby don't leave me now you can't leave me now I need you I love you." Jeanie's body shook violently as she drowned on her own blood.

John ripped the ropes from around his wrists, Matt still clutched his leg torn between the two John looked at Matt for guidance

"John go…go…" running into the kitchen the red river swam around his feet. "No…No...Jea. James what do we do JAMES!." coughing Jeanie exhaled, the breath diminished from her lips.

"Tell Elizabeth…I love her." James screamed violently

"Jea…please don't go stay with me baby come on." Olivia laughed as Jeanie slowly slipped away.

"You can't have her now!" Olivia smiled as John ripped the knife from her chest. "Fuck you! James…please we need to get her to a hospital."

Holding her close in his arm her lifeless blooded body draped over him like a shroud, the blood still dripping from her lips seemed to drown any life she had left.

"How am I going to live without you how am I meant to do this without you Jea. I'm sorry…I'm sorry..." Lifting her off the floor he ran to the car. John raced into the driver's seat; James ran his hand over her pale clammy skin, the sparkle from her eyes dwindled and as the car sped around the country lanes she clung onto him desperate to live.

John looked on anxiously not knowing what to say he felt powerless. Landing at the hospital the Signthorpe seen played out over and over again, this time James was then one in the waiting room. Catherine had disappeared into the night getting away with sordid plan. Search parties had been set up to see if she could be captured but all they could do was wait.

James paced the halls, he had left her to another doctor and on hearing the ticking of the clock it emphasised every painful minute.

"Doctor…..Doctor Watson….can I have a word..." James followed the doctor into a side room. "My name is Dr Hodgeskiss I've been seeing to Jeanie and I'm sorry doctor the bleeding was just too much. I'm sorry to have to tell you this but your wife has just passed away."

Wandering out of the room James dropped to his knees in the corridor, the screams of anguish where heard throughout the hospital. John slid down the hospital wall and as the gents sat in silence they couldn't contemplate what was next.
She was gone.
Matt had followed with Olivia's body and on seeing both gents he knew immediately. James stood as Matt stumbled towards him.
"She's…I mean. I need you tell Irene….I need to stay..." Matt placed his hand on James shoulder. "Its ok son I'll go."

Ivy stood at the door grabbing hold tightly of Elizabeth. The screams from the Rutherford cottage sent shockwaves into the night. Her daughter was now left without a mother.
She was dead.

As a town woke in shock, the news of Jeanie's death spread, Irene lay in bed surrounded by her girls as the emptiness inside consumed them all. Elizabeth lay fast asleep oblivious to her mother's disappearance. James wearily made his way through the door.
"Can I see my daughter please?" Ivy carried her downstairs Elizabeth was still fast asleep grabbing hold of her he pulled her close. Ivy started to cry as she felt his pain and more besides.
"I need to plan the funeral." as the grief engulfed him, Irene clasped her mouth.
"You did this. You killed my daughter." Ivy slapped Irene across the face. The last conversation anyone needed right now was who was to blame. Taking Elizabeth he sat at the front of the fire resting his head gently on hers, Ivy stood patiently watching.

"He needs us mum she was killed because…they wanted her dead not him." Irene walked away unable to comprehend what had happened. Ivy pressed her head against the frame of the parlour door, watching James rock his child. There was no explanation of their grief there was no explanation of his pain, the anguish inside felt empty and everything about James reflected it.

Chapter 37

As friends and family gathered Jeanie came home
for the final time. Her coffin laid out in the living
room and the flowers beautifully scattered around
her as if she was lay in a summer meadow.

   John arrived with Matt and as he lowered his hat
James welcomed them both. "Thank you I don't
think I can take much more of this." Matt held out
his hand pulling him forwards.
"I'm so sorry James I truly am..." James
straightened his tie, as if the action was going to
pull him out of his nightmare.
"How's your leg? I'm sorry I didn't get much of a
chance to ask," Matt smiled and patted him on the
shoulder.
"My leg is of no consequence." John stood at the
door unable to look at the coffin. "Do you have
anything stronger than tea?" James smirked and
nodded leading him into the kitchen.
"It's her mum's Brandy tastes like shit but in the
circumstances." Both of them sat at the table trying
not to exchange glances. The pressure of trying to
keep composed rippled through every tense muscle.
"James I don't think...." James placed his hand on
his shoulder
"I know the worst thing of all is the guilt." James
rubbed over his eye's trying to hold back the tears.
"Are you ready for this?"
"Not really. I never wanted to admit it but you're a
good man James. I know she loved you..." Gaining
composer James held out his glass raining in
whatever emotion was trying to escape.
"A toast from two men that loved you we're sorry
for what we did but what we did we did out of love
for you....." John clinked the glasses together in
response.
"Any news on Catherine?"

"I spoke to Matt on the way over and they still think she's in the area." Starring into the bottom of the glass James sighed heavily.

"She didn't get this finished John you know that don't you."

"I know." John threw back the tumbler hoping the brandy would at least numb some of the pain.

Reaching the Church gates both men stood arm in arm carrying her coffin, Elizabeth sat and played oblivious to what was happening. Eric had been asked by both of them to conduct the eulogy it seemed befitting as he was practically her father. Eric stood proud as he started to speak:

"To all of you that knew Jeanie she was a sweet loving girl with a constitution of a horse and as pig headed as her father and they where her better qualities.

No one tells you how to feel when you loose a child and recently with another Great War passing it should seem more reverent.

We all know Jeanie's death wasn't through war and it wasn't through an accident. Jeanie's death was cruel and uncalled for and at the hands of people who where only interested in their own self gain.

My darling girl used to stand on the gantry proud of the empire she had started to build but she had a kindness and heart that touched all who knew her. She was as open as a book and as complex as a piston.

My only wish was for her to find happiness.

For those of us that knew her loving her was simple, hurting her was easy and getting close to her was something you didn't do half heartedly.

Her beautiful daughter Elizabeth graced our presence at the factory but Jeanie didn't want her to follow in her footsteps. Jeanie was a talented

413

engineer who could work a piece of machinery out in minutes but for her daughter she wanted more.

If I had one wish it would be to turn back the clock for Elizabeth to understand how special she was and for everyone to understand that without her our light in our factory has gone out.

Her husband James asked me to do the eulogy and I have to say it has caused me some sleepless nights, but the one thing I do know is Jeanie loved you she loved you with her heart and soul. John take head from my words that my darling girl was more complex than you could understand and we thank you for looking after her and bringing her home safe.

I will leave you with this promise, I will look after your empire as if it where my own and I will guide all those that may sway from your path.

My sweet darling girl I will miss you more than any words could ever mention, your family are torn without you and your father and your beautiful son have received another angel into heaven.

Sleep well my darling and may your dreams be the sweeter form of your own life. "

The church full to capacity hung onto every one of Eric's words, John happy to have been mentioned stood at the back of the church trying to keep himself together.

As the procession left he lit a cigarette trying to settle his nerves. The passing crowds made his stomach churn and without question something wasn't right and he felt it. Capturing James's attention he stumbled into the procession. "James something's not right." feeling John's anguish he rested his hand on his shoulder.

"I know what you mean. I have seen Matt already and just in case…" John threw away the stub and pulled at his jacket. "Yep just in case."

"Glad we are finally on the same page."

John and James stood shoulder to shoulder on the hill her graveside had a beautiful view of the town and as the clouds parted the small concave roof of the factory could be seen.

"Now or never James"

"With you all the way. Ready. NOW!" As the figure fell from the crowd, both gents opened fire. As the screams deafened the sound of the bullets, the gents walked forward. Catherine lay face down at the side of the coffin, her gun displayed and her finger on the trigger.

"I wish I'd never met you." Handing John the gun James walked away.

"So what now…" throwing the gun in the bottom of the grave, John took a deep breath. "Now it's over…."

Irene and her girls sat quietly with Matt at their side in the church hearing the shots, Irene held her chest.

"Irene girls I believe I have some cleaning up to do. Again."

The funeral gave Catherine an opportunity to inflict more pain and knowing Elizabeth was the target made it all the more reason to be prepared

"It's done its over." James nodded kissing his daughters temple.

"I'm just glad your all safe come on Elizabeth let's go home." John stood at the door cigarette in hand.

"I never expected you to be someone I could trust James…" James held out his hand and looked back at the coffin still resting on the hill.

"You're welcome at my house any time John…we're family."

Walking away James pulled Elizabeth close, the only comfort he had was that the unlikeliest of friends had become allies and at least for now Jeanie was at peace.

www.ingramcontent.com/pod-product-compliance
Lightning Source LLC
Chambersburg PA
CBHW060140260626
47160CB00001B/55

* 9 7 8 1 8 4 9 1 4 6 4 1 8 *